A BILLION
Hot Kisses

WICKED Hot BILLIONAIRES

JANE McBAY

cat whisker press
Boston

First Paperback Edition
ISBN: 978-1-957421-52-0

Published by Cat Whisker Press
Cover: Philip Ré, Rex Video Productions
Book Design: Cat Whisker Studio
Editor: Chloe Bearuski

To my parents
James and Beryl

*for giving me a love of the beach
and the sea at an early age*

WICKED HOT BILLIONAIRES

A Billion Little Lies

A Billion Hot Kisses

A Billion Starry Nights

A Billion Second Chances

ACKNOWLEDGMENTS

I want to give a big *thank you* to the following beta readers who gave me the gift of their most precious asset, time: Toni Young, Philip Ré, Kyrstin Poyson, G. Feldma, Liz Osborne, April Frisch, and Jessica Guenther.

As always, thank you to my long-time editor, Chloe Bearuski, and to my proofreader, Julie Evans.

Your combined efforts, each suggestion offered or typo found, made this a better book. I am exceedingly grateful. All mistakes, of course, are my own.

1

Murray Island, off the coast of Massachusetts

Lindsey

"The tavern is open from three until whenever Dave decides to close up," I explain to the early tourists in my shop, a husband and wife, before handing the woman her change along with a brown paper bag of goodies.

I can tell them the hours of every business on the island, but I have intimate knowledge of Dave's Beach Bar, which I prefer to call a tavern. I'll be their server later if they choose to go there for dinner. And that's more than likely given the limited choices available at the moment. The few dining establishments left in town haven't opened yet after the winter. Others closed at the end of last summer and will never reopen. Every year, we lose at least one business.

The couple might be the only customers I have today, as we're still a good two weeks before the season begins. When it does, my shop becomes imperative to the island, standing proudly near the ferry terminal as it has done for three generations. With sunscreen, candy, and beach chairs, Whatnots and Such offers everything tourists need for a great summer. In my opinion, they don't get any greater than on Murray Island.

"It's perfect here," the woman says, while her husband holds the door open for her to precede him.

"Yes," I agree softly to myself.

They look happy. I can tell they're at the beginning of their vacation because a) everyone looks happy at the start of a week's vacation, b) the ferry just docked, and c) they bought the essentials along with Whatnots' proprietary map of the island.

The map is printed and laminated, and there are three heavy boxes of them that I would love to sell because they've taken up space for five years. Honestly, they're placemats that my father designed and ordered, thinking if tourists didn't buy them as an island memento, then one of the local breakfast or lunch places would. Nope!

Mrs. Tourist rolls the map up because it is impossible to fold seeing how it's really a large, thick placemat, which she now wields like a baton.

"Onward," she says to her husband, preceding him through the open doorway. "With this, we can explore everything."

That makes me smile because any local will tell you whatever you want to know, and the map is pure hogwash with silly names for pretend places that mean nothing but sound appealing.

Siren Sands, Lucifer's Lighthouse, Pirates' Cove, Mermaid Bay, and Haven Harbor where my store is located. We're lucky to have a deep and wide enough port for the summer ferries. But plain Murray's Harbor just doesn't sound as inviting.

The island is a mere eleven miles long and a mile wide at its belly, as we call the middle section where most of us live and work in the main—and only—town of Murray. Up at the northern end, it's two and a half miles wide and similarly shaped at the southern end. In truth, the town isn't so much of a belly as a skinny spine.

Most people can map it out for themselves, which they do by bicycle or by foot. That's why the neat stack of maps on my counter, with a tidy folded white card on top states in friendly blue ink, "50% off, this week only!" And I added a yellow smiley-faced sun in one corner.

When new tourists arrive next week, it will, of course, say the same thing, and for every week after that until they're gone. The maps, I mean, not the tourists, although they go hand in hand. With no one else in sight, I retreat into the back room to take stock. Despite having an ancient computer with slightly less-ancient software that tells me what I have and what I'm running low on, still, it's nice to have a visual.

Glancing at the shelves, I remind myself how damn efficient I am. There is nothing left to order before the deluge of eager customers, the official start of tourist season.

I conduct a brief survey anyway while humming along to the radio on the counter out front. Crouching low, I look at the boxes of sunscreen and candy bars. Up high, I have folded towels in bright colors. On the middle shelves are about a hundred other items, big and small. And in the corner, one of my most popular items, medium-sized beach umbrellas. Maybe next year, I'll think of something wildly novel to sell, but at the moment, I can't think of anything else I need to offer.

The sole cloud over my blue sky is caused by the summer deluge having shrunk each summer for a decade, until last year, it was more like a trickle than a flood. I hum more loudly to stave off the fear that one day, no one will get off the ferry at all.

Life is good. Damn near perfect, I remind myself. *Or it would be if I had someone to share it with.*

"Shut the hell up," I tell myself aloud as I reenter the shop floor.

"*Whoa,*" says a male voice from over by the front window where the sunglasses are displayed on a rotating wire rack.

I literally jump like a cat seeing a cucumber. I didn't hear the shop bell and shoot it a quick glance. The bell is certainly still there, hanging where it has hung for over sixty-five years since my grandfather installed it.

The owner of the voice approaches the counter, and I stop thinking about the bell. In fact, I stop thinking any thoughts, necessary or unnecessary, apart from focusing on this Adonis of a man.

Dark brown hair, light brown eyes, and tall enough with broad shoulders that my shop shrinks around him. He's got the classic, chiseled-chin good looks that most of us females admire. And my brain goes on a mini vacation until he speaks.

"Who were you talking to?" he asks.

"No one," I say a little sharply. "Myself," I add, feeling instantly stupid.

His golden-brown eyes widen. "You were rather harsh." He pauses. "And I didn't hear you say anything that warranted telling yourself to shut up."

I am not going to confess to shouting at the voice *inside* my head.

"Can I help you?" I ask.

"Sunglasses," he says. "I'm just picking out a pair."

"Gotta have 'em," I agree. "The reflection off the water can fry your eyeballs."

"Doubtful," he said, "but I don't want to squint the entire time I'm here."

He could squint without losing a drop of his handsomeness.

"You have your choice of glasses. Newly stocked and not yet picked over by the tourists."

"Picked over," he echoes. "Like vultures? Or hyenas?" With a lift of his dark eyebrow, he goes back to the sunglasses display.

"No," I call after him, not wanting to give him the impression I don't like my customers. "Not like that at all. But in a few weeks, the selection will be slim." That is, if my prayers are answered and I get more customers than last year.

"For your sake," he says, "I hope so. Seems pretty quiet right now."

Is he dissing Murray Island? The only island inhabited year-round off the coast of Massachusetts, north of Cape Cod Bay.

"We like it quiet," I explain, sounding a tad defensive. "We're not a celebrity island. Plenty of noise on Martha's Vineyard or Nantucket, if you like that sort of thing."

He sends me a querying look with his unusually intense eyes that shuts me up. Of course he likes *that* sort of thing. Who doesn't? The fancy B&Bs, the massive yachts, the busy shops and variety of restaurants, and the "beautiful people"—of whom he is most definitely one.

Maybe he got on the wrong ferry.

"Anyway," I say, "no one knows what this year will be like, what with all the changes."

"Changes?" he asks and slides on a pair of glasses.

They don't suit him, and I venture out from behind the counter. It's not a huge shop, taking me all of fifteen feet to reach him.

He puts on another pair, and this time he turns to me.

Nope. I shake my head. He removes them and keeps scanning, but I go closer and grab a pair I know will work.

"Try these."

He turns, looks at what I'm holding out, but before he takes them, his glance meets mine.

Zing! I suck in a deep breath, luckily through my nose, not loudly through my mouth. Not a loud *God-you-are-hot* gasp, which is what I'm thinking.

His broadening grin makes me believe he knows what that voice in my head is saying now.

Finally, he takes the sunglasses. No, our fingers don't brush. This isn't a silly historical romance like my Nan enjoyed reading.

"Thanks." He slips them on and looks in the small mirror hanging from the display. Our gazes meet again in the reflection.

"What do you think?" he asks.

Suddenly, I am too close. I can smell his aftershave or cologne. It is the bomb! One of those masculine smells that women without a man like to wear just to have the fragrance around. Maybe I have something like it tucked away in my bedside table to spray around my bedroom once in a while. Maybe.

I step back and turn away. Over my shoulder, I tell him, "I think they look fine."

They actually look amazing. *He* looks amazing! All European-model sexy, and suddenly, I feel a little blue.

Undoubtedly, there's a gorgeous woman waiting somewhere on the island, maybe already having a mid-day cocktail on the hotel patio, the only place that serves alcohol before three.

Tall, dark, and yummy follows me to the counter. "What changes were you talking about?"

I ring him up as I talk. "At the end of last season, some faceless corporation bought The Lady of the Light, the big hotel overlooking the beach, as well as a bunch of our cottages."

"That's where I'm staying," he says. "At the hotel."

"Then I extend my apologies on behalf of Murray Island. The new owner hasn't done anything with it yet, and even ordered Jim—he's the manager—not to do any upkeep apart from the barest maintenance." I recall him in the winter months, coming into Dave's for a beer and grumbling that The Lady was being neglected for the first time under his watch.

"I'm sure you'll still love the grand Lady," I add, hastily, not wanting to bad mouth our best island accommodations.

"But Jim has to wait for some corporate stooge to decide what the hotel needs. It's galling to think a company that has no connection to us holds her fate. Everyone on the island is wondering what the outcome will be."

"Sounds like someone has a plan to make improvements."

I snort, immediately wishing I hadn't.

"You don't agree," he surmises.

"Sounds to me like a half-assed, greedy off-islander thinks he or she knows better than the locals. Murray Island is just perfect. And I'm not the only one who thinks this way. What if some idiot deems the hotel to be too old and wants to tear it down?"

"Maybe the new owner will bring positive changes and more of those tourists you need to survive and pick over your sunglasses."

I stop myself from snorting again. "We have plenty of tourists," I mutter. Besides, this stranger has no idea what I need to survive. But I've said too much. That's what comes from being mostly silent in this store for too many hours.

Reaching for his money, I freeze when I see it's a hundred-dollar bill.

"Credit card?" I ask hopefully.

After a beat, he says, "Sorry, no. Phone app? Google Pay? Venmo?"

"Sorry, no," I echo his words, not having gotten the shop up to speed on alternate payment methods. To tell the truth, it's mainly because our internet is spotty.

"How much are the sunglasses?" he asks.

"Twenty-two dollars." Top of the line for my shop, but he looks at them again.

He clears his throat. "Do you have any that are more expensive?"

I nearly laugh until I see he's serious. It's the weirdest request I've ever had, until I realize he wants to pay more so I'll take the big bill.

"It's fine," I tell him, not wanting to make the customer uncomfortable, an ingrained rule my father taught me. I have the change, but it's a weird way to start the week.

"No worries, I can break a hundred," I say because suddenly I'm embarrassed by my small shop and reasonable prices. "It's just early in the season. Pre-season actually. You caught me off-guard. As I said, there aren't many tourists yet."

"Hopefully by next year, when the hotel is renovated and word gets around, there will be more visitors earlier in the season."

I bristle. "Renovated?" Now I'm giving him my narrow-eyed stare that my mother says makes me look like a disapproving librarian. In other words, squinting does not add to *my* attractiveness. "What makes you think it needs fixing up?"

The Lady of the Light, with her white-painted clapboard siding and her massive porch, is beautiful and elegant. You can take a photo and not know whether you're in the twenty-first or the nineteenth century.

He doesn't respond. Instead, he's already looking around. "Hold on. There are a few other things I need." In under five minutes, he's gone on a shopping spree to spend nearly one hundred even. And that's hard to do in my shop.

On the counter, he has placed two packages of mint gum, a box of tissue, which makes me wonder about his private-time activities, five chocolate bars with nuts, and a baseball hat that proclaims the wearer to be "Island Chillin'." I cannot imagine him wearing it, nor using the high-qual beach towel with a lobster pattern that he adds to the pile, along with a large tube of sunscreen, and one of the impractical—some might say, stupid—laminated island maps.

As I'm ringing all this up, he asks, "Is that enough?"

I feel myself getting a little bitchy. After all, I know he just wanted sunglasses, and he's doing me a favor. It's grating as hell. I want to appear to be a successful merchant. Which I am, thank you!

Instead, I feel like I'm fifteen again, working in my parents' store while some high-roller is trying to impress his summer girlfriend. Except there's no one here to impress.

Before I can respond, he adds two bottles of spring water. "I think you should raise your prices," he says and snatches a bag of pretzels from the display by the register, putting it on his pile.

"It's enough," I practically yell before bagging it all up in our plain paper sacks and giving him a couple dollars and some change, which he drops into the animal rescue donation tin.

Despite his insanely handsome face, I want him and his fat wallet out of my store.

"Can you cut the tag off?" he asks, removing the sunglasses from the top of his head. "Tag removal must be part of the price, right?"

I'd like to cut something off, I think unkindly. The talk of island renovations has unnerved me. My parents' big move off the island three years ago was change enough for one lifetime. Then Nan passed away a year later. And recently, I lost Max, my beloved yellow lab.

I reach under the counter and grab a pair of snips, clipping the plastic tag without taking the glasses from him.

We eye one another again. Damn if he's not one high-key sexy stud.

"Thanks," he says and slides them back up his head.

"De nada," I reply, trying to sound chill and friendly. I nearly blurt out that he can find me at Dave's, but I restrain myself.

He picks up the paper bags with handles and heads for the storefront. When he opens the door, the bell rings as it should. Then he pauses, and I swear, he sends me a grin so wickedly sensual, my toes curl.

"I'm staying for a week or two," he says. "Maybe longer. I hope I'll see you around."

Without giving me time to think of a glib comeback, like "likewise," he leaves. That's a good thing because my mouth has fallen slightly open. Is he interested in me? Or is he trying to toss me a bone, offering a torrid hookup with a horny tourist?

At least, I imagine it would be torrid, although I might be the hornier one of the two of us. But that killer smile tells me he'd be the kind to rip off clothes, his and mine, pretty fast. I am already picturing my legs wrapped around his lean hips.

Maybe he just thinks I want another of his hundred-dollar bills.

Ass-hat!

2

Marcus

I ducked out of the Whatnots store feeling like a heel. That pretty shopgirl was already a bit prickly. If she saw my name on my credit card, she might have recognized me as the off-islander intent on making those renovations she so plainly despises. Marcus Parisi isn't exactly a John Smith type of name.

On the other hand, I don't have anything to hide. It's not like I'm going to pave over the goddamned beach. Just making some upgrades by refreshing the old hotel, bringing its rooms and services into the here and now. Also, my real estate development company will improve the gray, weathered cottages as additional lodging because I hope to bring in plenty of new business.

This place is a jewel in the rough. It was once thought to be as nice as Nantucket or Martha's Vineyard. But those places have the rich population, the visiting celebrities, and the high-profile tourists. Murray Island, on the other hand, has fewer year-round inhabitants, a much smaller economy, and budget-style accommodations.

The budget aspect was apparent when I touched down two hours ago. Calling the pothole-infested landing strip "an airport" is being too generous. I'm only hoping my hotel isn't *infested* with any rodents or blood-sucking insects. If it is, I may sleep in the cockpit of my single-engine puddle jumper, which I flew over from the mainland.

With no tower or anyone there, merely a windsock for guidance, I chained the shining carbon-and-aramid fuselage under the sole available shelter, a glorified wooden carport. Despite it not being the fanciest plane I own, it looked like a spaceship tethered to an old hitching post.

After hefting my duffle bag over my shoulder, I'd started to walk. Not a single car, not even a bicycle passed me until I hit the edge of town. But by then, I could see the hotel and finished on foot.

The front desk of painted-white beadboard on top of well-worn flowery carpet appeared deserted. But there was a brass desk bell, which I found great satisfaction in pressing my palm onto a couple of times. The note resounded more deeply than the tinkling bell at Whatnots. Eventually, a woman older than me came out of a nearby room, brushing crumbs from her hands.

"Sorry, love. Just having a muffin and a cup of coffee. Do you have a reservation?"

"I do." I wasn't ready to announce who I was and make the staff nervous as cats. Confirming my assistant had booked me into and prepaid for the best room under her androgynous name, I followed the friendly clerk's directions, dumped off my bag, and was pointed to Whatnots for sunglasses.

The alternative had been undesirable, walking back to my plane and retrieving my favorite pair, stupidly left in the cockpit. I'm glad I went to the store. Meeting a feisty local gave me hope that the people here aren't as stuck in the past as the hideous, knitted bedspread and ugly lace curtains in my room might indicate. They might've been in style in the seventies.

As I stroll back to the hotel I own, I admire the good points that my assistant, Robin, told me about when she scouted the island last year, doing a little recon. The scenery of unspoiled beaches and cobblestone streets, the mild weather, the shabby quaintness that I intend to tweak and make less shabby. Murray Island has promise and then some.

While I walk, I know I ought to just leave the pretty shopkeeper alone. But there is something about her, something that tells me she'd be interesting to get to know. Then I let the matter drop. For now. Even if she was up for a drink with me and offered to be my own private tour guide, as soon as she found out who I was, she'd drop my *half-assed, greedy off-islander* self in the harbor.

I dump the bunch of unwanted junk I just bought onto the bed in my hotel room and notice the laminated map. Quick examination tells me it's not a map at all. Not to scale, nothing accurate, not to mention an X marking buried pirate treasure! I roll my eyes. I've been taken.

But it gives me an idea. Right now, Murray Island has one main set of clientele: impoverished college kids, who drink beer, eat hamburgers, and sadly, trash the place by the end of each summer. The beach I just admired across the street will soon be strewn with cans, wrappers, and loudmouths. Again, that's according to Robin. Her advice was to buy up some real estate, polish it, gentrify whatever I can, and sell it.

Smart advice, which I intend to follow. And although I only own the hotel and some cottages right now, I came to see what else I want to buy. I think I can bring both families and the wealthy, if I have the right attractions for the former and posh accommodations for the latter. Murray Island needs a blend of visitors who can afford to spend, keep the island economy growing, the beaches clean, and the locals happy.

That includes Miss Mary Sunshine at the shop. I'm sure she would be relieved to have a few extra weeks of customers at either end of the season, and a greater volume of people streaming in all summer. She'd be able to stock some pricier goods, maybe expand, even.

And a real map could lead people to actual places on the island, as well as have all the shops and restaurants, assuming there are more than what I've seen in the center of town.

I shake my head at my own expansionist dreams. I can't help it. Ever since I was young, I wanted to build and then build more. First with Legos, then working for my dad on construction sites, and then on a bigger scale as a developer. To my parents' delight, I've made a fortune doing what I love with real estate development.

Visiting Martha's Vineyard with my fiancée two summers ago and noticing little Murray Island on the ferry schedule, on the other side of the Cape from the expensive vacation places, I was intrigued. Last year was busy for me, so I sent my right-hand man, who happens to be a woman. Robin spent a week before suggesting, at the very least, that I start by purchasing the grand old hotel.

I'm even more stoked about the island's potential now that I'm here. Having stored my purchases, I take a bottle of water, don my new sunglasses, and head out to roam around the town.

From the air, I saw one main street running the length of Murray Island. Shorter streets cross through these from one side of the island to the other, shore to shore, here in town. Gray weathered or oil-painted clapboard houses are located on these side streets, interspersed with very few brick buildings and some wide timber dwellings, with some homes being almost on the beach. There are residents on the Atlantic side and on the side of the island that faces the coast of Massachusetts.

There's a shed near the hotel with a sign proclaiming, "Bicycles." But inexplicably, there aren't any to rent for another week and a half according to a piece of paper taped to the door. That irks me. How short-sighted. I consider going back in the hotel and finding out the easiest way to get that shed unlocked, even if I have to buy it and its contents today.

Since the weather's nice and I have nowhere to be for the first time in months, I decide to start walking. It's what I've been doing ever since I landed. There aren't a ton of stores, and the majority are as closed as the bike shed, although some have weekend hours.

Looking in the window of a shop diagonally across from Lindsey's, I see a lot of tourist bait. Called Island Treasures, the inventory looks to be anything but island-made. Frankly, the stock is unappealing. I know vacation destinations have to have this type of branded stuff as souvenirs, but this is particularly cheap-looking. A few well-made sweatshirts and tank tops with the island's name or likeness stenciled on them would be better than a large charm bracelet with the letters spelling "Murray Island" dangling from it. Someone should take a trip to Nantucket and see how it's done.

When I reach an open shop, it's a bakery. The enticing aroma wafts from the windows. Thinking I might grab a donut that I don't really need, I have my hand on the door when a sandy-haired guy pedals up on his bike, dismounting nearby. He leans it against an old oak, the roots of which have destroyed the sidewalk and part of the street. With nothing to lose, I get an idea and walk over to him.

"Can I rent your bicycle for the afternoon? You can name the price."

He looks me over, sizing me up, and shakes his head. But he's not saying no to me.

"Take it. No charge. Just put it back here when you're done." He starts to head into the bakery, which I no longer have an interest in. I want to go in the opposite direction from the air strip to see what the southern end of the island looks like.

"Thanks. I'm Marcus," I tell him, thinking we should be introduced if I'm going to borrow his property.

"Hey, there. I'm Carl. Enjoy."

Carl, who could be from forty to sixty, disappears inside without another word. I doubt such an exchange would've happened anywhere else but Murray Island or the smallest of small towns, USA. I guess he knows that even if I make off with his bicycle, I can't go very far. Probably half the people I pass will know whose it is.

So, I go on a bicycle ride, which I admit I haven't done since I was in Amsterdam about seven years earlier. Traveling through Europe after I'd made my first million, I went native. Gondolas in Venice, bikes in Amsterdam, and a sweet Ferrari for Paris, Barcelona, and Rome. And more than my share of gorgeous girls. It was a fun time.

I have to ride on the brick sidewalk because the street is mainly cobblestones. Some have sunk, some haven't. They're a nice touch, and I imagine they're authentically old, but I doubt a scooter would be safe on them, and certainly impossible to negotiate with a bicycle. A flat, narrow strip of bike lane between the road and the sidewalk would be a big improvement. Better yet, I start thinking about a bike path along the beach.

Even on the sidewalk, the front tire wobbles, and I nearly go over, regaining my balance as I pass the last commercial building. Or I think it is. About a mile out of the town, there's a squat, old stone-and-wood house with a brightly colored flag to attract attention. A hand-painted sign says, "Pottery."

Getting into the spirit of island exploration, I lean the bike, which has no kickstand, against the house and knock on the front door.

"Come in," says a female voice. "Don't stand on ceremony or on my front step."

Pushing the door open, I enter what must have once been the main room a couple hundred years ago, with a stone fireplace and light coming in the small, paned-glass windows. It's now a studio. An older woman with a blue scarf on her head of white hair is working a potter's wheel.

Behind her are shelves of her creations, cups and bowls and vases in glazes of varying colors, but predominantly rich blues and greens.

"Wow!" I say.

"Thank you," she says. "You have good taste."

That makes me laugh. "Sorry for barging in, ma'am, but I was cycling by and your flag caught my eye."

"As intended," she says. "Where are you from?"

I realize every local on the island can spot a visitor.

"Born in Virginia. Raised, schooled, and currently based in North Carolina."

"Lovely places."

She says it like she's been to both. Before I can ask whether she has, she shoots me another question, "What brings you to Murray Island?"

Weirdly, the mesmerizing sight of her hands working the wet clay and the hypnotic sound of the wheel make me nearly spill my guts. The pale gray clay almost seems to be a living thing, the way it moves and grows under her skilled fingers.

"Just looking around," I say. That part is true. "You're off the beaten path. Do you get many customers coming this way during the summer?"

"A few." She stops talking and uses a piece of metal to smooth the exterior of the pot from base to top. I'm fascinated by how quickly she's working. "Excuse me while I finish this, it's the tricky part. This is the skirt," she adds, cutting away the extra clay from the bottom of the vase.

"May I stay?"

"Please do." In moments, she uses wire to cut the finished pot free by sliding it underneath. "I have to keep the pressure low and even while lifting it off, and not use my thumbs because they'll make squash marks."

I watch her turn the wheel again slowly while she's barely grasping the base with just the middle of her fingers, not the tips, and then it's off. I release the breath I didn't realize I was holding.

She sets it on a wooden board next to her, which already holds two similar pieces.

"That turned out well," she says, stretching. "In answer to your question, not so many customers that I have to fend them off with a stick, but enough that I need to keep working to make more. I sell online, too." She gestures to the table beside the door, and a small blue bowl she's made, which holds her business cards.

The card, unlike the pottery, is uninspiring at best. "Jeannette James, Potter" with a phone number. No website and not even a picture of a pot.

"If someone buys something and it breaks or they want more after they get home, they can call me and order."

"Are their other artists and artisans on the island?"

"Quite a few of us. We have textile workers. You know what I mean, don't you? Knitters, mostly sweaters and beanies, and a weaver." She goes to a sink in the corner and washes her hands. "We have a stained-glass artist, another potter who's a bit more rustic than I am. Devon makes larger pieces for outside, mostly from red clay. I use his firing oven. Of course, there's a couple painters, always doing seascapes, which they sell to the tourists. Or they used to when we had more."

Then she looks at me. "I'm rambling. Comes from too many hours with pots and animals." She nods toward a chair under the far window. "Those are Sasha and Willy."

I hadn't even noticed a fat orange tabby curled on a cushion, nor the ancient-looking, grizzled dog, hardly larger than the cat, tucked under the chair. Now that I'm paying attention, I hear the latter's gentle snoring.

"Would you care for tea?" the potter asks.

First a free bicycle and now an invitation to tea. I wasn't on the mainland anymore.

"Thanks, no. I'll keep going. May I take a card?"

"Of course. And please call me Jeannette."

"If I thought it would survive the bike trip back to the hotel, I'd buy something."

She smiles, not pushing. Possibly not believing me, either.

"Do you sell in town?" I ask.

"In town?" She frowns.

"At one of the shops?"

She shrugs. "I sell here."

"You should have inventory where people can find it. Maybe all the island's creatives could sell in a shop near the ferry."

"Like at Whatnots and Such?" She shakes her head. "Lindsey might not have room for pots or paintings."

Lindsey? That must be the pretty woman I met earlier.

"Perhaps you could ask the owner for a shelf in the store."

Jeannette cocks her head. "Lindsey's parents own the store, but she has run it by herself for a few years."

I file that away and rearrange my thoughts slightly, because a shopgirl and an owner-manager view their businesses quite differently. We could probably have a discussion about other services the shop closest to the ferry might provide.

"If you could have some space at Whatnots and people want to see more, she could direct them to your studio." I shrug. "If not there, then maybe a store near the bakery." I almost add, *rather than the cheap junk sold with "Murray Island" stamped on it.*

I keep the negative thoughts to myself and say instead, "People would appreciate authentic wares of the island."

I earn another smile. "An entrepreneurial spirit," she says. "I like that. Upon occasion, I have set up a table near the hotel."

My hotel. *Hm.* I wonder if there's room to build out a gift shop near the main entrance. Would that be crass? It might be better to let the shops sell and the hotel provide first-class accommodations.

"Good idea," I say and drop the matter. Maybe after I've sorted out a few things and figured out how to attract tourists, then I can convince all the artisans to have a profitable co-op in the bustling heart of Murray Island. That is, if I can bring in the caliber of visitors with money to burn.

Then, before I can stop myself, I'm asking about the curvy shopkeeper. "Has Lindsey lived on the island for a long time?"

The potter nods. "She has, with her parents and her father's parents before that. But Lindsey's alone now. Her parents moved away a few years ago."

I'm shocked, maybe because my parents live about half an hour from me. Or it could be because the natural progression of things is for the child to leave, especially to fly away from a small nest like Murray Island, and go live her life in the big world.

"They left her?"

Another small frown from Jeannette. "What's your name?"

"Marcus." Again, leaving off my last name seems prudent.

"Well, Marcus, it's nice to meet you. I believe Lindsey had her reasons for staying, including having her grandmother still on the island at the time, although she has since passed away. Other than that, you'd have to ask her yourself. Anyway, I'm glad she stayed. She's a valuable member of our community, and the third generation to run that shop for our visitors."

"You don't go to her store?" I can't imagine locals find much value in the touristy beach items.

"Not much, but she's important to the social fabric of the island quite apart from her shop." She's looking at me like I'm puzzling her. "People are precious for who they are, not what they do. Don't you think?"

I think she's admonishing me. Am I being too capitalistic? My friends have accused me of that before a time or two. It's not that I care about the money because I have plenty. But I see the potential for everyone to make more, and it's hard not to try to "fix" their financial futures, too.

With the pretty, honeyed blonde on my mind, it somehow doesn't surprise me too much when I see Lindsey again later. After hours spent cycling, getting lost despite being on an island, and not talking to anyone after Jeannette, I reenter the town center, creatively named Murray Town.

I've had a necessarily longer-than-usual shower because the ancient shower head in the tiled tub delivered a tepid drizzle, barely enough to rinse the soap off my skin. At least I'm sweat-free when I follow the recommendation of the hotel staff for casual dining and enter Dave's Beach Bar.

Sadly, it has all the charm of a beer-scented dive. A paneled wall frames a Keno screen, and two folding trays hold bussing tubs of dirty dishes against a wall in the dining room. The cramped bar area at one end contains a single window facing the ocean. Someone has closed not only that shade but those in the dining area, too, darkening the entire place. And all the people, about half a dozen who are presumably locals, hang by the bar where a small TV flickers.

I could be anywhere, but I'd never guess I was a stone's throw from the ocean. What a waste of space! Why not just shutter the ugly place and call it a day?

I don't have high hopes for the dining, casual or otherwise. A sign says, "Seat yourself." But I wonder how long it'll be before anyone knows I'm here.

Seven long minutes to be exact. And that's when Lindsey strolls out of what I assume is the swinging door to the kitchen.

Her caramel-streaked hair is held high in a pony tail. She's wearing the same hip-hugging jeans she had on earlier, and a long-sleeve T-shirt that says "Dave's -- For Fun and Food."

Considering the top is on the tight side and hugs her generous breasts, stretching the words across them in an eye-catching way, I wonder if the slogan means something more. Maybe this Dave guy knows how to promote after all. She falters at the sight of me, then hurries over.

3

Lindsey

I swear Dave's dining room was empty a minute ago, like it almost always is on a Thursday night before the official start of the season. But suddenly, as if a handsome warlock has materialized in our midst, there's Mr. Hundred-Dollar Bill himself, seated at a table halfway between the bar and front door.

"*Jeez*, I'm sorry. Have you been here long?"

"No. I just had time to take in the ambiance."

Is he kidding? Yes, by the slight smirk, I would say he is. "There's not much open this time of year," I admit. "Tomorrow and Saturday, The Clamdigger serves dinner. In a week, it'll open Tuesday through Saturday. The food is much better there."

His mouth opens slightly, then closes. He frowns. "Do you normally badmouth the place you work and do it behind the owner's back?"

I'm puzzled. What's he talking about? Then it hits me. "Hold on." I go to the kitchen door and push it open. Dave is sitting on his stool, watching sports on his tiny TV. "Can you come out here a moment?"

Dave ambles out with his impressive girth. Actually, his legs and arms haven't changed much during my whole life of knowing him, but his middle has greatly expanded. I think it's due to a steady diet of his own greasy cooking, regularly washed down with beer.

We stand side-by-side in front of the know-it-all's table.

"This gentleman is taking umbrage with my saying that The Clamdigger has better food."

"He's taking what?" Dave asks me, bless his heart.

"He thinks I shouldn't say that The Clamdigger is better than our place, and that I especially shouldn't say it unless you're able to hear me."

Dave makes a face. The disapproving tourist looks ever-so-slightly embarrassed. Normally, I would never make a customer uncomfortable, neither at my shop nor here at the tavern. But this guy! Telling me off. Sorry, *no!*

"Have you eaten at The Clamdigger?" Dave asks Mr. Hundred-Dollar Bill.

"No, I just arrived today."

"Then how can you argue? They serve better food. Everyone knows that." Then he looks at me. "Don't waste my time on fools, Lindsey."

With that, Dave leaves us. My point made, my ruffled feathers smoothed, I am aware of the thick, awkward silence. Perhaps I went too far to prove a point, and I wish Dave hadn't used the word *fool*.

My customer looks unimpressed with the entire performance, and I wouldn't blame him if he walked out. Trying to turn the situation into a pleasant experience between patron and server, I nod and send him a small smile.

"Now that's settled, do you know what you want?"

"A menu," he says drily.

Wow, he *is* a comedian. But I also should have noticed. I know when I'm wrong.

"Sorry." I head to the cash register and grab him a menu, glance at a ketchup stain, and swap it for another one.

"Here you go." I hand it over. He's still staring at me. Those tawny golden eyes don't waver as they slice me up. I clear my throat. "Let's start with the easy stuff. Do you know what you want to drink? We have some beers on tap." I list them off. "And the rest are on the backside of the menu. Or pretty much any cocktail you want. Our bartender is fab. And we have a limited wine selection. House red or white."

"Black and tan, please."

"All-righty," I say, wondering why I do until I realize he's making me more than a little nervous. It's the way he's keeping his gaze fixed on mine.

I wish I'd said a much smoother opening line when I first came over, like, "Hey there, I'm Lindsey, I'll be your server." But it's not the type of place where we do that. Or maybe I'm just not that kind of person. I've experienced it on the mainland and found it cringey. Personally, I'm not trying to strike up a friendship with each tourist who comes in, and the islanders already know my name.

I also regret making a big deal out of the whole Clamdigger remark.

"I'll get your drink, and then you can tell me what you want to eat."

"I'm sorry I accused you of badmouthing," he says. "Stupid of me."

That's good. I'm not the only one feeling regret. "That's OK. All is forgiven." I start to walk away but want to give him some menu advice. Turning quickly, I catch him looking at my ass. It gives me boost of satisfaction.

"While you're considering, I recommend you stick to the simpler fare. Like the burgers or . . ." *Shit!* I can't lie. "Or the burgers." I laugh lightly, but I hope he takes me up on my suggestion.

Glancing at the menu, he asks, "Not the chicken parm, then, or fettuccine alfredo?"

I wish Dave would remove those things from the menu since we haven't let him serve either in over a year. Maybe two.

"Not unless you want to spend the night worshiping the porcelain god." I hate to be blunt, but I believe I've made my point.

While Dave knows this isn't a fine-dining establishment, he thinks he's all that and a bag of donuts when it comes to cooking the few things we offer. But he's not.

The locals know better, and anyone who serves here steers off-islanders clear. Sometimes, if someone is insistent, I say, "Sorry, it was so popular we're all out of it. And that. And that."

"I don't need any time to decide then. I'll have a burger. Onions and cheese, if they're available."

"Of course they are," I quip. "We're not savages." But I wink because I don't hold a grudge. "Tasty fries, too. I'll bring you some."

I walk away, knowing his gaze is on my rear end, which is appreciated since there haven't been any attractive, single guys around for a while. My last boyfriend was a year ago. A summer fling because I was lonely. Not like a one-nighter or any such desperate act on my part. Jacob worked with a small archaeological group from UMass Amherst. They came for six whole weeks to dig up one end of the island, past the airport and near the lighthouse where the natives lived hundreds of years ago.

They had a successful dig, finding some earthenware vessels and arrows, which are kept on the first floor of our town hall. Successful for me, too, since I was simply happy to be touched by another human being. Best part was not being broken-hearted when he left. It was too light and fluffy for that.

It's trickier dating a local because when it ends, you're stuck together on about nineteen square miles of land.

That's how it is with me and Conor, who owns Island Treasures, the *cheap-shit-sold-expensive* store, as I think of it. He orders it online from overseas.

I know I have some crap in my store, too, but at least mine is utilitarian, like a hat or a towel. His is just straight-up useless garbage. Everything is decorated with a generic lighthouse or a harbor that vaguely resembles ours, and no one needs any of it—acrylic, blue pineapple-shaped ice buckets, ugly garden décor shaped like whales and sharks, and massive "decorative" red lobster wall-hangings made out of ceramic. He stamps "Murray Island" on whatever he can with indelible ink for added authenticity.

We dated for not even an entire month, three years ago, and broke up over two issues. For one, he is greedy, which is ugly to be around. When he told me how much markup he makes on his child-labor-made junk and said it with a proud smile, I'd never been so disgusted.

And secondly, his kisses didn't float my boat, or my skirt, or any other part of me. I didn't think he would take it as hard as he did, but there's a deficit of single people in our age group on Murray Island. Conor went out of his way to make our break-up ugly, with a capital *Ugh*!

He still scowls whenever we run into one another, which is about three times a week.

After putting in my one customer's food order, I return from the bar with the black and tan. Mr. Hundred-Dollar Bill is texting someone, not looking up, so I leave him alone. He's still typing away when I bring his food, which is disappointing. Although some of our exchanges have been rough already, I generally appreciate having a gorgeous guy to interact with.

Hoping it's not psycho to sneak peeks through the corner of the window in the kitchen door, watching the man eat, I head over to his table again as soon as he's finished. Not surprisingly, I feel a little wistful while clearing away his dishes. He'll leave and, just like that, the evening—and maybe the rest of the summer—will be utterly boring again.

"What's the fun?" Mr. Hundred-Dollar Bill asks me out of the blue.

"Sorry?" My brain is blank.

He points to my breasts. *What the . . . ?* Then I realize he's reading my T-shirt. "Oh, that fun!" My cheeks grow warm because, for a split second, I thought he was taking the conversation in a different direction. "Keno," I say.

"Really?"

I agree with his disappointed expression. "Here at Dave's, that's about it, except for when there's a big sporting event with a New England team. Then this place is packed around the TV in the bar. Locals, of course."

"Seems unlikely summer tourists would come in here to watch the Stanley Cup or a baseball game. You'd need a more open layout and a bigger TV."

I play along. "Maybe we can rip the roof off and have an open-air court to coincide with Wimbledon."

He rolls his eyes, then smirks. "I can imagine if there was an inviting patio with a big screen TV, some folks would eat and drink while watching tennis or baseball when they're tired of the beach. But what would draw people in here earlier in the season?"

"You said that before," I remind him, "but it makes no sense. Do you feel the chill in the air?"

"Yes, ma'am," he says, which is kinda cute and sexy. "The sun's gone down."

Smart ass! "That chill is because it's May. If tourists show up earlier in the year, they won't be able to sit on the beach, which is the main thing people come here to do. That and swim, which they also can't comfortably do until late-June or July."

Undaunted, he picks up his nearly empty beer glass. "Maybe there should be some other activities and attractions."

"Attractions? This isn't Disneyland. And we don't want it to be."

"I know," he says, draining the last mouthful before setting the glass down. "Murray Island is perfect just the way it is. I believe you said that when you were telling me about the half-assed, greedy off-islander who might change it. To me, the island is stagnant."

What the hell! "I think the word you mean is *historic*."

He chuckles, which pisses me off further. I'm still holding the tray with his dirty dishes, and he's lucky I don't let it slip onto his lap.

"For your information, we already have activities for the early tourons . . . I mean *guests*." It's a stupid slip because I really do know which side my bread is buttered, and I don't mind people coming to visit the island. Polite people with credit cards. But he's rubbing me the wrong way.

Instantly, the unwelcome thought of rubbing my bare skin across his bare skin makes me feel prickly hot.

Clearing my throat, I add, "We have classic summer fun. And if visitors come early, like you, there's shuffleboard, tennis, bike riding." I've run out of ideas.

"The bicycles aren't available yet, which is lame," he states firmly, like it matters to him. "I saw the cracked and crumbled *remains* of a shuffleboard court behind the hotel. I bet the tennis court is in the same condition."

I don't respond because he's right. I can't say that I've seen the court in a few years since it's overgrown with weeds. Then I think of a favorite activity.

"Beachcombing."

He nods. "Basically, walking on the beach."

I shrug. "I enjoy that."

"Is there an arcade?" he asks.

I glance toward the bar where there's a pinball machine from before I was born and shake my head.

"How about virtual gaming?"

"*Ugh!* Why would anyone come to this beautiful island and then strap on goggles and go into a virtual world?"

"What if it's raining, cold, dark, or windy?" Then he asks, "Go karts?"

"Nope."

"Bowling alley?"

"Nope."

"Movie theatre?"

Thank God I can say, "Yes!"

"We don't have a movie theater," Dave says, passing through the nearly deserted room with a crate of empty bottles on his shoulder.

"What do you call the theater at the hotel?" I ask him.

"A shitbox," Dave quips and keeps on walking, disappearing out the side door to the dumpster area. I've told him not to walk through the dining room when we have customers.

Mr. Hundred-Dollar Bill looks like he wants to laugh but wisely doesn't. He leans back in the uncomfortable chair and says, "I'm staying at the hotel, and I haven't seen a theater."

"In the attached annex. There's a big screen and seating for about forty people."

I can see he's not impressed. "What's playing tonight?"

He's got me there. "Nothing. It's only open on Fridays and Saturdays."

"All year round?"

"Yes." I tilt my chin in the air. "Locals need to watch movies, too." But I never go. No one I hang out with does.

"First run movies?" he persists.

I'm not about to tell him it's a VCR machine hooked up to a projector, or some such contraption. "I have to get these into the dishwasher. Do you want anything else?" Before he can answer, I add, "I think it's too late for much except drinks. Kitchen's closed."

"Just the check," he says. "Since it's already going on eight, I better hurry off to bed. I'm exhausted from all the activities."

"Ha-ha." I return to the small kitchen and take my time loading the dishwasher. He can wait for his check since he's correct. There is literally nothing else for him to do but stay here and drink, which he doesn't want to do. Or go to bed.

Fortunately, he has the amenities of our finest hotel. He can take a long, scalding shower because I assume they have better water pressure than I do and massive hot water tanks. And my filthy brain instantly pictures him doing exactly that, imagining the water cascading over his broad chest, down the indentations of his six-pack before droplets catch in the thatch of hair over his manly parts.

My mouth goes dry, and I wrestle my thoughts back to what I'd been thinking before his naked body stormed into my lonely brain.

He can also avail himself of cable TV and internet where he's staying. I got rid of my cable after my parents left, and my internet is spotty at best. Basically, he has nothing to complain about.

Melinda, who tends bar, walks in to grab herself a few more limes, if her empty bowl is any indication. As usual, the bar is half-filled with the regular beer drinkers, as well as those who hit the harder stuff. All men, most of the time. And she handles them with ease.

"Who's the yummy man-candy?" she asks, setting the bowl down and stopping to lean against the stainless counter. Her hands go up to check that her curly brown hair is staying in its messy bun.

I know who she means. "Guest at the hotel. Seems to be by himself. A little cagey."

"What do you mean?" She fills the bowl with citrus from the cooler.

"No credit card at the shop today. Paid in cash."

She shrugs.

"A hundred-dollar bill," I add.

"*Hm.* Wealthy and well-built. Sweet."

Mel is about five years older than me, about four inches shorter, rounder everywhere, and married to Sam, who does something of everything. He fishes, runs the summer bike rentals, and does handyman jobs. I don't know how they eke out a living through the winter months on her bartending tips and Sam's unsteady work, but they do. She also stands in as a server when it's not busy enough to pay me, which is most of the winter until last week when Dave began ramping up.

"I don't know if he's wealthy," I say. "Why would he come before the season except to save money? Maybe he's dealing drugs. That would explain the cash."

Mel is staring at me. "You need a hobby," she says. "Oh, that reminds me. We have too much venison in our freezer. Sam's mom didn't take any this year. Do you want some?"

Sam is a hunter, too. "Sure. I'll take whatever you want to give." And then another thought flashes through my mind. I snap my fingers and hurry out to the hot stranger who has left his table and looking out the bar window toward the ocean. Since the sun has set, all he can see is his own reflection, but that's a pretty good view.

"Deer hunting," I say, feeling smug.

He turns, and I'm too close. I take a step back when confronted with his tawny eyes and slight smile.

"What are we talking about?" he asks.

"We have deer hunting on the island. It's popular. Even some off-islanders make the trip to do it."

He nods. "But no hunting now, right?"

Suddenly, I feel foolish trying to make Murray Island into more than it is.

"No. That's in November."

He's still staring at me.

"What?" I ask.

"My check."

"Oh!" I totally spaced. "I'll be right back."

"No, it's fine. If my math serves me, this should cover it." He hands me two twenties and a ten-dollar bill.

He had a burger, fries, and a single black and tan. So yes, it covers it. But now I'm puzzled.

"Why didn't you give me small bills earlier? At my shop?"

"I went to the bank. Guess what?" He leans closer until I'm treated to the gold flecks in his eyes. "Just when I thought I'd have to purchase some doubloons, turns out Murray Island has an ATM."

He's actually quite funny, in a wry way. "I'll get your change. I promise I'll be quick, but you've overpaid." I try to shove a twenty back into his hand, but he shakes his head.

"The rest is tip," he says.

A very generous one, but I'm not going to protest, except I must have a look on my face because he adds, "It's not that I mind waiting, but I flew in early and spent all day walking and bicycling. I'm going to go enjoy my world-class hotel room, that definitely doesn't need any renovations."

He's making fun of The Lady of the Light, but I don't say anything other than "Thanks."

I'm still gripping the cash while watching him walk out, unable to decide what looks better—his broad shoulders, his tight butt, or his sculpted thighs.

When I remember to blink and close my fly-catching mouth, which dropped open from thoughts of touching those muscles, I turn to see Mel watching me. With a shrug, I go back into the kitchen, knowing there is no way to hide or deny my obvious interest. OK, some might call it *lust*.

4

Lindsey

With the kitchen closed, my shift is done. And it registers in my tired brain as I'm getting my purse that Mr. Hundred-Dollar Bill said he flew in. Interesting.

I collect my tips, a better haul than usual for a quiet Thursday thanks to the cash-carrying stranger and to the couple from the shop who also came in earlier. They were surprised to see me, but took my advice on burgers, as well.

Leaving the bar, I'm glad I have my coat. It's not winter anymore, but it's not reliably shorts-weather, either, especially after the sun goes down. I have a quick ten-minute walk to where my family's house has stood for longer than the Coopers have lived in it. About a hundred and ninety years, in fact.

"I was thinking," says a voice, making me jump again. It's my handsome stranger.

"Are you a crazy stalker?" I demand, my heart racing. I wonder if I'll have to swing my purse and clunk him on the head. Since there's a bottle of water in it and a chocolate bar, I might do a little damage.

He shrugs. "I got caught up looking at the harbor lights."

I peer past him, taking in the sight that I barely notice any longer.

"Besides," he adds, his tone playful, "maybe you're the one stalking me."

I snort laugh. "You just keep showing up where I work."

"Do you work anywhere else?" he asks.

"Nope. That's it."

"Then if I see you in the hotel lobby, I'll know I was right and you're the one following me."

"I guess so." He's a bit odd, but I like the way he's teasing me as if we're already friends.

"I take it you and your family own Whatnots, but you moonlight working for someone else," he muses, and we start to walk, luckily in the same direction. "That's odd."

"It's not," I explain. "The island economy is more communal than on the mainland. Many of us do various jobs and work for one another. That's just how it is to survive."

In the dusky light, I see him nod. "Are you heading home? Or to the movies?" he asks.

There he goes again, trying to get a rise out of me over our lack of nightlife. "Home. Been a long day."

He looks around. There are very few people on the street. Off-islanders might find it eerie.

"Walking?" he asks.

"Yup. I live pretty close. But then, so does everyone else."

"May I walk you home?" he asks. "It's getting dark fast."

I don't laugh at his statement of the obvious. The island is certainly not brightly lit like a city, but it's what I'm used to.

Besides, how sweet of him. On the other hand, I still don't know him from a serial killer.

"Thanks, but no thanks."

"I get it. You don't trust me. You don't know my name yet."

"Yet?" I repeat.

"Well, as I said earlier today, I'll be here for at least a week. Might as well be friendly. I'm Marcus."

I can be friendly. "I'm Lindsey."

"Now that, I do know. From Jeannette James," he adds before I can ask how.

I wonder why I came up in their conversation, but I'll ask *her*, not him. We shake hands, and I get a zing from the skin-to-skin touch. I attribute the unexpected tingling to the fact that it's been a few months since I touched anyone. I saw my parents on the mainland in February for my father's birthday. But hugging my parents is comforting while this is sizzling with excitement.

"I'm going past the hotel," I tell him, gesturing to the looming building a few blocks up. "I guess I'll walk *you* home."

"That doesn't feel right," he says, "but I'm a guest in your strange land, so I'll go along with your custom."

Marcus has me laughing again. We walk along Spire Street in silence for a few feet, then he asks, "Is there a tourist or info office?"

"Not exactly. Louise, our town hall clerk, prints up a weekly calendar during the summer about what's going on. And any of the business owners can tell you pretty much whatever you want to know. Most people stop at my store when they get off the ferry, and I give them any info they need."

"You're the welcome-wagon lady?" he asks.

"I guess I am."

"With the maps that are actually placemats?"

"Yup. If you'd asked me questions, I could've answered them. Best place to stay, you're staying in it until the new owner ruins its historic elegance. Best place to eat, you missed it by a block, but since The Clamdigger was closed tonight, you got the second best. Also, the best bartender, but you didn't try Melinda's fancy drinks."

"Best server?" he asks, as we reach the stone path that leads to the hotel's front door and lobby.

I make a small bow and wave my hand in the air like a Regency lord. "You had her, sir."

Hearing the flirty words from my mouth, I straighten. His gaze drops to my mouth, and I feel the urge to step forward and press my lips against the slight stubble on his jaw before going in for an open-mouthed kiss.

It wouldn't be much of a leap from that to molding myself against his fit, hard body. I wouldn't need more than a hot, greedy kiss and a few seconds' blissful sensation of his hardness against my curves. Sure, only a second or two, and I'd be good to go home and imagine the rest.

"OK, then," I say, seeing his grin as if he knows what I'm thinking. When did the air become charged between us? I could accompany him inside and let go of every last thread of morality and all my inhibitions for a longer, more intimate taste of his company.

Instead, I say, "Probably see you around. Best breakfast is Macey's Grill, opens at seven-thirty, closes at twelve fifty-eight on the dot when Mrs. Macey and her sister call it quits. If you just want coffee and a pastry, go to Carl's Bakehouse. Opens at seven."

"I think he leant me his bicycle earlier today," he says. "And I'm impressed. You really are the head of island tourism."

For some reason, his compliment warms me, even if he thinks we're just too po-dunk for a real tourist office.

"Good night, Lindsey. See you tomorrow."

Why does that make me shiver? It's the certainty of it, I suppose.

"Good night, Marcus. Sleep well."

$♥$♥$♥$

Marcus

By the time I'm stretched out on the rough but clean sheets in my hotel room, enjoying the peace and quiet, I have an idea. While it's too early for sleep, even after I finally turn off my phone and plug it in, I try to spend some useful time pondering the notion that came to me while undressing: winning over Lindsey is integral. With a native islander on my side, it'll be much easier to navigate local politics and not step on the wrong toes.

Picturing Lindsey in her tight T-shirt does not advance my plan, nor do thoughts of removing that same shirt and filling my hands with her breasts. Effortlessly, she is one of the sexiest women I've ever met. Her ass in those jeans, her wry smile, those knowing eyes, and again, her generous breasts. If she's up for a casual relationship while I'm on the island, I'd be up for it in a heartbeat. One part of me is already up for it and I try to push her out of my thoughts and get some sleep.

I manage to relax while contemplating the horses in my stable at home. There is something about those large, spirited animals, especially the goofy ones, that makes me sincerely happy and stress-free.

Well rested from turning in earlier than I have since forever, I eat at Mrs. Macey's breakfast place just after she opens. Locals stream in behind me, but I get a table against the wall under a poster of two eggs with happy faces. They're wearing hats and are, in turn, sitting eating from a plate of eggs, bacon, and toast. It creeps me out a little.

"What can I get you, honey?" asks the server, a woman who might be my mother's age. She's already pouring coffee into the white cup next to my paper placemat.

I nearly suggest she get some of Lindsey's laminated maps. Instead, I point to the poster. "Over medium eggs and rye toast, please. No faces and no bacon, ma'am. Thanks."

She winks at me. It's a nice touch when my meal comes with hashbrowns, which I can tell upon first bite didn't come frozen in a bag. She also sets down a small bowl of something she calls "beach plum" jam, which I spread over my toast and devour. If someone on the island isn't already selling this by the large jarful, then I am going to lose my shit.

When my server refills my coffee cup, she says, "I forgot to ask whether you want an apple or a banana?"

I wonder if this is some kind of joke or a psychological test. "Neither, thanks."

She sighs. "My sister likes everyone to leave with a piece of fruit."

I look around and see that most people have one or the other on their table next to their plate.

"Why?"

My server shrugs. "Keeps you regular."

"I don't think a banana does," I argue.

"Maybe not, but some like it better."

"Nicky," hollers a woman from behind the counter where there are six stools of diners. A nanosecond after my server turns, a red apple comes hurling our way. She catches it without effort, setting it down beside my plate. "I guess my sister chose for you."

I laugh, deciding to go with the flow. "Super. I would've chosen an apple anyway."

"How long are you staying, Marcus?"

She shows a friendly interest like the potter from the day before. But I'm disconcerted that she knows my first name. For some reason, it seems rude to ask her how. I'm guessing either from bicycle Carl or someone at the hotel. I can't help wondering if she knows my last name and exactly who I am. If she did, I might be wearing the coffee refill on my head instead of watching her pour it into a cup.

"At least a week, but maybe more." I'm fairly sure I can meet with every business owner in a week. I'm deciding whether there are more commercial or residential properties

I want to buy and fix up, and also what land is available for sale.

After the delicious breakfast, I go straight to Whatnots and Such. The bell above the door rings, but Lindsey isn't in the back as she was yesterday. She's out from behind the counter and on only the second rung of a step ladder, which is laughable as it hardly puts her a foot above the floor. She's using the bristle end of a large, wooden push-broom to loop a cardboard cutout of a whale over one blade of the paddle fan.

"Good morning," I say before she can turn.

However, apparently, the mere sound of my voice is enough for her to swivel on the small step as she twists to look at me, wobbles, and loses her balance. The broom she's holding high overhead crashes onto the stationary fan, knocking the entire fan sideways while breaking off one of the paddles.

Meanwhile, she is toppling over backward, unbalanced by the loss of the broom. I'm already rushing forward to catch her, suddenly holding her warm, lush body in my arms and looking down into flushed face. Startled eyes, the dark blue of a stormy sky, gaze up at me.

"My hero," she quips, then struggles like a stray cat I'm holding against its will.

I set her down immediately. "Good thing I played football."

Having gone to sleep thinking about Lindsey, my body is humming from holding her close two seconds after seeing her. I wasn't wrong. She's the complete package of pretty face, curvy body, hint of sarcasm, and a great laugh.

On her feet, she's ignoring me and looking up at the cock-eyed fan and broken paddle blade.

"Well, shit!" she says.

"Are you OK?"

"Obviously, I am, but that looks like hell, doesn't it?" After staring at it for a moment as if she thinks it might magically fix itself, she looks at me, eyes narrowed. "What do you want?"

She's feisty this morning.

"You," I say, watching those eyes widen like quarters.

"Excuse me?"

"I want you to show me the sights," I say, despite suspecting she has zero interest.

"I have to stay in my shop, and now fix this fan, too, although that's clearly above my pay grade." She retrieves the broom, using the handle end to straighten the pendulum part of the fan. At least it's hanging straight down again.

"That's already better," she says. "If I order a new paddle, does it really matter if it matches? I should call Sam." She seems to be talking to herself until she asks, "Does it? I mean, wouldn't any piece of lightweight wood do the trick to push air around?"

"Might look a bit run-down," I say, "if it doesn't match the others."

She doesn't like that response and sends me a glare. "Seriously, what do you need? More snacks for the day? Because I'm busy."

"Seriously," I echo her. "I want you to take me all over the island."

"Why don't you use the map you bought?" she snaps back.

"It's not a real map, and you know it. I can't even fold it up and put it in my pocket because it's laminated."

"We're surrounded by water," Lindsey explains as if I'm stupid.

"Meaning?"

"It's laminated to keep it dry. You can take it to the beach or the rocky inlet or the caves or even whale watching," she insists, "*without* it being ruined by saltwater."

"I think you can eat a plate of eggs and hashbrowns off it without it being ruined by a splash of orange juice or coffee because it's actually a placemat. Admit it."

She tries to keep a stern, straight face, but she can't. And when this woman's smile appears, I swear it's like the clouds have parted after a thunderstorm. Wow!

"Come on," I urge, not afraid of challenge. And she's the most challenging and interesting thing so far on this island. "Show me around."

"I have to work," she points out, sounding somewhat less hostile.

"Do you have a day off?" I ask.

"Not a full day, not from both jobs at the same time," she returns, her tone still holding a waspish vibe.

When even she must realize she's being difficult, she adds, "I close the store at eleven on Sunday, after the morning ferry leaves. I'm open just to sell Dramamine and snacks anyway."

This is crazy. She should be open all day, seven days a week during the season, which means she should hire someone. I bet she loses business every Sunday afternoon in June, July, and August when weekend visitors want water and snacks. I bite my tongue because it's not my problem.

"Then you'll give me the locals-only tour on Sunday?"

She hesitates.

"I'll pay you by the hour."

"Deal," she says without even waiting to hear how much.

I laugh. "Deal. And I'll bring the map. We can use a crayon to mark off each place we visit."

She joins in the laughter. It's an enjoyable sound. A few moments later, she asks, "You know those names are all made up, don't you?"

I feign shock. "You mean I can't listen to seductive sirens lure me to my doom at Siren Sands or swim with enticing mermaids in the bay?"

"'Fraid not. Just some kelp-strewn beaches, although we get a lot of dolphins in the bay. Much better than prickly mermaids, if you ask me."

"Bummer. But you did just mention whale watching. Is that an option?" For some stupid reason, I gesture to the cardboard whale that she retrieved from the floor, and she scowls up at her broken fan again. "I didn't see any signs for whale watching trips at the dock," I say. "Nor were they mentioned on the placemat."

"Here, you can watch this instead." She hands me the whale cut-out, and folds up the step ladder before she adds, "Our small whale watching tour shut down during COVID and never reopened. But admit it. The map would be awesome, even if you dropped it overboard and fished it out."

I file away the info that Murray Island needs to revamp its whale watching business, something I can definitely remedy. I could help them purchase a sturdy, moderate-size boat and outfit it with a grill. The joy of seeing such magnificent creatures up close has stayed with me since I was eleven years old, along with the treat of a hotdog when I was extra hungry from the sun and salt spray.

For now, I'll have to try to spy whales from the land, which reminds me of the one impressive sight on the map that is real.

"I bet the lighthouse is worth looking at and offers a great view."

She nods thoughtfully. "It's a goodly trek out there, a lot of stairs to climb. Let me check the schedule and see who's manning it this week."

"Manning it?"

"Or *woman*-ning," she adds, carrying the aluminum stepladder behind the counter and tucking it inside the open doorway to the back room. "Every family with an able-bodied member takes a week."

"Living in the lighthouse?" What a cool if antiquated arrangement.

"Yup. Tending the light is serious business. It's important to keep boats from crashing into our island," she says, like I don't know what a lighthouse is for.

I have an image of a *Moby Dick*-era sailor in a strong gale, depending on the Murray Island light for his safety. And this curvy blonde up there in a hurricane doing her duty.

"You're not kidding, are you?"

"Nope. It's in the island's by-laws. Of course, there are a few who won't or can't, but very few. Some even look at staying in the small annex as a mini-vacay."

"What about you?"

"I've never done a week. My father did it once as a young man and again with my mother, but I wasn't alive. And there are enough islanders that it can be years before a family's turn comes up again."

I think that community spirit is the coolest thing about Murray Island. Apart from Lindsey.

"Then Sunday?" I ask, pressing my request while she still sounds friendly. "Is it a date?"

Her expression clouds over, and I wish I'd used any other word.

"I mean, do we have an agreement?" I'm looking forward to spending time with Lindsey and having her show me around her island. Soon to be *my* island in a different way, depending on how much I invest in it.

"For twenty-five an hour," she says, "yes, we do."

Ha! She's a businesswoman, after all.

"I'm sure I'll see you before then," I say, since Sunday is a few days away.

"Maybe," she allows, "but the better restaurant, The Clamdigger, opens at five. Give it a try if you want anything other than a burger."

"Are you trying to keep me out of Dave's tonight?"

She laughs. "Trying to save your stomach is all. Go where you like."

"Oh, I will," I say, returning the cardboard whale to her. "Why were you hanging them if you don't offer whale watching on the island?"

Lindsey shrugs. "Just for ambiance. And our visitors might want to go for a day trip to one of the southern islands or even to Boston Harbor, where they can go whale watching."

I change my mind. She's *not* a businesswoman. "Why would you send people off the island? That's asinine."

Her face grows ruddy. *Whoops!* I've offended her. "I mean, it's not smart to send your customers away to places that offer so much more."

"As an island business owner," she says, "sometimes, you have to think of what's best for your visitors and not simply your bottom line."

She's right in a way. "Agreed," I say, "but I think as a business owner, you should try your best to provide whatever your visitors need right here. And if you can't do it, then you should make sure who can, in this case, the boat owner, steps up. For the good of the entire island."

Not sure if I've pissed her off, I grab a bottle of water and a few granola bars.

She holds out her hand, then almost looks disappointed when I place a ten-dollar bill on her palm.

"Are you nearly out of money already?" she asks, pressing buttons on the antiquated cash register.

Now that *is* funny. "Don't I look like a billionaire?" I ask, heading for the door.

Her laughter reaches me, along with her words, "Not even close."

5

Lindsey

As expected, I see Marcus a few more times before Sunday. He seems to be everywhere in town. He's at the bank talking to the branch manager, Jeremy, when I go in to make a deposit. He's in a serious conversation with Jim, who manages the hotel, both for the prior owner, Mr. Newton, who, rumor says, is now in Virginia, and for the mysterious new corporation.

Marcus even comes out of the Boyers' ice cream store when I know they're not open yet. I was in a hurry, with no time to do more than nod. He waved back at me.

He's still as drop-dead gorgeous as when I first laid eyes on him in my shop. I wish I was immune to his type of clichéd handsome hunkiness, but I'm not. And I swear he gets better looking with each smile he sends my way in passing.

I'm getting curious as to what makes this guy tick and excited at the prospect of spending the afternoon with him by the time I close up shop on Sunday. The sound of the departing ferry's three horn blasts is still resonating as I put on my sunglasses. Sliding a straw bag I've stocked with lemonade and chips over my shoulder, I prepare to lock up when Marcus appears at my door. I should've known he'd be prompt.

Wearing gray cargo shorts, he's showing off muscular legs without a hint of excess fat. Not too hairy, either. Rather perfect, in fact. A royal blue, short-sleeve polo shirt leaves no uncertainty that he hits a gym somewhere in the world when he's not here.

"Not ducking out on our deal, are you?" he asks.

"Nope," I say, jangling my keys with nervous energy. *Don't I look ready?* I wonder.

My hair is pulled up in a ponytail because my Jeep is unzipped and topless. My face has sunscreen on it for the same reason. I'm wearing a comfy, coral-colored T-shirt and pale-blue shorts, even though my legs aren't exactly tanned yet. They are, however, smoothly shaved as of seven this morning when I showered. I keep a hoodie in my car for unexpected weather changes, and I have on my trusty, worn-in sneakers that were once white but are now more of a beige hue. Yes, I'm ready as I'll ever be.

"It's a glorious, sunny, warm day," I practically crow, "and I'm looking forward to being outside and showing you around."

I really am, but Marcus cocks his head, looking doubtful.

"Who are you, and what have you done with the curmudgeonly shopkeeper?"

I'm a little surprised he thinks of me that way. I'll try to change his opinion with a sunnier disposition to match the weather. At least for today.

"Are you thinking of buying a house here?" I ask because that would make sense as to why he's been questioning everyone on Murray Island. He probably wants to know if we have all the amenities he's looking for in a vacation home.

And he'll have a pretty good selection. Sadly, we've had a number of people moving away in the past few years, unable to make a living any longer. Their homes are standing empty, even one of my favorites not too far from my own. Now that would be interesting, having Mr. Hundred-Dollar Bill living practically next door.

"Maybe," he confesses as we step outside into the sunshine. "If I like what you show me?"

What *I* show him? A shiver runs down my spine despite the growing heat of the day. I bat away the image of getting undressed in front of this attractive man. *Cool it, Lindsey.* Apparently, it's been too long since I was with a guy, GQ-quality like him or even a regular mortal man, because my imagination and my hormones are going berserk.

"It's nice to get a real beach day," I say. "This time of year is dodgy, and the wind can whip up the sand making it sting your skin. But today will be just right."

"I think it's already just right," he says.

He's flirting, which is fun. Yes, I definitely needed this day.

"Tell me what you've seen," I invite him, "and where you want to start."

"I've mostly wandered around the town, poking into the stores, including the supermarket."

He puts air quotes around the word *super*, which I totally understand. *Basic* is actually the word that comes to mind. If he was looking for brie or coconut milk, he'd be shit-out-of-luck.

"I think in the four days since I got here," he continues, "I've tried all the food options, but except for a bicycle ride the first day, I haven't seen much outside of town."

"Which way did you go?"

"That way." He points to the south end. "I found a potter."

"Jeannette," I guess, since the others are off the beaten path. "She's the one who told you my name." She's had a hard life and a lot of loss, but that's personal, so all I add is, "She's very talented."

"Agreed," he says. "I think she and the other island artisans should sell their wares in a common shop near the ferry. Literally anything would be better than that store selling useless tourist junk,"

I blink at him. Not only is it a great idea, making me wonder why our local talent has never banded together to create a co-op, I'm also pleased he agrees with me about Conor's store. I'm about to ask him what he thought of the blue pineapple-shaped ice buckets when Marcus takes my bag from me like a gentleman.

"How are we getting around?" he asks. "By foot or bicycle?"

"Neither. I have a Jeep."

It was the first day in a long time that I didn't walk to work, although I do try to drive my Jeep at least once every two weeks to make sure the engine keeps running. But it's silly to drive the ten-minute walk and waste gas when it's expensive on the island at the one gas station a block from my shop.

"It's in the ferry parking area," I explain. The short walk from the store, down a slight incline toward the ferry, brings us to the upper lot, which is from the days when we had summer crowds. Many visitors brought their cars in the island's heyday, warranting two parking areas.

In the couple hundred spaces between us and the empty dock, there are merely a handful of cars, all locals, and an abandoned one that we just leave there because maybe somebody will come back some day for their Oldsmobile. I mean, how do you go home on the ferry from a week on Murray Island and forget you left your car behind? This person did.

"There's Bella," I say.

He laughs. "I take it the name is ironic."

I falter in my stride as we approach the ancient Jeep I inherited from my parents. The soft top is off as are the doors.

"No. Why?"

"Seriously?" he asks. "Lucky thing it started out red because the rust sort of blends in."

"Hardy-har," I say. "Every car in New England has rust issues, and here, with sea salt all around, it's worse."

"Yes, it is!" he agrees before climbing into the passenger side.

"Comfy," he adds, even though I know the seat is crooked from some bags of fieldstone my dad was transporting once.

"Good," I say with enthusiasm, "because this is it. Without Bella, it'd be a helluva long walk."

"Point taken."

I say a brief prayer as I turn the key in the ignition. It would be an awkward time for Bella to be temperamental. Luckily, after a heart-stopping long crank, the engine starts, and we're on our way.

"What do you want to see first? Your choice. Best beach maybe?"

"Let me check the map." He opens a pocket low on his cargo shorts and pulls out the laminated map. He has, in fact, managed to fold it, and now makes a show of unfolding it and smoothing it out. Of course, that's impossible, and we both laugh at the curled and bent map.

"All right, lemme take a look," he says. "I would love to see those pirates in their cove."

"There's actually a cave," I tell him, turning onto the main road.

"It's a cave in a cove?"

"You got it." I take a deep breath and smile. On a warm day, I love the feeling of the wind whipping at my hair. In the bitter cold of January, I detest it. In the middle of winter, I lose my appreciation for the island just a little, but today, it's easy to remember why I love it so much.

"And the pirates lived in the cave?"

I glance at Marcus, who's hanging on to the roll bar with one hand and the map with the other.

"Absolutely not," I tell him. "They hid their treasure there."

"And why not? That's what pirates do. But why leave it there?"

"That's the tricky thing, isn't it?" I say with my gaze back on the road as we turn onto Charles Street heading to the smaller beach road. "Who knows if they came back to claim it or if it's still there?"

"I bet you have a guess. Maybe there's no treasure and never was."

I shrug. "I think the point is the dream of pirate treasure. Most of us never get rich, but we can dream about finding treasure."

"Better to get rich, than dream about it," he says, and his voice sounds serious.

Well, OK then. We pass the airport, and I crane my neck to see his plane, but it must be in the lean-to.

"I walked from here the first day," he says.

I nod. "Nearly there," I say as we zip around a bend.

"Already?"

"Everything is five to fifteen minutes from town by car in either direction."

"Hold up!" he says suddenly.

I slam on the brakes. Before Bella has even come to a halt, he jumps out and walks right up to the lopsided, closed gate with rusty hinges belonging to Kathy Dooley. Over the gate hangs the old sign, Duke's Riding.

"Horseback riding," Marcus exclaims. "Why didn't you mention that when you were telling me about the island's activities?" He waves the map around. "It's not even on the map with some ridiculous name like 'Wild Mustang Meadow.'"

"No more horses," I say, then I amend my words. "I mean Kathy, who owns the property, does still care for two

51

mares, but she sold the rest and there's no more public riding."

"That seems like a great business," he says undeterred as we hear baying in the distance. Kathy's bloodhound, Sylvie, was one of my goofy dog's friends, and I used to bring Max here for doggy playdates while she and I had a drink and a chat.

"There's got to be a lot of people who would love to go around the island on a horse," Marcus continues, "not to mention riding on the beach."

"Yes, it's a perfect place for horses," I agree, despite having never been able to conquer my acrophobia long enough to get onto a saddle. "But Kathy's husband, Duke, died and then her daughter went to college on the mainland, fell in love, got married and stayed away. Kathy can't handle the business on her own."

"That's a damn shame." He touches the gate, and it seems to angle even more. "These hinges are about to give way. The screws have pulled right out of the wood."

I make a note to mention it to Mel's husband. I'm sure Sam could fix it and wouldn't even charge Kathy. Sylvie bays again, probably smelling us, even this far from the house.

"Do you ride?" I ask Marcus, thinking he would look wicked hot on horseback. A sexy, modern cowboy. On the other hand, like Mel said the first time she saw him, he's a yummy piece of man-candy just standing there by the rundown gate.

When he grins at the question, my pulse speeds up.

"I do," he says, climbing back into the Jeep. "In fact, I keep horses myself."

"Really?" That gets my attention. I realize how little I know about him, except that he eats burgers, chocolate, and pretzels, and drinks water and black and tans. But, of course, there is a huge world once someone gets off the ferry on the other side. "Where?"

"North Carolina," he says. "Outskirts of Tryon."

Which means nothing to me, so I merely smile.

"Do you think Kathy would be open to starting up again if she had help?"

My mouth drops. *What is it with this guy?* He is an entrepreneur on steroids. Every other word out of his tantalizing mouth is about fixing a business or starting one up.

"I don't know. I guess you'd have to ask her."

"I'll come back another day. I don't want to waste your time."

He sounds like he means it. Why does he care if we can ride horses on Murray Island? Even if he buys a summer place here, he has horses at home. I shake my head.

"Are you offering to be her stable hand? I think she could only pay you in free rides."

He simply laughs then asks, "Where to next?"

"Pirates' Cove." Once the road turns to sandy dirt, we have a bumpy trip with barely any suspension or springs left, or whatever part makes your teeth rattle when it's missing in your vehicle. Bella's missing that part.

"I feel like I've been through a blender," Marcus jokes as I pull directly onto the sand.

The tide is out, so we can pick our way across the rocks, and I show him the twenty-foot cave that all the island kids are sure has pirate treasure in it. Or, at the very least, it has ghosts of dead pirates who were searching for said treasure when the tide came in and trapped them. The floor is sand, not rocks, and you can stand up in it, even if you're as tall as Marcus and then some.

"Cool," he says, examining the back wall, using his cell phone to shine a light on it.

"There aren't any engravings or markings."

"It's still intriguing."

Just then, a rogue, medium-size wave brings water to the cave's mouth and then retreats.

"I hope you tell any families about the danger."

"Families?" I can't help asking.

"Tourists. Visitors. There should be a sign back along the beach, maybe fixed to the rocks that says what time the tide is high. Not everyone is lucky enough to have a local showing them around."

I shake my head, because in all my twenty-five years living on Murray Island, no one has ever got hurt or trapped. Not that I know of. Suddenly, it seems pretty lucky to me.

"Come to think of it, I think there was a sign when I was a kid, but we had a lot more visitors then. I'll suggest it to the board of selectman at the next meeting."

His eyes light up. "When is that?" Marcus thumbs open a calendar on his phone.

"I'm not sure. I don't often go, but the schedule is posted at the town hall, but the meetings are at the old meeting house. It's a brick building past Macey's Grill on the left."

"I thought that was an abandoned building. I knew you had a town moderator, but when I saw the size of your town hall, I assumed the moderator conducted business out of one of the restaurants or the church."

I can't help sending him a sour look. "We're not hicks. The town hall is small because it used to be Josiah Barkhum's house in the early eighteen hundreds, and he was the first town moderator. There are four rooms, two up and two down, all used as offices. The meeting house, on the other hand, may have a few bricks missing, but it's totally functional and holds a decent-size group." I pause. "When it's open."

"Which is?"

"Only for the town board of selectmen meetings."

I watch him send a text to someone before sliding his phone into his back pocket.

"You have better reception than I do."

"Satellite phone," he says. "I wouldn't go anywhere in the world without it."

Must be nice. I gesture around us. "Well, what do you think?"

"Of the slimy, dangerous cave? If I'd grown up here, I would've brought a shovel and been digging for treasure from a young age." Then he adds, "Or maybe go after a different type of treasure as a teenager. Seems like a good make-out spot. The added possibility of drowning or being washed out to sea probably heightens the excitement."

I can't help smiling.

"I'm right, aren't I?" he says.

I shrug. I'm not about to tell him that I had my first kiss in this cave. But I did. We start back to the Jeep.

"For the record, I thought you should see this local landmark. Not because I thought we'd get rich or make out."

And with that not-very-witty remark, which embarrasses me as soon as I say it, my foot slides off a wet rock, and I nearly go down. Marcus, who was closer behind than I knew, somehow has his arms around me, holding me up before I can even shriek.

"You're two for two," I joke, glancing down to see his hands clasped just below my breasts. It would be easy for him to palm them if he just . . .

I don't finish my thought because his hands unlock and disappear as he releases me. I take in a breath and get my feet steady under me.

"You OK?" he asks, still behind me.

Apart from being mortified and flustered, not to mention wanting his big hands on me again. "Yeppers," I say. "And I swear I'm not normally a clumsy person."

"It's your shoes," he says, sounding completely unfazed. "Turn around slowly."

I step onto the next rock which is broad and flat before I pivot to face him. To my surprise, he crouches down.

"Put your hands on my shoulders."

"What?" I squeal. After all, his face is now down near my crotch, and my lady parts are taking notice.

"Lift a foot," he orders.

"Oh, I see," I mutter and raise one leg, sticking it forward awkwardly while keeping my fingers dug into his shirt for balance.

"As I thought," he says, examining my dirty sneaker with its knotted laces, making me cringe. "The soles are completely worn out. Doesn't anyone sell shoes on the island?"

I pull my dirty sneaker back a little too fast and have to clutch him to stay upright.

"Of course they do. Again, we're not savages."

"You said hicks before."

"We're neither," I insist. Truth be told, my mom and I used to go to the mainland a couple times a year for clothing and shoes. But he doesn't need to know that.

On the island, there are mainly sandals and flip-flops for the summer visitors who lose both at an alarming rate. We also have a large supply of rainboots because Mickey at the hardware store, that also sells pet food, birdseed, and gardening tools, once bought a massive shipment of "wellies" at cost, convinced we were in for a few years of monsoons.

The storms never materialized, and the rubber has dried out on the pairs he left in his store's window. But a lot of islanders bought them. My mother used one of ours for an umbrella stand in the front hall. I don't think they'd be any better over rocks than what I'm wearing, nor would any of my sandals.

Once Marcus lets go of my foot, I release the man's shirt, now all puckered from my fingers twisting the soft cotton fabric. As he rises, we're facing one another. And we're close. Too close. His gaze goes to my lips for a second, and I part them, exuding my willing and welcoming vibe.

I wouldn't mind a kiss. That's all I can think while I keep looking at him until his eyes flicker back up to mine, and our glances lock.

I must be oozing desire and yearning, telegraphing loudly how much I want him, because a slow smile spreads across his face. I find myself mirroring it, smiling back. His brows raise. It's hypnotizing to watch. Truly, I'm fascinated while I wait to see what he does next, hoping it involves touching me again.

Yes. It. Does!

His hands glide under the fabric of my T-shirt, before coming to resting on my waist. His thumbs stroke warm circles against my stomach, which is currently housing about a billion butterflies. In record time, I'm growing damp down below while a persistent throb keeps time with my pulse.

His hand on my back presses me forward. I comply willingly and we're pretty much thigh to thigh and hips to his . . . *gulp!* . . . pelvis.

When Marcus tilts his head, I tilt mine the other way. And then my day suddenly gets a whole lot better.

6

Marcus

If a beautiful woman gazes up at me with a scorching look that could melt an iceberg, then I'm going to kiss the hell out of her. It's the gentlemanly thing to do. Anything else would be weird, awkward, rude, and stupid.

I anchor Lindsey in place and claim her sweet lips before the moment passes. I'm glad I'm entirely unattached, no longer engaged, and between girlfriends. I can kiss her freely, which I do.

I don't hold back, as if this is a tender moment between lovers. This may, in fact, be the only time we ever kiss, and I intend to make it count. Not that I usually kiss and run, but Lindsey has made her feelings clear about "the corporation" that's initiating changes on her island. It's not hard to imagine how annoyed she'll be when she knows who I am.

As soon our lips touch, a powerful sensation—fiery, craving, reckless, and steamy—gallops through me. I've had serious relationships, and I know how they felt at the start, pure physical attraction and curiosity. But as my fingers press the delicate curve of her waist, I know this is different, that *she* is different. This kiss is connecting me to someone very special.

I want to sink my teeth into her plump lower lip, but that would mean un-fusing our mouths for an instant. Instead, I tilt my head for a closer fit.

This woman feels good, tastes great, and smells like a tempting flower. The scent coming from her skin and hair reminds me of the wild flowers blooming on my estate this month, heady and gorgeous. I want to lay her down in the green pasture, under a brilliant blue sky, and strip her bare. I imagine licking my way across her skin in the bright sunlight before sinking into her wetness, and my body goes from tender to turned on in a heartbeat.

Fierce desire rushes through me as if I'm on the wet, slippery ride down the face of Sliding Rock waterfall in my home state of North Carolina. Intense, exhilarating, and a little dangerous, to say the least. But there's more to it than desire. More to Lindsey and this kiss. More to us.

All I know is my reaction feels . . . unique. If I'd felt this strongly for Greta, I'd still be on the path to the altar. Instead, we went from attraction to a warmth I mistook for love, to getting engaged, and then pretty quickly, to nothing more than lazy attachment until we gave our engagement a mercy ending.

Greta did not want a cowboy and a real estate developer, a man who likes the land. She wanted constant entertainment and a full-time companion for adventure. Flying in my plane was neither high enough nor thrilling enough. And what I mistook for a bright spark was nothing more than reflected light from all the camera flashes going off when she put us in the middle of whatever scene interested her, whether it was in Dubai, Paris, Milan, New York City, or Hollywood.

All that was a giant yawn.

Lindsey, on the other hand, is a stirring, complex, genuine person . . . who is going to hate my guts if I'm not careful. Maybe I can take this further than a kiss and see where we go *before* she figures out who I am, with all her preconceived notions of me as a villain.

Sounds like a plan. I sweep my tongue over the seam of her lips, demanding entrance. Let's take this kiss up a notch.

7

Lindsey

I'm not sure what type of kiss I expect because I wasn't expecting one at all. If I'd known something romantic or, more accurately, sexual was going to happen, maybe I would've worn more than merely mascara and colorless, peppermint lip balm. Perhaps I would have worn my hair down, too, instead of in a juvenile ponytail.

When Marcus plants his lips firmly on mine, there's a zing of what feels like static electricity. If we were standing in water, I might be worried about frying, and the dire warning on every hair dryer about not using it while bathing comes to mind. I wave it away. Let my nerve endings continue to sizzle. This is so worth it.

I appreciate how he's not crushing my lips into my teeth or moving his mouth around like an open-mawed carp. He's simply kissing me straightforwardly and firmly. Obviously a guy who knows what he's doing.

And it is a seriously intimate kiss like I've never had. A manly man taking the mouth of a womanly woman, with no bullshit.

I'm ready when Marcus adds his tongue to the symphony of sensations coursing through me. He isn't gross or overly forceful. But he is massively sensual. I just want to slide closer, if I could, and suck on his tongue, which is now gliding against my own.

My knees feel weak, and I wish we weren't standing on a bed of rocks. Far better to be lying on my lumpy bed at home.

When I think the kiss is over because he creates a sliver of space between us, I start to straighten. That's when he slips his hands into my hair, below the hair elastic holding my ponytail. Cradling my head, he anchors my mouth to his. Then he tilts the other way, and his hands helpfully angle my face in the opposite direction.

When he begins to nibble my lower lip, I sag against him. *Zing, zing, zing!* He sinks his teeth lightly into my now very sensitive lip, just as all of my body has become a heaping mass of sensations. And when he tugs gently, I moan a little. I can easily imagine his teeth tugging at my nipple next.

He groans and draws back.

"Nice," I say, then wonder if that sounds stupid or condescending. I know it's definitely an understatement, and I add, "Spectacular, actually."

"Ditto," he says. "Except for the wet shoes."

I hadn't even noticed, but with each minute, the tide has come in and already washed over our feet a few times. Guess I was wrong about standing in water and being electrocuted by the force of that astonishingly great kiss.

"Shit!" I exclaim because, in fact, wet sneakers feel awful.

We pick our way over the slippery rocks, holding hands and supporting one another until we're back at the Jeep.

"What's next?" he asks.

Given the way he's looking at me, I'm not sure Marcus is talking about the next sightseeing stop. But in case he is, I go with that answer.

"The lighthouse isn't far. Andy Rumble's in charge this week. His father owns the largest fruit farm on the island."

He smiles.

"What?" I ask.

"Just how you have that extra nugget of info. Like about Josiah Bunkum—"

"Barkham," I correct him.

"It's really charming," he says.

My face feels hot with happiness. This stud-muffin thinks I'm charming. That's pretty cool.

"As long as you don't mind continuing our day in wet shoes." Personally, I can't stand the feeling of soggy socks, and I'm already taking my shoes off.

"I guess I'll take mine off for a bit," Marcus says. He's not wearing socks anyway with his canvas slip-ons. "Are you going barefoot?"

I reach into the back of my Jeep. "Nope. Emergency sandals."

"Smart woman," he says. Then he gets a look at them. They used to be a natural leather color. Now they're blotchy with dark spots and a torn piece over my right littlest toe. "They look like they've already been through a couple emergencies."

I slide them on and slip the strap over my heel, while Marcus watches. His gaze makes me feel as if I'm dressing in front of him.

"Criticism from the man who's going barefoot."

"Touché," he says.

The first time I turn the ignition, Bella responds with a cough. I pause, pray silently, and try again with another long crank. My Jeep chortles into life, while Marcus is still looking at me, watching everything I'm doing as if I'm there for his entertainment. I try to keep my eyes on the sandy lane and then the road, but eventually, I turn.

63

"Now what?" I ask.

"Just admiring the view."

Which is funny because if he turned his head, he would see the sun dappled Atlantic, shimmering at this time of day. I send him an appreciative smile.

"Dear Lindsey!" he says emphatically.

Dear? Sounds a tad old-fashioned.

Marcus grabs the wheel, just as I turn to see a deer running beside Bella. Sure enough, as these stupid creatures always do, it darts in front of us. Luckily, with Marcus's warning, I avoid the doe.

"Sorry," I mutter. "I thought you were saying *dear*, not *deer*."

"What?"

"Nothing. Anyway, while you may have noticed we don't have any squirrels—"

"I hadn't until you mentioned it," he says. "That's weird though."

"Well, we don't, and to me, it would be weirder to see them running around. Whenever I'm on the mainland, it seems like you're overrun with them, and they make me think of rats."

"You need to get off the island more," he says.

I don't take offense. He's just joking. What's more, he's probably right.

"Anyway, I was saying we don't have squirrels, but we do have a lot of deer with no predators except our yearly hunting season. It's for two days, with limited licenses, and during that time only the hunters are allowed down this end of the island."

Marcus nods. "Sounds orderly."

"And necessary. Everyone has a deer collision story."

"*We* almost had one," he says. "I feel like an islander."

That makes me laugh. A few more minutes, and there it is—the Murray Island Light. Marcus puts his shoes back on as I pull into the small parking lot, next to Andy's scooter. I babysat him for a couple dollars an hour when he was six and I was going on thirteen.

The lightkeeper's house, with its red tile roof, looks like a boxy appendage, attached at the base of the tall tower. The house's walls and the tower are whitewashed in the classic New England style, but three-quarters of the way up, a thick red band encircles the cylinder. On top is the oil-black lantern, as the glass enclosure is called, and it houses our massive revolving light.

"Lucifer's Light," he says, referring to the map. "Nothing very devilish about it that I can see."

"My father came up with all those names," I confess. "And he didn't put too much thought into them, to be honest."

"What would be great out here is an information board," he says, "with all the history and details."

"You're right. I wonder how much that would cost to install."

"And maybe a couple porta-potties," he adds, his words draining all my enthusiasm.

"Is there room at the top for a dining room table?" he asks. "I've seen a lighthouse that serves meals for up to four people. They charge seven-hundred dollars for five hours, and that's without the food."

I'm gaping at him now, hoping he doesn't make any more hideous suggestions. "Maybe you should just enjoy the Murray Light as it is."

"I'm sure I will," he says, looking up at it, wearing the sunglasses he bought at my store.

With Marcus beside me, I knock on the glossy, red door of the tiny, white house. Everything wooden out here on the point is covered with thick oil paint to protect the structures from the ocean, the salt, and the weather, including this door.

I suppose we could go in without waiting. After all, we islanders consider this a communal place, and Andy is supposed to be ready and welcoming for tours and general information from nine to five.

"Coming." His voice is muffled by the thick door and the even thicker stone of the house, made to withstand hurricane-force winds. A moment later, Andy opens it.

"Hey, Lindsey," he says.

"Hey." It's no longer weird to see him as a grown man, at age eighteen, taller than me. He even asked me out once last year. Now that was weird! I nipped his inclination in the bud.

"Can you show my new friend around?"

"Sure," he says, his voice surprisingly deep.

Marcus and Andy shake hands.

"You want to go up?" Andy asks me. The gleam in his eye indicating he hasn't forgotten my fear of heights.

"Nope," I say quickly. "I'll just sit right here and wait."

"You're not coming?" Marcus asks. "Aren't you going to point out landmarks?"

"Nope," I say again. "But Andy will."

I plop myself down on the worn sofa, prop my feet on the old coffee table and fold my arms to make sure both men know I'm not budging.

Andy laughs. "She's not into heights."

Everyone in town had a good laugh when I got stuck in a tree trying to rescue a cat. The little beastie jumped down and left me clinging to the trunk until our volunteer fire department, consisting of Matt and Dave, arrived. One hundred percent mortifying at age sixteen. At least I tried. Before that, I'd hidden my fear rather well.

"That's all right," Marcus returns. "I'm not into depths."

"Huh?" Andy says.

"Scuba diving," Marcus clears up. "I had a girlfriend who loved it. It's all she wanted to do in her free time and was constantly pushing me to do it, too. We broke up over it, in fact."

"Whoa!" Andy says. "Brutal AF!"

Marcus laughs. "As long as we're climbing up and not down, I'm fine."

"We'll definitely be coming back down, dude," Andy says, but he knows Marcus is joking. "Right through here." He goes through the doorway to the base of the spiral stairwell.

Marcus hesitates, looking into my eyes. "Sorry you won't see the view with me," he says. "I would've skipped this if I'd known you would have to wait for me."

"Not a problem," I tell him, and I mean it. "I'm happy to sit here. I'll take a snooze, and when I wake up, you'll be back."

"OK. I won't be long."

"Take your time. It's sixty stairs and a gorgeous view, or so I'm told. And you can see down to the other end of the island, past Jeannette's studio, and right to Fort Mercy."

He frowns and waves the stupid placemat that's back in his hand again.

"I thought I'd taken note of everything on here." He glances down at it.

"Don't bother," I say. "It's not there."

"Why?" His brown eyes lock with mine, and I get a jolt of wicked-man sensuality.

Why are we talking about old forts? He should come sit with me on this couch and press me back into the cushions while he kisses me again. I rein in my naughty thoughts and answer him.

"Because we don't want people climbing all over a three-hundred-year-old structure."

"To preserve it?" he asks.

"Yes, and also because their touristy feet might go through the wooden floors."

"Then it's dangerous?" he asks.

"It's an historical artifact," I say, "and we keep it for locals only unless someone stumbles across it."

"Are you coming?" Andy calls, his voice echoing because he must be halfway up by now.

Marcus ignores him, waiting for my answer.

"Really, truly dangerous?" I ask, considering. Then shrug. "It's where you go as a kid or a teen and poke around, spook one another, dare each other to do stupid things, drink too much, smoke pot, etc. Most like, there's some ugly graffiti on it."

He nods. "Did anyone ever get hurt?"

"Before my time, someone leaned against one of the upstairs walls and it gave way."

"What happened to him or her?"

"I don't know. He died maybe? Some joker said he toppled into the sea, swallowed by the ocean. Except the sea doesn't come up that high. It's all just rumor now. You'll have to ask someone older than me."

Marcus looks pensive. "I'd like to see it. Maybe it should be fenced off with chain-link and a padlock."

"We won't make it down there today." I think of stretching out on my couch at home and having a snooze. "Don't worry," I tell him. "No one's getting hurt on my island tour. Now go."

He does as I say and follows Andy.

I rest my head on the couch cushion. Dave's was unusually busy last night, the first warm Saturday evening. To the untrained eye, it looked like the season had started, but the tavern was packed due to a birthday party. Not private, either, meaning anyone and everyone showed up, and we stayed open late. I'd expected Marcus to show up, but he didn't.

In any case, I didn't get to bed till after one in the morning. I needn't have bothered jumping up to open the store, either. The only people who left on the morning ferry, which won't return until tomorrow, were the early tourists from four days earlier and a few locals. None of them came into the store before departing the island.

With my eyes closed, I can hear the echoing sounds of Marcus's shoes on the metal stair treads. And then Fort Mercy floats into my tired brain. I haven't been out to it in years. About five years ago, our board of selectman called for a townwide referendum on whether to fence off the structure, just like Marcus suggested. Some even called for bulldozing it, but they were in the minority.

In the end, not enough people voted on what to do, and it was left as it has always been because it's a landmark, or it should be. I don't know how those things work or who gets to decide what's historic and worth preserving. I've always thought it was lovely in a ghostly sort of way. And it's the sole big structure at the south end.

When I think of it at all, which isn't often, I imagine the fort being like a sentinel protecting the island from invasion the way the lighthouse up here at the north end, protects those at sea from perishing on our rocks.

Rather poetic to have this protection by land and by sea.

Forgetting about Fort Mercy, I want to replay the perfect kiss Marcus and I shared, but exhaustion takes over, and I drift off to sleep.

8

Marcus

"Lindsey," I say near her cute ear with its blue and silver starfish earring. "Time to wake up."

I hate to rouse her because she is really knocked out, but I've already been a creeper, watching her sleep for a few minutes. I've been trying not to stare at her full breasts that stretch the T-shirt just above where she's folded her arms across her chest. But *not* looking is impossible. She's beautiful, her breasts are gorgeous, her thick eyelashes are darker than her hair—probably makeup magic—and they fan her cheeks, and her lips are flawless, both full and bowed. I could happily watch her for hours.

I spent about fifteen minutes at the top of the lighthouse, seeing the lantern and walking around the outer platform for a 360-degree view. Andy didn't know too much about the light's history, not even when it was built. Instead, he referred me to a guide book in the town hall, but I have a feeling I can ask Lindsey.

When we came down, I let her sleep another ten minutes while I walked around outside. But now I've whispered in her ear, catching the light scent of her perfume again. The floral fragrance may just be her shampoo or soap, but on her skin, it's sexy as fuck. I want to kiss her again right now.

"Mmph," she says with those luscious lips of hers that I now know taste of mint. A second later, her long eyelashes open and her blue eyes focus on me.

"Oh!" she says and startles to a sitting position.

"Hey, settle down," I tell her. "Everything's fine."

She looks around, then back at me with a frown. "Sorry, I was up till the wee hours. We closed Dave's kind of late. Where's Andy?"

"He mentioned something about video games and disappeared."

"Jackass," she mutters. I think she means Andy, not me for waking her. "How long was I asleep?"

"Don't worry about it. I saw everything I wanted to. It's glorious up there. Imagine being up there for the sunrise."

"Imagine," she says, with little enthusiasm.

I can't help laughing. This woman puts me in a great mood. "I'm guessing you wouldn't find it romantic being up there?"

She swallows and shakes her head. "Not unless you think lightheadedness, vertigo, sweating, and a pounding heart are romantic."

"Maybe the pounding heart," I say, but I feel bad for her.

Then she smiles. "Did you and Andy feel romantic on the catwalk?"

I laugh hard. "We did. I nearly dropped to one knee and proposed."

She grins at my joke, but I wish I could have shared the view with her nonetheless.

"You want me to drive?" I ask.

"No. I'm fine after my nap. Besides, Bella might not like you at the wheel."

"I'm pretty sure I could handle her, but it's your call." I step back and hold out my hand, which she takes after a moment's hesitation. As soon as our fingers touch, I'm ready to kiss her again.

What the hell is that sizzle between us? But all I do is pull her to her feet and release her. The top of her head comes up to my chin, making her about five foot seven, if I were to guess. Despite the slippery rocks, it had been easy to lean down and plant one on her.

The kiss was epic, in my humble opinion, but undoubtedly ill-advised. I didn't come here to hookup. And I have a feeling Lindsey wouldn't appreciate a fling with a short-term visitor. For all I know, she has a lucky islander boyfriend, although I would expect her to have pushed me away if that was the case.

As we walk to the car, I simply ask her, "Are you seeing someone?"

Like a comedian, she trips over her own feet, stumbles, but catches herself, giving me a double-take.

"Where'd that question come from?"

"Left field apparently. Why is it so shocking that I would ask you?"

We climb into the ancient Jeep, her cute ass settling into the well-worn driver's seat. Then Lindsey seems to be praying slightly before turning the key in the ignition. It starts on the second try.

"Not shocking," she says at last as she turns back onto the road, "but I wouldn't have allowed you to kiss me if I had a boyfriend."

"Fair enough and good to know."

"Why? Are you thinking of kissing me again?"

She is direct, and I like that about her.

"I've been thinking about it. While I climbed the stairs to the top, while I looked at the view, while Andy made up numbers about the strength of the light, while I came down, and definitely while I watched you sleeping."

She squeals. "*Ick!* Who watches someone they barely know sleep?"

"You should have told me you were up late and too tired to go sightseeing today."

Lindsey shrugs. "I'm not too tired. It just caught up with me because that couch is broken in and comfy." After a moment, she asks, "Did I drool? Was I snoring?"

"No and yes."

She hits the wheel with her fist. "Wow! Way to make an impression."

I laugh again, then tell her, "It wasn't like leaf-blower-level snoring. Just gentle buzzing, like bees at a hive."

"That sounds almost delightful. I must be as charming when sleeping as I am awake."

She is, so I tell her. "You are, actually. You're fun to be with. If you weren't trapped on this island with a small gene pool from what I've seen, then you would have your choice of dates and guys and most likely be married already."

When she swings an irate glance my way, I get a clue I've made an error in judgment.

"For your information, we are not a small gene pool! People marry off-islanders and come back or leave all the time. Besides, there are plenty of guys right here if I wanted them."

"I see. You have the opportunity, but you just don't want to date."

Lindsey's cheeks redden, and it seems she's flustered. Keeping her eyes trained on the road, she says through gritted teeth, "I have dated. I will date again. Just not seeing anyone at the moment. OK?"

"Then we can kiss if we want," I surmise, "unless you're against starting anything with an end date." I don't know why I'm pushing when I don't see a future in it.

Yeah, I do know why. Because Lindsey Cooper, shopkeeper and sassy pub server, is the most likable woman I've been around in a long time. Maybe ever. She's also pretty and smart and interesting.

"Maybe we could just get through today," she says noncommittally.

"We can try." I like how she's left the door open to something happening between us. "What's next?"

"I'm starving," she says. "Why don't we get some sandwiches or wraps, and then I'll finally show you the best beach, the one marked as Siren Sands."

"I'd like that." I'm also curious as to where this food is coming from since I don't recall a sandwich shop, and it's Sunday. Against all better business practices, when I was walking to Whatnots and Such at eleven this morning, it seemed as though the town had shut down and rolled up the sidewalks. I'm hoping everything stays open all weekend once it gets busier.

I get my answer when we head back to town and turn down a side street before parking in the small gravel driveway of a modest, shingle-covered house. A saltbox with gray, weathered shingles, it's not very appealing to my southern eyes, preferring Greek revival. But I note its charm and the great location.

"Yours?" I ask.

"My parents'. Mine for now."

The house is easily the most common style on the island. Totally flat on the front, symmetrically laid out, with a pair of small-paned windows on either side of the door and a couple smaller ones in the half attic above. A chimney arises from the dead center, obviously located directly in line with the front door in the middle of the house.

I know when I see the back, it will have the quintessential drastic sloping roof that sheds snow as soon as possible, but also takes away any chance of a second floor at the back.

Lindsey's home is in better shape than some I've seen. It has been kept up. All the old nine-over-six glass panes look original, the door has a glossy coat of green paint, and the chimney, painted black, isn't missing any bricks.

"How's the roof?" I ask, having slipped totally into real estate mode.

She shoots me a puzzled look. "It doesn't leak, if that's what you're asking."

"It is," I say, as we both get out of the Jeep. After all, a leaky roof means damage and lowers resale value drastically.

We get out, and walk up a short brick path with weeds growing between the bricks to the single granite step in front of the door.

"Casa Cooper," she says, jangling her keys.

"Would have better curb appeal with some native bushes on either side of the step and under the windows."

Another puzzled look. I need to turn work off and simply enjoy her company.

"I mean, if you cared about your neighbors," I add.

She pointedly turns and gestures. There's an oak tree on either side of her, and across the street is a path to the beach.

"I guess the whales and dolphins don't give a shit about curb appeal."

"No more than I do," she says, pushing the door open. She hesitates a second, then enters.

"Sorry, I'm still used to my dog rushing to greet me. Max would have tackled you with joyful exuberance."

I'm hoping her dog is merely on vacation with her parents. His existence explains the water bowl and blanket in the back of the Jeep.

As expected, the central chimney is dead ahead of me, coated with stucco and painted white. There's a room on the left and the right. She goes left to a small dining area and then her kitchen at the back. There's a fireplace on this side, and I already know without looking there's a fireplace in the living area on the other side, sharing the chimney. Maybe two more hearths upstairs as well.

"He was super old," she says, and I realize we're talking about her dog. "Max used to come to the shop with me, and I'd drop him home before a shift at Dave's. It's still weird coming home to an empty house."

"I'm sorry," I say, hating that powerless feeling that arises when someone tells me something I can't fix. "How long ago?"

She scrunches up her face. "Three weeks." She points out the window to her backyard, which I can't really see from here. "I buried him out there."

"By yourself?"

Lindsey frowns at me, then takes a deep breath and releases it. "I need to stop talking about Max."

She opens the single door of her old-style, Harvest Gold fridge, but not before I see photos of people who must be her parents, as well as a big yellow lab, all taped to the front.

While I'm having a visceral reaction to one of the ugliest appliance colors I've ever had the misfortune to see, Lindsey is taking stock of its contents.

"I have ham and turkey, pickles, mustard, mayo, Portuguese sweet bread because our market got a shipment by mistake, and romaine lettuce." She starts handing stuff to me without turning. I set everything quickly on the old white-and-gold speckled Formica countertop.

"I also have whole wheat and dried rosemary-infused tortilla wraps."

"Because they got sent to the market by mistake?" I ask.

Laughing, she closes the fridge with a plastic-wrap stack of tortillas. "No, I thought they'd go well with ham."

I consider. "Are they?"

"I haven't tried them yet."

"Then I'll be brave and try one with ham."

"And a little turkey?"

"Might as well," I say, going to her sink without asking and washing my hands so I can help.

She does the same, then side-by-side at the counter, overlooking her backyard, which is all sandy and dune grass and a few overgrown green shrubs that she tells me are glorious smelling beach roses—and, sadly, her dead dog— we make wraps.

"I already have lemonade and chips in the Jeep."

"Emergency rations to go with your emergency shoes?"

"Yes, but now *warm* lemonade," she adds.

"Not a problem." The sun isn't yet blistering outside as it will be, hopefully, in another month. But the problem of a warm beverage makes me recall an ugly souvenir I saw in town. "You should have a blue pineapple ice bucket," I tease. "We could take ice to the beach for our lemonade."

Her mouth drops open. "Tell me you don't find those attractive."

"Not in the least."

"Thank God." She nudges me with her shoulder. "I'd have to rescind my invitation for lunch."

"They're hideous. If I see anyone buying one, I'll tackle them and call you for backup," I promise. "By the way, you've been very thoughtful. And kind. I really appreciate it."

Her cheeks blush pink. It's a huge turn-on, and I want to pull her close, but I'm a stranger in her home, and that type of move might seem threatening. I keep my hands off as she puts our food into a straw bag.

"Ready?"

She doesn't offer a house tour, and I don't ask.

"How are your shoes? Dry now?" she asks, locking her front door.

"Fine," I lie because the canvas has been chafing my feet with damp sand for the past hour and a half. But I'd rather end up with blisters than end the day we're having. I start to get in the Jeep.

"No need," she says. "In fact, take off your shoes and leave 'em behind. And grab that bag out of the back, please."

I watch her toss her sandals into the back seat and tuck a tartan blanket under her arm. Doing as ordered, I follow her across the road and onto a path made of slatted wood, bamboo if I had to guess, leading through dune grass toward the ocean.

When my feet hit the soft warm sand, it's bliss. Ahead of us is about twenty-five feet of pristine beach and beyond the shoreline is the green-blue water I've spied from the side streets in town. It was worth the wait, and I'm happy to see it with Lindsey.

"Ahh," I say loudly, letting my feet enjoy the freedom. "This is the perfect beach. Lucky you!"

We don't walk too far, to the right a few hundred yards and not too close to the water that's still coming in. Lindsey flips open the blanket, which catches the gentle breeze like a sail, billows up, then settles onto the sand.

We both stretch out, leaning on an elbow, facing one another.

"I'm starving," she says.

"Me, too. All that climbing."

"I slept in as long as I could and skipped breakfast," she admitted.

"You should have told me. We could have eaten before sightseeing."

She shrugs in a way I think is her default move. "We're eating now, and that's just fine with me."

"Is it the island way to be so easygoing, or just how you are? Because any woman I've ever hung out with would have told me she was hungry or would have called this off altogether to take a nap."

Again, the Lindsey shrug. "Going around being bitchy or demanding seems like a piss-poor way to live. I'm sorry you've been hanging out with the bottom-feeders of my gender."

That's harsh. I don't think of any of my past girlfriends or my ex-fiancée as bottom-feeders. But I do have a feeling she's in a class by herself.

Rosemary wraps eaten—and proven to go well with ham—she stretches out flat and lays her arm over her eyes. But I sit up, managing to wrest my gaze away from her gently rising and falling breasts, and look at the *other* astonishing beauty of this New England late-spring day. The ocean is calm, with sunlight dappling the water, and the sky is cloudless.

It's not the rich September blue that has told me summer's over since I was a kid dreading the start of school. Rather, it's a pale, light-infused blue, indicating winter's fully behind us, and everything good is ahead.

And if my plans for Murray Island pan out, then that's never been truer than this year for these people. I only wish I'd had the time to turn my attention to developing right after Robin told me how charming it was and how much potential she saw. I bought the hotel but didn't have time to get my butt over here. If I had, my contractors could have worked in the milder winter months, and these people would be enjoying a more prosperous summer.

Anyway, I'm here now. And I'm surprised that someone hasn't spilled the beans about who I am, seeing how small the community is. I don't know whether Carl or Mrs. Macey and her sister at the breakfast place know my last name. But people at the hotel do and at the town hall. They probably assume Lindsey already knows it by now.

It shouldn't be a big deal. I'm making too much of it. She's not going to suddenly hate me because I own Parisi, Inc. I ought to tell her as soon as—

"Wow!" I exclaim, as three dolphins rise at once, and then disappear.

While Lindsey sits up, they do it a few more times before we lose sight of them.

"Better than squirrels, right?" she quips.

I turn to her and can't resist. "Can I kiss you again?"

Instead of going all soft and acquiescing, she looks appalled. "We just ate."

"It's not like swimming, is it? With a waiting period after eating?"

That tickles her into a chuckle. "No, but I'd have to go back to my house and brush my teeth, unless you have some gum?"

"'Fraid not. But I ate the same food," I remind her.

"I could swish and spit with the lemonade."

She is a trip! "We both could," I agree, because now she has me worried about ham breath.

After cleaning our mouths with what's left of the warm lemonade, each spitting it into the sand on our respective sides of the blanket, I turn to her again.

She grimaces. "Now it seems too premeditated."

I decide to back off for the moment. "It's OK," I say. "No pressure. But just so we're clear, next time I feel the urge to kiss you in a spontaneous moment—without asking and without premeditation—you're not going to slap my face, right? Or press charges?"

She shakes her head. "Not unless you're married. Are you?"

If I'd still had lemonade in my mouth, I would have done a spit take. Her brain is flittering on a whole other wavelength.

"No more than I was when we kissed at Dead Man's Cove."

"Pirates' Cove," she corrects. "So, are you or not?"

"I'm not." Then because her blue eyes are still questioning me, I add, "I was engaged once."

She takes that information in with a nod.

"I don't even know why I brought that up, but if your next question is, have I ever been close to marriage, then I've already answered."

"Thanks." She looks at the water. "What happened between you and her to end it?"

"Funny how people always want to know that," I say. "Because people do ask. As if the end of a relationship explains everything."

"Maybe, it's like when someone drops dead," she says softly.

There she goes, on another wavelength again. "What do you mean?"

She manages to shrug while resting on both elbows, still looking at the sea. "When you hear someone has died, don't you often ask why or how? You sorta want to know there's a reason, like heart disease or cancer, and that it's not random. Because randomness begets fear. If you can't control your surroundings or your body, then it's scary to be alive."

"That went dark quickly," I try to joke. "I know what you mean though, but I don't think it applies to relationships."

"Wait," she turns to me. "Is she the scuba girlfriend?"

"No. That was another one. I never asked her to marry me."

She raises her eyebrows.

"Hey, it's not like I've been married and divorced three times. Or even once. What about you?" Because Lindsey seems like the kind of together, interesting woman who would've had a proposal if not a marriage.

"Never married. Never engaged. Had a few boyfriends."

"Locals?"

She rolls her eyes. "Not exclusively."

Then maybe she doesn't mind a quick romance with a tourist. Before I risk putting my foot in my mouth and asking, she asks, "What ended your engagement?"

"Back to Greta, are we?"

"Greta?" Her tone is surprised, out of all proportion to the single word.

"Yes, why?"

"Just unusual. I wasn't expecting a *Greta*. You don't look like a guy whose fiancée would be named Greta."

Lindsey has me laughing again. And funny enough, my mom had said something similar when I had told her I'd got engaged.

"What name do you think my fiancée would have?" In that instant, I think *Lindsey* and *Marcus* go together rather well, which is a bizarre and disconcertingly uncharacteristic thought for me. It must be because I'm on a beach alone with a beautiful woman.

When her cheeks turn pink, and not from too much sun, I guess she's thinking the same thing.

She looks away, at the horizon to her left, and mumbles, "Some normal name, I guess."

"Like?" Because now I'm beyond curious.

"I don't know. Amber?"

"Amber?" I don't think I've ever even met one.

"Maybe a Brooke or an Olivia?"

"Better than Amber," I mutter. Then I yawn, giving in to the effects of the food, the warm sun, and the climb up Lucifer's Lighthouse, not to mention how the sound of the lapping water is doing a number on me.

Lying down, I finally close my eyes. I'm not asleep, merely resting, although I do, in fact drift off. I know this because however many minutes later, I'm awakened by the feel of silky soft lips settling onto mine.

Recalling I'm on Siren Sands, I reach up to take hold of the most irresistible siren I've ever met.

9

Lindsey

I can't resist him another second. Marcus is stretched out on the blanket on my favorite stretch of beach, and he looks freakin' hot. *Hot, hot, hot!*

His arms have muscular definition that makes me feel all girly, a total turn-on, and I want them around me. His rock-hard thighs are right there for me to climb onto. I can easily imagine him rolling me under him before settling those thighs between mine.

And his package! His shorts aren't tight, but with him lying on his back, the cotton fabric is outlining his cock, which is lying to the left. He's either a little aroused or bigger than your average bear.

Either way, I can't help myself. I lean over him and kiss him. It seems like a harmless move on a languid, almost helplessly relaxed man, a snoozing tiger.

Instantly, he's more like a clam closing its shell. His arms go around me and he pulls me across him. I lose my balance and sprawl across his body, unable to use my hands to push myself—or my mouth—off of his.

Can't beat him, so I join him. I release the tension, stop struggling, and explore his lemony mouth. Bravely, I am the first to add tongue this time. When he parts his lips, I take the initiative, stroking my tongue alongside his, sending pings of pleasure between my legs.

We kiss a long while. It's pretty great, especially when his hands slide down my back and grab hold of my butt cheeks with each palm.

Anchoring my hips over his, he grinds against me. *Mm. Me likey!* It gets better when he slides me over his hard ridge, back and forth. I may be the one with my tongue in his mouth, but he's in control, working my body and pleasuring us both with the good ol' fully-clothed hump, where friction is your friend.

I'm thinking I can come with the pressure of his erection rubbing against my mound when, just like I imagined, he rolls over, pinning me beneath him. Once I'm under his tall frame, he nudges my legs apart and settles between them.

I squint against the light behind him, but he's still a dark, dangerous, silhouette. Closing my eyes, I'm plunged into a world of pure sensation, a splendid place to be. He's on his forearms now, and my butt cheeks miss the touch of his fingers. Until he glides his erection across the thin fabric of my shorts and panties.

We're kissing again, but I want more. His tongue finds its way between my lips and is swirling inside my mouth. It's tormenting because my brain is already fantasizing about his tongue going south where I'm damp and throbbing and, frankly, feeling damned needy.

I cannot imagine getting off this beach without getting off. If he doesn't finish me now, then I'll have to stroke myself, I'm that aware of an exquisite ache where our parts are doing their best to stimulate each other through layers of fabric.

"Lindsey," he says against my mouth.

"Yup," I say.

"Do you want me to stop?"

"God, no," I say. The whole conversation takes place with our lips touching. "But I'm not on birth control," I confess.

"Not a problem."

In a smooth move, he rolls to his side, turning me toward him, letting me rest my head on his arm. Unzipping his shorts, he uses his free hand to place mine atop his now jutting cock.

I keep my eyes closed because I'm totally in a realm of feeling. My breasts are heavy, my nipples are hard, and my lady parts are quivering with anticipation. If he just—

He does! Marcus slides his hand into my shorts and into my panties in one movement, and then slips a finger between my pliant, wet folds.

"Yes," I sigh, trusting he knows what he's doing.

I get to work with my hand, encircling his thick erection, and I hear him groan. It spurs me on to grip him while sliding my fisted fingers up and down his shaft. At the very top, I smile because he already has a bead of pre-cum, and it's relieving to know he's as far gone as I am.

And I'm already about to sizzle and explode. As I use his own cream under my fingers while I stroke and squeeze him, Marcus is deliberately, delicately, deliciously feathering movements around my pulsing clit. He knows enough to go to one side, then the other, not right on the sensitive bud.

"Mmm," I start to hum.

His finger movements quicken, and I lean into his hand. And then I'm off, shuddering and bucking, but not letting go of his cock until I feel him surging and climaxing, too.

Since we're sideways, his cum shoots onto my bare arm and into the sand, pooling there. *Jeez!* The man had quite a load stored up, and I'm super glad that's not all over my T-shirt or shorts.

In moments, we both roll onto our backs, our hands no longer touching one another. I finally open my eyes as he's zipping up. He looks over at me.

"I didn't have any expectations," he says.

"I know. I could tell."

That makes him laugh. "Damn! I was so unprepared," he jokes.

"I would've been freaked out if you'd pulled a condom out of your pocket," I tell him.

"Talk about premeditated for a day of sightseeing," he quips and waggles his eyebrows.

As expected, I chuckle. Then I sit up, needing to move. "Take a walk up the beach?"

"Yup." And he's on his feet before I can stand, holding his hand down to me.

A girl could get used to such gentlemanly behavior, especially from a guy who just played my body like a maestro.

I take his hand and let him draw me to standing, but as he sends me a frisky grin, my thoughts catch up with me. I remind myself not to get used to any of his behavior. He won't be around too long.

"What's wrong?" he asks, while using his bare foot to push some sand over where he climaxed.

"Nothing." I turn away and start to walk, disconcerted that he can read my emotions. "Absolutely nothing. I'm on my favorite stretch of beach, with a full stomach and a handsome guy. And I just had an orgasm without having to clean up afterward."

"I guess from that perspective, this is paradise."

"Murray Island is great, even *without* a handsome guy." I say it, but I don't mean it. It's lonely sometimes. *Often* actually. And I'm missing Max, even though he started life as my dad's dog. He ended it as my constant companion.

Marcus slides his fingers between mine, and suddenly, we're walking the beach in an intimate hand-hold. I decide to just enjoy the moment and however many other moments we have over the next few days.

"I could see the dilapidated fort from the lighthouse," he says.

"Yes, I know."

"But how did you know for sure if you haven't been up there?" He is teasing me.

"Guess what? I also know there's electricity, but I haven't seen that either."

He squeezes my hand gently in appreciation of my joke. After a few more minutes of silence, he says, "Fort Mercy should come to a merciful end and be razed to the ground. For everyone's safety."

I try not to jump down his throat. Instead, as calmly as possible, I say, "That seems extreme. It's like the lighthouse or our meeting house or our church. Not in the best of shape but important to the life of the island."

"Is it though?" he asks. "Would anyone miss it? When were you last there, enjoying the view of it and all its historical majesty?"

I pull my hand out of his grasp. I don't like an off-islander with such a strong opinion about tearing down stuff that belongs to us.

"You haven't even seen it up close yet. Besides, I'm always going to argue for preservation and fixing up rather than destroying."

"From what I've seen, including the horse lady's gate, Murray Island has a lot of things that need fixing before tackling an old fort that no one seems to give a damn about. I mean, wouldn't you rather have the potholes fixed in front of your store?"

Yes, I would, but I'm not going to agree with him since I doubt either fort or potholes will be taken care of in the near future.

"Renovating that fort would be costly," he continues. "It won't get done anytime soon. Instead, it's just going to continue to deteriorate until it takes itself out, hopefully before anyone gets injured."

He's right, but he's also *not* right. There's something beyond practicality in the poetic areas of the island. And to me, the fort is one of those. Like the cave, which is also dangerous. And he hasn't even seen the small area of cliffs west of the lighthouse, with no barrier or fence. Or maybe he saw them from the air before he landed and has forgotten.

We go along as far as a rocky outcropping that makes it impossible to go any farther now that the tide is in. We've walked past the hotel and the backs of some of the stores. And then we turn around. In fact, the incoming sea has left us merely a narrow stretch of sand, keeping us close together, even though we've stopped holding hands.

Despite not appreciating his talk of destroying the fort, I don't feel the least bit angry with him because I know he's thinking of everyone's well-being. Apparently, that's his default position. As long as he's not overbearing, it's kind of endearing and chivalrous.

We've spent the entire walk alternately talking about the island or being silent in a comfortable way.

"Soon, you're going to know Murray Island better than me," I say, when he tells me about a new flavor, blueberry vanilla, at the ice cream shop. "They haven't opened for the season," I point out.

"I happened to go by when they were carrying in supplies. They're opening next week."

Mr. and Mrs. Boyer, who own Island Scoops, moved here from Canada before I was born. They're nice, and my parents used to have them over for dinner.

"You saw them unloading cream and fruit and sugar, and then they started telling you about their new flavor?" Why didn't that seem plausible? He has to be the nosiest tourist we've ever had.

"I asked what their most popular ice cream was. Do you know the answer?"

"Chocolate?" I guess, although I love their strawberry-nutmeg ice cream.

"That's what I thought. We're both wrong. It's vanilla."

I wrinkle my nose.

"It makes sense," he says when he sees my expression. "You can eat it plain or put it on any flavor of cake or pie, or add fruit and nuts. But I wouldn't put chocolate ice cream on a pie."

"I might," I mumble, because I have. But since he thinks that's weird, I won't confess.

"And when they heard that customers were buying their vanilla ice cream and eating it with blueberries, they decided to increase their market share by combining the fruit already. Very smart."

It's funny how enthusiastic he is about any kind of business.

"Are they using our local berries?" I ask, thinking of times I've spent picking with my mother.

"They didn't mention it. They'd have to wait until the berries are ripe, and they said they're already making ice cream. When's picking time?"

"Andy could have told you."

"Oh, yes, the fruit farmer," Marcus says. "He pointed it out when we were up top."

"They also grow strawberries, raspberries, and apples. As for the Boyer's ice cream, they'd have to wait until late July and into the beginning of August," I tell him, immediately feeling a little sad. Marcus will be far away from here by then, and this day will be a distant memory.

We're approaching my beach blanket now, and it seems unfathomable that not long ago, we'd been groping each other on it.

"Island Scoops should definitely start using island berries and promote the local ingredients. Pity you don't have dairy cows." Then he looks at me. "You don't, do you?"

"Nope."

He pulls out his phone, types a few lines, then pockets it again. I think it's a note about blueberry ice cream, although that seems sort of weird. But if the man's into fruit . . .

"We also have wild blueberry bushes."

Without warning, Marcus grabs my hand and tugs me around to face him, and then draws me close. "I like the wild ones best," he says, and crushes his mouth to mine.

My pulse goes from relaxed to galloping in seconds. Pulling my hand free, I glide both arms up his chest, until I can lace my fingers behind his neck. His hands are back on my butt where I like them, tilting my hips against his.

It's a purrrrfect sizzling, long, kick-ass kiss, and I don't care if it ever ends. But it does, and just when I'm melting against him and feel that insistent throbbing begin again between my legs, he leans his forehead on mine, looking down into my eyes.

Too close, he can see into my soul, so I look at the base of his neck instead, where I'm eager to nuzzle and smell his cologne again. I can't help sighing with contentment.

"You are a magnificent kisser," I say.

"Right back at you," he returns.

"I don't think I am," I confess. "I mean, not lying, the few kisses we've shared have been the best in my life, hands down. But if I was such a good kisser, then wouldn't all my kisses have been this spectacular?" I look up at him again, just as he straightens up. "It must be you who's the expert."

He grins. "That was a long exposé on why you're not a great kisser, but I've already experienced that you are."

I shrug. I want to say that it must mean we're great together, but that sounds like I'm a stage-one clinger, angling for an engagement ring on a first date. That's why I simply smile, having decided to ask him if he wants to stay for dinner. And overnight, because we're not teenagers.

Besides, gorgeous men who actually want to be with me don't exactly fall in my lap every day. Or year, for that matter.

"Lindsey," comes a familiar voice before I can issue my invitation. I turn to see a frantic-looking Melinda, and my heart starts to race again.

"Mel? What's wrong?"

"Thank God I found you. It's Dave. He's collapsed."

10

Marcus

We go from DEFCON five to one and remain in a state of high alarm for the next few minutes. Grabbing up the blanket, basket, and remains of our picnic, I chase after the women who are sprinting toward the beach path.

"How did you find me?" Lindsey asks the woman whom I recognize as the bartender from Dave's restaurant. "Why didn't you call?"

"I tried. Your phone just rang and went to voicemail."

Lindsey pats her pockets as we speed-walk back to her house. "Must have left it on the kitchen counter."

"When I saw your Jeep, I figured you weren't far."

"Thanks for coming to find me."

I'm still puzzled and cannot figure out Lindsey's role in this emergency.

"Where is Dave?" I ask.

"I'm Melinda," the woman answers. "He's at the medical center."

"We have a clinic with a full-time physician assistant, a part-time nurse, telehealth helps, of course," Lindsey explains.

I already know all that from Robin's notes before I bought the hotel. Their facility needs updating and more staff, not only during the season but year-round.

"What does Jenny think is wrong?" Lindsey asks, turning her attention back to the bar tender.

She winces. "Heart attack."

"Shouldn't he be taken to the mainland?" I ask.

"Our physician assistant has stabilized him," the bartender says. "And she's called for a MedFlight."

Lindsey looks at me, then back at Melinda. "Marcus is a pilot. He came by plane."

The other woman shakes her head. "I don't think Dave can sit up and be strapped in some little cockpit."

"No, of course, not," Lindsey says. "I don't know what I was thinking."

"You're thinking like a friend."

By this time, we're back at Lindsey's house.

Melinda gets on a scooter. "I'll see you at the clinic. Don't forget your phone." She zips away.

Lindsey and I climb into her Jeep.

"Let's go," she says, driving barefoot.

"Are you related to Dave?"

"Nope," she says.

"Then why?"

She shrugs, keeping her eyes on the road. "It's an old island by-law. Everyone who is single gets a partner for emergencies. I'm Dave's partner. It makes sense in a hurricane and for medical issues. If he can't speak for himself, then I am his voice, just like any husband or wife would be."

"So, you know everything about him and what he wants to have happen in such an emergency?" It actually seems like a really well-conceived plan. And what a community of trust and caring it builds on Murray Island.

"I have everything in my phone. We had to fill out forms."

"Is he your partner, too?"

We've pulled up outside the tiny clinic.

"No, that wouldn't make sense. It's always someone else. Dave couldn't do me any good right now if something happened to me, could he? The person who has my back, so to speak, is Jeannette. After my parents left the island, I still had my grandmother, but then she died. And when Jeannette's husband passed, she got saddled with me."

I nod, watching as she puts on her sandals and gets out of the Jeep.

"I'll see you later," she says over her shoulder, and I realize I've been dismissed.

After the door closes behind her, however, I can't think of what to do with myself. For one thing, it's Sunday and everything is closed. Again, I hope this is because it's the week before the *real* season. Because if they close up like this during the summer, they're missing out big-time. Day-trippers and weekenders need both Saturday and Sunday to make the most of the island.

I don't feel like walking around anymore. Instead, I stay put, leaning against the Jeep. Drawing out my phone, I answer some emails, text my parents and my sister because I haven't spoken to them in a couple weeks. This type of medical emergency is a stark reminder not to let too much time go by.

I've just hit send when I hear the sound of a helicopter approaching. It lands on the square of asphalt with a red-and-white *H* painted on it between the back of the clinic and the beach. I'd seen the landing pad when I flew in.

Although I don't go inside, I stroll around the corner and out back, passing Melinda going in the opposite direction. People in medical garb, I assume they are the nurse and the PA, are already placing Dave onboard, but Lindsey is huddled by the clinic's backdoor, looking ashen.

When I go to her, she lets me put my arm around her, and we turn to go back inside. At least everything is bright and clean and welcoming despite the pervasive scent of disinfectant that most of us have come to hate.

"You're not going with him?" I ask.

She shakes her head. "Not even if I wanted to. No one's allowed on the flight but medical."

"You didn't want to go?"

She gives me a shaky, nervous laugh. "God, no! I couldn't. I just . . . can't."

"The heights thing?"

She nods just before the nurse comes in behind us.

"OK, Lindsey. Here's a copy of everything we've done here. Give us a call when you get to the hospital. Keep me posted."

"I will," she promises. Forgetting me, she heads for the front door. Naturally, I follow.

"How are you getting there?"

"The civilized way," she says. "By boat."

"Not on the ferry?" I glance to the empty harbor.

"No, Sam's ready to take me. I just have to grab some stuff from home, including my purse. He'll drop me off and come back before it gets dark."

She'll be alone on the mainland. Without thinking, I ask, "May I come with you?"

Her dark-blue eyes widen. "Why?"

"Because I have nothing better to do, and I want to."

For a moment, I think she's going to say no, but then Lindsey nods. "That's really nice of you. Can you pack a bag for one or two nights and be back at the main dock in ten minutes?" Then she drops me at the hotel lobby.

$♥$♥$♥$

A quarter hour later, Sam, who I find out is married to Melinda, and among his many jobs is a commercial fisherman, pushes the throttle on his trawler and the four of us are roaring away from Murray Island. It's surreal. An hour later, we dock in Boston, having threaded our way through so many small harbor islands that I've lost count. And then it gets interesting and busy, until we're tied up at a wharf surrounded by buildings, both warehouse and commercial.

Melinda and Sam hug Lindsey before shaking my hand.

"Safe travels," Lindsey tells them, and we walk away, each carrying a duffle bag.

"What's your plan?" I ask as we start walking.

"*Uh.* Get a taxi, I guess." She's clearly distracted by the noise and the sheer volume of people and cars.

"I ordered us an Uber," I tell her, hoping she won't mind. A quick look around, however, reveals that Robin ordered a stretch limo! *Dammit!* Apparently, my assistant thinks I'm too rich for a regular Uber.

"When? How?" Lindsey asks, not seeing the monstrosity blocking everyone's way. But I know it's for us.

"I texted before we got on Sam's boat," I say. Now I have to explain away a limo with a driver holding up a sign that says "Lindsey and Marcus," like we're a married couple. At least Robin is good at following some instructions, such as no last names.

Putting my hand on Lindsey's lower back, I steer her toward the black limo.

"This?" she asks, before shooting me a querying look. "This is an Uber? I don't think so." Then she stares from our names to the smiling driver and back to me.

"I may've made a mistake," I say vaguely, "but it's here. We might as well take it."

The driver opens the back door, and we slide in. Lindsey reads him the name of the hospital off her phone, and the door closes with a firm snicking sound.

"This is going to cost a fortune," she says, dropping her voice to a whisper as if the driver is going to care.

"Not a problem," I say, and suddenly, it is a problem.

"Dave is not going to want to pay for this," she frets. "Jenny and the Murray Island hospital don't have the extra funds. I certainly don't."

"It's all paid for. By me. It's fine," I add because she opens her mouth to argue. "Dave makes a great burger, and I want him back on the island. That's all."

She stares at me, and I cross my arms, looking out the window until she finally turns her attention to the interior. It's a regular rental limo, probably used for weddings and proms. I'm simply relieved it's clean.

"I've never been in one of these before," she says. "To be honest, it's even kind of weird to be in a vehicle with real doors."

Talk about a low bar to impress a woman. I guess everything seems deluxe compared to her ancient Jeep. Instantly, I'm sorry it's not my private limo, which is state-of-the-art and fully stocked. I'm also sorry that her first time is because of this tense occasion.

We maintain a somewhat strained silence until the driver pulls into a semi-circular drop off in front of a massive medical center. I sure hope Dave has insurance, or I see a huge bill in my future.

Inside, I can't help taking over. Lindsey seems shorter on the mainland, less substantial. I go to the info desk, mention the MedFlight from Murray Island, and soon we're in the elevator to cardiology.

On that floor, I explain again who we are, and that Lindsey is the patient's "partner." From then on out, they assume she's romantically involved with Dave, twenty years her senior.

We're shown to a place where we have to wait.

After filling out yet another form and doing an intake interview with the help of the info on her phone, she asks a passing hospital staff member, "Can I see him?"

The answer is *yes, sometime this century*. We wait and then wait some more. Finally, they call her back. Not me. Two visitors aren't allowed. And only his *fiancée*. She and I glance at one another, and then she disappears further into the unit.

I pace. I'm not good at waiting and doing nothing.

I know by now that Lindsey hasn't thought forward about a place to stay. I text my assistant, and a few minutes later, we have a suite at the Ritz-Carlton. It has two bedrooms, so I don't feel badly about not booking a second room.

At last, she reappears. Instead of devastated as I expected, she looks relieved.

"Not the worst heart attack in the world," she says as soon as we're together. "More of a wake-up call."

"Next time, tell Dave to get an alarm clock," I quip.

When she returns the smile, I know he's not in any danger. She's lost the brittle tension since Melinda found us on the beach.

"What now?" I ask, as it suddenly occurs to me that Lindsey might have had a plan after all.

She shrugs in classic style, and says, "I guess we use an app on our phones to find a motel."

"Motel?" I echo. It's good to be rich. Money doesn't make you happy, but it erases a lot of problems and provides some perks that sure seem like happiness. For instance, when I say, "I've already booked us a place," Lindsey's expression is relieved.

However, after she sees that the limo is still downstairs waiting for us, she tenses up again.

"Going to cost a fortune," she says, as if telling me something I don't know.

"Don't worry about it." Because her idea of a fortune and mine are vastly different.

That's made even clearer when we turn down a side street across from the Boston Common, and she sees our hotel. Two uniformed doormen are standing in front of the large glass-and-chrome doors. Grabbing my hand in a death grip, she cranes her neck, trying to see the top of the building without opening the window.

"Who are you?" she snaps, turning to me with eyes that appear bluer since her face has paled. But she doesn't wait for an answer. "What the hell are you doing? I know you're from North Carolina, and maybe things are cheaper than in New England, but this place is going to be super-pricey, even the worst room."

I think she might faint when she sees we're definitely not in the worst room. During the elevator ride up, Lindsey presses her lips together tightly, visibly distressed, and I curse under my breath for not thinking to get a ground-floor room, if they have any.

Seeing me staring, she says, "I'm fine. It's not the height. Well, not *only* the height. Just, you know, everything."

In fact, after the bellhop leaves us with our seawater and salt encrusted bags, Lindsey stands in the middle of the suite's living room and starts to cry.

Shit! I rush over and wrap my arms around her. "Hey," I say uselessly. "Come on. What's wrong? Stop, please." I rub her back, feeling her trembling against my chest.

And then she takes a big breath and pushes away from me. "You're a scammer!"

"What?" I can't help smiling at her outrage.

"You came to Murray Island, talking to all the business owners and getting in tight with people, always coming up with helpful money-making suggestions."

"I sound terribly devious," I say, not reading the room.

But as she shakes her head and takes a step back, it dawns on me that she's serious.

Narrowing her eyes and gesturing around us at the luxury, she says, "And then this!"

"Yeah, I still don't get it. How am I a scammer?"

"You took advantage of Dave's heart attack to get a free ride back here, and now you think you're going to get a free night in a hotel suite with me as your sex partner."

Well, she got the last part right. I don't see why we can't pick up where we left off on the beach now that Dave is safely in one of Boston's best hospitals. But I don't say that since the timing is obviously not right.

"When I wake up in the morning," she adds, "I'll be here alone with the bill and a bunch of regrets. You bastard!"

With those words of righteous indignation, she picks up her bag and goes storming for the door.

Because I'm momentarily shocked, I let her reach it before I catch up, slam my palm against it, and hold it closed while she tugs on the handle like we're in a movie.

"Lindsey, calm down. I promise you I can afford this room. And the limo, too. Besides, Sam's boat wasn't the smoothest ride in the world, and certainly not worth trading my plane for. I left it behind, remember? That's a big piece of collateral, don't you think?"

She freezes, having forgotten that little aerodynamic fact.

Resting her forehead on the door, she gathers her emotions. Finally, she straightens and turns. We're close enough to kiss, but this might not be the moment.

"You're really not scamming me out of an expensive night in this hotel, are you?"

"I'm really not." I relax and lean back against the wall, crossing my arms.

Lindsey touches my shirt where it covers my upper arm, smoothing her fingers over it and the muscle beneath. "It looks expensive," she says quietly. "It's the softest cotton I've ever felt."

I swallow. I don't think she's asking me a question, simply processing. Then she looks down at my shoes. "Also, super nice," she says. "Pricey shoes."

I nod because they're not cheap.

Finally, she looks me in the eyes. "I'm sorry I overreacted. This is all just too weird. And we don't know each other."

She's right about that. For one thing, I own an obscenely expensive, boutique hotel nearby that I recently stayed in for a few days before I flew to Murray Island. I told Robin explicitly not to book us a room there. With the staff fawning over me. I would have had to explain a few things.

"We don't have to do anything more than eat dinner, take showers, and go to bed."

Her eyebrows rise.

"I mean, go to sleep," I clarify, although that would suck. But to put her mind at ease, I add. "It's a two-bedroom suite."

"A two-bedroom suite," she repeats softly. "Sweet mother!"

I want to laugh at her adorable wonderment. Instead, I push away from the wall.

"Come on. It may be only for one night, but we might as well enjoy it."

As casually as I can, hoping she doesn't slip out behind me, I walk to the other side of the living room, where the windows overlook the Common. The park view is adequate but not amazing. Not like looking out and seeing the Seine and the Eiffel Tower or the Arenal Volcano of Costa Rica. But I do know there are great restaurants in this city, and I'm going to take this lovely lady to one of them.

It occurs to me, as I turn to see whether Lindsey has come away from the door, that she won't appreciate the bird's-eye view in any case. Closing the floor-to ceiling-drapes, I decide to take her attention off of where we are.

"You getting hungry?" It had been a lot of miles and a long time, both on the water and in the hospital, since our rosemary wraps on the beach. "Doesn't it seem like yesterday when we were sightseeing?"

To my relief, she puts her bag next to the sofa. I guess she's staying.

"Are we supposed to go back to the hospital tonight?" I ask.

She shakes her head. "Not until morning."

"Won't your fiancé miss you?"

"*Ha!* That was weird," she agrees. "Dave was fully conscious and kinda pissed off that we'd brought him to Boston."

"What did he expect? That he'd just stay in the clinic on the island?"

"Yes, actually. He said he would've preferred it. And he vowed it's the last time he has a heart attack around any of us clowns." Then she grins, and it's a stunning sight.

"Sounds like he's doing well."

"Yes and no. He was ornery, but the doctor said there's bound to have been some damage to his heart. On the other hand, he may not even need a stint. Just a better diet and some medication. How he fares tonight will tell them more."

She rubs her hands up and down her own arms, and I have the insane desire to hold her again, for no other reason than to comfort her. Insane because, as Lindsey said, we don't know each other, and none of this is my problem.

"You know what?" she adds. "I *am* starving, but I think I'd like to shower first. I bet the bathroom is top notch."

"Bathrooms," I correct. "Take a look at the bedrooms and see which one you want."

"Wow!" she says. "Just wow." Then she picks up her bag and goes toward the closest of the open doors on either side of the living room.

"This one's fine," she calls out.

"Don't you want to see the other one?"

She reappears with a genuine smile on her face. "If you insist. Are you afraid I'll get the better one?"

"Lady's choice," I say.

She sprints across the room to the other one. "I think this one is more masculine. I'll stick with the other one."

Sharing a room seems to be off the table, at least for the time being.

"I'll shower, too. I think we got used to the smell, but I'm pretty sure we both have the distinct odor of fish." I don't joke about the extra cleaning fee for the limo, because she'll get all freaked out again. "Besides, I'll welcome a decent spray with hot-as-Hades water for a change."

Maybe her water pressure is better than elsewhere on the island because Lindsey shrugs.

"Meet you back here in ten," she says. Then she hesitates. "Thanks, Marcus. You've been great. I hadn't thought beyond getting to the mainland."

I shrug, although I'm feeling like a hero.

"But I'm locking my bathroom door," she adds.

Just like that, I've been relegated to possible creep again.

11

Lindsey

The spacious tile shower with all the hot water a girl could want is exactly what I need. I'm taking longer than ten minutes to get ready, but there's heavenly smelling shampoo and conditioner, silky body wash, argan oil-infused moisturizer, and razors. *Free razors!* I'm not going to look a gift-horse in the mouth. Then again, that's what the Trojans said, and see where that got them, stupidly bringing a horse full of soldiers into the heart of their city.

Not that I'm thinking of Trojan condoms or how my heart feels warm toward this guy. But Marcus has been pretty remarkable if this is really all on the up and up. But it's crazy over-the-top.

He's right about something being fishy, and it's not only our clothing. And while his good Samaritan routine is hard to accept, what can I do but go with it?

Thank goodness I rolled jeans, another pair of shorts, and a skirt into my bag, along with two T-shirts and one sweater, plus the windbreaker I wore on the boat. Since it's not exactly balmy at night, I put on the jeans and a T before tugging my sweater over my head.

The hotel has provided a hairdryer, which I use. No ponytail tonight. I leave my hair loose around my shoulders, and it does what it always does, hangs in long, gentle waves. And because I am female and single, and he's a lava-hot male, I take the time to put on mascara, which is in my purse at all times in case I'm going from the shop directly to work at Dave's.

My thoughts return to my employer and friend, which is why I'm undoubtedly looking serious when I finally return to the living room. Marcus is on the couch, hair still damp, wearing clean jeans and a long-sleeved T-shirt. I half expected him to appear in a James Bond suit because he's handling everything so smoothly.

Looking up from his phone, he doesn't make mention of how I stretched ten minutes into almost thirty. Instead, his glance flickers over me, head to toe. My skin prickles as if Marcus is touching me.

"Feel better?" he asks. "Yes, thanks. I was until I suddenly thought about work and wondering . . . I don't know. I know Dave's not the best cook in the world, but man, we need his casual bar food. What's Murray Island going to do if . . . ?" I trail off.

He jumps to his feet. "Don't go getting ahead of yourself. My uncle had a heart attack about five years ago, and it was the best thing that could've happened. He started taking care of himself, and he looks better than ever."

I nod. It's reassuring. Plus, Dave didn't look as terrible by the time I saw him in the hospital as when I first saw him at the Murray Island medical center.

"What do you feel like eating?" Marcus asks, already heading for the door.

I'm struck again by how little we know one another. Apart from ham and turkey and a burger, I have no idea what this man likes. As for me, I'm pretty limited in my palette due to what's available on the island. But whenever I've come to the mainland, I've enjoyed trying things.

"You know what," I say, as I grab my purse and we head out. "I'll try anything once."

"A woman after my own heart," he says.

I feel his hand on the small of my back while we wait at the elevator.

"I promise," I say, "I'm not after your heart."

He sends me an unfathomable look.

"Just a joke." *Stupid joke,* I admonish myself. Now, he's gonna think I'm totally into him.

The elevator arrives in the middle of our cloud of awkward silence. We get into the smoky-mirrored, shiny stainless cage, and the doors close. There's nowhere to hide, and I wish the floor would open and let me fall through.

My imaginative brain immediately gives me a picture of the dark elevator shaft beneath me and how high up I am. Thirty-six floors to be exact. A flat, brushed nickel railing as low as my thighs is the single safety precaution. *Pathetic!* I need a parachute and a glass of wine, or a seatbelt at the very least.

I'm about to have a genuine freak-out when, to my surprise, Marcus moves closer.

"Maybe *I'm* the one after *your* heart."

Say what? Is he flirting with me? Now? While we're plunging to our deaths?

With his hands on my shoulders, he turns me to face him and, at the same time, backs me up against the elevator wall.

"May I kiss you again?"

I stare into his gorgeous brown eyes, seeing his pupils dilate. What can I do but nod?

He starts to lean down, but then he stops, just before I shut my eyes.

"What?" I ask, my heart pounding for a variety of reasons.

"Do you need to brush your teeth or gargle or floss?"

All the tension leaves my body, grateful for his teasing.

"I just brushed," I say, reaching up and drawing his head down with my fingers in his hair.

His mouth covers mine. *Zing!* It's another perfect kiss. Somehow, our mouths are already open and devouring each other in seconds. His hips press mine against the mirrored wall, and now I'm not at all unhappy about the placement of the railing. At least, I don't have a bar in the middle of my back.

But I cannot get him close enough, so I part my legs. Marcus takes the cue and nestles between my thighs, fitting like he was always meant to be there. His hands cradle my head and his thumbs stroke my cheekbones while our tongues stroke one another.

When the ding sounds and the doors open, I cannot believe my feeling of irritation at the interruption of our snog-fest. Also, disbelief that I forgot entirely about my fear of dangling over a high elevator shaft.

Someone nearby coughs, and I realize we're still entangled. In a heartbeat, we are moving past those who were waiting, and I turn to see Marcus is wearing an identical grin to my own. He's fun to be around. That's for sure.

"We didn't decide on food," he says.

"Except for eating it." And because I want to know more about him, I ask, "What do *you* feel like eating?"

His glance is downright wicked. But I'm glad he doesn't say any lewd line as cliché as what he seems to be thinking. Still, I feel an answering tingle between my legs, imagining his firm tongue getting busy. I am almost ready to say *Forget finding a restaurant*, but my stomach grumbles loudly.

He looks around, then lifts his nose, looking like a hunting dog. Like Max when he caught scent of a deer near our back door.

"Smells like there's a restaurant right in this hotel," he says.

I consider the inflated prices of a hotel dining experience. I want to repay him for being with me by buying him dinner. I wonder how Marcus feels about a pizza.

"This place is probably pricey," I begin.

He laughs. "Lindsey, everywhere in Boston is pricey. Don't worry, my treat. Just tell me what you feel like eating."

"I want to pay," I insist, feeling small for having accused him of trying to take me for a ride.

"Not going to happen. I pushed my way into this trip, and I bet you would've eaten in the hospital cafeteria."

I can't say I wouldn't have, so I stay silent.

"Darlin', we're going to have a feast. If you won't decide, then I will."

I'm not usually attracted to someone, meaning a *male* someone, taking over and making decisions. But right now, when I'm tired and starving, it's fine. Better than fine. Besides, no one has ever called me *darlin'* before. It's super sexy.

We get a taxi for the short ride to the North End. Marcus holds the door for me to enter an Italian restaurant that smells like heaven.

In short order, we have a bottle of red wine and some warm, crusty bread with garlic-herb butter and olive oil for dipping. I don't think you're supposed to use both, but I do. I'm happily wolfing down my second piece of bread when I realize he's staring at me.

Holding my hand over my mouth, I ask, "What?" I must have already gotten a piece of oregano from the butter stuck between my teeth.

"It's nice to see you relaxed and happy."

"I'm both," I say, shooting a few bread crumbs into my palm. Glad he can't see, I slow down, chew, swallow, and drink some of the best red wine I've ever had. Totally giving up worrying about the cost, I didn't even suggest he order the house wine. He looked at the list and ordered something Italian.

When I'm no longer in danger of speaking with my mouth full, I ask, "Time to tell me about yourself."

If I'm not mistaken, he freezes like one of Mrs. Boyer's snow cones. After a moment, he says, "I live in Tryon,

North Carolina, when I'm not traveling. You've probably never heard of it."

"May I ask how you afford to travel?" Would he tell me if he's a drug dealer or a gambler or a—

"Real estate," he says, easing my mind. "My dad was a builder before he retired. I worked construction on some of his jobs."

"Hence the muscles," I say before slapping my hand over my mouth. Gulping red wine on an empty stomach *before* soaking it up with bread was clearly a lip-loosening mistake.

Marcus smiles, and my stomach flutters, not from hunger, either.

"Thanks, but it's been a few years since I swung a hammer." Then he says, "No, wait, it hasn't been that long. I built a playhouse for my niece and nephew last summer."

"You have siblings?"

"An older sister. She lives in Greensboro with the man she met in college and their two kids."

He asks me about my parents and what they're doing since abandoning ship—my words, not his. I tell him how my mother is currently teaching at the University of New Hampshire in the MFA Program in Writing after spending last year as the writer-in-residence at Philip's Exeter Academy.

"Dad is semi-retired, by which I mean he occasionally finds a way to make money. He thinks like you, always wanting to improve or streamline something." Then I steer Marcus back to his career, and he tells me about the natural progression from building houses to going into real estate development.

"I've done well," he says with a shrug that lifts those wide shoulders.

I decide to stop fretting over any money he spends for the remainder of the evening. The house-made pasta is sublime, melting in my mouth, while the *fra diavolo* sauce lights up my tongue, and the asparagus is perfectly roasted. I could not be any happier.

And then the dessert arrives. I was wrong. My happiness level shoots up another notch. We ordered tiramisu and affogato, and go back and forth with dueling spoons between the creamy, marsala-wine-and-cognac-soaked lady fingers topped with rich mascarpone and the ice cream dish.

I've never had affogato before, but it is amazing. All opposites of bitter espresso and sweet ice cream, hot and cold at the same time. Absolutely fabulous, and I wish there was a chance in hell of getting Mr. and Mrs. Boyer to make anything like it at their ice cream shop.

I savor each bite of both, licking my spoon, catching Marcus watching me.

"I am so full," I admit.

"But we're not done," he says.

As if the server was waiting, she comes over with a tray and two small cups of coffee—espresso, if I'm not mistaken—and two small shot glasses.

"Caffè corretto," she says, "with sambuca."

When she walks away, I groan. "You will have to roll me home." But I watch as he pours the clear liqueur into his coffee. I do the same, and we drink the after-dinner concoction.

"Delicious," I say. "And at least I won't fall asleep on the ride home."

"There's a reason espresso is served in a small cup," he says. "Plus, it helps your digestion after a big meal, and the liqueur will soften the caffeine effect."

"Does it?"

"Sounds plausible," he says, leaving me wondering if he's making it all up. Then he adds, "You know there's one more thing coming, don't you?"

At my astonished expression, Marcus is nearly laughing.

"Italian *digestivo*," he says.

"Marcus." I level him with a stare. "I know that's another liqueur, and I have to say no."

Too late, the server is at our table again, setting down small, frosted glasses of pale-yellow liquid.

"House-made limoncello," she says, pronouncing it like *lee-mohn-chehl-loh*.

"Really?" I ask, looking at Marcus, who is smirking slightly. He raises his hands, in a gesture of "what can I do?" But I know he must have ordered all this when I excused myself to the ladies' room after the main course.

"It removes the taste of the caffe," our server says, "and cleans your pallet." She raises an eyebrow at me and nods toward Marcus. "You will thank me on the car ride home, yes?"

Like I'm fifteen on a first date, I feel myself blush. Somehow this matronly Italian woman knows we're going to kiss before I even know.

In another few minutes, we're in the back of another taxi, sharing lemon-flavored kisses, like on the island, which now seems a world away. I don't even mind the ride up in the elevator because Marcus's tongue is in my mouth, and my hands are sliding under his long-sleeve shirt.

Ding! We manage to break apart and get out just in time before the doors close again. I'm feeling giddy as he takes my hand, and we make our way to one of only three doors on the entire floor. Then he shoves the card key into the slot so hard, I think it's going to snap before he pushes the door open.

In what can be described as a whirlwind of clothing, we're almost naked before we're on the bed in his room. He's tall, but once we're lying down and his body is over mine, we fit like puzzle pieces. He nudges my legs apart and rests between my thighs, and then we're kissing again. Perhaps we never stopped.

I thread my fingers into his thick brown hair and suck his intruding tongue, while relishing the weight of his body on top of mine. But I want more. He smells good and tastes better. And his hard muscles have me wet and wanting even before he rubs his erection against my mound.

111

Then I think about what held us back before. I tear my mouth from under his to say, "Still not on the pill," before I go back to kissing him. His lips are that perfect blend of firm and soft and sensual. He's giving and taking, and I'm trying to keep up.

"We're all set," Marcus says mysteriously, and I decide to trust him.

He sucks on my lower lip, then tugs at it, making my clit harden and pulse. He nibbles and kisses his way down my throat, making me tilt my head back to give him better access. I'm barely breathing, my eyes squeezed closed, enjoying the warmth and moisture he's leaving on my skin until he reaches the valley between my breasts.

"Lindsey, may I take off your bra?"

My eyes pop open, and I smile at the question. "Yes."

It's a regular, pale-pink cotton, unsexy bra, but he's looking at me like I'm a Victoria's Secret model. When he slides his hands under me, I arch my breasts up and lift my chest until he undoes the clasps.

A little too practiced, I think. But when his firm lips gently latch onto my right nipple, with a hint of his teeth grazing my sensitive flesh, I'm grateful for any and all experience he's had.

He is not like any guy I've ever been with, all two of them. Marcus takes his time but moves at a pace that keeps my body humming. In that instant, his mouth starts teasing my other nipple while his capable fingers roll the first one.

I'm already beginning to feel that taut, pent-up sensation low in my stomach that says a climax is on its way. No vibrator, and he hasn't even touched me yet, but somehow, I'm in a state of heightened bliss, both relaxed and excited. My lady parts are ramped up and overly sensitive, under his torso. I lift my hips to better feel whatever manly parts I can.

Knowing I'm doing nothing apart from receiving, I grab his butt under each of my hands, wishing he'd already removed his boxer briefs. When I squeeze him, he gently bites my nipple, making me gasp.

Spreading my legs further allows me to wrap my ankles around the back of his calves and stroke my satiny smooth skin up and down his legs. *Thank you for the free razors,* I say to the hotel management. Then I try to lace my fingers at his back, but he's suddenly on the move. Downward.

I try to swallow, but my mouth goes dry. The planes of his body take their time moving down over my mound while he is kissing my skin again. Below my breasts, across my ribs, around my navel, making me squirm because I'm ticklish, and then . . . he raises up as he hooks his thumbs under my bikini panties and slides them down. He leaves them tight across my thighs, and I had no idea that would feel so erotic and naughty, almost like I'm bound.

I try to grasp his shoulders, but he's too far away.

"Relax," he says, and then his deft fingers open me right where I'm desperate for his touch. A puff of his breath makes me moan, and his next kiss blows my mind.

I cannot help bucking off the mattress when his mouth closes over my clit. But he anchors me to the bed with his weight on my legs. And his thumbs still hold me open while his broad hands are splayed across my hip bones, also keeping me in place.

His tongue laves my hardened nub. It is torture and joy, and I can't think of any better thing happening. Ever.

The loud sounds in my ears are coming from me. I'm not embarrassed. I don't care. Not about anything except him continuing what he's doing. If he stops, I'll shrivel up and die with disappointment.

He doesn't stop. He doesn't rush. He doesn't change the speed of the flicks of his tongue, so I don't lose ground. He doesn't start poking around all over. He is methodical in a good way, allowing me to wind up and wind up and wind up. When his teeth graze my clit, I call out something unintelligible, even to me.

Just a rebel yell of release as my climax unwinds, and everything tense in me relaxes into jelly. It's spectacular. I groan and open my eyes, look down the length of my body, and see him smiling up at me.

"Jeez!" is all I can manage.

He continues moving down, taking my undies with him. I go up on my elbows to watch. He shucks his close-fitting boxer briefs and lets loose the same long, thick erection I held on the beach.

"Tell me you have protection," I say.

He nods enthusiastically. "When I packed my bag, I grabbed a condom from my room."

"Only one?" I joke, with nervous excitement.

"Maybe a couple dozen," he says, dead-pan and not cracking a smile.

I decide not to be bothered that he had condoms in his hotel room. He's a gorgeous single man. Why shouldn't he? I watch him grab a shiny packet from the pocket of his duffle bag and think, *Now we're getting down to business.*

12

Marcus

When I watch Lindsey climax, it's stratospheric, and she's so far gone, I wonder if my cock—hard and ready as it is—can manage to repeat the success of my mouth and make her come again.

I'm game to try. As they say in horse racing for a first win, we've already *broken maiden*. Now, it's time for me to catch up with her on the backstretch.

Condom on, willing woman waiting, I gently grasp her slender ankles and spread her legs wider before settling between them. Dropping kisses across her now damp skin, I travel up her body until the tip of my erection encounters the wet and inviting heat of her pussy. Nudging her entrance, I'm looking directly down into her languid blue eyes.

When I pause, she raises an eyebrow.

"You are amazing," I tell her. With her hair spread out around her, she looks like a golden goddess. I don't tell

Lindsey the rest of my thoughts, that I've never been this turned on by any female ever, and I have no idea why. Better to show her.

Leaning on my forearms, I rock against her drenched pussy, dipping into her slick channel. But I want to be kissing her when I enter. Lowering my head, I claim her mouth.

Like an insatiable siren, she sinks her teeth into my bottom lip while I sink my cock inside her. It's awesome. When she gasps and releases me, I slide my tongue inside her mouth. Soon, our tongues are stroking while I bury myself in her snug but slippery sheath, an erotic glove that's been tailor-made for me.

"Yes," she whispers, softly like a summer breeze against my mouth.

When she lifts her hips to meet mine, sex has never felt closer to perfect synchronicity. Her fingers on my shoulders squeeze or tap depending on my movements. When they sink into my flesh with a surprisingly strong grip, I can tell she's coming again. Her moan is so sensual and her body so open and supple, I follow her over the edge.

I have to raise up for the final surging thrusts, breathing hard, as my climax rolls through me from my lower spine to my tight balls through to my pulsing cock that's deep inside her.

"Yes!" I echo, but a lot louder.

And then I collapse to the side, pulling off the condom and dropping it on the nightstand.

"God, I'm exhausted." Lindsey says exactly what I'm thinking. "This day has lasted forever."

"Too tired to brush and gargle?" I joke, with my eyes already closed.

"*Ugh!* I am," she declares. In the next instant, she changes her mind. "No, I have to. After all that food."

She jumps out of bed, and I watch her pert ass as she sprints for the door.

"Come back after," I call out, thinking she might not, but wanting her close in case we feel the urge again.

"Maybe," she yells back.

I roll over and nearly fall asleep, but I want to still be conscious in case she does return to share my bed. Hauling my ass into the bathroom, I brush my teeth and wash my face. When I come out, the bed's still empty.

Shit! That shouldn't be as disappointing as it is. I mean, we just had great sex. We're not dating. And she's only yards away. *Calm the hell down, Parisi*, I tell myself.

I get back under the covers, thinking about the day. I couldn't have imagined it playing out like this in a billion years.

"Here I come," Lindsey says a second before she enters at a run, wearing a thigh-length T-shirt, and hurls herself onto the mattress like a kid would do.

Laughing hard, I snort while she struggles to pull the covers out from under her. Finally, she wriggles beneath them. Another few long moments are spent as she arranges herself, plumping her pillow and moving her hair out from under her shoulders.

"I guess you don't usually have espresso in the evening."

"Nope," she says.

"Don't worry. It was very little. You should be asleep in no time."

"Yup," she says, rolling onto her side and facing me.

We talk for a minute about how good the dinner was, although what just happened surpassed any meal I've ever eaten.

Soon, her words taper off, her eyelids drift closed, and her thick lashes rest on her cheeks. After clicking off the bedside lamp, I banish the unexpected thought that I wouldn't mind seeing her face last thing before I sleep every night. And, of course, first thing in the morning.

"Marcus," I hear against my ear, waking me instantly. For a second, I have no idea where, who, what, why. I'm on my back. Not home. Not Murray Island.

"Marcus," comes her soft voice again. *Lindsey.*

"Mmph?" I ask because my brain and tongue haven't connected yet. I can tell by how I feel that it's early, like 3 A.M.

"Are you frisky?" she whispers, and her hand is suddenly on a quest, patting my stomach, stroking my hip, and then encircling my cock, which, given the circumstances, does me proud. My arousal is instant.

She giggles. "I guess you are."

"I am now."

Her breasts are pressing against my upper arm as she leans into me and nibbles my earlobe.

I move fast for someone who was deeply asleep ten seconds earlier. I flip her onto her back and nestle between her legs. Tugging her nightshirt up, I can't see her breasts in the darkness, but soon I have a nipple in my mouth. She makes a cute sound, like a sigh of pleasure. When I pinch her other nipple, not too hard, just a roll and a squeeze, she moans. In the darkness, it's the sexiest sound ever.

"Still not on the pill," she reminds me.

I can't help smiling. She wants it right now. Leaning over, I grab another foil packet off the nightstand, and roll it on. In seconds, I'm buried balls deep in her wet, tight warmth.

Another moan from Lindsey. I thrust and retreat while she lifts her hips to meet me. With her fingers curling around, trying to reach my butt, she pushes and pulls my body. I let her set the pace until she relinquishes all attempts at control.

In the inky blackness of the light-blocking curtains, our senses are heightened to the point I can feel her surrender as her arms fall to the mattress and her legs spread wider. She's almost there, so I slide my hand between us and give some attention to her clit with my thumb while I rock against her. Almost as soon as I begin to stroke her taut button, her stomach muscles and her thighs tense.

"Marcusss," she hisses in gratitude. And then, "Yes, yes, yes!" as her pussy grips my cock while she comes, followed by her groan of release.

I withdraw my hand from between us. With my cock rigid as a fucking fence post, I fill her softness and withdraw, over and over, until my orgasm builds to the point of shuddering tension. I let go with a pistoning motion of my hips, enjoying another mind-blowing climax.

"Thanks," she says, making me laugh even as I roll off her and discard the condom.

"You're welcome." I know that sounds like a prick, so I add what I really want to say. "Thank you for the best middle of the night wake-up I've ever had."

I swear I can feel her smile in the darkness, and then we drift off to sleep again.

13

Lindsey

I sleep later than I have in a long time. While I'm still struggling to wake up, feeling drugged by the amount of rich food, alcohol, and sex, combined with a late night and pre-dawn climax, I discover Marcus's side of the bed is warm but lacking his killer body.

"Marcus," I call out, but it devolves into a yawn.

"Stay there," he says from the bathroom. "I've called room service and ordered breakfast. I'm gonna shower and shave."

"*Mm-OK,*" is all that comes out of my mouth before I drift off again.

When I startle awake the next time, probably less than ten minutes later, it's to the sound of knocking at the suite door. Since I can hear the shower still running, I run from his bedroom to mine and grab the bathrobe hanging behind my bathroom door. I feel like a movie star when I go to the door in the thick, white, and luxurious belted robe.

"Room service," the man says unnecessarily after I open the door. He pushes in a cart laden with covered platters and a coffee pot. It smells divine, and my mouth is watering instantly. He wheels it to the small dining table by the windows and places every dish and cup and pot onto it.

"Do you want me to open the curtains?" he asks.

"That's OK," I say, embarrassed that I was lounging in bed while this man was working and people were cooking my breakfast. "I'll do it."

He nods and wheels the cart toward the door.

"Tip," I blurt out before he leaves. I may be a Murray Islander, but even I know you tip hotel staff. "Hold on a second." *Where is my purse?*

But he shakes his head. "No worries, ma'am. Mr. Parisi took care of it already."

Marcus has a way of taking care of everything. And effortlessly, too. I could get used to it. When the man leaves, I open the curtains, shocked to see how high up I am. I never even looked out of these massive windows yesterday evening before I showered and we went out. Swallowing the unreasonable surge of fear, I turn away.

Pouring a cup of coffee, I add sugar and creamer, deciding to wait to eat until Marcus joins me. Meanwhile, I keep my back to the view of the Boston Common and roll my shoulders, knowing it's silly to get the least bit anxious and tense because there's merely a single pane of glass—no doubt a thick one, maybe two panes—between me and a many-story drop to the pavement.

Something else is distracting me, too, but I can't put my finger on it. Sipping the coffee, I look at the breakfast feast. Having never had room service before, I think it's magical. Each plate has its own steel cover. The aromas wafting out from the small round holes in the lids promise bacon, sausage, and other delectables.

Hanging around my new . . . friend is going to put pounds on me if I'm not careful.

I sip the coffee. It's superbly smooth.

Maybe I'll just peek and steal a piece of bacon. I hope it's crispy. There's an order slip on top of one of the lids. *Parisi. Suite 36-1* is scrawled across it.

Seeing the name in writing tickles loose a memory in my mind. Parisi. I take another sip of coffee. Parisi?

Parisi! Oh. My. God! Parisi Development, Inc. bought The Lady of the Light Inn and a bunch of cottages all over the island. They're rumored to become weekly and monthly rentals for all the many tourists that Marcus has been dreaming of.

I guess he's been doing a lot more than dreaming. Before he ever arrived, he'd been buying. What's more, he's been snooping around the island, doing recon, talking to fellow business people. Probably trying to buy them out for cheap.

I slam my cup down.

Jokes on him. There's a reason those cottages sold easily. With the number of tourists dwindling in the past decade, they were often standing empty. For a while, some locals lived in the one-bedroom bungalows in town because they didn't want to pay to heat their larger houses. It's more than likely they were thrilled to sell to him, and I hope they charged him top dollar.

And those cottages farther from the town center hadn't been used in years. No doubt they need an entire overhaul to make them inhabitable. Of course, that's right up his alley, real estate development. I just wish so many hadn't gone to a lying off-islander.

I hear Marcus whistling. He'll be out in a second. Setting my cup down, I make a beeline for the wallet lying next to my purse and sweater on the coffee table. I don't recall divesting myself of those things last night, but we were in a passionate—*i.e.,* lust-infused—hurry to get to the bedroom.

Without stopping to think, I snatch up the slim leather wallet and open it. A driver's license with his face, not smiling but as good-looking as ever, is the first thing I see, along with his name: Marcus Parisi.

It's true. I just slept with the freakin' enemy! He wants to change the island, bulldoze the fort, put porta-potties next to our lighthouse.

The next thing I see are a couple credit cards, proving he's a liar.

"I'm famished," he says coming out of his room and stopping short when he sees what I'm holding.

"Hey, great news, Mr. *Parisi*," I say. "Your credit cards have miraculously reappeared. If only you'd checked your wallet for them, you wouldn't have had to break out that hundred-dollar bill and buy a bunch of crap from my store."

"Lindsey," he begins.

"Please don't," I say, taking one more glance to see he has plenty more hundreds, too.

And I was going to try to treat *him* to dinner. What a laugh!

"That's why you said you had to go to the men's room last night, and then paid the bill before you returned to the table. You didn't want me to see your credit card. Admit it."

"I did have to use the men's room," he says. "We drank a lot of beverages. But yes, I found our server after and paid her, mainly because I didn't want you to see the sizable amount and get weird again about money."

Oh, I'm weirded out. No question, but *not* because of the size of last night's restaurant bill.

"I'm going to the hospital. By myself. And then I'm going to visit my parents." I don't know why I make this statement, but I emphasize my solo intent because we're finished. *Finito!* He can find his own way back to the island.

"Let's eat," he says, purposefully ignoring my attitude. "Nothing has changed."

"Everything has changed," I say before heading to my room. But I stop. I'm too practical to be a martyr. Turning around, I return to the table, pick up a covered plate with one hand and retrieve my coffee cup with the other.

In silence, I go in my room and manage to slam the door with the heel of my foot. Not without spilling drops of dark coffee on the cream-colored rug. For a moment, I feel a sense of panic, then take a deep breath and let it go. I'm sure Marcus has the money to pay the cleaning bill.

Setting the plate on the dressing table, I lift the lid. My nose was right. There's a full breakfast. Without a fork—because I'm not ruining my killer exit by going back out there—I shovel a few things in my mouth with my fingers, devouring all the bacon, a sausage link, and some fluffy scrambled eggs.

Now, I can face the day.

Taking a quick and miserable shower, I ignore the stupid razor that now seems like an enticement for me to be a class-A slut. It worked! Dressed, bag packed, I go back out to the living room.

Marcus is drinking coffee, appearing relaxed, and he's eaten most of what was on the other plate. And he's reading the newspaper that room service provided.

"You ready?" he asks, putting it down on the table.

He's persistent, like an annoying fly. I glance around to make sure I have everything.

"See ya, Mr. Parisi," I say, picking up my purse and heading for the door.

"Really?" he says, sounding totally pissed off and getting to his feet. "You're going to flounce out of here like a child."

That frosts my cookies. "Children don't flounce. You're mixing your metaphors or clichés or whatever."

"Fine, when you took your breakfast to your room, you were having a tantrum and sulking like a child. And now you're flouncing like a prima donna."

"Whatevs," I say, opening the door.

"Can't we talk about this?"

"About you being the big bad developer who is trying to take over my perfect little island? Ready to bulldoze the hotel, are you?"

He has the decency to look ashamed, probably at being caught in a lie rather than having second thoughts about destroying the place I cherish.

"Yes, about that."

"What?" I exclaim. Alarm trickling through me like icy sea water. Is The Lady's head really on the proverbial chopping block?

"I mean, *no*, I'm not bulldozing anything, except maybe the fort. But yes, I want to talk about it."

My ire only increases. "You haven't even seen the fort. How dare you!"

"Then we'll go see it together when we get back, and you can show me how it's worth saving. Otherwise, I'm going to suggest the land is repurposed at the next town meeting."

What a bastard. And a bully. Not to mention poking his nose in where it's not wanted.

"Lindsey, please, can we talk like rational human beings? A couple of mature business people who shared—"

I hold my hand up. I swear, if he mentions last night and how important that was, I will scream or simply kick him in the nuts.

"No, thanks. I'll admit I don't feel rational around you." I feel sexy and full of wanting and desire, but of course I don't say that. Instead, I add, "And frankly, I think you've screwed me enough."

Congratulating myself on another great exit, I stomp across the corridor to the elevator. I do feel childish. More than that, I feel foolish. He knew my thoughts about the new hotel owner from the first time we met, and he went out of his way to conceal his identity while getting under my skin and making me like him.

He branded my mouth with kisses and gave me the best sexual experiences of my life.

I press the button again with a vicious stab. That's when I sense him beside me.

"I didn't set out to lie to you," he says. "Or have sex with you for that matter."

"Well, then you're two for two without even trying."

The elevator doors open. When I step on, I have to turn because of the rules of elevator etiquette. He has his hand on one side, stopping the doors from closing.

"Will you hear me out when we get back to the island at least?"

I roll my eyes. But he has to return for his stupid plane.

"Why don't you send someone else to pick up your plane?"

"I'm coming back," he says.

I shrug. "I can't stop you. But I can ask you not to buy any other properties on the island."

The look on his face tells me he's going to continue doing whatever the hell he wants to do.

"Jerk," I say softly.

"I'm doing what's best," he says. "You can't deny that the island's source of income is drying up and putting everyone at risk."

The fact that he comes to Murray Island for five seconds and thinks he knows best is what infuriates me the most. "Step back!"

His face is as stony as the walls of Pirate's Cove.

"Please," I add, my tone shrill.

With a sigh, he drops his hand. I keep staring into his gorgeous tawny eyes until the doors close.

$❤$❤$❤$

Three days later, Dave and I get off the ferry and are met by Melinda and Sam. Dave, despite being pale and with circles under his eyes, is walking under his own steam and obviously much improved. Even my own mood lifted with each nautical mile closer to the island.

"*Damn*," is his first word. "It's good to be home."

I agree as I hug Mel.

"What's the plan?" she asks.

"I have to make sure my partner, here, checks in with Jenny first and then goes home to rest."

"I thought I was now your fiancé," Dave jokes, and I quickly explain to Mel and Sam about our new inside joke.

From the Ritz-Carlton, I'd returned to the hospital, trying to put Marcus out of my head and focus on Dave. I sat with him while we heard the treatment plan, which mostly consisted of medication and exercise. Also, a change in diet was recommended. He grumbled about all three.

"No reason for you to stay," he'd said from his hospital bed. "I'm just going to lie here and learn some stupid fitness regimen. I'll see you back on the island."

Then he'd looked at the doctor. "When can I reopen my pub?"

"Give yourself two weeks at a minimum," the coronary specialist advised.

I could see by Dave's face that would only happen if Mel and I tied him down. In front of the doctor, I asked, "What happens if he goes right back to the kitchen when you let him out of here?"

The doctor frowned at me, as if I was suggesting it. "Then your fiancé here could drop like a stone. His heart muscle has been through trauma. He needs to rest. You wouldn't run a marathon if you sprained a calf muscle, would you?"

I nodded and stared pointedly at Dave. "Are you listening?"

Dave folded his arms, but he looked like he might just obey.

"I'll be back as soon as this nice doctor releases you," I tell him, having just learned it might be three days. "We'll take the ferry home *together*."

Then I left him in capable hands. Having called my parents on the way to the hospital, still in shock from the big breakfast reveal, I was relieved to see them waiting downstairs. We drove to their home in Portsmouth, New Hampshire, about an hour away. For the brief respite, I ate

Mom's wonderful cooking, we three played cards and talked, and I slept a lot.

It was wonderful to be with family again, especially after the mind-fuck experience I'd had, getting too close to someone and trusting him way too fast.

That's what loneliness will do to a single woman.

Now that I'm back on the island, I've decided I should make an effort to be more social outside of my two jobs. Maybe another long-term visitor will come for the summer, like my archeologist friend from last year.

As a group, the four of us walk ten yards from the ferry dock to Sam's car.

"Jenny wants you to stop by right now," I remind Dave. I'd already spoken to our PA, impressing on her the need to corroborate what the doctor said. "Dave trusts you," I remind her, "so please put the fear of dropping dead into him."

"*Bah!*" Dave says, but he lets us drive him up the hill from the harbor and across the main street.

"You realize," he adds, looking back toward the harbor, which is diagonally across from the clinic, "that we wasted gas driving from there to here."

I turn and catch sight of Marcus, who must have just disembarked the ferry. On a motorcycle! *What the fuck?* I watch him park it in a vacant slot. My stomach flips. I've spent three days trying to pretend he doesn't exist and that I didn't let him lick every inch of my body. Now I find out he was on the same ferry as us.

How bizarre! And sneaky, too! Obviously not a coincidence. He must have been keeping tabs on Dave. At least Marcus knew better than to approach me on the boat where neither one of us could walk away without diving into the Atlantic. If he had, it would've been an ugly scene.

I'd intended to get Dave settled at the clinic and then drive by the airport to see if a certain unwelcome plane was still there. Part of me thought the worst of Marcus, that he would have already returned to the island while I was on the mainland and flown away.

On the other hand, I was half hoping for that very scenario. So much easier if I never have to speak to him again.

While I've been standing here gawking, Marcus leaves his motorcycle and walks up the hill.

When he glances over and sees me, I turn my back. Dave and the others have been talking, and I didn't hear a word.

"Anyway, you're back now, and things will return to normal in time," Mel says. "We'll check with you later." Then Sam takes her hand.

Before they can walk away, however, Dave states, "I want to set up a schedule for reopening." Dave is looking squarely at his bartender. "Tomorrow, after Lindsey closes up shop, we'll meet at the bar."

I clear my throat.

Dave sighs. "We'll meet at my house tomorrow."

This time I cough.

Dave looks at me. "In two days?"

I shake my head.

He tries again. "In three days," he tells Mel, "we'll meet at my house."

"Aye, aye, sir," Mel says, holding back a grin.

As I suspected, she and I are going to have to tie Dave to a chair to keep him from exerting himself.

After they leave, I resist the urge to turn again and see where Marcus is. Instead, I follow my fiancé into the medical center.

14

Marcus

The comparison between the Ritz-Carlton and The Lady of the Light is rather drastic. Lobby, drapes, mattresses, linens, lighting, and carpeting for a start. I realize that's not fair, because most places won't live up to a top-notch city hotel suite. The only thing Murray Island has that Boston doesn't, of course, is Lindsey.

And her first glance at me is pointedly disapproving and then disinterested. I stayed at the Ritz after she left and made sure Dave's insurance covered all his bills. It didn't, so I took care of the rest. Then, having already met with many of the islanders, I used the time for conference calls with my staff. I made some decisions and had Robin email a couple purchase offers to one of the executive services' printers at the Ritz. I'm certain the Murray Islanders will want to see my offers in writing.

I'm mostly interested in buying The Clamdigger, which is a successful restaurant, and a shuttered shop in the middle of town that brings the whole street down. I'm not sure what I'll do with it, but I want to at least update the derelict storefront.

As soon as I was notified Dave was being discharged, I hopped on the same ferry as him, surprised to see Lindsey. Delighted, actually, even though I didn't approach her. I can't help wondering where she stayed after she stormed out, and hope it wasn't some fleabag motel.

With nowhere more important to be, and with unfinished business between me and the island's resident sexy siren, I bought a BMW motorcycle, with a quiet purring engine for getting around, as well as more clothes for a longer stay. She's not going to like my plan, but I can deal with that.

After Lindsey goes into the medical center, I board the ferry again to collect my new baggage. There's no one I can pay to take my stuff to the hotel, so I leave my bike and walk over. I've got the bag I left with over one shoulder, a new laptop in one hand because working on my phone was getting old, and my new suitcase in the other. It gives me an idea to set up lockers near the ferry where people can store bags either before or after checkout. Also for day-trippers who bring too much stuff to carry around.

After dumping off my stuff at The Lady of the Light, it's time to come out of the shadows and let everyone know I'm doing an island makeover. *Parisi style!* That's what my sister calls it whenever I buy something that's rundown and restore it to its former glory or create some pizazz where none ever existed.

A glance at Whatnots and Such tells me it's not open. I don't want to track Lindsey down yet, as she's probably helping Dave, maybe getting him settled at home. So, although she's the first thing on my list, determined to make things right with her, instead, I head over to The Clamdigger. It's the nicest restaurant on the island, but it could be better. It's all potential. And I want to have somewhere to send hotel guests when The Lady of the Light is revamped.

An hour and a half later, I'm close to making a deal with Mr. and Mrs. Rigley, the older couple who own it. Their cook, Benny, even made me lunch. He was basically auditioning to keep his job, but there's no guarantee. My gut tells me I will need a better-trained chef to punch things up. Maybe Benny can take over at Dave's, offering palatable choices on the pub menu besides merely burgers. Win-win!

Regardless, although they want to retire and seem thrilled by my initial offer, they said they needed to think it over.

"If you sell to me," I ask, "will you remain on the island?"

"Oh, yes," Mrs. Rigley says, glancing at her husband, who nods. "It's our home, you understand. We don't want to make anyone angry."

Understanding dawns in my brain. The former hotel owner had said he'd have to think twice about selling to me if he'd intended to remain on Murray Island. Ultimately, Mr. Newton accepted my offer and my money, retiring to Virginia to avoid any hostile blowback.

When I come out of The Clamdigger, Lindsey's shop is open. I can tell by the small blue *Welcome* sign in place of the red *Closed* sign. I think she'd do well to have a brightly colored flag outside to let people know more easily.

Mentally girding my loins like a gladiator, I head across the street and push open the door. The cheerful bell does nothing to make me think this is going to be easy.

At the sound, she comes out of the back room and stares at me.

"Mr. Parisi," she says, clearly reveling in saying my last name like it's a curse word.

"It was a bonehead move not to tell you who I was," I confess, hoping to catch a break or find a chink in her armor with some old-fashioned groveling. "I'm really sorry. At our first meeting, you made it clear you didn't approve of whoever bought the hotel."

"And you thought your best course of action was to hide the fact that it was you?"

"Just until you got to know me a little." I offer what I hope is a charming smile.

"A little!" she exclaims, slamming her palms onto the counter. A bottle of sunscreen topples over. "I had you inside me! Don't you think you should have told me you're staging a coup of my home before you fucked me?"

I wince. "I didn't expect us to get so close so fast. But I'm not a bad guy. I'm not a villain. And I'm not staging a coup."

She comes out from behind the counter until we're two feet apart. Even though she's genuinely furious with me, I want to draw her close, brave her claws, and kiss her.

"Don't look at me like that," she orders. "What do you own besides the hotel and cottages?"

I'm glad I didn't close the deal yet on The Clamdigger.

"Nothing." Then because it's only a matter of time, I'm about to add the words *not yet*, when the bell tinkles again.

I turn to see a couple of college-age guys, who go over to the snack section. I saw them on the ferry, getting wasted despite the early hour. Directly behind them is Melinda, the bartender, whom I haven't spoken to since the boat ride to Boston.

"Something wrong with Dave?" Lindsey asks when she sees her friend.

"No," Melinda answers quickly. "You saw him last. I'm just wondering if you have some ones. Bank's closed and I'm trying to keep the bar open for Dave. Honestly," she shoots me a glance, "people aren't really missing the fact that there's no food."

"I have ones," Lindsey says, taking the twenty-dollar bill that Melinda holds out. "In the safe. Hang on a sec." She disappears into the back.

Melinda looks at me. "So, how's your stay going? That was nice of you to go with Lindsey to the mainland, but you didn't come back together."

She's on a fishing expedition, but I'm not going to be reeled in. "Murray Island is great. I did go with her, but I haven't seen her or Dave since Monday."

Out of the corner of my eye, I see one of the guys slip a candy bar in his shorts' pocket. The other one picks up a bag of chips and takes it to the register with a soda. His friend follows him and pockets some beef jerky along the way.

When Lindsey returns, she hands the bartender an envelope.

"You're still here," she says to me, causing Melinda's eyes to widen before the woman shoots an awkward smile in my direction, thanks Lindsey, and leaves. "Don't you have some business to buy or a landmark to tear down?"

"I'm not tearing anything down." Then I think about the fort and clench my jaw.

"Ah-ha!" Lindsey says. "I knew it."

Before I can explain, she strolls back to the counter.

"Hey there," she says to the newcomers. "Did you arrive today?"

"Yup," says the one who has stolen a few things. "Finished exams early and decided to explore."

"Welcome," she says. "Do you need a map, some sunscreen, or a spare towel?" She's already ringing up the chips and the soda, but I admire her attempt to upsell.

"You'll need some water," I tell the thief.

Lindsey sends me a glare. It's a damn good one, but it doesn't faze me.

"Trust me. After you eat the jerky and chocolate," I add, "you'll be thirsty."

Lindsey frowns and looks at the guy, puzzled, as does his friend. The college kid's cheeks turn ruddy. He's been caught, and he doesn't pretend otherwise. If he'd tried to run, I would've felt compelled to tackle him.

Pulling the items from his pockets, he doesn't protest when I add a bottle of water. His friend punches him in the arm.

"Not cool, bro."

After they pay and leave, she turns her attention to me again. By her conflicted expression, she sure doesn't want to thank me, nor like me, nor even speak to me.

"Thanks for that," she says at last as if the words are dragged from her.

"You're welcome. Does it happen often?"

She shrugs. "Price of doing business."

"Maybe you should put up cameras."

Lindsey rolls her pretty blue eyes so hard I fear she'll hurt herself. "How would that help?" she snaps. "Am I supposed to get off work at Dave's and spend the next few hours looking at video? And if I see a crime on tape, then what? Go hunt down some tourist and accuse him of stealing a candy bar?"

"Well-placed cameras, visible to everyone who comes in, along with proper signage will act as a deterrent," I explain. At that moment, she seems more like an ostrich than a savvy business owner.

"If they don't steal because they know they'll be caught, then you won't have to hunt anyone down. And if anything big ever happens, like someone breaking in when you're closed, you'll be happy to have a recording."

Lindsey shakes her head as she comes out from behind the counter again. "You don't get our island way of life. I don't want people coming in here and seeing a bunch of security cameras, let alone signs saying they're under surveillance. This is often the first destination when they get off the ferry. I want them to think happy thoughts and not worry that Murray Island is an unsafe place. Because we're not."

I see her point. Damn me if she's not one hundred percent right.

"I'd rather lose a few candy bars," she adds as she goes toward the windows and straightens up her display of beach towels and a small beach chair that has a book on it, "than put up warning signs telling my customers this is a shoplifting zone."

I don't mind admitting when I'm wrong. "You know more about hospitality than I do."

"I guess I do," she agrees, crossing her arms. "But you now own our hotel. What are you going to do with it?"

"I'm going to polish it till it shines."

"What does that entail exactly?" Her tone is clipped.

"Basically, it needs an overhaul. The roof is leaking into rooms on the third floor. The carpets are all worn. Wallpaper is peeling off left and right. New mattresses are a must, and a plumbing upgrade so there's more than a mist in the shower."

By her expression, she didn't know.

"The island guests deserve a decent place to stay," I remind her. "A luxurious place, in face. And The Lady of the Light deserves to be restored."

"Hm," is all she says. "But someone at your company told Jim not to make repairs over the winter."

"True. I don't want duct tape and a coat of paint. I want skilled renovation and meticulous restoration."

She sighs, and I wish we were friends again.

"It's going to be great," I add, trying to win her over. "I'm adding a lounge with a bar—"

"Taking Dave's customers," she snaps.

"No, I'm bringing in *new* customers," I promise. "And I'm rebuilding the dining room entirely. Maybe make a full-service restaurant out of it instead of merely a place to eat the free breakfast, which, by the way, is coffee and a prepackaged muffin. Not at all worthy of The Lady. Also, I'm putting in a boardwalk to the beach, directly from the hotel."

Her face is not reflecting my enthusiasm, but I keep trying.

"And I'd like to add a big patio on the beach side obviously. It'll have umbrellas and, if need be, heat lamps."

Her expression is growing more sullen.

"Then you're not restoring as much as *changing* everything," she says.

"Improving," I explain. "And not only the hotel."

Because she stiffens, I don't mention The Clamdigger. Instead, I say, "The hotel will rent out scooters to augment the bicycle rentals, *if* that ever opens. And I'm considering a gazebo, so the hotel could be a wedding venue."

"Gazebo," she echoes, sounding disgusted. "There's a beach and orange-tinted water at sunset. Why the hell do you need a gazebo for a wedding on the island?"

She's right about that. "OK, forget the gazebo. It was just an idea for photo ops. Maybe a picturesque cabana though. I also have to renovate the cottages I bought. Most are in rough shape. They'd be ideal for wedding parties or large families who want to stay for a week."

"Some of them are a hundred and fifty years old," she says quietly.

"Meaning?" I ask.

She throws her arms up. "Meaning show them some respect."

I can't help it. I start to laugh, which makes her turn and storm away from me, back behind her counter.

"Get out," she says.

I stop laughing. "Lindsey, come on. There are a hundred and fifty years of repairs needed, and I'm willing to pay to make them."

"Everything old doesn't have to be repaired or renovated. What about the lighthouse?"

I take a breath. "I do have some suggestions to make it a little more tourist-friendly."

"Arghhhh!" she groans. "It's a historical landmark. It doesn't have to become more touristy. We don't want your smelly porta-potties. I suppose you want to put in a café next to it."

"Not a bad idea," I say. "The lighthouse is away from everything, and people get thirsty climbing stairs. I was thinking of merely a refreshment stand, but perhaps a full-fledge café is better. By the way, the public bathrooms are a common courtesy."

I think she's going to lose her shit, but she simply makes a sour face, her mouth puckered as if she ate a full lemon. "What other ideas do you have?"

I can see whatever I say, it won't be received well at this moment. Maybe over a glass of wine.

"Have dinner with me, and I'll tell you."

"Absolutely not," she says with obvious satisfaction at turning me down. "You need to go away, and I need to get things ready. I've been away for a few days and the dust has settled."

She starts tidying shelves that clearly don't need tidying.

"Get ready for what?" I ask, picking up a pack of batteries and checking the date. They're expired. I wonder how long they've been there for sale.

Lindsey makes an exasperated sound, which grabs my attention. I hate to say it, but it reminds me of the noise she makes just before she climaxes. It makes me want to kiss her again.

"You realize that our busy time starts in a few days, don't you? Everyone on the island is getting ready."

"I looked at the hotel's bookings. Not as busy as you might think."

"Everyone doesn't stay at The Lady of the Light," she says with a haughty tone. "We have tent camping at the south end of the island, and people stay in the other two motels. And a lot of private houses turn into rentals, too, Mr. Smarty-Pants. And don't forget the day-trippers."

It's my turn for an open-mouth stare. I'm stunned by what she said about the two motels. "Are you saying The Crusty Seashell and The Mermaid's Tail still take guests? My scout said both were closed last year." They're on my list to purchase except I hate to own that high a percentage of the lodging, as that does smack of an island takeover.

Lindsey squirms a little. "It's not *crusty*. It's *curly*. The Curly Seashell. I suppose they had some issues last year. Plumbing and wood rot. And Marie who owns The Mermaid's Tail went on a long vacation to stay with her son."

My head nearly explodes. "During the peak of summer? She closed the motel? And no one cared that two places of lodging took the season off? Without those rooms, you had less business, as did the ferry service, and all the other businesses. Fewer diners, fewer bike rentals, fewer ice cream cones and beers. You all have to think of this as one connected entity. Everyone affects everyone else."

"A rising tide lifts all," she murmurs, looking into the middle distance. Then she snaps out of her private thoughts. "My dad says that. I've always believed it."

I see an opening in her armor. "Then think of me as the tide. I didn't buy the hotel to destroy Murray Island. I want it to flourish. I want all the businesses to do well."

She's frowning again and chewing that luscious lower lip. I have to hold back from stepping forward and kissing it.

"But if you buy everything up," she begins.

"I'm not interested in doing that," I promise her. "Although if those motels aren't going to get their shit together and reopen, then they're lowering the tide for everyone. In which case, I'll either buy them or talk to the owners about letting me invest in their properties. Then they can retain ownership while fixing them up to attract guests. I might need your help for that, though."

Amazingly, she nods. "You would definitely need the help of a local to speak to Stan Brie, who owns The Curly Seashell."

I know that Robin already tried to speak with the man last year, and he slammed the door in her face. "Not too friendly?" I ask.

"That's putting it mildly, and he's no fan of mine. You may have to get Dave to speak with him."

I can't imagine why someone wouldn't be a fan of Lindsey's.

"What's his problem with you?"

She shrugs. "He thinks my parents are 'traitors' for moving off the island. He's sure I'm next to go."

"That's harsh. Why would he think that? You're passionate about Murray Island."

"I had a bit of a fling with an off-islander. A stupid rumor went around that I was going to get engaged and move."

This is news. Unwelcome but intriguing. "What happened?"

"Nothing," she says. And she turns away, ending that particular line of conversation. I realize how long I've been talking to her and how few customers I've ever seen in her place.

"Does it really pick up for you in a few days, enough to earn a living?"

Her usual shrug is followed by, "Being frugal is key. The store's slightly overstocked, but I'm optimistic. And my family owns the building, which means I have no rent."

Suddenly, she gasps and her hands go to her hips. *Perfect, curvy hips* in pale jeans rolled up at the bottom.

"You've got me spilling my guts about Whatnots. Are you intending to seduce me so I'll sell it to you?"

I can't help laughing. When I regain my composure, I ask, "Do you *want* me to seduce you—*again!*—and make an offer on your business?"

I dodge sideways when the first thing she can lay her hands on comes flying my way. Luckily, it's just a pen.

"Out," she says.

"Lindsey, if everything goes well, then I hope the ferry will deliver a ton of customers to your door. I have to go see about zoning for a marina."

"A marina?" she gawks. "With loads of smelly motor boats and massive yachts?

"If we're lucky, yes. With more summer jobs for islanders to run it, pumping gas, selling snacks, etc., and more wealthy tourists to come to your store and my hotel. Do you want to have dinner with me tonight since you won't be working at Dave's?"

She lifts her chin, the epitome of female stubbornness. "No."

15

Lindsey

Marcus looks like he's about to try to convince me to eat with him, when the bell tinkles. *Hallelujah!* But it's not a customer. It's Jeannette, our potter, and following behind is her old dog, Willy.

I've known her—and her dog, for that matter—all my life. She even let me throw a pot on her wheel once. I was terrible at it, but it was fun.

She nods at me in greeting, but speaks to Marcus. "You're still on the island?" She sounds surprised.

"I am. It's a pleasure to see you again, Mrs. James."

"Please call me Jeannette. I'm actually here because of you." She turns her attention to Lindsey. "Marcus cleverly suggested I sell my pottery near the ferry. No one closer than you, although I won't push it if you don't have room."

I'm speechless, while Marcus makes an attempt at hiding his smug satisfaction. It makes me want to clobber him. I'd love to tell him off for being in my business and offering up

Whatnots as if he has a say in the matter. But I won't bicker with him in front of Jeannette. Next thing I know, the whole island will think we have the hots for each other.

"I don't mind clearing a shelf for your pottery," I tell her, crouching down as Willy ambles over for a scratch behind his ears. He makes me miss Max with a sharp pang around my heart because he's such a lovebug, like my lab. "Didn't my mom ask you to bring some stuff up here one summer?"

"Barbara did, indeed. But it was for a table outside, and I was more protective over my wares then. Now I know they are merely things that can be replaced, remade. Nothing to get upset about if a whole shelf fell to the floor."

I nod, totally understanding her change of perspective. Sometimes I groaned about spending my Sundays off keeping my grandmother company. But I'd give anything to be seated across from Nan at her dining table, working on a puzzle and shooting the shit.

"I'll leave you ladies to it," Marcus says. I hope he doesn't ask me out again in front of Jeannette. The answer will be the same. But he doesn't. "Just think of me as the tide going out," he adds before he leaves.

Funny guy!

"Seems like a nice young man," Jeannette says. "And handsome, too, unless the standard of attractiveness has changed since I first fell in love. Perhaps you'd rather have a man with a tattoo or an earring. But that one has a winsome smile. And those eyes!"

I don't bother to tell her I've seen his whole body, and he doesn't have a tattoo, not that I would have cared. Instead, I tell her the most important thing that she may not know.

"He's the new owner of The Lady of the Light."

"Is he?" She thinks a moment. "Then he's Marcus Parisi. Good for him. Hopefully good for us, too. When was the last time you stayed there? I had family come for Robert's funeral. Too many mourners for my small house. And I was embarrassed by the condition of some of the hotel rooms."

I had no idea. One of my first jobs, when I was fourteen was being a chambermaid. That was eleven years ago, and I thought the place was elegant. I don't like to think about Marcus being right.

"Back to your pottery. You know I don't get a huge number of people, especially not big spenders," I tell Jeannette. "But I would love to feature some of your pieces."

Then I get an idea. "We could set up a 'Take me home' shelf. I'll make a sign. Your pottery will be authentic mementos of the island." Another thought hits me. "I could offer to ship it, too. You could show me how you pack them. Or give me the same packaging supplies that you use."

I tap my chin with the same pen I threw at Marcus. "If they choose the item when they first arrive and don't want it shipped, I could offer to store it for them until the end of their stay and pack it up for the ferry ride home."

"I think those are all great ideas," Jeannette says.

I get a weird notion that I'd like to share my thoughts with Marcus and make him proud of me.

"Plus, that means they'll have to stop in again on the way home to pick up their pottery. They might grab some snacks for the ferry ride," I point out, thinking aloud at this point, as I look around for the best shelf to give to Jeannette's mugs and bowls and platters.

She nods. "It could be beneficial for both of us." She sighs. "Suddenly, I'm hoping it'll be a busy summer."

I like the gleam in her hazel eyes. We spend a few minutes talking and decide we should put a few pieces in the window, but since we want people to be able to examine them, we'll put the majority on a side-wall shelf, high enough that little kids can't grab it.

I have to admit, I'm thinking more fondly of Marcus than I have since that moment I realized who he was at the Ritz-Carlton. It was simply such a shock to find out I was hanging with a billionaire real estate developer. Hanging *and* having sex with. Obviously, it was too soon to let my heart get involved, but he seemed so caring and thoughtful that I could easily have fallen for him if he were a regular guy.

But billionaires don't hook up with shopgirls, at least not with the intention of a long-term or permanent relationship. Not even with one who will inherit ownership. Maybe if I'd been a Manhattan socialite—whatever the hell that is.

Besides, what I took for caring was his controlling nature. Just the same as how he's trying to control Murray Island. He'll do it, too, if someone doesn't stop him. Namely me.

Let him fix up The Lady of the Light. But change the lighthouse, itself? No, I don't think so. I'll be at the next town hall meeting to cast my vote if necessary.

And a marina? A bunch of fancy sailboats with their tall masts blocking the view sounds terrible. Worse even will be stinky, loud powerboats buzzing around Mermaid Bay.

I manage to get myself worked up into a lather of outrage. Why doesn't he just go to Nantucket or Martha's Vineyard if he wants all that?

After Jeannette and Willy leave, I have only two more customers before it's time to lock up. It made no difference that I opened late, after Dave and I got back, and it wouldn't have mattered if I'd locked up an hour early. In fact, I would have saved money by turning the lights off sooner.

Pondering the last few days, mostly Marcus, of course, I walk home in silence. If Dad had sold the store and I'd moved with them, what would I be doing tonight? I would've moved out of their Portsmouth home by now, probably working some crap job since I have an online business degree that may not be worth the paper it's printed on. Besides, I enjoy being my own boss, even if the pay sucks and there are no holidays or paid vacations.

But I would have friends who weren't in their fifties. Apart from Mel, who's only five years older, nearly every other person my age went off to college and didn't come back. At the very least, I would be dating, maybe going to clubs, seeing guys at bars.

I take a glass of wine onto my front granite step for the view of my favorite beach, and my heart blooms with contentment. The sound of the waves is much better than loud club music. And the sun-dappled water beats flashing dance-floor lights any day.

My dog's company was better than just about any guy I've ever met, too.

Except maybe Marcus.

When Jacob left after a summer's archaeology dig, I missed him for a time. I had to get used to not having a guy to hold hands with, and all the other good stuff that comes with having a man around.

I felt lonely for a while, but it wasn't overwhelming. I've only known Marcus for a week, but he's intense. And the feelings he evokes in me are off-the-chart intense, too. If I hadn't immediately broken it off with him, I already know how sad I would've been when he finally left, far worse than missing Jacob or losing any of my childhood friends to the lure of the mainland.

It would be right up there with losing Nan and Max or when my parents told me they were moving. Of course, they gave me the choice—stay here or go with them. But the store had been my life, and knowing I would run it was ingrained in me. It was the reason I got that associate's degree in business, because I was destined to own Whatnots and hoped to make it flourish.

Plus, I wouldn't have missed Nan's last year of life for anything. I know my mother has regrets about timing.

I take a sip of wine. It's white and fruity. I brought it back with me in my bag because it's cheaper off-island. I feel guilty. I should have spent my dollars here. On the other hand, Marcus has made me see that I can't make a silk purse out of a sow's ear. If we don't have tourists, it doesn't matter how bright and clean my store is, nor how well-curated my stock. Nor does it matter if we locals buy each other's stuff. That's not enough.

As if my thoughts conjure him, he turns the corner onto my short street and my pulse speeds up at the sight. I'd forgotten about the motorcycle.

He kills the engine and climbs off before removing his helmet.

"Hey," I say, staying casual. Inside, I'm screaming, *Oh my God! Marcus on a motorcycle is the hottest thing I've ever seen.*

"Hey," he says back. "You look lovely sitting there. Would be a stunning promo photo for Murray Island. *Come meet the pretty, friendly islanders.*"

I can't help it. I laugh. "Friendly, huh? I think I told you to get out of my store."

He shrugs. "You also told me you weren't interested in going to dinner with me, but I'm here. That should earn me some points."

Marcus is wily, and I'm not giving him an inch. I'm still thinking how quickly my heart got entangled in what ought to have been simply great sex. He's too perfect for me not to fall for him.

All I say is "Nope."

"I'm not easily deterred," he says. As if to prove this, he comes over and sits beside me. I scoot over—and quickly— or we'd be crammed thigh to thigh and shoulder to shoulder. As it is, there's only an inch of air between us.

"What a view!" he says, staring out toward *my beach*, as I think of it. The sun sets on the other side of the island, but right now, the long fingers of rosy-tinged light are bathing the sand and sea. It's glorious.

To go along with the feast of a vision, now my body is all tingly from his close proximity, and my thoughts could easily become muddled if he starts sweet-talking me.

"I can see why you love it and fight to protect it."

There he goes, trying to get me to lower my guard by agreeing with my point of view.

"I will," I say. "I don't want to look out and see a bunch of yacht masts. And I definitely don't want to hear or smell motor boats zooming just off the beach, scaring the dolphins."

"Agreed," he says. "The marina will not be in your line of sight."

I sigh. "It's not only *my* line of sight I care about. What about my neighbors?"

"The hotel windows will look out over a state-of-the art marina," he says as if it's a done deal.

It's disheartening. Oil and gas will leak into our pristine waters. But maybe not. Marcus might not succeed. I understand that he has a firm plan, but I picture empty slips, devoid of boats. First, he has to fix up the hotel, and then he has to convince a bunch of his rich friends to come eat Dave's burgers and Boyers' ice cream.

Why would they, when they can go a few hundred miles south to the Vineyard?

"Whatever you say," I mutter.

That makes him laugh. "Oh, ye of little faith." Finally, he turns to me, and my heart skips a beat. If I turn my head, we'll be within kissing range.

"Are you hungry?" he asks.

I shake my head, refusing to be distracted. "You know Sam and a few others have fishing boats. They don't need a fancy marina."

"Sam and his fishermen friends aren't the ones we're trying to get to come."

"We?"

He shrugs. "I wish you would help me. If you were on my team, then people wouldn't think I'm some crazy outsider trying to ruin their island."

I sip my wine, so I don't say it immediately. Then I do anyway. "But you are a crazy outsider trying to ruin our island. I won't help you, Parisi."

He looks up at the sky, as if asking for otherworldly help. Then he focuses on me, and his light brown eyes are soaking in the sun's rays, looking golden.

"Then help yourself. This island is dying. Do you really think those dilapidated motels will reopen without financial assistance? And some of the cottages I purchased are ready to fall over. How long before you lose the last of your small retail shops? I noticed a lot of packages from Amazon and big box stores on the ferry."

I think of my traitorous bottle of wine, again wishing I'd bought from the local market where there's an aisle of beer and wine.

"What will you do if the last market closes and you have to have all your food shipped over weekly, or the ferry stops its regular service, because they're not running a charity? They used to come every day, right? Now, it's every other day for most of the year. It's only going to get worse unless all the Murray Islanders get their heads out of their—"

Wisely, Marcus interrupts himself. "Out of the sand," he finishes.

Maybe he sees what I haven't noticed. Or maybe he's trying to scare me. Either way, it's still not his business.

I'm tempted to pick up my phone and scroll through the Murray Island barebones website that Carl manages to see if there's a town meeting on schedule. But Marcus still has his glance locked on mine, and I think he's waiting for an answer.

"I've listened to you, and I'll think about what you've said."

He appears mollified. For a ruthless, greedy, bulldozing businessman, he's pretty zealous about making things better.

He smiles, which I see because I'm suddenly staring at his lips.

Slowly, giving me time to move away, he reaches up and slides a hand into my hair, cupping the back of my head. Then he holds me still while he leans closer.

"I'm going to kiss you," he says quietly. "I'm not going to ask this time, because I think you'll tell me to go to hell."

I smile back. "I will."

"I thought so."

His mouth claims mine, and my body feels like it's been plugged in and switched on. Sizzling warmth washes through me, my legs start to tremble even though I'm sitting, and my breath catches in my throat.

All from a kiss. I want to thread my fingers in his hair, but I'm still holding my wine glass half full of off-island, traitor's vino. When his tongue traces the seam of my lips, I open to allow entrance. As soon as he slides in, I grow wet between my legs, as if his tongue is teasing me down south.

With his other hand, he's not being gentlemanly at all. Marcus palms my breast through my long-sleeve cotton shirt and discovers my secret.

"No bra," he says against my mouth, sounding pleased, then resumes kissing me.

My preferred post work, relaxation state is to be braless. But having his thumb and finger rolling my nipple is my new favorite post-work activity.

When he eventually stops ravishing my mouth, he asks, "Will you have dinner with me?"

Caught between his penetrating gaze and his warm hands, now resting on my back, it would be easy to say yes.

"At The Clamdigger?" he presses. "Benny might not be like a Boston's North End Italian chef, but he'll do for a salad and roast chicken dinner."

Alarm bells go off.

"When did you eat there and meet Benny?"

When Marcus hesitates, a sense of foreboding penetrates the warm fuzzies brought on by his kiss.

"Lunch time," he says.

I rise to my feet like I've sat on a nail. "They're not open for lunch," I tell him, backing away, still clutching my wine glass.

"I went in there to discuss buying the place."

"You said you didn't own any other business."

"Not yet," he says, leaving it hanging in the air.

"But you're going to? Is that right?"

"As soon as I can convince them that they won't be treated like pariah if they sell to me."

"And that's where I come in," I realize. "You want me to be the local stooge who helps you wheedle your way into making deals with the islanders."

"Stooge? Wheedle?" he repeats and starts to smile.

He is not reading the room at all. There's nothing funny about what he's doing.

"That wonderful old couple. You just want to take their restaurant from them, and you'll be doing a happy dance up Spire Street as soon as the ink is dry."

"That's not how it works," he begins.

"I suppose you think the best restaurant in town needs the same Parisi polish as the hotel?"

"Less than the hotel," he says, rising to his feet, "but it needs new furniture, a paint job, and a chef, not a cook."

I can't help the sad twinge low in my stomach. I'm helpless to stop this in the face of Marcus's billions. "You're firing Benny?"

"Maybe. Probably," he says, sounding as if it's unimportant.

His nonchalance fuels my anger until I think I might break the stem of my wine glass. I have to get away from him before he gets close enough to kiss me again. I need distance and icy resolve to put up some defenses and figure out how to stop Murray Island from becoming *Parisi Paradise*. I wouldn't put it past him to rename the place.

Skirting him, I reach my front door.

"Have a nice life," I say because I can't think of anything better that doesn't involve futile swear words. With that, I go inside.

With my back to the door, I listen. Part of me expects him to knock. I hope I won't give in for company and sex.

Thankfully, despite how quiet the pretty, shiny machine is, I hear his motorcycle start up.

And then my glance falls on Max's leash hanging by the door. For some reason, even though it's now been over a month, tears flood my eyes. I hate change, and I hate loss. The two seem inextricably linked.

And Marcus Parisi is exacerbating both.

16

Marcus

I'd hoped for a better outcome. At least dinner with Lindsey if nothing else. Although the *something else* isn't going away. We have amazing chemistry. I'm not going away anytime soon, and she's fighting a losing battle regarding the island. There's no way I'm backing down when I can see even more clearly how great this place will be.

The next day, I steer clear of her store and meet with Mr. and Mrs. Boyer, finally cluing them in that I bought the hotel. Like everyone else, they're leery. When I recommend they buy up any blueberries from Andy's family that the tourists don't eat, freeze them, and use them in their ice cream, they look less doubtful.

"I know the cost is higher than the frozen berries you buy, but people love to eat local. You can raise the price on a cone or a pint. You might as well not stop at blueberries, either. Not if you can buy their raspberries and strawberries, too."

Next, I intend to meet with Dave to see if he agrees he would more than make up for paying the wages of a good cook like Benny by serving better lunches and dinners to a larger number of diners.

It's easy to find his home. Not only because Mr. Boyer gave me directions, but also, Dave is sitting out front. It's a different style house to Lindsey's. It doesn't face the beach, but it has a covered porch with two chairs.

"There's the man himself," I say as I approach.

Dave's smile means, I think, that he doesn't know I'm the big, bad real estate developer Lindsey believes me to be.

"Hey, there," he says. "Come on up."

I take the three steps to his porch. He's in one chair, but the other one is unusable with a broken seat. It's emblematic of Murray Island, sort of friendly and welcoming but then again, not so much.

No matter. I lean against the railing after testing it for sturdiness. I don't want to go ass over heels.

"Glad you came by," he says. "I wanted to thank you for accompanying Lindsey to the city."

So that's why he's friendly.

"You don't have to thank me," I say. "She was supporting you. I wanted to support her."

By the look in his eyes, I wonder if he knows we're interested in one another. Emotional support was definitely not the only thing I did for her in Boston.

"I didn't come by to be patted on the back. I came by to talk business."

His bushy brows shoot up. "Really?" He crosses his arms in a classic move expressing caution and defense.

"I bought the hotel last year," I confess.

He nods. "I know."

"Oh." I wasn't expecting him to have heard. But I shouldn't be surprised. Word will spread quickly now my last name is out there.

"Jim's my friend," Dave adds.

"Jim?"

"Hotel manager," Dave explains.

Glad I didn't start by launching into all the problems with the hotel. Most are not Jim's fault, in any case. Before the former owner headed to Virginia, he simply handed the manager all the keys and told him I'd eventually stop in.

"It's going to be fully renovated," I tell him quickly, in case Dave thinks I'm bulldozing it. That was Lindsey's word.

"'Bout time," he says. "But what's it to do with me?"

"I want all the business owners on the island to be on board with what I'm doing."

"Which is what exactly?" He levels me with a stare that reminds me of one of Lindsey's suspicious looks.

"Naturally, I want a return on my investment," I admit. "Which means sprucing up a few things around the island. I think it used to be more of a popular vacation destination than it is today."

"It was. About twenty years ago. Still did a fair but not bustling business a decade past. Dwindling each year. There used to be two other places to eat in the town center. A seafood restaurant called The Hungry Whale that actually had tables in the sand. It was delicious, but COVID killed it. And a deli. Super popular for getting a sandwich and pickles."

"What happened?"

"They moved away in the dead of winter without talking to anyone. Just don't ever mention The Dilly Deli. People are still pissed off."

"I think I can help," I say.

"To get the ROI you mentioned."

I smile. "Yes. Beyond that though, there's satisfaction in helping to improve something. To be honest, I get a lot of pleasure in improving things. Which brings me to your bar."

"Not for sale," he says without rancor.

"I don't want to buy it," I tell him, "so that's perfectly fine."

He grunts. "Did Lindsey send you?"

"No. Why?"

"She's been telling me for years that I need to do this or that, but it's easier not to and a helluva lot cheaper."

I'm curious. "What's the *this* or *that*?"

He shrugs. "Put a big window down the bar end to see the beach. But most people sit in there at night. When it's dark out, who cares about the window?"

"Maybe it's a chicken-or-egg scenario," I say. "People will sit in there for lunch if there's a view, and you could serve the full menu down the bar end. If you put some torches out on the beach, light will reflect on the water, then people might be more inclined to stay for dinner, too."

"That's the other thing," Dave says. "Lindsey says I should remove the fancy things from the menu, like the chicken parm, and offer more of what I can make well." He laughs for a second. "Problem is, there's not much I can do well. I'm not a trained cook. I fell into it. Began as my own bartender. When my grill cook up and quit on me, I hired Mel behind the bar and took over the kitchen."

I tell him I'm buying The Clamdigger. He nods. "They're good people with a nice place. Also, they're not competition."

I'm relieved he understands that. "I think you should hire Benny. He's a capable cook, but he's not a fine dining chef. He doesn't want to elevate the cuisine or create a different vibe. He wants to make filling, tasty food, and it seems like he'd be a great match."

Dave is already shaking his head.

"Can't afford Benny."

"And that's why I came to see you. I think your place is all potential. If you're willing to attract more people, let's put in a patio with seating. Extend your space to the beach's edge. Then give Benny a chance to cook the dishes you want to offer. He can handle a variety of pub food, and even the chicken parm."

"You said 'let's put in a patio.' How do *you* figure into this? I told you I don't want to sell. Smacks of defeat, and as the only bar left, I think I'm sitting on a gold mine."

"I agree, or I wouldn't be interested in investing, which is what I'm proposing. Although I confess I'm putting in a boutique bar in the hotel."

That earns me a glare until I explain it won't have pub food. "Fancy hors d'oeuvres and high-end cocktails at The Lady," I explain.

He's amenable to a silent investor. We work out my percentage, and just like that, I have a stake in Dave's Beach Bar.

"If the Rigleys know they'll be supported rather than blamed, then they'll sell to me." Feeling confident, I've already texted Robin, and she's speaking to a chef headhunter. "I intend to hire a new chef as soon as possible so he or she can have a say in how I revamp The Clamdigger," I explain. "I guess I'm stuck with the name."

Dave nods. "Unless you want half the island coming at you with pitchforks."

"With Lindsey leading the charge," I say.

He laughs harder this time. "She giving you a hard time? That girl has grit."

I shrug, feeling sheepish. "I admit I'm not her favorite person right now."

Hopefully I'm still her fav bed partner, I think to myself, but that remains to be seen.

"She thinks I'm trying to change things just for the sake of change. I'm really not. I think Murray Island should keep its general character, but be more welcoming."

"Sounds reasonable," Dave says. "Do you want a showdown with her?"

"What do you mean?"

"She's on her way over. In fact, she's about three yards behind you and closing the distance fast."

I straighten and turn. Sure enough, Lindsey Cooper, all five-feet-seven inches of her, is coming my way. Her expression is furious, and I can easily imagine her carrying that pitchfork Dave mentioned.

"What the hell are you doing here?" she asks, coming right up the steps. "He is not supposed to be stressed." She points to Dave. "No cooking, nor worrying about the bills and deliveries, and certainly, no Marcus Parisi trying to buy his tavern out from under him."

"He's not trying to buy it," Dave protests. "He's just investing in it."

She throws up her hands. "If it's more than fifty percent, Dave, then he may as well own it."

She gets up in my face, by way of standing on her tiptoes, which is seductive as fuck, to be honest.

"What's your problem? You shouldn't be over here when he's vulnerable."

"I'm not vulnerable," Dave says from behind her back.

She ignores him. "He needs to remain calm and take his medication."

"Damn pills," he mutters. "Haven't taken one yet."

Lindsey whirls to face him. "What the fuck, Dave? You better be taking that blood thinner."

"Is that what it is? Thin blood, eh?" He makes a face. "I suppose for the hot summer months, that won't be such a bad thing."

"In another week, you have to start the exercises, too," she tells him.

"Who has time for that?" he asks.

I'm grateful to the guy for taking the heat off me, even though I don't think he intended to do it.

Without looking at me, she points behind her. "If Mr. Parisi is buying you out, then you'll have all the time in the world."

"I promise you, I'm not buying him out," I say, and she swings her attention back to me. "And I'm not a majority investor. Dave can still run his business however he wants.

But since he won't be in the kitchen anymore, he'll have time for that exercise you talked about."

She scowls at me, then turns back to her friend. "Why won't you be cooking?" She doesn't sound displeased though.

"Because we need a better cook, and I'm ready to admit it."

"Where are you going to find another cook?" Lindsey barely pauses before she comes up with the answer. "Benny!"

And she's back to looking at me again. "Is that right? You're firing him from The Clamdigger, but you want him to work at Dave's?"

I nod, hoping she'll see the wisdom in it. "More of a lateral relocation than a firing."

"Why didn't you tell me that before?" she demands.

Is she nuts? "Was I supposed to talk to your closed front door?"

Dave lets loose a laugh. "You two are more entertaining than any show on TV."

Just then, Melinda shows up.

"You started the meeting without me?"

"I didn't," Lindsey says, "but these two did."

Mel eyes me curiously. "What's Marcus got to do with Dave's?"

"Oh, didn't you hear? Mr. Parisi is an investor in the tavern now. Switching out personnel and . . . what else?" she asks me.

"Dave and I were talking about a patio with heat lamps and opening up the bar area with a big window for the view."

"Cool beans," Melinda says. "We'll be busy every night all summer." She looks at Dave. "That's a lot of hamburgers."

"Won't be my problem much longer," he says. "That is, if Butch and Donna sell The Clamdigger to Marcus. Then I'm going to poach Benny for our kitchen."

A play of emotions cross Melinda's face, finally settling on approval.

"Seems like a good plan." She looks at Lindsey. "But after the mean things said about your parents and about Newton, they might be nervous to sell."

I recognize the name Newton as the man I purchased the hotel from, but I didn't know Lindsey's parents got any grief simply for moving away.

She sends me a sideways glance like she didn't want me to know. But she tells Melinda what I told her. "Mr. Parisi said they are somewhat hesitant."

"You should talk to them," Melinda says to Lindsey, and I give a silent cheer.

"Even if I did," she says, "I can't guarantee that the rest of the business people won't be annoyed."

"They're not planning on moving off island," I say.

"That's fine, then," Dave said. "Everyone knows they wouldn't shit in their own pool if they're staying to swim."

"That's true," Lindsey says.

"Just to be on the safe side," Dave continues, "you should take Marcus around with you, to smooth the way. Unless you're against him making some improvements."

Way to put her on the spot, Dave. I want her to help me to help the island, but perhaps she's a bit touchy if these same islanders were snide about her parents.

"If she's not comfortable," I say, "then someone else can go with me when I talk to the business owners. I've already spoken to most of them on my own, but I'm starting to understand how this insulated island culture works."

"Once Donna and Butch sell, everything else will become easier, especially when they stay put rather than moving away," Melinda says.

"You don't want a Dilly Deli on your hands," I offer, feeling like one of the group.

Dave winces, while Mel and Lindsey send me identical shocked looks.

"Don't ever mention that name again," Mel says into the awkward silence. "Not if you know what's good for you."

"Yes, ma'am," I say because she sounds as though she means it.

Lindsey nods, eyes wide. "Not a smooth move, Parisi."

It seems that either she or Melinda or both are still extremely pissed off about those people leaving without so much as a goodbye.

Then Lindsey adds, "Despite the fallout from my parents leaving, I have friendly relationships with the other businesses. I stayed, and they see me as loyal." She shrugs and doesn't look at me when she finally says, "I'll go with him."

She's putting up an icy front in front of her friends, but I intend to chip away at it.

"Please," I say, as if I haven't been balls deep in this enticing woman, "call me Marcus. After all, we've crossed the ocean together."

Lindsey shoots me a withering look that, due to the angle, neither Dave nor Melinda can see.

"Don't you have employees who do all this trivial work, like buying up properties?"

The bartender smiles, but I know Lindsey is serious when she adds, "Shouldn't you go home now and find other places that need the Parisi polish and let your minions take over?"

Dave is laughing hard. "Minions? Makes him sound like an evil overlord."

"If the adjective fits," Lindsey says.

"Am I missing something here?" Melinda asks. "Aren't we on Team Parisi for fixing up Dave's bar? Not to mention the hotel. The last time I was in there running a takeout burger to that woman who sprained her ankle a year ago, I was pretty shocked by how rundown The Lady is."

Lindsey sighs hard. She knows she's lost this round.

"I'm not on Team anything," she says, "except Team Murray Island." With a look of resignation, she adds, "I guess I'll help."

I know that pained her to say. Then she levels me with another hard stare. "The three of us are supposed to be meeting to talk bar business. So, unless you intend to exercise your new investment interest in Dave's by tending bar while Mel takes over the cooking, then you can leave."

But I'm going to press my advantage. "When can you go with me and start paving the way for my complete and utter takeover?" I cough exaggeratedly. "I mean, my attempt to spruce up around here."

Dave and Melinda laugh. Even Lindsey cracks a reluctant smile.

"Tomorrow, I guess," she says.

"Why don't you go now?" Dave suggests. "All I wanted to tell you gals was to keep on keeping on. Mel handles the bar, and Lindsey keeps serving tables. And I'll sit on a stool at the stove and flip burgers until we get Benny."

The shouting erupts at once. Melinda and Lindsey are incredulous. Frankly, I am, too.

"You're not setting foot in the tavern for another week," Lindsey tells her boss as soon as she's calm enough to speak. "If you don't cooperate, then Mel and I are walking. We won't open at all. Right?" She turns to the bartender.

"Right," Melinda says.

"It's my place," Dave begins.

"It is," Lindsey says. "But you won't have a place if you so much as put your hand on the door. And if you want us open for the tourists who'll be arriving over the next few days, then it'll be however Mel and I decide to handle it."

Dave starts groaning. "It's going to get busy."

"Not that busy, not yet," the bartender says. "And you know it."

Lindsey squats in front of Dave, so they can talk eye-to-eye.

"For a week, or longer if you don't behave and rest, your menu is going to be pared down to burgers, a few sandwich choices, and the fryolator."

She's sexy as hell when she's laying down the law.

"And I have no say in the matter?" Dave asks.

"Nope," says Melinda, backing her up.

"You going to cook?" he asks Lindsey.

'Yup," she says, sounding a little less certain. "I'll see if Andy Rumble can wait tables. OK?"

"Like I have any choice. I guess we're done here," Dave says, not looking happy in the least.

Lindsey glances at Melinda, who nods.

"OK. As long as you don't try to slip behind the bar or go into the kitchen," Lindsey says. "But we can't open tonight."

Dave moans loudly.

But Lindsey doesn't cave. "I'll need to get in fresh supplies and make sure we have Andy on board." Then she looks at me. "Let's go."

Yes, ma'am.

17

Lindsey

I'm beyond surprised that I'm walking beside Marcus, intent on helping convince Mr. and Mrs. Rigley to sell their restaurant to him. But we need to talk to a few others first and bring the couple some assurance they won't be on the receiving end of nasty remarks, nor hearing the word *traitor* at the next town meeting.

I'm overly aware of this man beside me, all oozing confidence, tall and fit, strolling along like he already owns the island.

Ugh! But Dave and Mel have a clearer perspective. I can acknowledge that and trust them. They weren't blindsided after having the best evening—basically the quintessential, ideal date—then waking up next to an evil business-grabbing developer.

"We should stop at the town hall and see when the next meeting is," I say.

"Already did. It's in two nights."

I'm impressed but annoyed that he knows something I don't. *Get over yourself, Lindsey.*

"I'll be there, watching you lay out your plans," I tell him.

"Keeping your eye on me, are you?"

My cheeks feel warm. I know he doesn't mean anything by it, but it's awkward and weird to have jumped into a . . . a *liaison* too quickly and then abandoned it just as fast.

"I can't help wondering what's next after The Clamdigger," I say. "The bakery? The ice cream shop?"

"No, neither. But I think if I make some bigger investments, maybe put in a bike trail and the full-service marina I told you about, then we'll get enough big spenders that the bakery and ice cream shop can fix themselves up. The town center would look more inviting with lighting, though. Not sure if the town has the capacity, but I could bring in my commercial electricians. Old-style streetlamps, of course."

My mouth has dropped open slightly. "How rich are you?" I blurt out before quickly adding, "No, don't tell me."

Thankfully, he doesn't. In a few minutes, we pass by The Clamdigger, still dark inside. Clearly, the prep staff hasn't arrived yet.

"Probably another hour before anyone shows up," I say. "That's OK. Let's start by talking to Mr. and Mrs. Boyer. If they're amenable to your buying the restaurant, then we'll have their support along with Dave's before we talk to the Rigleys."

"Great idea," he says. "I don't want to be responsible for making their lives miserable if it turns out the sale isn't going to be taken well."

Just like that, he surprises me again. After another block, however, before we enter Island Scoops, I ask Marcus, "Are you sure you don't want to wait until *after* the town meeting?" I'm not entirely sure I want to stick my neck out before I know if any particularly vocal Murray Island citizens are going to object.

"Are you saying that there'll be anyone in the meeting who can stop me legally from purchasing property?"

His brown eyes stare at me in earnest.

"No, I don't think anyone has the power to do that. I think you would've already checked on that. Correct?"

"Yes, I would have."

"But there could be a groundswell of people who don't want you to make the changes you're hellbent on making?"

He shrugs, and I watch his muscles flex under his shirt. My mouth goes dry. I know precisely how they feel under my fingertips.

"I've never made over an island before," he admits. "But I've gone into some towns that needed help although the people weren't always welcoming. That's putting it mildly. I've been shot at, nearly run over, and even seduced by the mayor so she could convince me to leave her little fiefdom alone."

My mouth has dropped open. I should be more concerned about him being shot at. However, since he's healthy and in one piece, I ask, "Did you sleep with her?"

"Thanks for worrying about me." He sends me a wry grin. "The shotgun owner only had one good eye and his round of buckshot missed to my right by about three inches. I had to run headfirst into an alligator-infested swamp to avoid the angry Pontiac driver. Luckily, the reptiles weren't hungry. And no, I didn't sleep with her. I don't like being told what to do by a corrupt official. She lost her next election, by the way."

I nod. I guess this isn't his first rodeo, as they say.

"And you were successful in those unfriendly places?"

His smile makes my insides flutter. "I was."

Then Marcus's glance drops to my mouth. Lordy, this man is tempting. Just his light-brown eyes looking at my lips makes me part them. I have to turn away before I say something stupid and needy.

He holds the door for me, and I enter the ice cream shop that I've been going to since before I could walk, when my dad would carry me in on his hip, then his shoulders, then holding me by the hand.

For the first time, it strikes me that I've grown up, but the place is exactly the same. The three small tables are in precisely the same spot against the left wall of the narrow shop. Straight ahead is a floor-to-ceiling freezer for hand-packed pints and gallons. It's about a third full right now. And the entire right side of the store is taken up by the ice cream counter with space behind it for the servers.

For a couple busy summers, the Boyers' grandkids stayed with them and helped out, but all the rest of the summers I can recall, it's been only the two of them. In truth, Mrs. Boyer looks tired, and the season hasn't started yet.

I get a flash of myself in thirty years, still standing behind the Whatnots and Such counter, and a shiver runs down my spine. Is that what I want?

"Hello, Lindsey," Mrs. Boyer says. "And the man with the butterscotch-colored eyes."

I feel like I'm back in middle school coming in with a friend.

"You've met Marcus Parisi," I say.

"I have." She nods at him. "We had an interesting discussion about berries."

"How's business?" I ask. "You stepping up production?" I know they typically start making ice cream about three weeks before the season starts and then keep producing until the last two weeks. They don't keep ice cream over the winter. I know because I've tried to get one of the special summer flavors in December.

Mrs. Boyer laughs. "We only opened on weekdays starting yesterday," she says. "So far, not too busy."

"If you decide to buy berries from Andy's parents," Marcus says, "you should make a colorful sandwich board for the sidewalk that states you make your own ice cream and use island fruit. Mentioning *handmade* and *fresh, local fruit* will draw people in. Maybe stencil it on the door, too."

He's so enthusiastic and helpful, it's a little sickening.

"Then you know he's a real estate developer?" I ask.

Mrs. Boyer nods. "I know he now owns the hotel." Her pleasant expression doesn't falter.

"We came by to tell you about some," I can't get myself to say *changes*, "some renovations he wants to make and see how you feel. In particular, he intends to buy The Clamdigger."

Her smile definitely wobbles. "Just a second. John's churning in the basement. I know he'll want to hear what you have to say."

She disappears from view to go down the small back stairs. I went down there once on a school fieldtrip to see how ice cream was made. I learned later that other kids went places like Washington, DC, to see the Smithsonian and the memorials.

Marcus and I share a glance, then I head to the case and look through the glass at the flavors. There's the blueberry-vanilla he was talking about right before we learned of Dave's heart attack. It seems like a long time ago.

Then I spy my precious strawberry-nutmeg. Suddenly, my mouth is watering. I hope we can order *before* the discussion in case the Boyers' get angry and toss Marcus out. But we don't.

Once they return from the basement, John Boyer gets down to business, and a discussion ensues about one person, namely Marcus, having too much power over the economic health of the community.

"I understand your concern," Marcus says. "On the other hand, the larger my stake in Murray Island, the more I'll want it to succeed beyond everyone's wildest dreams. I'm not going to invest here and then do anything half-assed."

Everything turns out fine in the end. Mr. and Mrs. Boyer, whom I could never call by their first names, are enthused by all the things Marcus discusses.

"We'll hire someone to have an ice cream cart at the marina," Mr. Boyer says. "The Scoop Cart," he adds, looking at his wife for her opinion.

"I wonder if Dave would start serving our ice cream at the beach bar," Mrs. Boyer says. "Will you ask him, Lindsey?"

"I will."

Marcus says he'll put in a standing order for French vanilla if his new chef puts a buttery apple torte and a flourless chocolate cake on The Clamdigger's dessert menu.

It's heart-warming to see them excited at the prospect of growing their business. They said they would totally support Mr. and Mrs. Rigley selling him their restaurant.

After Marcus asks whether they make ice cream with beach plums—"No, they're too difficult to work with"— Mrs. Boyer tries to give us each a free serving.

"Thank you," Marcus says, "but I want to pay you, not merely for our ice cream but for being supportive. You've been very gracious with your time."

Each of us is carrying a cup of strawberry-nutmeg ice cream, which Marcus was keen to try, as we walk side-by-side down Spire Street. I'm impressed by him. He seems genuinely nice, the polar opposite to the man whose store is coming up on our left. My footsteps quicken as I try to pass Conor's Island Treasures without pausing. Just when I think I've made it, Marcus stops.

"What about this place?"

Taking a breath, I turn around. "The owner's no fan of mine."

"Because of your parents?" he asks. "Angry like the motel owner?"

I squirm. "No. Because I don't want to go out with him ever again."

His eyebrows raise. "Is he a real estate developer, too?"

"You think you're really funny," I fume. "There are plenty of reasons for me not to like a guy. Wait, that didn't come out right."

Before I can say more, the door opens. There's Conor, tall, a wiry build, blond hair, blue eyes. He must have been standing near the front window. He looks from me to Marcus. While we might not be together, and could have simply both been walking by at the same time, we're holding telltale matching ice cream cups.

"No eating in my store," Conor begins by way of greeting. He looks older than his years. Like me, he inherited the role of shopkeeper, although under different circumstances. His parents divorced but stayed on the island. Since neither wanted to give the other one the shop, they gave it to their son who had already turned eighteen.

It was a useful, general store, but over the decade of owning it, Conor changed it to cheap candy and taffy, none of it made here, to its current Chinese-made, junky inventory.

I roll my eyes and show him the cup. "Empty," I say.

"Mine, too," Marcus chimes in, then he holds out his hand. "I'm Marcus Parisi. I bought The Lady of the Light last year and may be interested in some other properties."

The expression on Conor's face is one of surprise. He's already mid-handshake when his eyes narrow. He withdraws his hand too quickly. "You can't have my store."

Marcus chuckles. "No worries. I didn't come here to make an offer. I came to meet fellow business owners and also to let you know I'm buying The Clamdigger."

I notice Marcus doesn't leave any room for doubt or discussion the way he did with the Boyers. But he does mention his desire to bring more tourists, more guests, more buyers. Conor nods, taking it all in, undoubtedly seeing dollar signs.

I look past him through the open door. The general store had been a welcome compliment to the market and had always been frequented by more locals than tourists. Conor thought the money was to be made in catering to visitors. My shop depends on off-islanders, too, but I've always kept my prices reasonable and provided good quality items in case locals need anything I offer.

Refocusing on the discussion, I almost wish Marcus would buy this godawful place and make it better.

"Are you all in?" Conor asks, addressing me.

For a second, I think he means in a relationship with Marcus. I pause, flustered.

Before I realize what Conor means, Marcus fills the silence. "Lindsey has graciously decided to introduce me to fellow islanders. But she's not responsible for what I'm doing. Nor does she necessarily condone it."

That was kind of him to take me out of the equation. In this case, it's a good idea.

I fold my arms across my chest and nod. I'm an innocent bystander on the Parisi polishing tour.

Conor shrugs. "Hey, if you beef up our tourists, I'm not gonna stop you. If the Rigleys want out, that's their deal. Seems to me if you can do what you say you can, then they're foolish to sell. In a year, we might be rolling in dough. No fool like an old fool."

What a disrespectful asshole! I recall our dreadful date at The Clamdigger. He was buttering up Mrs. Rigley who was hostessing that night. Conor went all islander-to-islander, looking out for one another, giving fellow locals a break.

After he persisted, he still didn't think they gave him a big enough discount, nor did they comp him our drinks. To my mortification, he said loudly what cheapskates they were and then low-balled the server's tip.

I was beyond humiliated.

Marcus clearly doesn't want to be part of Conor's worldview, either. He says, "I assure you I don't do business with fools."

And he's done, walking away without a goodbye. I offer Conor a satisfied smirk and follow. When I catch up to Marcus in a few steps, he's muttering under his breath.

"Where next?" I ask.

"I cannot believe you went out with him. He's beneath you in every way. Looks, personality, intelligence. And obviously in sheer niceness."

That warms me, until he adds, "You must have been lonely and damn desperate."

Wait, did he just insult me?

"I wouldn't say desperate," I defend myself.

"Really? Because he's obnoxious. And you . . . ," he trails off.

"Me, what?"

"You're not. How long did you date him?"

"I've known Conor all my life, and we went out about three times over a single month."

He shakes his head. "I'm shocked it took three times before you ended it."

I loosen up and relax. Marcus is annoyed on my behalf, and it's endearing.

"So am I, to be honest. But the third date was at The Clamdigger. I thought I should get a fine meal out of the disastrous experience before I dumped him."

Marcus laughs. "I hope you ordered the most expensive thing on the menu."

"Nah. Once we got in there, I wasn't sure he was going to pay for mine after all."

He shakes his head. "Forget him. You decide, The Crunchy Seashell or The Mermaid's Tail?"

"Curly, not crunchy," I say, "but we might as well try it."

Marcus's head is on a swivel, looking at everything, occasionally, pulling out his phone and typing a note. Seeing the town center through his eyes, it is decidedly dated. Not in a quaint, antique way, though, as I've told myself. It's actually neglect due to lack of funds.

"I don't know if there's anyone in the office of either place right now," I remind him. Sure enough, we get to Stan Brie's place, and it's dark. Crossing the road, we have no better luck at The Mermaid's Tail.

"You probably know where both owners' live."

I still feel like I'm helping the enemy, even if I'm not sleeping with him any longer.

"I told you that Stan Brie is a bit of a prick," I remind him. "But we can go talk to Marie."

Luckily, Marie's one-story house on the harbor side of the island is a short walk. There's no way I'm getting on the back of Marcus's motorcycle and wrapping my arms around him to hold on.

When we get to Marie's house, however, I do immediately drop to my knees and wrap my arms around her dog, Flint, who's lying on the patch of grass in her front yard. He should be called Squishy because there's nothing hard about him. He's a yellow lab, like Max. If I close my eyes and hug him, I can pretend for a moment. So I do. Then I give him a kiss on the top of his head and rise to my feet.

Marie, who is in her mid-sixties, immediately offers us coffee, which we both refuse after the ice cream. She asks how my parents are doing, and then Marcus launches in to the "Parisi polish" rah-rah speech.

She nods, having heard that The Lady of the Light was going to be renovated. Marie has no issues with that, nor with Marcus purchasing The Clamdigger.

"I think it'll be great for the tourist business."

"Will you be opening again this season?" Marcus asks.

She makes a face. "I know I should, but it was nice not having the responsibility last summer. I didn't have to hire maids and front desk staff or a pool person."

Honestly, I'm shocked. After the Rigleys and now Marie, I can't help wondering if anyone's happy. Conor seemed miserable, too.

"Is there any problem getting staff?" Marcus asks.

"No, not really. We have enough young people needing summer jobs. If we don't provide them, then they have to commute by ferry to work or even leave altogether."

Then she sighs. "I also don't want to face the crack in the bottom of the pool."

"Oh no!" I blurt. All three of us can imagine the difficulty of renting out rooms with a closed pool. "It's too late to do anything about it," I muse.

Marie shrugs. "I was thinking of discounting the room rates because there's still the beach, but it's hardly worth opening when I do the math." Then she smiles at Marcus. "I don't suppose you want to buy my motel, do you? Cheap?"

She isn't serious, but he is. Like a heart attack.

"Yes, as a matter of fact, I do want to. But at a fair price, not cheap."

Just like that, her expression grows hopeful. She *was* serious. And like the Rigleys, she seems relieved.

"Maybe I should go and let you two discuss price and do some negotiating."

Marie stops me with a hand on my arm. "If this handsome fellow can afford The Lady of the Light and The Clamdigger, I'm sure we can come to an amicable agreement." She sticks her hand out toward Marcus. "Sold before you change your mind."

He laughs and shakes her hand. "Sold before *you* change your mind."

"Will you stay?" I can't help asking. Flint barks like he's wondering the same thing.

"Now that is a question I'll have to think about." She claps her hands. "I'm very excited that someone else will be taking over the burden—" she stops, then winks at Marcus. "I mean taking over the *wonderful* opportunity. I can't sit still any longer. Flint and I are going for a walk and calling my family. Phone reception is better if I head toward the ferry."

Marcus's enthusiasm is contagious, and we're both laughing as we approach The Clamdigger. The lights are on now, but the restaurant is still locked. I tap on the glass, pressing my face to it until Mrs. Rigley sees me. Soon, we're inside, drinking an aperitif at the bar while I explain how so far, no one I've spoken to is going to be at all critical of them selling to Marcus.

Just like that, it's a done deal.

I lift my glass of unfamiliar Kir Royale and sniff the pale-crimson beverage. I learn from Mr. Rigley that it's crème de cassis and champagne.

"We are beyond ready to retire," Mrs. Rigley says, sitting on the barstool beside me while her husband stays on the other side of the dark wooden bar. "But with the downturn in the economy, we didn't think we'd ever get a buyer. We never even tried."

I take it Marcus is offering them a fair price, too.

"You should know that I intend to hire a new chef," Marcus says. "But Benny will have a job waiting for him at Dave's pub if he's interested."

Mr. Rigley laughs. "I think he'll be relieved. He loves the island, but the pressure of cooking above his abilities has stressed him out."

"Win-win," Marcus says.

"Win-win," the Rigleys echo and hold up their glasses again in a toast.

"Now you just have to solve the water issue," Mr. Rigley says.

I glance at Marcus on the stool beside me, but he doesn't look at me. He's staring straight ahead into the mirror behind the bar. Still, I manage to catch his eyes in the reflection. He winces slightly.

"Water issue?" I ask, stung that he knows and I don't.

"You know how bad the pressure is," Mrs. Rigley says. "I can hardly rinse the shampoo out of my hair."

"I figured it was just at my house."

"Oh, no," Mr. Rigley says. "We used to have much better pressure. The island's going to need a new well or find another aquifer."

Marcus remains silent, but our gazes are locked.

"Of course, the water treatment plant is as old as Moses, too," Mrs. Rigley adds.

Each word is making me more concerned. Murray Island can do without a lot. But not without water. I should have been more aware.

"Ask Marcus how he likes showering at the hotel," Mr. Rigley says.

But I don't need to. I know the answer.

Finally, he downs the last of what's in his glass, winks at me in the mirror, and then gets off the stool.

"I'll do my best," he says.

He'll do his best! Who is he? Poseidon?

"I'll bring papers over tomorrow," he tells the couple. "Do you have an attorney on the island? Or we could facetime with one."

A minute later, I ask him, "Do things always work out for you?" We're ambling along with no specific destination, mostly because I have no idea what he wants to buy next.

Unexpectedly, he grabs my hand. "I don't know, you tell me. Are we good again?"

18

Marcus

Lindsey gives me a long look.

"I'm not sure what you're asking?"

"I'm fairly sure you do. Can we go back to the path we were on before you discovered that I own a credit card?"

"Don't be flippant," she says. "Besides, it wasn't a path. It was a quick diversion."

"Really?"

She picks up the pace, not looking at me.

"Yes, really. Of all the things you've bought on Murray Island, a permanent home isn't one of them, is it?"

She's right. And she's being cautious about getting involved with me if I'm not staying. Smart lady. But just because I have an end-of-stay date, that doesn't mean our relationship would have to end, should we get into one.

"I already own a beautiful house." More than one, but only one I think of as home. "I'd like to show it to you some day." It's true. I would love to give her a tour of Tryon,

North Carolina, and have her stay with me. Although at this moment, I'm having trouble thinking of her anywhere except in my bedroom.

"And I have a lovely house, too," Lindsey reminds me.

"With one of the best views," I agree. I try to come up with a few things to entice her to come away with me besides the satisfying time we could have in bed. "Wouldn't you like to see my horses? Also, I have a pool and hot tub. And I have a vineyard. Scuppernong grapes."

She shrugs at my attempt to impress her.

"What are we going to do about the water problems?"

OK, we're done talking personal stuff already. But I do like how she said *we*.

"I'm going to bring it up at the town meeting and find out what the long-term plans are."

She nods. "Seems like a big deal. I have to admit that shower at the Ritz felt decadent."

When she mentions the hotel, my neanderthal brain goes right back to sex. Specifically, our off-the-charts, awesome sex. Secondly, my thoughts meander over to how much fun we had at the restaurant. When I first saw her in her shop, she was just a pretty woman swearing at herself. But as soon as we started talking, she was interesting and funny, generous with her time. Drop-dead sexy, too. And a great kisser, on the beach or off it.

"I own a few superb showers in North Carolina." I try again.

She stops and turns to face me. Then she shakes her head.

"You're persistent," she says. "I'll give you that."

"I want you to give me a helluva lot more than that," I say the truth out loud. "Let's start over." I offer my hand. "Hi, I'm Marcus Parisi, and I intend to help bring Murray Island into the twenty-first century."

After the briefest of hesitations, she takes my hand and shakes firmly. "I'm Lindsey Cooper, and I intend to make you respect its nineteenth-century historical aspects."

I can't help grinning. "I can deal with that."

Glancing around the empty streets, I consider our options.

"Dinner tonight?"

"Pizza?" she asks, surprising me.

"But I'm almost officially the owner of a nice restaurant."

She wrinkles her nose. "I don't want to go back in there tonight. Smacks of desperation."

Oh man! "I'm sorry I ever said that about you. I don't think you've ever been desperate in your life."

Raising an eyebrow, she nods. "You're right about that."

Her fortitude is absolutely alluring. I want to back Lindsey against the clapboard building behind her and kiss her senseless. By the wicked smile on her face, she knows it, too.

"Did I miss a pizzeria when I was touring the island?" I ask.

"Don't judge, OK?" she starts. "In the market, they sell ready-to-bake. But it's not frozen. The whole thing, dough included, is made fresh by the market's manager. Very popular, both with us locals and with visitors, if they have access to an oven. Believe it or not, if they don't, there's a pizza oven in the corner of the market just for this one purpose. Sal will start baking some in June, and they fly out of there."

A gold mine, I'm guessing, tucked in the corner of the market. This island needs a full-blown pizza parlor. If it's any good, I'll talk to the market's owner tomorrow.

"I can see the wheels turning, Parisi," she says. "For tonight, just eat the damn pizza without planning a pizza restaurant."

She knows me well already. Back to our plans for the evening.

"I have some work I have to get done before dinner. I'll work for an hour in my hotel room."

"Your room in *your* hotel," she quips.

I decide it's not the time to tell her it's one of many I own.

"Shall I pick you up for dinner . . . at the market?" That sounds ridiculous even as I ask her.

"I'll get the pizza," she says. "You can come by my house when you're done working. Say, seven o'clock."

"Shall I bring anything else?" I ask. *Like a box of condoms?* I add silently.

"That's OK. You looked after me on the mainland. I can do the same here."

I like the sound of that, but I'm still going to take a bottle of red wine, even if I have to pilfer it from the hotel, assuming they have some there.

In the end, I do better than that. I show up at her door with a salad of fresh greens and, sadly, *no* goat cheese, but also a fruity bottle of red and some brandy for afterward. Ownership has its privileges.

"Helps with digestion," I tell Lindsey when I unpack the bag from the hotel and put the brandy on her kitchen counter. I'm happy to be back in her house. Plus, it smells mouthwatering.

"Pizza should be done," she says, turning away to switch off the oven, open a cupboard, and extract a couple of wine glasses.

As she reaches up, the hem of her blue-and-yellow flowered dress skims up her thighs. I can't take my eyes off her slender legs. I know it's silly, but simply being in her kitchen again feels extremely intimate. Like we're already a couple.

When she turns, glasses in hand, I'm still staring.

"What?" she asks, setting the glasses down. Then she turns in a circle trying to look at her own backside. "Oh, shit, is this the dress Max chewed a hole in?"

I can't help laughing. "I don't see any holes. You look amazing, that's all. And I'm glad you let me back in your home."

Her cheeks grow pink. She's blushing. Damn, if it's not the hottest thing, and I get hard just looking at her lovely face. I'm trying not to rush things this time by moving in for a kiss, but it's hard when I know how sweet her lips taste.

Lindsey pushes the corkscrew toward me over the counter. "Make yourself useful."

"I can think of better ways," I grumble, which makes her laugh.

In a few minutes, we're in her dining room because it's too breezy outside for dining al fresco. Her table is rustic, scarred oak, laid atop with cork placemats.

"Surprised you're not using those laminated maps," I say, as I put down our plates of pizza and salad while she lights a candle.

Her easy laughter comes again, trickling over me. It goes straight to my groin. Or rather, her happiness does. I need to think of something besides getting Lindsey naked.

Since we're now seated beside one of her four fireplaces, I ask, "Do you light fires in the winter?"

"You're wondering if the chimneys are in good shape," she guesses. "The answer is yes. Chimneys are safe, roof doesn't leak, and the floors are solid. But you cannot buy my home."

"I promise I wasn't going to try. Although everyone has their price."

Her brow furrows. "Not everyone."

"You don't think so?" I ask. "It's been my experience over the past decade that anyone can be relieved of nearly anything they hold dear if you offer them enough zeroes behind a number."

"You mean property, of course." She takes a sip of wine, and I hate to disillusion her about humanity.

"Living things, too. I wanted a horse that everyone said the owner would not part with. Now I'm the owner."

"I wouldn't have sold Max," she protests. "He was both family and friend."

I nod. "OK, we'll stick with real estate, and things, like cars and boats. People will sell for the right price because they can always buy another one."

She mulls it over. "Do you think I'd sell my home for an exorbitant sum?"

I consider. I can almost believe the answer is no, but if she were to become a millionaire and have freedom to go anywhere, then I think I know the answer. In any case, I'm diplomatic.

"Perhaps if the money were needed for something else you love. Like the shop or a medical emergency, then you'd sell."

"That's not a fair hypothetical. Anyone would sell in an emergency. But money for money's sake? No, I wouldn't sell." She spears some lettuce and starts on her salad.

I believe her. After all, she already has the view people go on vacation to enjoy.

"Back to your winter on the island. Here you are, in your cozy home, with a fire roaring in the fireplace—"

"Usually in at least two of them," she interrupts. "I buy two cords of wood from the mainland when it's at its cheapest, early summer, then bring it over on the ferry and use it all winter."

"Clever and economical," I say. I'd love to sit with her before a roaring fire, so toasty that we can strip down. I want to see the reflection of the flames lick across her skin and follow with my tongue. "Maybe we'll enjoy a lit hearth together sometime."

She frowns. "I'm saving what's left of my wood for next year. No more fires until October."

"Smart, frugal, practical," I say. "But apparently not too romantic. Nothing like a crackling fire."

She shrugs. "Maybe we can have a beach bonfire before you leave."

And Lindsey has just dumped cold water all over my crackling fire by mentioning my departure.

"Not going anywhere for a while," I tell her. "I decided there's more on Murray Island to learn about than merely which businesses to buy."

"Yeah?" she asks. "Like what?" Having finished her salad, she takes her first mouthful of pizza and moans. My cock stands at attention. To distract myself, I take a bite, too.

"Wow, that's good," I tell her, glad it exceeded my expectations.

"Hot, cheesy deliciousness," she agrees. "What else do you need to learn about?"

She's fishing to discover my level of interest, and I don't want to hold back.

"Hot deliciousness called Lindsey Cooper." Cue another blush-fest across her cheeks.

"Oh." She remains quiet after that.

We eat in companionable silence for a minute, and then I ask, "Do you want to live here the rest of your life?"

I expect her to snap at me with a fervent, "Yes!" But she shrugs and continues eating. I wait. I can see she's ruminating. Finally, she picks up her wine glass again and looks me in the eyes.

"You know, I've been thinking about that a lot lately. When I left the Ritz, after I saw Dave, I visited my parents. Life is definitely easier for them on the mainland. Funny enough, they spent the time asking me everything that was happening here. They might be homesick, come to think of it. Anyway, if not ecstatic, they seemed happy in their new life. I don't begrudge them the move. In fact, I don't judge anyone who sells to you and leaves, like Mr. Newton."

That's refreshing. I'd been putting her in the camp of "Murray Island or die."

"I believe remaining on the island is also a valid choice for Mr. and Mrs. Rigley," she continues. "But I'm not sure I want to picture myself working at Whatnots right up until I drop dead, with a bottle of suntan lotion in my hand."

"And a laminated placemat in the other," I joke.

She snickers. "Exactly. In the past, I haven't thought much about it because it's always been a given. Family store, and I'm family." After a sigh, she asks, "You want to see my living room?"

She says it as though it's a grand tour and a long trip from one room to the next. But since I haven't so much as poked my head in there yet, I say, "Yes!"

Jumping up, I draw out her chair.

"Now that's funny," Lindsey says. "My mother would think you're the swankiest gentleman."

We go around the chimney in the center of the house, and in a few steps, we're seated on the couch. There are photos on the mantel in this room, including one of her as a youngster with her parents, and I ask her more about them.

"Mom has a fine arts degree in writing. She's currently teaching at the college level." Lindsey tucks her legs under her and turns to face me. "My dad is fishing and cooking. Mostly cooking the fish he catches. And he's loving retirement."

She picks up a cushion with a mermaid embroidered on it, giving it a punch before shoving it behind her back. "They were lucky to have enough money to move without selling the store," she says.

"But if they had sold it," I remind her, "you'd be totally free."

She nods. "To do what? That's the question, isn't it?"

Her question frustrates and saddens me because she is smart and could do whatever the hell she wants, but her world is narrow at the moment. And she's taken on the responsibility by default of being a shopkeeper. It almost makes me want to buy her store after all. And I find myself saying precisely that.

"Lindsey, do you want to sell me your store?"

I don't expect her reaction. She jumps up from the blue-and-white striped couch we just settled onto.

"Are you kidding me?" she asks, sounding genuinely outraged. "Did you do all this," she gestures to the wine glass on the coffee table as if I've showered her with presents, "to lull me into thinking you're a good guy, only to get your hands on my store?"

With her hands on her hips, she's gone from relaxed and friendly to suspicious and annoyed in a heartbeat.

I rise to my feet. "Hasn't anyone ever brought you a bottle of wine and a salad before?" I ask, taking hold of her hand and then her other one. "You're a strange one, Miss Cooper. I can't imagine how valuable you think the brandy is, but I promise, even that isn't a bribe. And the only thing I want to get my hands on is you."

I pull her close, release her hands, and place my own firmly on her ass. Its utter perfection has made an impression on me, and I'm a happy man to have it under my fingers again. I squeeze gently, tilt my head and—

"Wait," she says, sounding breathless already. "Promise me you don't want my store."

"I promise and pinky swear that I don't want your store. But if you wanted out of it, I'd buy it to set you free."

She takes in my words and then I feel her body relax against mine.

Finally, I lower my mouth to hers and kiss her.

19

Lindsey

I grab onto his back and hold on for a kiss that makes the floor seem to tilt. We are smooshing our mouths as if we can't get close enough and making hungry sounds that I've only seen in movies. And then, the room does tilt because he sweeps me off my feet.

Not figuratively, either, but really.

I shriek because I've never had a guy do this before. And except for when the fireman rescued me from that obnoxious tree that seemed to grow farther from the ground as soon as I was in it, no one has carried me since my parents when I was a toddler.

Marcus heads for my sturdy but narrow stairs at the back of the house, next to the bathroom. He doesn't pause to mention how poor the design is for resale. But he does have to set me down at the first step. There's no way he can carry me up the two-hundred-year-old staircase without hitting my feet on one wall and my head on the other.

"Well, shit," he says, but he's laughing, too. "A guy makes a passionate gesture, and it's for nothing."

I lead the way up. "Not for nothing. It was romantic and a first for me."

With each step I take, his hands are playing with the hem of my cotton dress, and I am all tingly inside.

"I'm glad," he says, "to be the first to carry you."

A sharp turn at the top of the stairs, and we're in my bedroom.

"I'll do it again some time," he promises, "when I have room to make it more than a few feet."

For now, he's backing me onto my queen bed, which fills the room meant for either a single or a double, back in the day.

"Not a mattress filled with straw, I hope," Marcus says, as he climbs atop me.

I look up at him. "No, but the walls are horsehair plaster."

He lifts his head from where he was nuzzling my neck, and I immediately regret mentioning something remotely interesting about my house.

I take his face between my hands to stop Marcus looking around.

"I'll show you later," I promise. "Every historical detail, including heart of pine flooring."

"I love it when you talk real estate to me," he jokes.

But I swear he's only half kidding. Moonlight streams in my bedroom window, and the sparkle in his eyes suddenly seems brighter, turning them from pale toffee brown to gold. And his erection, already hard against my thigh, becomes like granite.

"You're weird," I mutter, before pulling his head down so we can resume the kissing.

When his tongue sweeps between my lips, my body seems to melt like molten lava. His scent is already familiar to me, a crisp, citrus cologne that tickles my nose. Because I smelled it when we had great sex in Boston, I'm like

Pavlov's dogs with the bell. Instead of salivating, I become damp between my legs where an insistent throb has begun like a drumbeat.

Maybe I am salivating a bit, too. I suck on his tongue and widen my thighs for him to settle more snugly. The downside to our rush to the bed is that we're both still clothed.

Reading my mind, Marcus breaks the perfect kiss and rears up to start divesting himself of his shirt and pants. I can't help staring when he reveals the flat planes and sculpted bulges of his muscles. I swallow, and my heartbeat increases, knowing his heavenly body is about to be joined with my mere mortal one.

For my part, while still watching him, I shimmy out of my panties. Yet before I can remove my dress, he's back. Resting between my legs, Marcus pushes my dress up to my hips. Having my upper body still covered when my lower half is bare, with his mouth close to my pussy, is erotic as fuck. I take in an excited breath, letting it out in a soft moan of neediness.

My core goes from damp to drenched just from the way he's looking at me. I'm desperate for his touch.

"Can I kiss you?" he asks softly, looking me in the eyes.

"Mmph-hm," is what comes out because I can feel his breath against my skin, but he knows it's an affirmative.

First, he blows gently, a little puff of air to my lady parts that sends me to the moon. I swear I'm already lightheaded. When he kisses my inner thigh, I groan. He kisses the other side, then closer. He parts me with gentle fingers.

"Marcus," I breathe out his name as his mouth closes over my clit in a hot kiss. My hands go to his soft hair, my fingers thread through it. I'm not anchoring him there so much as holding myself in place in case I float away.

As his tongue makes magic, swirling and gliding over me, I close my eyes and enjoy the ride. It doesn't take long, a few firm, sweeping licks around and then directly over my aroused nub, and I've climbed the mountain. When he nibbles my clit, then sucks it, I'm gone. I explode, I fly, I soar, and then I start to come back as relaxed as a feather.

Marcus pushes my dress up the rest of the way and undoes my bra before dragging both garments up and off my shoulders and over my head. It's not exactly graceful, but we're both too far gone to care about optics.

"Still not," I say the shorthand for not being on birth control.

"I know," he says, prepared with a condom beside us on the bed.

"Let me," I say, wanting to roll it down the length of him.

"Next time," he rasps, too charged and aroused to allow me to fumble and take my time.

He settles along my entire trembling body, leaning on one forearm as he guides the head of his penis to my slick entrance. I know he's ready to thrust, but he bows his head to kiss my breasts, each in turn, while easing gently inside me.

When he's filling me, his mouth moves up from my nipples to my lips. As he ravishes my mouth, I get to grasp his soft brown hair again, his hips rock, and his erection spears and retreats. It's like we're dancing, moving in synchronicity, even breathing the same air.

It's a whole new level of intimacy for me from anything I've ever before experienced during sex. We take our time, he strokes, my hips lift, and back again. Over and over, until he has to raise his head and take a gulping breath. I feel his back muscles grow taut and know he's about to climax.

"Touch yourself," he orders.

It never occurred to me that I could help myself along at the end. But it's sexy as hell when he commands me to. I slide my hand between our bodies and caress my clit. That's all it takes to join Marcus in a shuddering climax, which makes us both groan as the tension leaves our bodies.

He collapses beside me, and I reach down for my comforter, dragging it over us.

We're silent for a moment, just breathing in the twilight.

"Nice," I say finally.

He laughs. "Good God, woman! How do I earn an A plus if that was merely nice."

"It was much better than nice," I confess. "It was the best."

He turns on his side and looks at me. "The best," he agrees, before tracing my mouth with his thumb. For a moment, I think he's going to say something else, even more romantic.

Jeez, Lindsey! I chastise myself. What do you want? A declaration of love?

After a few seconds, he asks, "Are you ready for a glass of brandy?"

$♥$♥$♥$

After dressing, we sit on my sofa, sipping brandy and talking. I hear all about his North Carolina home, learn about his parents, Carolyn and Ricardo. His married sister, Bianca and her husband. He tells me his personal journey from construction worker to contractor to real estate developer. Marcus has traveled all over the states and internationally, too. He's gone back to his father's home in Sicily, and even owns a small villa there, in Taormina.

Actually, he doesn't use the word *small*, but my provincial Murray Island brain hopes that's the case. I already feel inferior in every way possible, having only been off the island a couple dozen times, rarely leaving New England. We had a trip to Florida once, and I found it overwhelming. Also, I had to take Benadryl for the flight. Otherwise, I would've taken one look out the plane's window and been in hysterics.

When I start to yawn, Marcus takes my empty glass along with his to the kitchen and puts them in the sink. I rise to my feet, wishing the evening didn't have to end.

"You have a store to open in the morning, lady," he says. "I have a lawyer to meet with and a restaurant purchase to finalize."

Nodding, I walk him to the door. I don't offer the rest of his bottle of brandy. That would be crass, and he wouldn't take it anyway. But I can use it as a lure.

"I hope you'll come back and have another glass of brandy while you're on the island."

His face grows serious. In a heartbeat, he takes hold of my upper arms and, with a graceful arc, has me backed me against my own front door. When Marcus looks down into my face, I catch my breath at his expression.

"Lindsey, I'm not leaving right away. Even if I was, I wouldn't disappear from your life without telling you."

Not exactly reassuring that I'm much more than someone to play with in the short term.

"If you're happy with *this*," he continues, sending a golden-eyed glance to my lips and giving my arms a gentle squeeze where his fingers are wrapped around them, "then I don't see any reason why we can't enjoy ourselves while I'm here."

To prove his point, he kisses me. Not a swift, goodbye kiss, indicating he's eager to get out the door. It's as languorous and sensual as if he's just walked in. My toes curl in the slippers I put on when we came downstairs.

Sighing, I relax against him, enjoying every second of being sandwiched between Marcus and the oak door. That's what I need to do for the remainder of our . . . association. Enjoy the moment.

When at last he lifts his head, he rests his forehead against mine for a second and then he steps back.

"I'll see you tomorrow."

"Will you?" I ask, wondering when.

"At the town meeting. I know you're re-opening Dave's, but I hope you'll make the meeting."

Shoot! I'd forgotten that both are happening within a half hour of each other. My promise is to Dave and Mel, but perhaps I can at least catch the beginning.

"And maybe after you close up." He leaves that hanging.

I don't want to be coy, but I also don't want to suddenly be taken for granted as a sure thing.

"Maybe," I say.

"Lock the door," he reminds me as he leaves.

I nod, then watch him put on his helmet and drive away.

"Don't," I tell myself. It would be easy to say these strong emotions are already love. Even easier to get attached to this man and want to see him every day and night while he's here.

He won't be leaving anytime soon, he said. But he will be leaving.

I close the door and tidy up the kitchen. But when I climb the stairs to bed, I can't help smiling at just how great we are together. It certainly feels like more than a summer fling.

20

Marcus

"I haven't hidden my intentions," I say about ten minutes into the town meeting, when asked by an older man I've never met before whether I'm doing a land grab.

He introduced himself as the town moderator, Mr. Gardner. By his appearance, sparse hair, thin pale skin, and watery eyes, he might have been here when the town was first established in the mid-seventeen hundreds. He is seated behind a long table with a few other people to his left and right, the board of selectmen.

"I want to improve Murray Island for the good of all its inhabitants," I explain, leaning against the back of the incredibly uncomfortable wooden bench seat, the rail of which hits me just under my shoulder blades. I can't help thinking it's on purpose, to make people squirm when facing the men and women who run Murray Island.

Lindsey is here. She's dressed for work with that eye-popping T-shirt stretched across her full breasts, proclaiming that Dave's is the place for fun and food. After waving to me when she came in, she took a seat in the back by the door of the single-story, plain wooden building. The only thing modern are the windows and the electric lights.

"But you're not an inhabitant," Mr. Gardner says. "Do you intend to become one?"

"No." I'm truthful, but the word sounds harsh. I glance over to see Lindsey listening intently. She's not judging me, but she doesn't look happy, either.

"That's a problem," the town moderator says. "We've never had an off-islander own any of our businesses."

"My assistant came last year and combed through your bylaws and spoke with one of the selectmen." I don't name which one because I haven't met or spoken to him personally, and I don't wish to get him in trouble. Not unless asked.

Taking in the board members, I notice Carl, the man who leant me his bicycle and who owns the bakery, as well as Jeannette James. But I don't recognize anyone else.

Brass name plates, a surprising touch, tell me one is Andy's father unless there are other Rumbles on the island. Another is Stan Brie, the owner of the Crusty Seashell Motel. I tried to find him today, but he wasn't at his motel or answering his door at home.

And suddenly, he's the one talking. Loudly.

"A monopoly. That's what's going on here. This foreigner—"

"I'm American," I interject.

He sends me a withering look while some people laugh.

"This off-islander," he begins again, "is trying to kick us all out. He has his tentacles in The Lady of the Light, The Clamdigger, and now The Mermaid's Tail. He came knocking at my place today, no doubt trying to scoff up my motel, but I didn't answer."

I try to keep the smile off my face, but my reply is snarky. "Were you worried my tentacles would take a hold of you if you came to your door?"

More laughter ensues. No doubt a mistake on my part because the man's face turns red. Time to diffuse the situation.

"Legally, I could buy every single house and business," I inform them, "if I wanted to."

A general hush falls over those in attendance. I glance back at Lindsey whose eyes are wide. She even gives an almost imperceptible shake of her head.

"But I don't want to," I continue. "Everyone who has sold to me has done so with relief because they can no longer make a viable living here. For the many businesses that remain, I intend to get Murray Island's economy back on track. But I can't do it by myself."

Actually, I probably could, but I wouldn't be making my life any easier by boasting.

"Mr. Brie, I came to your home today because your motel is closed up and your busy season is purportedly starting tomorrow. How are your fellow islanders supposed to conduct business with tourists if you don't open and give visitors a place to stay?"

Heads swivel in Stan Brie's direction. He's never going to be a fan of mine, so I might as well knock him out of the way.

"I have some plumbing problems," he says.

"Why didn't you fix them over the winter?" asks the town moderator. "I didn't know you weren't opening for a second summer in a row. After that, people will assume you never will, and that's the end of that."

Mr. Brie sniffs. "It's a big undertaking. You know we all have water problems of one type or another."

"Did you ask anyone for help? Perhaps a bank loan?" Mr. Gardner persists.

"Nope." For some reason, the grumpy bastard stares at me, like this is all my fault.

I might as well get to the elephant in the room. "Mr. Brie brings me to the water issue, which is my other reason for coming here today, besides getting to meet all of you in person. What plans are in place for building a new wastewater treatment plant and digging a new well?"

Silence. The town moderator coughs, then says, "Personally, I'm kicking that can down the road a ways until I'm six feet under."

Someone gasps, another person behind me laughs nervously, most remain silent—maybe with shock. Because that is a shocking way to handle a problem that affects every single person on the island.

"Now, Joel," Carl says, like the voice of reason, "Mr. Parisi is going to think you're serious."

"Isn't he?" I ask.

"He better not be. We paid for a study three years ago, and the consultant said the aquifer is good, but we need a deeper well. Our three island wells go to seventy-five feet, but he suggested tapping down to a hundred and fifty."

The first thing that comes to mind is *expensive*.

"And the water treatment plant?"

The town moderator sighs. "No getting around that. We need a new one. But I suppose you knew that and yet you bought those properties anyway."

"Either a fool or a charlatan," Stan Brie says.

"I was made aware of the plant's age," I say, ignoring his remark. "But I figured that one way or another, the town would be addressing these issues, or everyone will have to move off Murray Island in the next few years. I'm betting that's not the choice you'll make."

The people in the room who didn't know about the extent of the water issues erupt in discussion.

I wait until the moderator uses his gavel and restores order. Then I ask, "You've raised taxes in recent years to pay for it, I assume."

"Some," he says.

Which means *not enough*.

"I've cut down on irrigation," Mr. Rumble speaks up. "I can't water any less or I might as well give up on farming altogether. But I also can't pay any more for the land than I already do."

Another round of murmuring goes through the room. Mr. Gardner smacks his gavel again.

"Assuming we can raise the money or get a loan," Carl says, "we'll have to get the new plant built before we take the old one off line, meaning we need a new site."

I've had an idea about that since the day I rode around the island on my motorcycle when Lindsey still wasn't speaking to me.

"May I suggest tearing down the dangerous fort?"

I hear a gasp and recognize the sound as coming from Lindsey. It's a sound I've heard when we're having sex, but I have a feeling if I look at her now, the light of desire won't be shining in her blue eyes.

"It's an eye sore," I continue, feeling like a traitor to her, but it's for the best. "The structure is falling apart and strewn with trash. Apart from that, it's a massive liability should a tourist climb on it, get injured, and sue the town."

"He's right," Andy's father chimes in. "Plus, it's practically the same distance from town as the current treatment plant, with any noxious breezes going out to sea or over basically empty land."

As if the location is a done deal, I say, "First step is to get bids on both the new wells and the plant."

After a pause, the moderator says, "I'll have some names by the next meeting."

Personally, I'm not waiting a month. I'll find out the name of the consultant they've already paid, get the details from him or her, and call my favorite structural engineer. Perhaps it's possible to retrofit rather than replace the plant. In any case, I intend to locate some contractors who are willing to come over and bid, and I'll present Mr. Gardner with the names next week and the bids as soon after that as possible.

"You don't feel so happy having snapped up The Mermaid's Tail now, do you?" sneers Stan Brie.

What did I ever do to him? I know what I want to do. Smash my fist into his face.

"I bought The Mermaid's Tail to give Murray Island's guests at least one open motel. Otherwise, the tourists will have to rely on The Lady along with any private rentals for this year's guests."

General grumbling ensues. But at least no one is talking about whether I should be allowed to own businesses any longer.

"The Mermaid can be opened as soon as Mr. Parisi staffs her," Marie speaks up from a neighboring bench. "I've kept it in good order. I mean, it's not fancy, but I've had inquiries for availability over the last few weeks." She winces. "I'm sorry to say I didn't confirm with anyone."

My can-do instincts kick in. "I have a friend in Boston who owns an international ad agency. I'll ask Adam if he'll get someone on his staff to create an enticing marketing campaign. If you don't have any suitable photos, then I'll bring one of my employees over here to take photos," I offer, "or I'll ask Adam to handle that for us, too. Just tell me what areas of the country your guests typically come from."

I send Robin a text to contact Adam at Bonvier, Inc. Then I express my other concern. "If I find guests, both for The Lady and the motel, will I have cleaning and front desk staff?"

Carl from the bakery answers. "There are plenty of islanders who are semi-retired or fully retired who love working the summer jobs. We usually have a sign-up list." He looks to the moderator.

"We have one. Tons of folks are ready."

I wonder what *tons* means on an island with only about fifteen hundred full-time residents and shrinking. But I trust that they've done this before.

"What's in it for you?" asks Stan Brie.

I have to stop myself from rolling my eyes.

"Money," I say simply. Because that's something every person in the room can understand. But it's much more than that. In my mind's eye, I already see Murray Island in a couple of years, completely transformed and full of vivacity, instead of that whiff of decline.

Regardless, a buzz of murmuring crisscrosses the room. And Brie wears a smug expression. What did he think I was doing this for? A suntan and some home-made ice cream?

"I'm a businessman, first and foremost," I point out. "But as a friend of mine says, a rising tide lifts all boats. I'll only make money if we all have viable businesses that bring people to the island."

I glance back to see what Lindsey thinks, but she has left already.

$♥$♥$♥$

I stay and speak to people after the meeting. They're curious to know more if they've already met me. And if they haven't, then they're a little wary, as though I really do have business-stealing tentacles.

Like a politician, I chat with anyone who wants to. I answer their questions and allay their fears. I do not mention that I'm prepared to offer the town low-interest loans for both projects. That's premature.

At the end, Marie and I end up discussing the motel. I confess I've already summoned my concrete guy, and he'll be here in days with his crew to patch the pool.

"It'll do until I can revamp the whole thing in the fall. I hope you're not annoyed that I jumped the gun."

"Not at all." Then she smiles and waves over another woman, maybe my mother's age with faded blonde hair in a loose bun.

"This is my friend Kathy. She owns Duke's Riding."

"With the wonky gate," I say.

Kathy cringes. "I'll get to that."

"I'm pleased to meet you." I'm actually thrilled to talk to a fellow horse-lover. "I keep horses. My stable is in North Carolina."

Kathy's eyes light up. "My husband was from South Carolina. It's nice to meet you. Everyone else around here is all about fishing and beaches."

"I'm going to Dave's," I say. "Will you ladies join me? My treat."

I want to see how Lindsey is doing running the kitchen without Dave there.

"That would be lovely," Marie says. The three of us leave the town meeting house for the short walk in the early evening.

"You've made some friends," Marie says.

"And maybe some enemies," I add.

Kathy laughs. "No maybe about it. I would say definitely."

"Is it me?"

"I don't like to speak ill of anyone," Kathy says, "but Stan isn't the most pleasant person at the best of times. The Bries were once very well off. His family was considered to be one of the first families."

"Not first as in first settlers?"

"Oh no," she clarifies as I hold open the door to Dave's, and the women precede me. "As in first in win, place, and show. But no longer."

"The come-down has made him bitter," Marie agrees.

I'm only half listening now as I scan the nearly empty room for Lindsey. There are two people seated, but it's early. There may be four people in the bar. And I think I've seen some of them before, which means they're islanders.

Then, unexpectedly, I see Andy Rumble standing beside the kitchen door. He looks awkward by any measure, wearing the same black T-shirt that Lindsey wears, except his looks like it's one of Dave's and hangs like a loose dress on his gangly form.

"Hey," he calls across the room, "sit anywhere."

I let the women choose our table. It's against the wall, and even though it's still light out, in here it's dim. And not in a romantic way. I'm itching to brighten the place into a beachy vibe, rather than a dingy, dark bar atmosphere. The paneling needs to go for a start. After that, the place needs paint, new flooring, new furniture, attractive lighting, big windows.

I have to laugh at myself. It would be almost easier to bulldoze it and start over.

Andy shuffles across the well-worn, unequivocally hideous carpet and gives us menus. They are, as they were before, laminated and somewhat sticky.

"Are you serving here now?" Kathy asks.

"No, ma'am. Just helping out while Dave's on bedrest or whatevs. I'll take your order, Lindsey will cook it, and Mel will mix your drinks as always."

"Burgers all around?" I ask.

"You bet," Marie says.

"And fries," Kathy adds, then wonders, "Does Mel have a specialty drink tonight?"

Andy shrugs, looking as if he has no idea how to proceed.

"After you put our order in, why don't you ask her?" I say. "I'll have whatever she's making."

"Make that two," Kathy says.

"Three," chimes in Marie.

We're certainly making it as easy on the kid as possible.

"Cool," Andy says and ambles back toward the kitchen at what I have come to understand is simply an Andy-pace.

And then Kathy and I talk horses while Marie listens. I hope to convince her to start up her riding stable again, even if only for the summer, by letting me bring over a few of my gentle mares and my oldest colts since I don't keep geldings. In reality, we probably couldn't get a rental program going until next year, since I haven't yet seen the state of her stables. However, I haven't got to the nitty-gritty before Melinda, herself, brings over three cocktails on a tray.

"Andy's not old enough to serve alcohol yet," she explains, "and I don't want to get Dave's closed down on my watch."

"What are these?" Kathy asks.

"I call them Whale's Breath," Melinda says, then shrugs. "Because why not? If you can guess what's in them, another is on the house." She leaves with that challenge.

I take a sip and try to focus, but I'm tempted to excuse myself and poke my head into the kitchen. I want to see Lindsey. But she's making our food and the orders for the other couple, too, so I stay put.

The three of us take turns suggesting the ingredients. We keep guessing until the drinks are nearly done. Meanwhile, Andy has served the other table and ours. And the food is at least as tasty as I had before. I'd hoped Lindsey knew it was me, maybe that Andy had told her, and she would come out to say hi. I can't imagine she's too busy.

While we eat, another couple comes in. I never thought I'd feel relieved to see four diners in a restaurant, plus us. It's amazing how having a stake in something ups my interest.

Mel comes over and tells us we've all guessed wrong. "My secret ingredient isn't pear liqueur or anything else you've mentioned. It's elderflower."

"Clever," I say. "And subtle."

"No one has guessed it yet."

"Busy?" I ask.

She glances around. "Not yet in the bar, too early, although this is a pretty good turnout in here."

When we're ready to leave, I offer to walk them home, but Jamie has an old Mini, and Kathy has a scooter. I'm glad that they turn me down. As soon as they leave, I go back inside and head for the kitchen. Lindsey can't possibly be in a harried state with only two more people to cook for.

Since she's at the stove, her back is toward me, offering a luscious view. Two long ends from the apron tied at her waist hang down over her shapely ass. My body reacts to the visceral image, and I'm hoping we can get together tonight when she's finished here.

"Hi, there."

I swear I see her straighten and stiffen from across the small kitchen. She turns, and her face is a mask of disapproval.

Raising a hand, pointing a spatula at me, she spits out two words, "Get out."

21

Lindsey

Marcus smiles. He doesn't realize I'm not joking around. After stabbing me in the back over the fort, how can he think I'll be welcoming and totally OK. If I'd been able to tell which burger Andy would give him, I would've dumped some Tabasco sauce on his.

"No. Really," I say. "Get out of here."

"Territorial about the kitchen?" he asks.

"I meant out of Dave's. You two-faced shithead."

His forehead creases. "Are you serious?"

"As serious as Dave's heart attack," I say. "You knew I thought the fort was an important artifact of this island, and you just threw it under the bus."

"Have you seen it lately?" he asks.

"Have you?" I shoot back without acknowledging that I haven't.

"Yes, in fact. It's barely standing. And what is standing, while fort-like in shape, couldn't protect anyone. Quite the opposite. It looks dangerous and ready to cause harm."

"Looks dangerous, but maybe it isn't. Maybe it's just a historical treasure. *We* have a fort. Other islands don't. That should mean something to you. Why is a motel worth fixing up and saving but not an old fort?"

Realizing I'm walking toward him and waving my spatula around like a lunatic, I stop and wait for an answer.

"We'll go out there together then," he says, "and I'll welcome your expert opinion."

I open my mouth and close it. I guess I better take him up on the offer so I can convince him to leave the fort alone.

"OK. We'll go. As soon as I have a free moment, which won't be until next Sunday."

"Fine. I have plenty of other things to do," he says.

"I bet you do," I say.

"What does that mean?"

"I have no idea." And I don't. I'm just pissed off and want to keep fighting. But he's being too reasonable. Speaking of which . . .

"Getting new wells and water treatment plants are beyond the town's means right now, if I were to guess."

"You're probably right," he agrees.

"Then why even bring up tearing down the fort? Nothing can be done for years."

"The town can't wait years. I haven't mentioned this to anyone else, but I could provide Murray Island with a low-interest loan if there's no other option."

My mouth drops open.

"You have the money for an entire wastewater treatment plant, not to mention surveying for wells, or whatever it's called."

He nods.

Well, shit!

"How rich are you, Parisi? Because I'm guessing you're not just a millionaire real estate mogul."

"You'd be guessing correctly."

I swallow, but my mouth has gone dry as beach sand.

"You're a b . . . a b . . ." I can't even say it. It's too ridiculous.

"A billionaire," he finishes helpfully.

Except now I want to faint on the spot. There's a billionaire standing in front of me in Dave's Beach Bar. In the kitchen. On Murray Island.

My knees feel wobbly, and I swear I'm lightheaded. My brain is getting around to the truly astonishing truth. I made out with a billionaire on the beach. I yelled at a billionaire in a hotel room. I served pizza to a billionaire in my house.

I had sex with a billionaire!

Even more intimately, I've shared kisses with a billionaire. About a billion spectacular, hot kisses.

I think I stopped breathing because I'm dizzy.

"Lindsey!" He says my name and darts forward to grab me before I sink to the greasy, linoleum floor.

With his arms around me, I take in deep breaths. Although my eyes are closed and I wish I could crawl away to be by myself, preferably lying down, after a few moments, I start to feel better.

One more deep breath and I open my eyes. I'm looking directly into his.

Golden-brown *billionaire* eyes!

"You can let go of me now," I say. "I'm fine." Although I'm not.

He is so far out of my league in every way possible, I realize he had to have been playing around with me the whole time. Not that I thought a rich real estate developer was truly interested in a future with Lindsey Cooper, shopgirl. And now fry cook. But I could pretend we were equally attracted and equally turned on. I was going to fool myself for as long as he stayed on the island.

Now I know there's just no way. He lives in a rarefied world. He's practically a different species.

As he's slowly releasing me, Andy comes in. He stops dead when he sees that Marcus is touching me. I step away quickly, smoothing the front of my canvas apron.

"It's OK," I say. "Mr. Parisi was just leaving. He shouldn't be in here anyway."

But Marcus doesn't look like he's going to go quietly. He snatches the order slip fluttering in Andy's fingers.

"Out," he tells the teenager in a voice that allows for no argument.

Andy doesn't even look at me for permission or guidance or confirmation. He shrugs and leaves.

"Give me that." I hold out my hand.

"Come get it," Marcus says, and a ghost of a grin touches his mouth.

Without hesitation, knowing surprise is the best attack, I lunge for it. My fingers touch the paper before he yanks it away, holding it above my head.

"This is not a joke," I tell him, fuming. "It's a business. Give me the damn order and get out of the kitchen."

"Stop making me out to be a bad guy," he says. "Promise you'll cool down and come with me to the fort on Sunday."

"I said I'd go with you," I remind him.

"Will you cool down, too?" he asks again, still holding the order slip out of my reach.

I count to five. "Yes!" It comes out like a hiss, the opposite of cool.

"And you'll let me kiss you before I leave?"

"What? No!"

He laughs softly and hands me the paper. "You can't blame a guy for trying. But you better get on those hamburgers and fries before you lose customers."

While I'm seeing red, Marcus leaves. Yes, I watch his sexy ass, but recalling it's a billionaire's ass, I stop gawking and turn to the stove.

Oh, I'll cool down all right. I'll be an ice princess by Sunday.

$♥$♥$♥$

A few days later, I finally ride on his motorcycle. He tricked me into it, saying I'd promised to go with him, which meant on *his* ride, not in my Jeep.

After he hands me his helmet and makes sure I have on a warm sweatshirt despite the sunny Sunday, we're off. As expected, I have to hold onto him tightly, snuggle up against his back, lean when he leans, and put myself entirely in his hands.

The short ride to the south end of the island is exhilarating. My hair is flying out from under the helmet, and sometimes I have my eyes closed, but it's fun. I don't think I'd like being on a motorcycle on a real street or a highway though. Here, on Murray Island, it's perfect.

We arrive at Fort Mercy, and the only thing to stop us from driving up to it is . . . nothing. We drive from the road to gravel to a sandy trail to grass. Up close, the fort is a hulking structure. A two-story stone and wood stronghold built when there was still a Massachusetts Bay Colony, by settlers for protection against the French, although eventually, it was turned against the British. Long since abandoned except, as I once told Marcus, by the island's teens.

It's a short walk to the place where a door used to be. Not really dark inside because there are window holes, too, yet it's cool and dim inside. The stone room has no floor apart from the packed sand.

When we enter, with me looking for low-hanging cobwebs, I remember the stone staircase in one corner and the thick wooden ceiling through which more sunshine is filtering through. It's also the floor for the room above, and it has planks missing.

"Do you want to go up?" he asks.

I realize he means because of my phobia, not because I think it's dangerous.

"Yes, indoors, I'm fine." Mostly, unless I go out on a crazy-high balcony or a rooftop. I think of the thirty-sixth floor of the Ritz-Carlton. I was more than fine in his bed at that height. "Especially just one floor up," I add.

Regardless, when he reaches for my hand, I let him take it because, frankly, I am a little nervous. Crossing the packed-sand floor, it's hard not to miss the alcohol bottles and other trash, such as chip bags and candy wrappers. None of which makes Fort Mercy look very impressive as a landmark or an historical site.

When we have to step over a fallen post, I pray it didn't support the entire room above us.

"I'll go first," he says. "Lucky these are granite steps. Wooden ones would have long since fallen apart."

He has to let go of my hand since the steps narrowly hug one wall. Obviously, there's no railing. In thirteen steps, a stupidly suspicious number that I think the builders would have known better than to use even centuries earlier, we have reached the upper level. There's more trash. The sunlight shows through gaps in the walls and the roof. In fact, the roof is more gap than wood.

But it's *my* island's fort, so I say, "It's not that bad."

Marcus laughs. "It's not that good, either. Why would anyone come here to look at the view when they can go to the lighthouse?"

It's a fair question, and I've already made sure to have my answer ready. I looked up Fort Mercy the night before. Strangely, there's not much info on the internet. Or maybe not that strange, after all, now that I look at the place. It has most likely been forgotten by the rest of the world.

"An older fort was built here in the mid to late sixteen hundreds, but this one was built in 1705, as the most northern US *island* fort, although obviously those on the coast of Maine are farther north."

He just stares at me. I clear my throat, proceeding like a tour guide, except I'm not sure I should move from this spot in case I go through the old oak planks.

"There aren't that many forts still standing from this period. But all those that are have been turned into historical sites."

"Really?"

"Yup." At least I think so. I hope so.

Feeling more confident, I take a few steps toward the wall facing the south. When a board bends under my sneaker, I step quickly to the left and tread lightly until I reach what might have been a window. At the very least, an oil skin would have been hung over the gaping opening during the winters.

"Be careful where you step," I say, "but come look at the view." I keep my eyes firmly on the horizon. If I give in to the insane urge to look down at the beach below, then my irrational fear will tell me I'll tumble out the window.

Marcus suddenly takes my hand again.

"Going to push me out?" I joke.

"No, more like I'm anchoring you in place."

I'm grateful he understands the phobia.

"It is a nice view," he says. "But as I said, nothing near as remarkable as from the lighthouse, although it's the southern tip, showing more of the ocean and the Mass coastline. Anything else about this place that makes it more than a pile of old timber?"

Sighing, I fear I've lost. "I don't suppose the tale of the fort's second commander would stir you." It's my ace in the hole if Marcus does care about my feelings.

"I don't know. Tell me."

I explain what my father told me, about a young lieutenant tasked with commanding a small group of rowdy soldiers, who mutinied because of the severe conditions during the winter. They tried to kill him before abandoning their post and setting out in boats for the mainland, taking all the provisions with them.

"They stranded him alone. Or so they thought. But at the other end of the island were natives. Given the area, they should be and maybe were Wampanoag, like those on

Nantucket and Martha's Vineyard. But for some reason, it's always been said they were Abenaki from New Hampshire."

"Said by whom?" Marcus asks me.

"My father," I mumble because otherwise he's going to think I'm nuts when I tell the rest. "The Abenaki trail connects the area around Ipswich, Massachusetts, to Maine, through the New Hampshire towns of Hampton, Rye, and Portsmouth. But *Abenaki* is a catch-all term for many tribes who spoke a common language, so they might have actually been Apikwahki or Kennebec."

"That's already more interesting than how old this place is."

Good. "The wretched commander without any provisions left the fort to scout the rest of the island and came upon the natives. Luckily, he didn't bring them a disease that killed them, as happened to the Abenaki on the mainland and to the Wampanoag on Nantucket. Instead, the daughter of the leader of this small offshoot fell in love with our hero."

"That's an interesting story," Marcus says.

I can tell he doesn't believe it. I know it's true because I've seen the records, and more importantly because I'm part of the lineage. "We have a cemetery on the island. Have you seen it?"

"It was on your placemat map. The Founders' Burial Ground. I went by on my motorcycle, but I didn't stop in."

"It's worth a look if you like history. The first burials there were in 1707, according to the church records. But the oldest headstones are from 1741."

"Now I *am* impressed," he says. "Is the cemetery still active?"

"The dead pretty much stay in the ground or in their urns," I respond, straight-faced.

He pauses, then laughs. "That's funny. But seriously, if and when people die, hopefully not tourists on holiday, are they allowed to be buried here on the island or is the cemetery closed to interments?"

"You are a weirdly inquisitive guy. Are you thinking of developing the cemetery, too? Maybe a café and gift shop?"

"No, I promise—" He breaks off when he realizes I'm teasing.

"In answer to your question," I explain, "yes, it's all very normal and still open for business, so to speak. The only restriction is on where someone can be laid to rest. Meaning, not amongst the founders' original section."

"Got it."

"Except for my family, of course," I add, feeling a blush of pride. "In fact, my grandmother was buried there two years ago."

Marcus's eyes open wide. "Seriously? Your family are among the founders?"

I can't help smiling. "My dad can trace us back to the young commander, Lieutenant William *Cooper*, who stayed alive by marrying . . . ," I trail off.

"Go on," he urges.

"Her name was, as best I can say it, *Kwai Megeso*, meaning Friendly Eagle. Or that may have been her father's name. The records are confusing. Anyway, the commander called her "Kay." When the army came to find him, or rescue him, he said he wanted to stay on the island. Her headstone says she died about seventeen years later."

"Again, officially impressed," Marcus says.

I add what my mother told me. "The lieutenant's headstone states he died the day after. My mom said it must have been from a broken heart." Our gazes lock. "My dad says that's nonsense. Must have been an illness. Maybe a fever. In any case, they had two sons."

Marcus nods silently. Then he asks, "You said he was the second commander? What happened to the first?"

I shrug. "No story there. He left after his tour of duty. And before you ask, I don't know what happened to the soldiers who went AWOL. But Lieutenant Cooper was sent new troops, and he commanded the fort until he died."

Marcus nods. "Did the commander actually live here?"

I'm not too sure of many more details, but since he seems to be coming around to my way of thinking, I gloss over my lack of specifics and say, "He might have. Right below our feet."

He looks around the room, and I wonder if he's picturing Fort Mercy all fixed up. Hopefully *not* with a gift shop, but who knows?

Finally, he looks at me again. "Why's it called Murray Island?"

"Legend states it's a bastardization of the Abenaki's word for red, *mekwi*, to do with a red moon that hung over the island. Beyond that, I don't know."

Marcus nods. Then without warning, he slides his hands into my hair and kisses me. His firm lips press mine open, and I tilt my head, enjoying the feeling of his tongue caressing mine.

As usual, I melt in seconds, with my body heating up to scorching and a breath-stealing pulsation starting its insistent beat between my legs. My knees are ready to give out when I recall that we're not on the best of terms. I'm standing here at Fort Mercy because he told the town to tear it down.

Pulling back, sucking in a ragged breath, I look up at him. "You didn't ask that time whether you could kiss me."

His eyes flash. "I didn't. Sorry."

"*Are* you sorry?" I persist.

"Not really."

If I give in easily, then I'm just a big marshmallow doormat. So, I don't tell him how much I enjoyed it or that I'm not sorry, either.

"Let's go," I say.

Marcus doesn't try to stop me as I make my way cautiously to the stairs. "Now I know I'm with island royalty," he quips, "I'll start behaving better."

I guess he means starting *after* that panty-dampening kiss.

"Ha-ha," I return. He's teasing me, but I'm glad he has stopped thinking of tearing down the fort. Then I hear a

cracking sound and turn while Marcus is still lunging to the side. A plank has caved in where his foot was.

"You OK?" I ask.

"Nearly ended up going downstairs the quick way."

What can I say? Relieved he's not hurt, I wish the fort hadn't chosen that moment to deteriorate further. Going outside without further mishap, we walk around the building to the ocean side. The water laps against the *cliff*, as we call it, a four-foot-high bluff to the golden sand below.

There's the other issue, though, since I care about what happens to the island. "If not here, where could the new wastewater treatment plant go?"

"Not my call," Marcus says. "Not yet, anyway. I assume that's the board's decision, or whoever gives them a sizable loan. But I've contacted an engineer who'll do a thorough surveillance. What if this turned out to be the only place?"

Since he's being reasonable, I try to be the same.

"We'll cross that bridge," I say. I hope he doesn't have an ulterior motive for no longer pushing to raze the fort because I could start to like him again.

Except that he's a billionaire who'll break my heart as surely as the death of Friendly Eagle broke Lieutenant William Cooper's.

22

Marcus

The one downside to traveling by motorbike is Lindsey and I can't talk while we're riding. The upside is that her arms are around me. The fort didn't go at all as I'd expected. I thought she'd see what a trash heap it has become and agree it would be for the best if it were torn down.

Not only does she remain convinced it's worth saving, she believes I agree. I don't. Not because it tried to kill me, but because it's just an ugly eyesore. There isn't even a single cannon left. The first floor could as easily be an old latrine as a fort. It smells more like one, anyway.

I drive us straight to the Founders Cemetery and let her show me around. It's intriguing and humbling to read the headstones. I hope any souls who might still be hanging around approve of the changes I want to make to the island.

After the cemetery, I take her home.

"Do you want to get a bite to eat?"

I can see she's reluctant even before she shakes her head.

"I'm tired," she says. "Have you noticed how everything has picked up the past few days. Even the store bell rings more than once an hour."

"That's good." But for once, I don't want to talk about business or developing a property.

"Thanks for spending your one afternoon off with me."

"You're welcome. I'm glad you see the worth in keeping Fort Mercy."

Internally, I wince at her assumption, but she continues, "Besides, I might not have Sundays off soon. If we get super busy, then Dave's Beach Bar stays open seven nights. It's silly not to."

She's right, but there are other ways. "Don't you think Dave should hire a second crew to give you and Melinda a break?"

Lindsey leans against her front door.

"Benny will be working with us soon, thanks to you, and when Dave is fit again, he can do my job. I won't always go directly from Whatnots to Dave's."

She's still an immovable force, and now she crosses her arms, looking even less inviting. I wish she'd let me in and go back to the way things were before I stupidly said I thought the town should tear down the fort. And before she found out I was a billionaire, which freaked her out.

While I still think the fort should go, I could've been more diplomatic. Even if half the story is hogwash, William Cooper is Lindsey's distant relation. I try to imagine how she feels, living this close to where a great-great-great-great-however-many grandfathers ago was mutinied against and then found love and started her line of Coopers.

But I cannot imagine that rundown, ramshackle place can ever be an asset to the island.

In any case, right now, the sole island asset I want to focus on is her.

"I could rub your neck," I offer. "Or your feet."

"No, thank you. I couldn't relax knowing a billionaire was rubbing my feet. Don't you hire someone to do that for you?"

I can't help sighing. "Do you want me to hire someone to rub your feet? Would that make you feel better?"

Uncrossing her arms, she scowls. "Good night, Marcus."

With that, she turns to go inside.

"Lindsey," I say.

"What?" she asks without turning.

"I'm still the same guy who made you climax twice in a row. Or was it three times?"

That makes her whirl around to face me. "I know you're still the same guy, but I didn't know that guy was you, did I?"

"What? I think I need that in writing."

She snorts. "*You* knew that you were an incredibly, obscenely wealthy guy, but I didn't. You're the same as far as *you're* concerned, but not to me."

"Come on," I say. "You knew I had money."

"Having money and being a billionaire are two different things."

"I suppose. But why can't you like the obscenely wealthy guy the way you liked the guy who was merely rich?"

"Because there's no way we can be on an equal footing. You can't take me seriously as the owner of Whatnots."

"You're wrong. I admire you as a business owner."

She puts her hands on her hips. "So much that you don't even want to buy my business."

What?! "You don't want to sell me your store. Do you?"

"Of course not. But even if I did, you don't want to buy it. Why don't you want Whatnots? Your lack of interest is offensive."

Maybe I'm the one who is super tired because I cannot follow her logic. Besides, she's wrong.

"Of course I want your store."

"*Ah-ha!*" she exclaims. "You knew I'd be a hold-out till the bitter end, until *after* you'd bought everyone else's business or invested in them making the islanders beholden to you. And you've been trying to seduce me into a false sense of trust. And then—*bam!*—you'll make me an offer I can't refuse."

She's starting to sound like me. And in some instances, I've done that, minus the seduction part.

"I've never seduced anyone into selling me anything," I protest. "I'm simply saying that any smart business person would want Whatnots, at least for the location if nothing else. It's the closest commercial property to the ferry and to the parking lot. It could have tourist info, scooter and bike rentals. You could get a commission from all the businesses you refer visitors to."

"That's not legal," she snaps.

"Yes, it is. They'd pay you to have their menus or store cards on your counter. Or you could have coupons with your store name so when tourists use them at those other places, the business owners know they came from you. And you could put their shops and restaurants on the next printing of your map."

She silently mulls over my words, unfolds her arms, and even takes a step away from her door. I move closer.

"You sure you don't want to get a meal together. I've never been to the chicken and chips place that re-opened yesterday for the summer."

I'm pretty sure Robin said she dined there, and everything, including the pickles, were lightly fried to perfection and really tasty. It's a shame they can only do business about twelve weeks a year.

Lindsey wrinkles her nose, but I can see she's considering. I don't pump my fist yet. But she's tempted. It's not like I'm trying to get back into her bed. Wait . . . yes, I am. But that's not the sole reason I want to spend time with her.

There are a billion reasons. And if I kiss her again, she might agree.

I start to reach for her, and she darts away to her front door again.

"I knew it."

"Knew what?"

"Nothing," she says darkly. "And don't go telling my fellow islanders I'm going to charge them to tell visitors about their businesses. It's a terrible idea."

With that, she thrusts the door open, goes inside, and slams it shut.

$♥$♥$♥$

It's time to call in reinforcements. I'll have Robin here in a day or two. Then I think about something special I'd like her to bring when she comes, which means it will take longer. But it'll be worth the wait.

Meanwhile, I meet with an engineer, a well-digger, and a surveyor. I'm not going behind the town moderator and the board's collective backs. I spoke to Mr. Gardner, and he was happy that I've started the process. On my dime! I'm sure he thinks the more the town stays out of it, the less they will have to pay.

The results are in a few days later. The well can be dug no problem. The wastewater treatment plant has to be replaced, not retrofitted. The fort is still the best site for the new plant. In a few days, I have more than one proposal, which I submit to Mr. Gardner. Ultimately, it's not my call, unless he does nothing or cannot secure a loan. In which case, I'll be forced to make the loans to get these two vital projects started. And they will be loans, not gifts.

I have no doubt that Murray Island overall is a sound investment. Even with it just as it is, visitors have come in the past, and my hotel is a third full already. But I'm not a sucker, willing to revamp the island's entire infrastructure in hopes I'll see a return when I'm ninety.

When Robin arrives, she'll do what she always does, listens thoughtfully and gives me sound advice. It doesn't hurt that she went to law school and has a good head for business. I'm lucky to have her in my organization. In a platonic way, my capable assistant is the main woman in my life apart from my mother and sister.

And now there's Lindsey, too. But she's steering clear of me. Naturally, I'm hesitant to approach again because she's going to find out soon enough that Fort Mercy is most likely going to be torn down. Not that a stiff wind wouldn't take it out anyway.

Besides, she doesn't have a lot of time between closing the shop and going to Dave's, although he's now back in his kitchen and eagerly awaiting Benny. Getting a full-time chef on short notice, one who is willing to relocate, isn't as easy as I'd anticipated.

Again, Robin is on that, offering a sweet deal to the right person.

But after a few days, I can't wait any longer to see Lindsey. Every day that I don't has felt like wasted time while I'm on the island. When I enter her shop, she has customers. She sounds happy telling them about how to find Jeannette's studio. I notice a shelf of pottery, too.

When she looks past the two women in front of the counter and spies me, her smile disappears. Her obvious annoyance is visible, causing the ladies in sunhats to swivel to see who has caused it. Clearly, they're expecting a monster.

I turn on the Parisi charm, taught to me by my father.

"Greetings and welcome to Murray Island, a place where dreams come true."

One of them laughs, the other eyes me up and down despite being old enough to be my mother. "I thought that was Fantasy Island from that old TV show," she says.

"I think it's the Disney World slogan," her friend says.

"*Vacation* dreams," I add, just to clarify. Although Lindsey has made some other hot and heavy dreams come true, too.

"Are you the welcoming committee?" the first one asks.

"No, you're already talking to her, the island's resident font of helpful information," I explain. "I'm merely a fellow visitor who has fallen in love."

They both turn back to Lindsey whose cheeks are growing red.

"He means with the island," she says.

I'm rendered speechless from having so blithely spoken about love. My mouth ran away before my brain could smack on a filter. She's mostly right, I suppose. Yet after saying the words, which came right from my heart, I accept that I'm falling for her. She's suspicious and prickly, but also warm and fun and generous. Basically, she's the best part of every woman I've ever known, all wrapped up in one gorgeous package.

She also happens to be glaring at me. *Damn!*

"I'm sure you both will love it here, too," Lindsey tells them. "I'm sure Marcus will hold the door and then escort you to the hotel. He owns it," she adds, trying to get rid of me.

But I have no intention of leaving. I may be kind, but I'm no one's lackey. In any case, I hold the door and go outside with them.

"Is it your first time on Murray Island?" I ask.

"Yes," they both say.

"I do own The Lady of the Light, but I have done nothing by way of renovations yet. Please let Jim, the manager, know that I said you'll be telling him of any issues you encounter during your stay. In return, I'll give you each a complimentary weekend, all expenses paid next year. You can come back and see how we've improved."

They look as if I just offered them the moon. "Don't hold back on what you find unsatisfactory," I tell them. "I apologize for not being able to accompany you now, but I hope to run into you later. Don't forget to speak with Jim."

I give them each my business card, and they stroll away, dragging small suitcases on wheels behind them. We desperately need a way to transport luggage from the ferry to all the lodgings. I'm thinking about that as I open the door again, bearding the dragon in her den.

"Really?" she says. "Don't you have anything better to do?"

"Like playing bellhop to hotel guests?"

She rolls her eyes.

Shaking my head, I approach the counter. "You can't get rid of me that easily."

"Why?" she demands, tallying her register. "What do you want?"

"Are you closing?"

"You know I am."

I do, in fact. "Then I'm not bothering you."

"Oh, you're bothering me, all right."

She isn't going to make this easy.

"I've found someone to dig the new well, and even given some proposals to the town for that and for the treatment plant. How about dropping the shit-on-Marcus attitude for now. Until I do something else that pisses you off. Which I'm sure I will. It seems I can't help it."

Finally, Lindsey looks like she might relent and stop sending dirty looks my way. I approach closer.

"My mother would be surprised that you don't adore her only son. She thinks I'm perfect."

Lindsey rolls her eyes. "No one can be as perfect as you seem."

Do I understand that she thinks I look perfect? Or that I behave perfectly? Or that I give her the perfect orgasms? "Then you do have the hots for me."

"Get over yourself, Parisi."

"I would rather get over you, my body on top of yours. What's upstairs?"

"Are you insane?"

Ignoring her hesitation, I add, "I'm about to get a crack chef for The Clamdigger, and I've already paid the mason to fix the motel pool."

"Why are you telling me this?"

"To make you happy, so you'll let me kiss you again."

Finally, at long last, she smiles. It's not a huge one, but I'll take it as a win. She puts the cash register money in a zippered bag, and I follow her into the backroom.

"Hey," she warns. "I'm putting this in the safe. If you want to be helpful, you can turn the sign to closed and lock the door."

"Yes, ma'am." I believe she's thawing quite rapidly.

"Just turn the catch and pull the door closed *behind* you from the outside."

Guess not. She's still frosty and wants me gone. I do her bidding, but I lock it from the inside and turn the small blue sign to red.

It's quiet except for the gentle whirring of the old paddle fan, still hanging slightly askew and with a broken blade.

When I meet her at the backroom doorway, she purses her lips.

"You don't follow orders well."

"Some orders, I do, Lindsey. If you ask me nicely, in that breathy voice you have when I'm kissing my way down your soft skin to your—"

"Did you turn the sign?"

"About that? I think you ought to put out a colorful flag when you're open."

She crosses her arms. "I suggested that to my dad."

"And?"

"He never got around to it."

"But you think it's a good idea, don't you?"

Lindsey nods grudgingly.

"I'll order you one," I say.

She bristles. "That won't give you a stake in Whatnots."

"How about if I fix your paddle fan, too? It looks shabby for the premiere gateway retail shop on the island. Not for a stake in the island, but for a kiss."

She shrugs. I step forward, which brings me directly in front of her. Gently taking hold of her wrists, I uncross her arms, one then the other. And I draw her soft curves against my body. I nearly sigh with relief. Holding her feels right.

"I'm not evil," I promise. "I'm not seducing you for your store. I just really like you."

She sighs and slides her hands up the front of my shirt.

"But you are seducing me, right?"

"God, I hope so." I glide my hands down her back and over her curvy ass, before squeezing gently. Finally, I take her lips beneath mine, demanding access to her sweet mouth.

When she opens for me, I suck her tongue gently. I can't help groaning as her light floral fragrance rises up from her skin, and I'm already hard as a flagpole.

After a few minutes, I lift my head. "Am I succeeding?"

"*Hm?*" she asks, looking dazed and aroused with her lips red and a little swollen from the long kiss.

"In seducing you?"

She nods, going up on tiptoe to kiss me again, but I'm ready for more. By her pearled nipples, which I can feel through both our shirts, I think she is, too.

"Is there a place we can take this seduction?"

"*Hm-mm.* Follow me."

Yes, ma'am. Wild horses couldn't drag me away.

23

Lindsey

I'm eager for his touch. Beyond ready to get naked with him, I've missed everything about Marcus since I closed my front door in his face. He follows me up the narrow stairs through the open hatch in the ceiling. For as long as I can remember, we've kept a single bed up here. My dad snoozed in between the rush times from ferry traffic in the old days when the island was busier. My mother rested here when she was helping in the store while pregnant with me. And if both my parents were working, when I was a toddler, I was sent up the stairs for a nap.

Basically, it's a partly finished attic, with a blue-curtained window under each peak, front and rear. The bed is in the middle of the room because it's the only place you can stand up without hitting your head. Around the edges are stored items, the shop's Christmas decorations that I didn't bother with last year, an old welcome mat, and a torn awning that I've lost the framing for.

We ignore the cluttered, dingy surroundings. I collapse onto the dusty bedcover, trying not to think of mice or spiders, and drag Marcus down on top of me.

For a moment, I wonder if the old bed will hold us, and then I don't think of anything but getting naked. Ultimately, without getting up, we manage to shed our clothes. And before I can think straight, Marcus is kissing a tantalizing trail down my body, stopping at my breasts to tease my nipples. Just as I arch, offering my breasts to him more easily, he changes pace and kisses a path along my ribcage and down further.

Stopping again, this time to nibble on my left hip bone, he splays his hand across my other hip. My heart is pounding. I'm sure he can hear it. And my juices are flowing with anticipation of where his mouth is heading.

His tongue traces a searing zigzag up to my belly button and then down to the trimmed hair over my mound. I lift my head and watch, which makes it that much sexier when he glances up at me from under his dark lashes right as he settles an open-mouthed kiss on my lady parts.

I shudder with pleasure. When his tongue flicks across my clit, a gush of desire soaks me, and the low moan I hear is my own. I don't know how this man makes me go from not being sure I like him to wanting him desperately in seconds. But he does. My legs are trembling. I'm a heartbeat away from climaxing, but I need him inside me when I do.

"Still not on anything," I mumble by way of invitation for him to put on a condom, which I hope is in his wallet, and sheath himself deep inside me.

His hands grip my butt cheeks and tilt my pelvis up for easier access to his talented mouth. Taking control, not letting me dictate when it's time to fill me with his cock, Marcus uses the flat of his tongue to send me quickly over the edge into a full-body-shaking climax.

I'm still breathing hard and shaking when he rises up and over me, lowering himself on top of my tingling body. I stare up into his burnished-brown eyes, feeling every hard muscle of Marcus's body plastered to mine. We're in sync and so sizzling hot together, I can almost smell smoke. I wrap my legs around his hips.

"Lindsey," he says, and nothing more, just a caress that happens to be my name before he lowers his mouth to mine. I can taste myself on his lips and tongue.

A shiver dances through me when he nibbles my throat. Taking in a big breath I sigh, thrilled to be under him again.

That's when I realize I can actually smell the unmistakable aroma of something on fire. And it's not from the flames of our passion. It's not us, after all. But it could be any second.

"Marcus," I hiss, going from relaxed to panic mode.

At the same time, he is already bolting upright, saying one word, "Smoke!"

That's when I hear the alarm going off below. There's one up here, too, but not enough smoke has reached it to set it off.

My head is spinning in disbelief while I leap from the bed and start putting on my clothes. If I'm going to roast like a marshmallow, I intend to do it wearing my favorite cotton T and my cute shorts.

Marcus is doing the same, but I realize I can hear a whooshing, sort of engine-throttling sound, along with loud popping noises. It's the fire gaining strength. And every movie I've ever seen with a building in flames comes to mind.

"Hurry," he says, going to the open hatch at the top of the stairs and looking down. "Nope."

I can see smoke rising from it. "Window," I say, finding it hard to believe that downstairs, right underneath us, there's a blaze. That's my family's shop. It's not possible. But my bare feet tell me the truth as the heat from below is coming up through the attic floor.

Marcus opens the window, and voices rise from outside as a gathering crowd sees movement. We both have our phones, but there's no need to call the island's volunteer fire department. I can tell it's already arrived by the siren.

"They're putting up a ladder," Marcus says.

"I don't like heights," I remind him. "Not even a bunkbed. I don't climb trees. And definitely not ladders."

He shoots me an encouraging grin that's also a bit of a frown, because this is a serious situation.

"Lindsey, we're not climbing up. We're climbing *down*." Then he turns back to the window and answers a question, "Two of us, both up here."

Great! Now the whole island will know I'm banging the real estate developer who's buying us all out. I'll never hear the end of it. The distinct voice of Mike, our fire chief, and retired banker, comes back to us.

"Push out the screen," he orders, and Marcus does it instantly with a hard shove.

Just then, I hear an explosion, and the floorboards that have been growing hotter shake slightly.

"Shit," Marcus says. He grabs my arm and shoves me onto the window sill.

I can't help my panicked scream, and for a moment, I'm fighting him.

"Lindsey," he says. "Hurry."

My hesitation could cost Marcus his life, and that's the only reason I swing my legs out and get a footing on the ladder while he keeps hold of my shoulders. Shaking like a wet dog, I waste precious moments turning since I'm facing the wrong way. I shriek again when strong arms engulf me from behind, and Marcus releases me.

Sam, who's one of our volunteer firefighters, starts the descent, taking me with him. Looking up at Marcus's concerned face framed by the blue sky behind him, I don't let myself consider that I'm on the outside of a building, two floors up.

I hear another loud sound, and the building shakes with waves of heat. I know by the debris flying around me as Sam clings to the ladder while shielding my body, that the shop ceiling—meaning the attic floor, has caved in. At least partially.

I'm still looking up. To my horror, Marcus disappears for a second, causing my third and loudest scream in five minutes. But he's back a moment later, swinging himself onto the ladder at the same time as my feet touch good old *terra firma.*

Sam shoves me away from the building while remaining to hold the ladder securely for Marcus. Stan Brie, of all people, catches me, dragging me back and away from the heat and flames shooting out the front windows, which have already blown out.

I keep my eyes on the man high up on the ladder. It's surreal to see flames shoot out the attic window, right where I was mere seconds earlier, backlighting him in garish orange. And then Marcus does some stuntman trick I've only seen in movies. With his hands, now wrapped in blue fabric—*it's my mother's homemade curtains!*—and his ankles positioned on the outer edges of the ladder, he slides down. His khakis protect his calves, the only part of his legs touching the metal ladder.

Landing with a thump in the midst of Sam and Mike, Marcus is hauled back as the front wall of my grandfather's store collapses inward, taking the ladder with it.

I stare at the sight that my brain cannot comprehend. Despite our firefighters spraying water, Whatnots and Such is literally going up in flames. I do a mental inventory of any truly important things in there and feel a catch in my throat. There are some irreplaceable photos hanging on the wall behind the counter. Or there were. And my purse is in there, with my wallet that holds photos of my parents.

I can't think of anything else that will bother me except . . . losing the entire beloved, familiar building. I know every inch of it. Every floorboard that creaks. Every shelf that my grandfather put up by hand and that my father reinforced. The counters that my mother used to wax, and the walls that I've helped paint countless times.

Marcus approaches me, looks at my shocked face, and draws me away from Stan, enveloping me in his strong arms. He saved our lives. I can't speak, but I release a few loud sobs before I get myself under control.

His big hand rubs up and down my back.

"Let me take you home," he says.

Instantly, a whoosh of gratitude goes through me that this disaster happened to the store and not to my house. I'm also thankful that Max wasn't alive because he often came to work with me. He would've been trapped downstairs.

Tears stream down my cheeks again at the thought of my dog. I rub my face against Marcus's smoky shirt and then step away from him.

The clinic's nurse, who works with Jenny, appears in front of me. Ruth is holding an oxygen tank, which she sets down. "Did you inhale much smoke?"

"No."

Without hesitating, she looks in my eyes, I guess checking my pupils. "Headache, nausea?"

"No, neither."

She whips the stethoscope from around her neck and puts it to my chest. "I just want to hear how fast your heart's beating."

I stay still, but I recall how my heartrate was elevated even before the fire.

"Fast" she says, "but I don't see any signs of carbon monoxide poisoning."

She takes a step toward Marcus, but he holds up his hand. "I promise you I'm fine, too."

"I bet you have some bruises on your legs from your ladder slide," she says.

He shrugs, keeping his gaze on me. "I'm fine," he says again.

"You OK?" Mel asks.

I hadn't even seen her standing nearby. Her expression possibly matches how I feel, which is stunned.

"I'm alive," I say lightly.

"You are, Lindsey. And that's the most important thing."

I gulp down another sob. "I know."

She puts her arm around my waist, and we watch as the firemen put out the last of the flames. Some framing is left at the back, but other than that, Whatnots is a pile of smoking, charred ruins.

What the fuck!

"This is going to hit you hard in a little while," she says. "Go home and put your feet up. Do you want me to walk you over there?"

I glance at Marcus. I'm going to lean on his strength since he offered.

"No, it's OK."

Mel nods, looking from him to me. "I'll call you later." Then she asks, "Wait, do you still have a phone?"

"Yup. Back pocket." I pat it, nearly confessing how I made sure it was there when I got dressed. Luckily, I recall I'm surrounded by townspeople within hearing distance, hanging on my every word.

Not only has my emergency captivated them, but escaping out of the window with Marcus, for everyone to see, has given everyone a front-row seat to my sex life.

I turn in a slow circle, seeing so many friends. "Thank you, everyone, for your concern." I look at Sam in his gear and nearly start crying again when he comes over and hugs me.

"Thanks," I say, my throat clogging with emotion.

Marcus shakes his hand, followed by Mike's. Then I let him lead me away from the inconceivable scene of destruction. It's a ten-minute walk to my house. He doesn't suggest taking his bike. And my Jeep is parked in my driveway since I didn't take it to work.

As we approach my front door in silence, I realize my house key and car key are on the ring with all my others in the shop.

Perhaps guessing, Marcus asks, "Can we get in?"

I nod and go to a regular looking rock. It's not a hide-a-key fake rock. It's real, and the spare house key is mashed into the sandy soil beneath.

I hand it to him, noticing my hand is shaking when I do.

He opens my front door, and more than ever, I wish Max would rush out with his big paws and doggy breath, bouncing around me with love and joy.

"I held him when he died," I say, going past Marcus into my house. I think he knows who I mean.

Everything is the same at home as when I left this morning, but it feels different. Like it knows the other part of my life just got obliterated. I eye the fireplace, thinking of its destructive power and turn away. In the kitchen, Marcus is already heating up water in the kettle.

Silently, with nothing to say, I sit on the kitchen stool at the counter and watch. He barely lets the water get hot before he pours a few inches into two mugs and then tops it with a healthy pour of the brandy he'd left here before. He slides a cup my way.

I've never had warm brandy in water, but I blow on it and take a sip. It's comforting, as he knew it would be.

Twice, once with Dave's heart attack and today, I've found out this man is good in an emergency. After I've downed half the potion, I am feeling more stable.

Marcus can probably see the improvement because he asks me a practical question.

"I'm assuming you have full insurance."

"Yes, although I don't know too much about it. Dad set that up." Then I wince. "I better call my parents."

He nods. "There's no rush though. Although if somehow, they hear about the fire, they'll want to know you're fine."

Speaking of fine, I look at him, straight in those golden, tawny-brown eyes of his.

"Everyone's worried about me, Parisi, but you were up there longer." His shirt has a tear in it, over his stomach, and his pants are worse for the experience. But he's not sooty or burned. "Are you really OK?"

"Yup." He leans his hips against the counter and drinks some brandy.

"You scared me when you disappeared for a second," I tell him.

"Scared myself," he admits. "The floor gave way under the bed, and where I was standing became a tilted ledge."

The terror hits me all over again, especially when he adds, "It was like looking into the pit of hell, or what I imagine it might be, but less intense. Also, no demons or pitchforks."

He's telling the truth but making light of it.

"Did you slide toward the hole?" My voice is high with tension.

He nods. "Got closer than I wanted, and then I grabbed at the window sill and the curtains to haul myself up. The fixture came away from the wall, and I realized I needed the fabric because I was going to use the ladder like a pole. Once I slid them off the rod, I climbed out."

"You cut it pretty close," I say. "If the wall had caved in while you were on the ladder . . ."

"It would've been BBQ Parisi, for sure."

My eyes widen. I want to cry but also to laugh because he's being calmly nonchalant. Setting my cup down, I get off the stool and go around the counter, then I can slide my arms around his waist.

"Thank you. And I'm glad you're safe."

He sets his cup down, and I feel him rest his chin on the top of my head. We stay this way for a few minutes. I don't know how long.

"I'd like to stay with you tonight," he says.

When I stiffen, he adds, "No sex, just . . . in case you freak out at one in the morning."

"I won't," I say.

"You might."

"Yeah, I might."

"Or we could stay at the hotel," he offers.

"Nah. It's better to be home. I'll dig up the insurance papers and treat you to another pizza for getting me out of the attic."

"I'll get dinner," he says. "Why don't you call your folks first and then call the insurance company while I let you have a minute to breathe. I'll go get my toothbrush and pick up dinner."

"Marcus," I begin, but I'm not sure what more I want to say.

"It's OK," he says. "I'll sleep on the sofa."

I shake my head. "It's not that."

"What then?"

I shrug. He confuses me. He's like the mythical knight in shining armor, but also, he brings emotional upheaval that I'm not prepared for.

"Before I call my parents, I'll find the insurance folder," I say because I cannot tell him that he confuses me in every way except for how much I want him.

After he leaves, I go to the cardboard box in my parents' closet, hoping it's in the box of important papers. *Good thing it wasn't in the shop safe,* I think, quickly locating what I'm looking for. Then I call my parents.

Despite thinking I'm calm and stable, as soon as my mom answers, I start to cry again. It's hard to get the words out. I don't feel guilty exactly, but as the messenger, I do feel responsible.

I can hear it in my mom and then my dad's voice, that this is beyond unexpected. They're frightened for me, even though it's over. To my surprise, and it's weird I didn't think of it, they say they'll be here shortly. That's another clue that this is a big deal, a life-changing event.

When I hang up, I'm glad Marcus is returning soon. He is quickly becoming my rock as well as my friend.

And there's no doubt in my mind he won't be sleeping on the sofa tonight.

24

Lindsey

Marcus is standing beside me when the ferry deposits my parents on the dock two days later. I run in for big hugs, and then they shake his hand. I told them on the phone who he is, a reliable friend.

He stayed that first night. No sex, just as he said, which turned him into Saint Marcus in my eyes. The following day, I sent him back to his hotel. He had work to do, and I . . . I had a lot to think about. Like what I was going to do with the rest of my life. Now another day later, it seems forever ago that he and I were in the store's attic.

"You've beaten the insurance assessor here," I tell my parents. "Some guy is coming tomorrow. They also want a report from the fire department. Mike will see us later today to tell us if they discovered any cause yesterday."

We turn, all four of us, and look across the parking lot to where Whatnots and Such is no longer smoking but is still a sad sight.

"Oh my," my mother says, and we walk toward the charred remains. My dad is carrying a suitcase in each hand, but Marcus offers to take them both. Dad relinquishes one, my mother's mauve-colored bag. Knowing Mom, it's most likely heavier than his.

Soon, though, the men set the bags down again. There's not anything much to look at except burned lumber and unrecognizable blackened lumps.

"I wonder if Jeannette's pottery will be intact," I say.

"Why is Jeannette's pottery in our store?" my dad asks.

"So I could sell it," I explain, glancing at Marcus. He winks at me reassuringly. I hope the insurance will cover what I owe her for the seven pieces I was displaying. She shouldn't lose out.

"Good idea," Mom says, as if it's still a viable possibility.

"Have you been able to pick through it?" Dad asks. "The safe is probably OK."

"Wasn't much in it," I explain. "And no, Sam told me yesterday to stay clear for another day in case there were any hotspots.

My father makes a face. Even though he's wearing sneakers, he lifts the tape and goes under.

"Careful, Nate," my mother says. "What if your shoes melt?"

He ignores her and climbs over some debris. Much of it has been shoveled aside yesterday by the volunteer firefighters.

"Mike will see us whenever you're ready," I say. Dad ignores me, too. I realize he's taking stock of something that's been there his whole life. I know what he's feeling. Disbelief, and the ridiculous notion he can make it all go back to being the way it was by sheer willpower.

"It looks much smaller," Mom says.

Marcus remains silent. I wonder if he feels awkward, like a stranger at a funeral.

Eventually, my father comes back to us. "Let's go see, Mike."

His voice sounds thick with emotion, and I send a worried glance to my mother. She pats his shoulder.

"I'll take your bags to your home," Marcus offers.

"Where's the Jeep?" my dad asks.

"My keys were in the shop when it burned. If we sift through that mess, we might find them eventually."

My father rolls his eyes. "Lindsey, there's a magnetic spare key holder under the Jeep's back bumper."

How did I not know that? If I couldn't find my key ring when I finally started poking through the pile, then I was going to call Chrysler for a new key.

"I'll handle it," Marcus says. "Back bumper, and I know where the house key is."

He picks up the suitcases. "I'll park the Jeep back in the same spot. Good to meet you both. Sorry it's under these circumstances."

My dad nods, and my mother says, "Thank you." I fight the urge to kiss his cheek.

"Thanks," I say.

As Marcus walks away, Mom says to me, "I wonder why he knows where our house key is."

Feeling like I'm sixteen years old, I cringe, hoping Marcus didn't hear her. But she'll have much more time to embarrass me later when we have dinner at The Clamdigger. I already told him we'd eat with him.

$♥$♥$♥$

It's busy, which shouldn't surprise me. Marcus hired a Boston marketing company to put out ads before he opened the motel, and nearly every day, a dribble of visitors have disembarked the ferry. They're coming for the "pristine, uncrowded beaches," and the "sanctuary of stillness," as the company he hired styled our modest island.

"That's pretty good," my dad commends him over baked cod and garlic mashed potatoes.

We'll be serving this at Dave's soon, and they'll be dining on fancier fare here, like grilled salmon and asparagus.

"It's true," Marcus says. "And this may be the last summer they get to enjoy the island for cut-rate prices."

My mom and I exchange a look. His words make me feel a little queasy, like we're going to lose something intangible but priceless.

"I don't think Murray Island should become another Nantucket," I say. "I want people to be able to come here without having to go into debt."

"There will be moderately priced accommodations available and great food at all price points," he says cheerfully.

I've learned this about Marcus—he loves planning for a brighter future. He can imagine more clearly than most of us can see what's in front of our noses.

"I can't believe Whatnots isn't going to be part of whatever comes next," I say.

"Why won't it?" Marcus asks. Then he looks at my parents. "The insurance adjuster is a formality. After he or she sees what's left tomorrow, you'll be reimbursed and able to start rebuilding." Then he speaks to me. "I know you'll miss this summer, but no reason the store can't be back up by winter."

I shrug. I've been thinking I might be done with my old life, but I haven't told him that yet because I'm not sure. More than that, I'd have to have a long talk with my parents first.

"Did your fire chief have any insight into what caused the fire?"

"Paddle fan," my dad says before I can. "Old wiring."

Marcus shoots me a questioning look. When I heard what Mike had to say, I certainly wondered if I hadn't done some damage practically hanging off the thing that day Marcus spooked me. Now he's furrowing his brow.

"It wasn't anyone's fault," I tell him just in case he thinks he is somehow to blame.

Of course, I also haven't told my parents what Marcus and I were doing in the attic. They think he was helping me get some stock from upstairs. Although by the way my mom raised an eyebrow when I said that, I think she might have guessed.

My cheeks grow red simply thinking about it now, and I dip my head to push my mashed potatoes around with my fork.

This entire day is surreal, right down to eating with my parents and a billionaire at the same table. I let the conversation flow around me while I eat and think. My parents tell Marcus more about the island and confirm my tale of our ancestor, Lieutenant Cooper. I'm glad Marcus is willing to preserve the fort and am about to ask him where he thinks the wastewater treatment plant will go, when Dad launches into a story about the time he manned the lighthouse in an actual hurricane. As he fills Marcus in on storms and shipwrecks, it occurs to me he ought to jot down notes and let Mom write a book of Murray Island's history.

My father has a hard laugh over the map when Marcus says they'd make superior placemats.

"Now that they're all gone," my father says, "I guess the map will become a collector's item."

I'm still trying to picture what other job I could do, either on the island or off it, because I don't intend to wait tables as my main career, but I hear his last comment.

"Hate to break it to you, Dad, but I have two boxes of the laminated horrors at home."

Marcus laughs along with my parents. During the meal, he keeps giving me a funny look. I think it's because I'm so quiet. But before my parents commit to rebuilding Whatnots, I need to make a decision. I've never had such a clean slate before. A frighteningly open future!

My parents definitely know that Marcus and I are involved in some way because first chance they get, they say they're going to take a walk and turn in early after the long day. When I say I'm ready to go home, too, they go all nuts.

"Don't rush on our account. We certainly know the way," my mom says.

"Why don't you two take a beach walk or go for an ice cream cone?" my dad says.

I'm embarrassed that they're being pushy. Marcus, however, immediately asks me, "Will you let me buy you some ice cream?"

Feeling like I'm in high school, I nod. And that settles it. I see the back of my parents as they walk along Spire Street toward our house. I've already moved out of the master bedroom for them. It would be too weird otherwise.

As we head to Island Scoop, he says, "You're thoughtful today."

"Yup. Hey, do you know if insurance money has to be used to rebuild what was originally insured?"

"Don't you want to rebuild Whatnots?"

I shrug. "I honestly don't know. I took online classes for a business degree, which I didn't need for the store. On the other hand, without the family store, and without my family, why am I still here?"

"That's a lot of questioning," he says. Then we fall silent as we enter the shop.

After that, we walk toward the beach.

"Nice to have a warm spell," I say, holding my cone in one hand and taking off my sandals with the other.

"Your parents are good people," he says. "Do they know you might not want to run the shop? Do they want you to move in with them in New Hampshire? Or are you thinking if you left the island, you'd go somewhere else?"

"That's a lot of questioning," I repeat back to him. The sand is cool between my toes, and I keep my thoughts to myself for a few minutes while I finish my dessert. But then, he takes my hand. We ate fairly early, and the sun is only now going down. We are, I believe, having a romantic beach stroll.

"Are you going to give me any answers?" he asks finally.

"Not at this moment," I say. He accepts that with a small shrug.

"Did I tell you I spoke with Kathy about bringing over some of my horses during the summer for visitors to ride or take lessons? Then I'd take them home each winter."

I think about the logistics of horses on the ferry. But I'm struck by his words. "*Each* winter? That sounds like you plan on being part of Murray Island for a while."

"It does sound that way. The longer I'm here, the more I like it. The island has a lot to recommend it."

He stops walking, takes my hand, and draws me close.

"We were reconnecting when the fire broke out," he reminds me.

Reconnecting must be a euphemism for torrid sex. My brain dances swiftly from us on the bed to the escape from the attic to the store being gone. It keeps happening that way, a weird sideways skittering of thoughts leading me to the fact that Whatnots is gone.

I shake my head, looking down at the sand between us. Our bare toes are inches apart. Just like that, I distract myself from the shop being gone.

"You don't want to continue with me?" he asks.

His words bring my attention and my gaze up to his face. I wasn't shaking my head about that, but maybe I should be.

"Everything was weird enough with you sort of settling in here, but not really. I mean, as a business owner, but not a local, not someone who intends to live here. And you've been behaving like my friend, almost a boyfriend, but that's impossible, given our circumstances."

He frowns slightly. "Which are what exactly? Besides you being a single woman and me being a single man?"

"A single billionaire who no doubt has an empire to run. You were engaged recently," I add.

"Not that recently. And so what?"

"Meaning you have a huge life out there that I don't know anything about. Not to be cliché, but I will anyway.

241

The world is your oyster. Me and Murray Island are more like shrimp or mussels."

He laughs, which I didn't expect. Finally, he says, "If we were off the island and we met—"

"That would never happen. I am one billion percent sure, even if I was on the mainland, we wouldn't move in the same circles, hardly on the same planets."

"Another cliché," he says.

"Because they're true. I searched your fiancée on the Internet," I confess, slightly embarrassed by snooping.

"*Ex*-fiancée," he interjects.

"She was *not* an online college grad or a shopkeeper. And I bet if I searched your entire long history of dating—"

"Probably not as long as you think," he interjects.

"Short or long, I would find gorgeous women, models, social butterflies, other super rich people."

"You have me all figured out, do you, Miss Cooper?"

"Just saying what's true. Your women are smooth."

"What?"

"Smooth. They have glossy hair, perfect skin, the finest clothing. Do you know why I wear my hair long?"

"Because it's pretty this way," he hazards a guess.

"Because of its waviness. If I tried to cut it into a short, sleek style, it would become a poofy nest on my head. But even long, it's never going to be smooth. I'm never going to be smooth like a billionaire's woman should be."

He heaves a sigh. "You were saying how it was all weird before. And now apparently, it's all even weirder?"

"Yup. It was almost providential, how we were doing it upstairs while my livelihood was going up in flames."

He winces. "I feel terrible about the paddle fan. I startled you and made you jump and tug on it."

"I knew you were going to say that. But it wasn't your fault. I've been hanging things off it for years, just like my dad did, and some stuff was likely too heavy and tugged a wire. Anyway, occasionally, I've turned it on and it hasn't even worked. I had to turn it on and off a few times to make it spin. Clearly, something was happening, and I should have had it checked out."

"Making the ceiling rock above it didn't help."

I know he's teasing since we didn't actually get that far. The best I can dredge up is a small exhalation of a laugh. The unknown future is keeping my mind anxious and busy, constantly trying to solve an unsolvable riddle, like a PC caught in a loop. Tumultuous change has been going on, even before the fire. Since Dave's heart attack, nothing has been as it was. To be precise, ever since Marcus set foot in my store – that's when everything started changing.

I have to tell him.

"I'm having an existential crisis. Once Whatnots is rebuilt, then I'll feel obligated to run it. Forever."

He takes my chin between his fingers and holds me still, then he leans down and kisses me. I drop my sandals, freeing my arms to slide around his hard, warm torso.

The kiss sparks my body, jumpstarting my heartbeat as his kisses always do. But it also gives me comfort, reminding me that Whatnots is, after all, just a store. And I'm alive with plenty of opportunities ahead of me. Life, this moment on the beach, a spectacular kiss, I need to be grateful for all of it.

"What was that for?" I ask when we're walking once again, nearly at the point where the path leads through the newly blooming beach roses to my house. The vivid pink buds have barely unfurled but already the scent is heady.

"Because I've never stood on the sand with a woman who said 'existential crisis' before, and I had to kiss the mouth that spoke those words."

I can't help laughing. Marcus has a nice way of looking at things. But he's also an agent of change, whether he's kicking my pulse into high gear or doing some billionaire deal. Right now, I crave some boring steadiness.

I don't want him walking me up to my front door with my parents inside, maybe looking out.

"You should walk back along the beach. It's faster to get to the hotel than on the street."

He looks past me toward the house.

"OK." He backs up a few feet from me. "By the way, in answer to your question, since your family owned the building outright and didn't have a mortgage, you don't have to answer to anyone about what you do with the insurance money. You and your folks can decide."

"Thanks." More choices. More decisions. That's all I need.

With a lift of his hand, he turns away. I watch him for a little while, and then I go home.

I can't help noticing that Marcus couldn't say I was wrong about the two of us. Different worlds and all that. The divide caused by wealth applies as much to the twenty-first century as it ever did.

He could literally fly away tomorrow to anywhere in the world, and I would have to be content with waiting for him to return to check on his properties here.

"Disengage, Mr. Spock," I mutter before entering my front door.

25

Marcus

I'm trying to give Lindsey some space. Yesterday, she made it clear she has a lot on her mind, thinking about her place on the island—or off it—and also her future. Having been driven to succeed and clearly seeing my path for my entire adult life, I cannot imagine what she's going through.

In any case, until her parents leave, we're not going to resume the one thing we do so effortlessly and without conflict. Instead, I'm suddenly spending more time using my head with a brain rather than my other head, which has been focused on Lindsey Cooper's body.

Getting my order in just before the kitchen closes at Macey's Grill, I'm eating breakfast for lunch with my laptop open, reading stock market news. When I finish, I read the briefs my staff sends me on my company's projects around the country and around the world. Parisi is doing well everywhere except for one development in the city of Iris, in my own home state, being blocked by an asshole.

Unfortunately, it's a personal vendetta. And Dan Bradley, the aforementioned asshole, is not only blocking an affordable new golf course and an over-fifty-five community of homes, he's also a congressman who's spreading vicious rumors while he's at it.

Yes, I slept with his girlfriend. She was out at a bar with her friends and up for some fun. I didn't know she was in a relationship. Would it have made a difference to my horny self at the time? I like to think it would. I'll never know except I don't normally sleep with other men's girlfriends or wives.

And we were in college, Dan. Get over it!

After I send another email to an Iris official who is asking for the same damn builder's license number, I'm relieved to get a text from Robin. She'll be here within the hour. In other welcome news, she has hired a chef for The Clamdigger. He'll be on tomorrow's ferry. More of those changes that constitute Lindsey's existential crisis are on the horizon.

So much for not thinking about her. I keep replaying what she said on the beach. There was the ridiculous part about my needing "smooth" women. Obviously, I know what she means because I've dated some sleek ladies, perhaps with their make-up a little too flawless, their hair too chic, and their clothing always in style. I even got engaged to one of them.

But just because Lindsey's not wearing designer shorts, she's no less desirable. Her hair falls in natural waves when she lets it out of its ponytail. No, it's not smooth; it's untamed. For some reason, she doesn't know she has the sexiest hair on the planet.

Since making a fortune, I've never thought about what I cannot have because I can pretty much have what I want. But Lindsey makes it seem like I shouldn't want her and, worse, can't have her.

Naturally, to me, that's a challenge, one I'm willing to take on and win.

$♥$♥$♥$

My smallest yacht, The Rough Rider, is now tied up near the island's ferry terminal. It had to dock there amongst the commercial fishing vessels and the ferry because I haven't built a marina yet. Any other private berths and slips around the island are too small. Even when I've built a state-of-the art dock, I doubt Murray Island will ever end up with facilities for the superyachts, like my 213-foot, Italian-designed Bliss. That's the one I want to be on if I ever take Lindsey cruising the world.

But The Rough Rider is my favorite. Only fifty-eight feet, a John Hacker-designed antique, I fell in love with her on sight. Everything on board the 1926 yacht has been renovated, refurbished, or redesigned to my specifications. A combination of original mahogany, teak, and white pine, everything that should gleam does, and everywhere I want elegance and comfort, it's there.

I can't wait to give Lindsey a tour. Since I can't dazzle her in the air with my flying skills, I told Robin to bring this unique vessel from a by-gone era, so we can enjoy a day on the ocean. Maybe with Lindsey's parents, too, if they stick around long enough.

Robin appears from inside the saloon as I board. It's nice to see a familiar face. She's wearing a tailored, coral-colored dress that contrasts with her dark skin. And despite the strappy sandals and sunglasses, I know she's in work-mode by the earbuds, her intent expression, and the staccato way she's speaking to whomever's on the other end of the call.

When she sees me, she smiles in greeting before saying, "Get it done, and let me know the final cost." Then she hangs up and yanks the earbuds, sliding them into a holder dangling around her neck.

"Hey, boss."

"Enjoy the trip?" I ask.

"Oh, man! Yes, I did. Feel free to make The Rough Rider my Christmas bonus this year."

"Not gonna happen," I say. "Are you eager to get on land, or shall we talk here?"

We decide to take a beach walk, letting Robin stretch her legs as she's been on board the yacht for three days. With a wave to the captain, we disembark and leave the harbor area. I don't have to point out the unmistakable remains of Whatnots and Such, having already filled her in on Lindsey and the fire.

"I remember the store from last year," Robin says as we pass. "I went in to buy water and some other stuff. Lindsey was very helpful. It's awful to see it gone."

"No one was hurt, and that's the main thing." When I think of that day, I recall the last time I touched Lindsey's bare skin and watched her climax. It's starting to seem like a fantasy that couldn't possibly have happened.

We stroll across the street and past Island Scoop, take a left and then a right to go to the beach on the other side of the island.

"Lindsey might not want to run the shop anymore," I say because it's a relief to have someone who's a fellow outsider whom I can talk to.

Robin stays silent a moment, looking at the ocean.

"So, you have the hots for this woman?" she asks.

"What? Why would you assume that?" I sound like a flustered teenager.

Robin cheesy big grin shows her perfect, white teeth. "Oh bossman, you wouldn't have me bring your cozy jewel of a yacht over for just anyone. You're crushing on this girl hard." She laughs at her own juvenile humor.

"You think you're really smart," I say, which isn't much of a comeback. Besides, she's right. "Can't a guy try to impress a girl with his smallest yacht?"

"If it doesn't work, we'll bring in something bigger," she says. "How's the heart-attack cook?"

I've been keeping her apprised of everything.

"Dave is back in his kitchen, but as soon as the new chef gets here, we'll be shuffling people around. Tell me that's happening."

"Yes, very soon. I think you'll like him. I *know* you'll love his food. He was looking for a change."

"Did you send him the photos of the houses for sale?" I ask.

"All settled. He made a choice. I've already bought it, and the locals had some people who could fix up anything that needed fixing."

"Sam?" I guess.

"Yes, that was his name, and two others. We were lucky there were some properties available," she adds. "But you always say, everyone has a price."

"I'm not sure about that anymore," I say, thinking of Lindsey. "Besides, the houses were already on the market. We didn't have to strong-arm anyone into selling. Glad he liked one. We want to keep him happy."

She gives me a long look. "You're really into this place, aren't you? Or is it just Lindsey you're into?"

"Shut up," I say. "For an assistant, you're mouthy and fresh."

"But I get results, don't I, boss?"

We've reached Dave's Beach Bar, and he's already put a couple tables outside. The overall look is not good. The tables are warped and the chairs are mismatched, and there aren't any umbrellas. I don't even know if anyone, namely Lindsey, will come out and serve us outside. We sit anyway.

"This could be very nice," Robin says.

"It will be. You made great suggestions," I tell her, giving praise where it's due. "Everything here has been easy. Well, apart from a man having a medical emergency where there's no real hospital and me nearly getting fried to a crisp in a fire. Other than that, everything, as I said, has gone smoothly. And the people—"

"Have they been easy, too?"

I chuckle, thinking of the town meeting and Stan Brie. To a lesser extent, I think of Lindsey's first reaction to realizing who I was.

"Nothing I couldn't handle. Eventually, everyone comes around to seeing things my way."

"The Parisi way," she teases.

"The right way," I say. "All this place needed was someone with forward thinking."

"Not exactly, boss. It needed someone with deep pockets. Or a fairy godmother."

"I don't look my best in sparkles, but I get your point and you're right. The islanders would have done the same things I'm doing if they had the money."

I glance toward Dave's. A cold beer would be welcome.

"Now that you've got the islanders towing your line, boss, what about Congressman Bradley?"

Robin brings up the biggest pain in the ass I've ever encountered and puts a dark cloud directly over my head. I guess Dan was more into his college girlfriend than she was into him, and he's making me the reason they broke up. I think I did him a favor. But all these years later, twelve to be exact, he's out for blood. And he's finally in a position to throw his weight around.

But I've got power, too, and right is on my side.

"How are the Iris officials this week?" I ask.

"Which ones?" she returns. "I think I've spoken to about twenty-five from every department in the city in the past few days. And they're still asking for clarification on specs that were signed off on already."

I'm fuming, and Dan knows it. All the contractors suddenly want money up front because they've heard that, personally, I'm "not good" for it. That Parisi, Inc. isn't a safe bet to extend credit to.

"Whenever I think we're proceeding," Robin continues, "another problem arises. The delays are costing us thousands a day.

And Dan is behind all of it. I didn't know at first, but he couldn't handle quiet, anonymous revenge. Like an egomaniac, he sent me a text, hinting strongly he'd bleed me dry before I built anywhere in his district again.

After all, he's a congressman.

But I'm a billionaire, and that's a lot of bleeding. He won't win, and what he's doing is hurting our state.

"Robin, you're a go-getter and one of the most capable people I've ever met."

She nods. "And?"

"Why is that ass-hat still up in my grill? I'm sick of it. I want this matter taken care of. Find out who I have to bribe to get this jealous jackass off my back?"

"I know you don't mean that," she says. "Anyway, it would be better to pay a hitman. Far more permanent."

I laugh. "Not my style. I'd rather fight fire with fire. We could dig up dirt on Bradley and spread it around, ruin his reputation. If he's busy protecting his own ass, he'll have less time to interfere with my development."

"Or you could do the ultimate double whammy and sleep with his woman. Again!" Thinking herself funny, she laughs.

I had to tell Robin why the costly vendetta was going on. For some reason, her calling it a "double whammy" strikes me as amusing. I start to laugh, too, imagining Dan's fury if he were to discover by poking the bear, namely me, I poked right back in a different way.

"Sure. Why not?" I say, all pretend swagger, which Robin sees right through. "Text me a photo of his current woman?" I fold my arms and look out at the ocean. "As long as she's smooth, I'm in."

"Smooth?" she questions.

"Nothing." Robin knows I'm kidding. I go silent, thinking of Lindsey and how I can't picture myself with anyone else. Maybe never again. It sends a razor-sharp slice of worry slashing through me. Her life is in flux right now, and she might consider that I bring chaos while she tries to sort it out. I should focus on business.

"Let's take this bastard down any way we can—short of a hitman—because I'm putting in that damn golf course and housing development, no matter what. And Congressman Dan is not going to stop me, even if I have to play dirty as it gets. Basically, I'm this close," I hold my fingers together, "to wanting to obliterate him entirely. I'll buy his damn congressional seat if I have to."

We lapse into silence because it's so lovely here. Well, not right on this particular six square yards of asphalt. But the amazing view in front of us makes it hard to think of the trouble I'm facing on the mainland.

"Do you think we'll ever get a drink here?" Robin asks.

I stand and turn to see a group of six twenty-somethings enter the main door. Lindsey will have her hands full.

"Is The Rough Rider fully stocked?"

"As ordered, boss."

"Let's go back there, then. Are you staying in our new hotel with lumpy mattresses and even lumpier pillows or on the yacht?"

"I should be asking you that," Robin says.

Sometimes, I'm too good to my staff. I could move onto the yacht, with its macked out stateroom. "You're right, but I'm fine with my set-up right now."

"You mean being whisper-close to Lindsey Cooper?" she teases as we head back to the harbor. "The dock isn't that much farther away."

"When are you leaving?" I ask, because she can be too much in my private life.

Her hearty laughter peals out again. A great assistant is almost like a business partner, advisor, mother hen, and wife—all rolled into one.

"Never mind, I'll tell *you* when," I say. "Four days of helping me, which includes some downtime for you on the beach, and then you're gone."

"I come on a yacht, but I leave on a ferry. Such is my life," Robin says dramatically.

"And you love it."

"It beats sitting behind a desk all day, boss. Meanwhile, I'll get to work on easing our company out of Congressman Bradley's sights. I have a few ideas."

"I had a feeling you would. But no hitmen."

26

Lindsey

When I go back inside Dave's, I'm shaken. Rattled enough, in fact, I screw up the order of the three guys and three girls who come in ten seconds after me. I don't forget any of their meals, but I do put the wrong burger down in front of each of them. So unlike me because I usually have an elephant's memory. Often, too good, making me a class-A ruminator.

Apologizing profusely, I hope Mel's liquid-heaven cocktails will make up for it.

In the end, when everyone gets the right hamburger or cheeseburger cooked as requested, I have a second to think about what I overheard. Mel had said there was a couple on the "veranda," her teasing term for the patch of blacktop with two tables on it, which she can see from the bar window.

When I went outside, I heard Marcus speaking. Before I rounded the poorly placed dumpster, I heard a woman's voice, and then . . . I froze and listened.

I'm not proud of myself for doing that. But the more I heard, the less I wanted to let my presence be known. Marcus sounded like a world-class jerk, scheming, and demanding he get his way. No matter whom he hurt.

When I heard him laugh about sleeping with some congressman's wife, I learned what it means to have your insides grow cold. Plus, he's a repeat offender! It sounded as though he'd targeted this man's wife before.

Right now, with my heart hurting, I understand that I have carelessly and stupidly fallen in love with him. With a man who has a far more complex life on the mainland than I could imagine. I'd fought even going as far as liking him, when all I thought was that he might be a player, a tourist who wanted a fling. Then I relaxed and trusted him, deciding to enjoy the happiness I felt in his company. Until I found out he was a billionaire developer.

I should have stuck to my better instincts. Why did I let him get close again? If I look at things clearly, instead of through the rosy haze of desire, I can conclude I lost the shop because of Marcus. If I'd stayed downstairs where I should have been, I'd have seen sparks or smoke and used the fire extinguisher. Instead, I was stupidly climaxing, all gaga and googly eyed, still believing he might possibly see a future with someone he was screwing in a dusty attic.

Finished with the loud, but jovial group of six for the moment, at least until they need more drinks or dessert, I walk through the dark bar and peer out the window.

"Was that Marcus with someone?" Mel asks me over the soft hum of voices and the sportscast on the TV in the corner. "Didn't they want to order?"

"No," I say. "Just a place to sit and talk." I don't want to tell her that I didn't go over to ask them.

Every doubt I've had about Marcus comes flooding back like a fast tide. He was so quick to start throwing his money around. He wants Murray Island to be a certain way, and he's not letting anyone stop him.

On the other hand, he agreed not to tear down the fort.

Because he likes me. Or at least, he likes having sex with me. Beyond that, I don't know. If he would sleep with a woman simply to irritate her husband, then he would certainly play around with me if it helped him further his interests.

I'm ruminating and driving myself crazy. But the kisses were sizzling.

Maybe I truly am too sheltered and don't have enough experience to know whether he can kiss me like that and not really give a damn. All I do know is I didn't like the man I heard talking outside.

Belatedly, I realize the woman must be his assistant, Robin.

I wonder why she's here. I couldn't see her from my cowardly place behind the dumpster, but they were thick as thieves. She's the one who first scouted our island for him. It sounds like she'll do anything to help him succeed.

I feel sick. What if Robin arranges for him to sleep with the congressman's wife? *Again*, as she put it.

Not my business. Nor is it my problem if he spreads dirt around about the man or . . . What else did he say? *Obliterate* him.

$♥$♥$♥$

"Well, will you look at that yacht?" my dad says when we walk into town the next day. It's weird not having the shop to open. Weirder still hanging out with my parents each day until I go to work at Dave's.

"Wow!" my mom exclaims.

"Jeez," I mutter when I see what's tied off at the slip on the other side of the dock where the ferry will come in shortly. A large white hull rises out of the water, with a

forest-green stripe at the waterline. From the deck upward, it's all varnished, natural wood that has weathered to a rich, warm burnished tone. There are obviously cabins below deck with five portholes showing, and a spacious deckhouse with windows all around running across two-thirds of the deck. Another flight up is a bridge with radar on top of that.

And on the bow in a pink bikini is a stunning black woman, whom I recognize from the previous year when she came into Whatnots and also strolled around town for a few days. And with her is Marcus!

He's not in a bikini, of course, nor even in swim trunks, but he does look relaxed, leaning against a low railing. It seems a cavalier and downright dangerous thing to do. He could go over backward into the water.

Robin, whose name I recall him mentioning, sits on a deck chair holding a bottle of what looks like orange juice. She's gesturing with it while talking.

Marcus appears captivated and taking in every word. Nodding, then he laughs. My stomach hurts. This is jealousy. Not because I think they're romantically involved, but because of their obvious relationship. The feeling sucks.

"Is that your friend Marcus?" my mom asks.

"Not my friend," I mutter under my breath, then say, "Yes, it's him."

Marcus Parisi, land developer and apparently ruler of the seas, as well.

"I wonder whose boat that is," she says.

"Yacht," my dad corrects her.

"No doubt, it's his," I say.

"But he came in an airplane," my mother points out.

"I guess his friend in the bathing suit brought it over. He's a billionaire, Mom. He can crook his finger and probably get a whole fleet to surround the island and take it over by force if he wanted." I speed up my step. "Let's eat."

Turning away is the best thing I can do. Let the two of them plot the ruin of a member of the U.S. Congress, as long as Marcus can make a fortune—*another* fortune, I mean—by building a golf course for his wealthy friends.

"Wouldn't you like to go over there and see it?" my mom asks.

"I would love a tour," my dad chimes in. "It's a beauty. An antique. I'd guess it's from the early thirties."

"Can we eat first?" I say, sounding like a child. "I'm starving."

"Afterward, then," my mother insists.

Fine. They can go over there without me after we've eaten. I don't see how I can be polite. At least, I doubt I can chit-chat without bringing up what I heard yesterday when I started my shift. Then what would happen? The veneer of civility would disappear damn quick.

By the time we're done with a leisurely breakfast and leave Macey's Grill with a banana and two apples, the ferry has docked. It hides Marcus's yacht from view, but my parents are determined to go take a look at it.

We wander down the gentle slope past the roped-off remains of the shop, which will be cleared away by week's end. But I don't go any farther than where we parked the Jeep. Dad had been sifting through the charred ruins the day before and found the safe intact as well as a few other things under the rubble that he'd salvaged. He'd used the Jeep to bring it all to the house before driving back here to meet Mom in the early evening.

"Aren't you coming with us?" Mom asks.

"No, you go on."

"Suit yourself," my father says like I'm the strangest creature he can imagine having for a daughter.

From this vantage point, I turn and look back at our shop, or the place where it should be. People start to disembark and move around me, going up the hill to the town center. Not a ton of visitors, but enough to spend a little money on ice cream, dining, and pottery, too, if they make it out that far.

I see some people dithering, looking lost. Whatnots and Such ought to be there to greet them. This is when I would step out of the store and give directions or answer questions. Usually, they'd come inside for sunscreen, water, or a candy bar.

A gush of emotion wells up in me. The corner just doesn't look right without the shop there.

"Excuse me," a man's voice says from behind.

I spin around, expecting Marcus. But it's an unfamiliar face. A man of medium height, a couple inches taller than I am, with ginger-colored hair and blue eyes. He has a suitcase in each hand, and a duffle bag over his shoulder. One serious tourist.

"Are you a tourist?" he asks. "Or do you live here?"

"Full-time islander," I say.

He looks relieved. "Can you direct me to The Clamdigger?"

I know immediately who he must be. "You're the new chef."

His face breaks out in a smile. "I am. How'd you know?"

"Lucky guess," I say. "We're all looking forward to your cooking."

"Great! I feel welcome already. I'm Jeff Burberry."

Now I can't help smiling. "Chef Jeff? Really?"

He shrugs. "I'm used to it."

"I'm sure you are. Sorry about that. I'm Lindsey Cooper." We don't shake hands because he hasn't set his cases down. "Are you sure you want to go to the restaurant and not to wherever you're staying?"

"I don't have the keys, but I know my new home is at twelve Dearmark Street."

I'm surprised. "I didn't know it had sold." The couple had put their house on the market last fall and left for the mainland. "There's a key under a brick beside the front step." Mel and I had made a chunk of change by cleaning it to sell, but that was over seven months ago.

"Wow! You're amazing," he says. "Is there a taxi?"

I don't laugh. I simply shake my head. "I can take you there. It's just up the hill and down the street. That's my Jeep."

"Wow!" he says again.

Next thing I know, he lets out a long, slow whistle. "What happened there?"

I sigh. "Believe it or not, that was my family's shop until recently." It seemed like a long time since the fire, but also as though it happened yesterday.

"I'm really sorry," he says, looking at me. "Are you going to rebuild?"

"Yes," I tell him. Because we decided as a family that we were, even though I'm no longer sure I'll stay to run it. Dad wants to make it "quainter and beachier" than it was and loves the idea of having Jeannette's pottery and other island wares for sale.

Chef Jeff's head is on a swivel, looking at the cobblestone streets, the buildings, the people, while I take a right, making sure to point out The Clamdigger as we drive by. We go south a couple blocks, and then another right. He's on the opposite side of the island to my house. I pull up in front of the cape style house, surprised to see it appears to have been spruced up recently.

"Let's see if the key is still here," I say. "Otherwise, I know where we can find your new employer."

"You know Marcus Parisi?"

Too well. "Yep."

Finding the right brick, I get the key and let us in. It's a tidy house on a pretty street, but I can't imagine coming here and not knowing anyone. That's one reason I'm scared to go to the mainland. I certainly don't want to depend on my parents for company. I suppose I could look up old friends who moved off the island or make new ones.

Mentally kicking the can of my future down the road to deal with later, I take note of the interior. Someone has waxed the floors since Mel and I were there. And new curtains have been put up. The furnishings are the same as the ones the previous owners left behind.

"You bought all the furniture, too?"

"I didn't buy any of it. Mr. Parisi paid for the house in exchange for my promising to stay for two seasons."

Made sense, and it was no skin off Marcus's wallet, I'm sure.

I notice that someone has thoughtfully left a bottle of red on the dining room table with a bowl of apples.

Predictably, Jeff heads for the kitchen.

"More wine in the fridge," he says. "A bottle of white and some champagne. That's dope. Parisi is a thoughtful guy."

He's full of thoughts, all right. Like sleeping with other men's women just to dig at them. But I'd bet Robin made all this happen.

"Pretty basic stove," Jeff says, "but I've been given free rein to get new equipment at The Clamdigger if there's anything that doesn't work for me."

"I'll leave you to get settled in," I say, heading for the door.

He hurries to catch me. "Thanks. I don't know what I would've done if I hadn't run into you. I might still be wandering around with my bags, wondering what the hell I'd gotten myself into."

"Glad to help."

My cellphone rings as I'm leaving. Pulling it out of my back pocket, with a jolt of surprise, I see that it's Marcus. I ignore it.

But I hate to leave Jeff if he needs help. Before I can offer, he says, "Can I take your number, seeing as how you're my lifeline?"

I laugh and give it to him. He texts me quickly so I have his number, too.

Then with due diligence, I add, "Mr. Parisi is staying at The Lady of the Light hotel. And his assistant, Robin, is on the island. I don't know where she's staying, but if you saw the yacht beside the ferry—"

"I did. It's a beauty."

"That belongs to Mr. Parisi, too. I'm sure you won't have any trouble meeting up with your employer."

"Thanks, Lindsey."

"The Clamdigger opens at five if you want to go take a peek at your new place."

And then I jump in the Jeep and . . . have absolutely nowhere I need to be. What a drag.

27

Marcus

When Lindsey doesn't pick up, I leave a friendly voicemail.

"I'm showing your parents around The Rough Rider. That's the name of my boat. Come over if you're close by. I guess, on Murray Island, no one is ever far. Hope to see you soon and introduce you to Robin, my right-hand."

It wasn't awkward at all, showing Nate and Barbara around the yacht and having Robin play hostess. They appreciated the historic beauty combined with the modern amenities. And then we had a cup of coffee before they left.

Nate intends to have one more look through the burned ruins before he lets it all be carted away. Lindsey's mother seems less nostalgic than either Lindsey or her father. She thinks the store will be much improved.

About an hour after they leave, I get a text.

Ran into your new chef and took him to his house. Nice guy.

And that's it. Impersonal. Unfriendly, at least toward me. And now, I'm wondering about the new chef.

"Hey," I say to Robin, who is seated opposite me in the saloon, typing on her laptop. She'd put on a cover-up over her bikini when the Coopers came aboard, and still manages to look professional. It may be her prescription glasses that give her a studious appearance, and the way she frowns slightly whenever she's at her computer. In any case, she presses a key and then looks up.

"Yes, boss?" she clips, as if I'm interrupting her.

"The chef has arrived. Lindsey has already taken him to his new home."

"Cool," she says. "I like how people work together here."

Something in my expression, makes her add, "He could have called me when he got here." She sips the iced coffee the steward made for her. "I told him to, in fact. Do you want me to zip over there and see how he's doing?"

"You can just call him," I say. "Tell him I'll meet him at the restaurant at four o'clock."

"You don't have to do that," she says. "The Boseman proposal just landed in my inbox. If you want to look it over, the time difference will be perfect for you to speak to the contractor at four. I'm happy to handle a meet and greet at The Clamdigger, and show Jeff around."

"Chef Jeff?" I say in disbelief, as it's the first time I've heard his name.

Robin shrugs. "He's probably heard that a billion times, boss."

"I won't say it to him, then. But I'll head over there myself." I want to check the man out. And I tell myself it's not because Lindsey said he was "nice," a tepid word that could mean anything.

But she *was* with him when she could have been here with me and her parents. More than that, it's been two days since I've seen her, and I'm feeling antsy. I want a moment alone before she starts her shift at Dave's, to find out if she's made any decisions about her future. Her parents seem to think she's going to be back behind the counter when they rebuild.

I text Lindsey back. *Where are you now?*

Receiving nothing in return, I rise. "Go through the proposal. Flag items that need my attention. I've got a few things to attend to." I don't know why I'm explaining myself to Robin. "I'll see you when I see you. If the proposal looks good, send them an email that I'll talk to Brad tomorrow. Why don't you come over to the restaurant tonight, too?"

Robin nods but says, "You're acting weirdly."

"How so?" I slide my phone into my pocket.

"You're not hyper-focused on work like you usually are. I planned on going through the proposal, of course, but normally, you would do it, too. You have time before four."

I level her with a look. "I trust you to evaluate the proposal. Do you trust yourself?"

She straightens. "Of course I do. I'm happy you trust me with a thirty-million-dollar project."

I smile at her. "That's why I chose a lawyer-slash-businesswoman as my assistant."

She smiles back. "Got it, boss. I'll come to the restaurant later. I hope you approve of Chef Jeff."

As long as he's gay, happily married, or older than Fort Mercy, I'll like him just fine. Otherwise, if he has an interest in Lindsey, we're going to have a problem.

$♥$♥$♥$

But I go straight to Lindsey's house first. The lack of her Jeep in the driveway doesn't stop me approaching the door because I saw it parked by the store. Her parents were combing through the store's rubble wearing masks and rubber boots. With a somber nod in their direction, I kept on walking.

JANE MCBAY

She doesn't answer. On a hunch, I turn around, cross the street and walk the short path through the thorny beach roses to the beach. The ugly shrubs have transformed into powerfully fragrant blooms that I can smell all over the island. I realize they are the base of Lindsey's floral perfume.

Sure enough, I see her sitting in the sand, staring at the Atlantic.

When I approach, she notices me out of the corner of her eye. Strangely, I don't receive a welcoming look. More like a scowl, making her appear like the Lindsey I first met, not the woman who has gone off like a rocket during heart-stopping sex and taken me with her. I drop to the sand nearby.

"Penny for your thoughts."

She snorts derisively. "Is that the best you can do, Parisi? How about a cool grand, at least?"

I might think she was being witty, but her tone is one of sheer annoyance.

"Are you mad at me?"

It looks like she's going to snap back with a resounding "Yes!" Instead, she takes a breath and looks away.

"Nope."

"Really? Because you seem kind of mad."

She is running her fingers through the sand, slowly, over and over, reminding me of how she sinks them into my hair when we're having sex.

Out of the blue, she asks, "How long are you staying?"

Now it makes sense. We were having a good time. Then shit happened. The days are passing, and she wants to protect herself. Because there is an end date on this summer, although I've been thinking more and more that we can continue past the time I'm supposed to leave.

"I'm not sure," I say, probably making her worry more. Quickly, I tell her what I've been thinking, hoping it makes her feel better. "When I do leave, there's no reason I can't fly back here."

266

Jumping up, she brushes the sand off her legs, bringing my gaze to the trim and shapely length of them.

"Don't come back on my account," she says. "I'm just trying to get a gauge on how long I have to put up with your presence on Murray Island. And on my beach! It seems as though you must have some important work to do somewhere else. Don't you?"

Her words are like a slap in the face. Dismissive, rude, not at all the Lindsey I've come to know. "What the hell is going on?" I ask.

Shaking her head, she walks past me toward her home.

I'm not in the habit of being a bully, but her snit has definitely rubbed me the wrong way. We've been through a lot. Not that long ago, she was thanking me for saving her life. And when we parted on this very beach two days before, she was hesitant, but not rude or belligerent.

Without thinking, I follow, reach out, and take hold of her arm. When she tries to pull away, I don't let go despite knowing a few well-placed kicks from her would put me in a world of pain.

Half turning, she's like an angry cat. "Handsssssss off," she hisses. "How dare you!"

Feeling like a neanderthal, I draw her backward until she's wedged against my chest and I'm looking over her shoulder at her upturned face. Because that puts our mouths close, she quickly faces forward, away from me, giving me the back of her lovely head, and nearly poking me in the eye with her high ponytail.

"Let me go," she says, while I breathe in her floral scent.

"Tell me why you're mad. At least do me the courtesy of explaining why I'm being subjected to the wrath of Lindsey Cooper."

"You don't deserve courtesy. You're making fun. I'm a joke to you. The entire island is small potatoes."

Where is this coming from? "Not true. To me, Murray Island is big potatoes. Russet, in fact."

She shrieks in frustration. I realize I need to take her seriously. Pronto. No matter how silly her accusations.

"If I let you go, will you stay and talk?" I ask.

"No. I'm not bargaining with you."

"Then no deal. We can stand here all day, and you'll miss your shift at Dave's."

"You're insane. And don't bother going to Dave's because I won't serve you."

"What in the hell!" I'm getting pissed off by how spiteful she sounds. "You work there, and I'm a stakeholder. In truth, you now work for me. You *have* to serve me."

"Please tell me I didn't hear you say what I just heard you say," she fumes. "And I don't have to serve you. There's a sign near the front door that says, 'We reserve the right to refuse service to anyone.' I'm reserving the right, so fuck off!"

"Then you're fired." I'm kidding, but I want to shake her up.

Unfortunately, Lindsey is one unshakable woman. "You can't fire me because I quit." She struggles in my grasp, but I still don't let her go.

"I knew you were an asshole," she rages. "I knew this whole Mr. Kind and Do-Gooder Billionaire was merely an act to get what you want. You've fooled people into selling. You're buying houses for your employees. Eventually, you're going to make it your own private island, aren't you? You'll have to bring a bigger plane next time. The second Lolita Express can't be a two-seater!"

Seriously? That's a low blow. The last time I had sex with someone under eighteen, I was underage myself.

"Lindsey, I didn't really mean you're fired. I lost my cool."

"Doubtful! You meant it when you said it because I don't want to *serve* you. And when someone thwarts your wishes, it's either the Parisi way or the highway—or in this case, the ferry. People will leave in droves once they realize what a snake they've let in."

Stunned by her vitriol, I finally open my fingers. Because she's been tugging hard, she staggers back and nearly sprawls in the sand. Normally, I'd be a gentleman and make a lunge to save her.

But not now. I watch Lindsey go down on one knee before she regains her balance and starts stalking away. I'm beginning to think she's batshit crazy!

"Don't follow me!" she says, backing up while still facing me. "And stop making nice with my parents on your stupid yacht. You don't need to impress them because you can't get anything from them. The shop is gone, we're not selling our house, and I'm no longer available."

With that, she turns and walks away.

Of course I consider following, but I don't. I'm not in the wrong here. I'm the same man whom she let between her legs before the fire, and I don't see why I'm suddenly an evil demon. Weirdly, I recall thinking it was sexy when she was laying down the law to Dave, being all bad-ass about him not going into his own bar. But it's not endearing when directed at me.

Whatever's gotten into her, she'll have to work it out. I'll leave her alone until then. And maybe hold out for an apology.

As I walk in the other direction so she can't possibly think I'm following her, I yank out my phone and text her. *You're not fired. Don't take this out on Dave by not showing up for work now that business is picking up.*

Then I add, *I promise I'll stay away.*

I don't expect a response, but about half a minute later, she texts back. *You better.*

I shake my head because that sounds like an "or else" statement, and I can't imagine what she can do to me that's worse than giving me the cold shoulder. The woman I was falling for to the point that I was ready to split my time between Murray Island and my home in North Carolina has gone missing.

Vanished like the sun during an angry, insult-spewing hurricane.

In place of the sweet and sensual island girl who I could easily see having a permanent place in my life, Lindsey morphed into an irrational hellcat who holds no appeal at all.

We've only known each other a few weeks, but I'm missing the previous incarnation of this woman the way I would someone I've known all my life.

This unfamiliar feeling really blows.

28

Lindsey

"We've decided to move back," my mother says the following day while we're sitting on the beach with coffee and muffins from Carl's bakery.

I literally drop my muffin, but swiftly retrieve it and blow off the sand sticking to the crumbly outside. As I process this absolutely unexpected statement, numerous emotions follow in swift succession, which is no surprise. I've been running on nothing but emotions since the shop burned down. Actually, since Dave collapsed, then the surprise that Marcus heads Parisi, Inc., then the fire, saving the fort, and back to Marcus again.

Even before all that, Max up and died on me.

Down, up, down. Never neutral. Maybe I should rethink my stance on edibles—too powerful—or maybe get a prescription for valium. Couldn't hurt to numb myself for a few months, could it?

My parents are coming back to Murray Island.

It'll be great to be three Coopers again.
I will be twenty-six next year and living with my parents.
Our house is not big enough for three adults.
There aren't any single guys I'm interested in on the island.
Maybe Chef Jeff?
Marcus is an asshole.
I had the best sex of my life.
With an asshole!

"Say something," my mother urges.

"Let her be, Babs," Dad says before sipping his coffee. "We've just blindsided our daughter."

"It's only us, coming home," my mother says.

"But why?" I ask, wishing that didn't sound whiny. "I mean, you've built a new life on the mainland, and you didn't say anything about not being happy when I visited during Dave's hospital stay."

"It's partly because we still feel like fish out of water," my mother says.

But Dad makes a sound like that's not the issue. "It's more because of Marcus Parisi," he says.

My stomach clenches. "Tell me."

"We like the fresh inspiration he's brought to the island. There'll be variety, more thriving businesses, new blood, a decent shower."

"You heard about a new well and everything that goes with it," I say without question.

"The Lady of the Light is going to be the way it was when we were kids," my mother says with enthusiasm, "except better. I wish you'd come onto Marcus's boat—"

"Yacht," my dad says.

"Whatever," she says. "He was explaining all his plans, and they're exciting."

"We want to be a part of it," my father adds. "And we're going to do the shop up better than ever."

I'm drawing patterns in the sand with my free hand, seeing how the grains always fall back into the small troughs I'm making. I nod at his words, not because I'm onboard with whatever Marcus is doing, but because I'm genuinely happy for my parents. They lived here their whole lives, and finally, they're hopeful the island's economy will go in the right direction.

"And you'll sell the house in New Hampshire?"

There's a long pause. "Unless you want it," my mom says.

My head snaps up. "Wait, are you kicking me out? And off the island?"

My mom puts her hand over mine while Dad laughs.

"So dramatic," he says. "We're giving you choices."

"And freedom," my mother adds. "You don't have to stay here and work in the store, nor do you have to live with us."

Tears well up, and a lump sticks in my throat. To wash it away, I retrieve my cup that I stuck in the sand and take a sip of now lukewarm coffee. When that doesn't work, I finish my muffin even though it chokes me.

"You don't have to make any decisions now," my mom says.

"If I want to stay," I begin.

"Then we'll live together for as long as you want," she says.

My father adds, "Or we can help you purchase another house if you want a place of your own."

Oof. Not expecting that, either. This generous offer sends another wave of emotion crashing over me. But they know the store hasn't made much profit the past few years. They know I haven't managed to sock away money for a rainy day. I'm no billionaire. Or millionaire. Or even thousandaire for that matter.

Jeez! Maybe I'm just a failure. Would I be able to make it on the mainland?

$♥$♥$♥$

I have to ruminate for a good long while after that discussion with my parents. But every time I ask myself what I think I should do, I don't like my answer. I should leave. Let them enjoy their house and let Dad make over the store however he wants.

Working at Dave's part-time is one thing, but I'm not prepared to do that full-time. I have a head for business. I know that. I suppose I could create a halfway impressive resume with my associate's degree and my real-world experience as a store manager. I could get a job in New Hampshire while living in my parents' Portsmouth house. I couldn't pay the entire mortgage each month, but some of it.

"There she is. My savior." It's Chef Jeff, finding me sitting in my Jeep, parked at the dock. I'd taken a ride out to the lighthouse and back while thinking. This newcomer is a welcome distraction.

Seeing Marcus would have also been a distraction from my circling thoughts, too, but far less desirable. I need to stop liking him and wanting him. He's an awful human being.

Without being invited, Jeff grabs the roll bar and swings onto the passenger seat.

"I didn't mention it the other day, but this seat needs some serious help."

I laugh. "I know. How'd it go at the restaurant? Do you like your new domain?"

"It's the bomb," he says. "I'd already worked up a couple menus, and Marcus was down with everything. I just need to find out what I can source reliably without worrying about a key ingredient suddenly not being available."

"Probably won't be too busy this season, not until the renovations are done at the hotel," I guess. "And there'll be a new marina by next summer."

"Yup. All good. But with the ads Marcus is running promoting the island as a day-tripper's adventure, there could be some solid tourism in the upcoming weeks. Also, he said one of the motels is up and running."

I nod. As Jeff said, it's all good.

"He should offer a package deal for lodging with a discount at the restaurant," I say, thinking aloud.

"That's a great idea. I'll mention it to him."

I nearly ask him not to attach my name to it, but then Jeff will ask why. Hopefully, he'll just claim the idea as his own anyway.

"Where are we going?" he asks.

"We?" I raise an eyebrow at this ginger-haired man with his engaging smile.

He shrugs. "I mean, if you're free. I've got nothing to do. Benny is finishing out the week, while I make test recipes and the new menus are printed. We won't be changing any décor until after the season ends." He runs a hand through his hair, making it stand up. "If you're busy, I don't want to intrude. With your shop gone, I thought you might have too much time on your hands."

A stiff breeze momentarily whips my hair over my face. After I wrestle it into a ponytail and fasten with an elastic from my pocket, I take a look around. There are dark clouds, but they're still a long way off.

"I was heading out to Fort Mercy. I think I lost my earring out there, and I'm hoping to retrieve it."

"Cool. I'm into history. I'd like to see it before it's demolished."

I think the blood drains from my head in about five seconds. "What are you talking about?" But I get a sick feeling that I already know precisely what he's going to say.

"Marcus said they're putting the new wastewater treatment plant there."

"Did he? When?"

Jeff shrugs. "Yesterday."

Wow! I guess I called it—the billionaire is a top-level liar and a jerk. My mind starts racing. Should I go confront him now? Then I rethink. He's not the town moderator, not even a board member. I'll go to the town hall in the morning with my plans for the fort.

Jeff is still talking while I'm thinking, but I catch the word *girlfriend* and start to focus.

"Your girlfriend?"

"Yes, Jackie, always says I take too long reading the informational guides at museums. She's coming in a week. I know she's going to love it here."

Well, that's a surprise, and also not. It makes a lot more sense that he would relocate to an unknown place with a partner than by himself. I start up Bella.

"Sorry to tell you, but there are no informative plaques at the fort. Not yet," I add. "Luckily, since I know everything about it, you're with the right island guide."

"Cool," he says again.

As I turn onto Spire Street, we pass Marcus coming out of the town hall. I wonder if he was in there sealing the fate of Fort Mercy. I consider flipping him the bird, but Jeff unbuckles and puts his head out of the open roof.

"Hey, there!" he calls out.

Marcus breaks his stride and stares at us. If I thought some small part of him was truly into me, then I might wave and smile, like I'm having a joyful time with anyone who isn't him. Instead, I remain sullen, not into playing games.

"We're going on a treasure hunt," Jeff yells when Marcus says nothing, "at the fort."

I can tell from his dour expression, even yards away, that he's not pleased. He's determined to take the fort away from me and the rest of the islanders.

But Jeff is not reading the room. "Wish us luck," he calls out.

By the time, he's shouting about luck, we're too far past for Marcus to respond. I see him in my rearview mirror as he walks in the opposite direction.

Oh well! Sucks to be him.

I'm fooling myself. It never sucks to be Marcus. What's more, I'd have to be one of those smooth and sophisticated women to make him the tiniest bit jealous. If I thought a billionaire who gave up a scuba-diving girlfriend and a wealthy, gorgeous fiancée could ever have deep feelings for me, then I have lost my ever-loving mind.

It takes us a little longer than normal to get to the fort because I slow down to point out the houses of people Jeff will want to meet, telling him who they are. Also, Jeannette's studio is open, and we pop in so he can see her pottery.

Ten minutes later, he's put in an order for two dozen unique salad bowls, expressly for the Caesar salad he intends the restaurant's servers to mix tableside.

"What about big bowls for the actual mixing?" I ask.

Jeff shakes his head as we climb back into the Jeep. "Those are traditionally wood, which is the ideal surface for pasting the garlic, anchovies, and salt. I like walnut or cherry. Did you know it was invented in Mexico?"

"The salad? I had no idea." I don't tell him I've never even eaten one before and assumed the name had something to do with the famous Roman general Caesar. I know I'm provincial, not from choice, just situational result. I'm mortified to think Marcus must have noticed that going to Boston's North End was like a trip to Italy for me. It sure felt that way.

When we finally arrive at Fort Mercy, the thunderheads are a lot closer than I thought they'd be, due to the high winds and our slow journey. But we're here, and we might as well take a look around.

"I'll tell you the history while we look for my earring," I say. "I don't think we'll be able to stay long. Let's put the top on first in case it starts to rain."

We attach the Jeep's soft-top, zip up the windows, and go into the fort's ground floor.

"Sorry for the trash dump." I nearly add that it's going to be cleaned up soon before remembering it's more likely the whole thing will be flattened and hauled away. I explain briefly about Lieutenant Cooper and the natives as we climb the stone steps.

It's weird, even uncomfortable, to go back to the spot where Marcus kissed me, but I think that's the place I lost my earring. He must've knocked it out of my ear when he put his hands in my hair. At least, I'm hoping it's right by the window because I really like this pair.

Because the impending storm has made it abnormally dark, I have my phone out as a flashlight, shining it down on the old wooden floor. Jeff does the same.

"Avoid that spot," I tell him when I recall the squishy spot and step over it. "And you see that broken plank, right?"

"Imagine if this place was reconstructed," he says, speaking loudly because the wind is whipping through the fort's many gaps, making whistling sounds. "What if it could be fixed up enough to serve food here? *Dinner at the fort catered by The Clamdigger.* The restaurant could sell tickets for a fixed-price, three-course meal."

I wince. To me, that sounds perfect. "Great idea." Jeff's as entrepreneurial as Marcus. "Maybe you can talk your new boss into sparing the fort."

I've made it to the spot where I think . . . *Ah-ha!*

"Found it." Sure enough, the silver wire with a green, sea-glass dolphin dangling from it is on the floor by the window.

"That's amazing," Jeff says.

I'm glad he doesn't ask me how or why it's here. Retrieving it, I shove it into my shorts pocket. And turn to see he's not referring to my finding an earring but the massive gray clouds nearly upon us.

"Awe-inspiring," he adds, "like we're on a ship in the middle of a hurricane."

Not exactly my favorite analogy, but he's right. Through the window, we watch the churning waves crash against the bluff below. Meanwhile, rain is coming down in dappled sheets, moving toward us across the sea.

"We better get out of here," Jeff says.

"Or we stay here until it blows over," I say. "Might be safer."

A gale-force gust of wind shakes the old fort, and suddenly, I don't want to be on the second floor.

"Let's at least go down below," I suggest.

Turning, we hurry toward the granite steps. I make sure to skip any dodgy areas, as does Jeff. But like an echo of the past, a loud crack makes me jump. Just like when Marcus was behind me. But turning, I see Jeff is fine.

A moment later, I realize it's thunder and not the floor giving way beneath us.

Jeff actually laughs. "Almost gave me heart failure."

The driving rain reaches land and splats heavily on the roof . . . and *inside* the fort. Naturally, the roof leaks like a sieve, and we're both under some impressive holes.

"You're right about going downstairs," he says. "We'll probably stay drier."

Ahead, however, rain is coming in directly over the smooth, stone steps, gushing down in a rivulet, which I should have known would be slippery. Almost as soon as my sandal hits the second step, my foot goes out from under me. I flail. It all happens at high speed. The next thing I know, I'm pitching backward over the side with no railing to stop me.

And then, nothing.

29

Marcus

Why did those two idiots go to that dilapidated, leaky fort in this bad weather? At first, I think, it's none of my business. In fact, I know it's not. If my new chef and the lovely Lindsey Cooper want to go on an adventure together, there's nothing I can do to stop them. Nor should I try or even give a shit.

I've been in a foul mood ever since seeing the ginger-haired Jeff in *my* seat, as I think of the Jeep's uncomfortable passenger side. Who am I kidding? I've been short-tempered since Lindsey called me a snake, among other things.

But I have to ignore my innate instinct to jump on my motorbike and go after them. I have no right to feel jealous or protective. Instead, I walk down to the dock to check on The Rough Rider, making sure everything is battened down appropriately. I assume the man I hired to captain my yacht knows there's a storm passing through and is familiar with all the peccadillos of this nearly one-hundred-year-old vessel, but I need to be sure.

It doesn't take long to see that everything's in order, and I try to relax in the saloon with Robin, who's grumbling because this was supposed to be one of her beach days before she leaves.

When it's been fifteen minutes and the wind is growing stronger, I pull out my phone. The top wasn't even on Bella. Maybe they're sheltering at Jeannette's pottery studio.

Finally, I can't help texting her. *You OK?*

I'm not surprised when I don't get any answer. Even if they went slowly and did some sightseeing along the way, they must be at the fort by now. Or better yet, they went quickly and are on their way back. Any minute, they'll pull into the harbor's parking lot, which I can see from the saloon window.

"You're pacing," Robin says from where she's working on her laptop. "No one paces on a yacht. It's almost illegal. Yachts are for fun and relaxation."

Her words make me think of Lindsey's T-shirt, "For Fun and Food."

I try to focus on the here and now. "Do you want to go to the hotel? We're about to feel like we're in a carwash."

"Nah." She lifts one arm and makes a fist to show me her arm muscle. "I can handle it, boss. Look how strong I am."

At least she makes me smile. As if her sculpted but girly arm can do anything against a force of nature.

"Thanks, Wonder Woman. I feel super safe now."

With a snort of laughter, Robin goes back to typing. We're a good team, with zero sexual tension between us. When we met, we were both with other people, and rather immaturely talked about those people who became our exes, Now, we're like siblings.

I try to settle down, but I can't. The feeling that I have to follow them grows until I'm shrugging into my jacket.

"What's up?"

"Nothing," I say. I hope. "I'll text you later. Keep my yacht from sinking, OK?"

"Yes, boss. Stay safe."

In moments, I'm flying along Spire Street on my BMW bike toward Fort Mercy with the growing dread that something is wrong. I hope to pass them so I can turn around, but I don't. And then the rain hits as if a faucet has turned on above me. I swerve once or twice but each time, I regain control. In another minute, the fort appears like a dark and ugly beast, and I'm nearly there.

There's no one outside, meaning they're wisely sheltering indoors. I'm relieved to see Lindsey's Jeep has the top up and also that they stayed put instead of trying to drive back through this deluge. But I'll be antsy until I see her precious face. Even if she's glowering, as the case may be when she sees me, her least favorite person on Murray Island.

Entering the ground floor of Fort Mercy, I hear Jeff's frantic voice in the murky gloom.

"Hello, hello. Can anyone hear me?"

No way a regular cell phone is working at this end of the island. What's more, his frantic tone kicks my pulse into overdrive.

"Jeff," I say loudly, to let him know I'm here because the sound of the pelting rain is like drum beats. At the same time, I click on my phone flashlight, directing it toward him.

Before I can ask where Lindsey is, the beam of light illuminates her, lying unmoving at his feet. My heart starts pounding as I rush over. My first thought, that he attacked her, I instantly dismiss since he looks miserable and scared. The second one, that she's injured, isn't as easily let go. Especially when I reach her side and see her unconscious.

"She fell off the wet stairs," Jeff said. "Knocked herself out, and I can't get a signal to reach anyone."

"How long?" I ask, seeing she's breathing shallowly. In the dim light, I think her face is pale, but it's hard to tell.

"A few minutes," he says.

"Normally, I'd say it's dangerous to move her, but we need to get her back to the health clinic."

At that moment, Lindsey moans but doesn't open her eyes.

"Can you hear me?" I ask her. She doesn't respond.

"Open the Jeep," I instruct Jeff. "Lean the passenger seat back as far as it will go. I'll carry her."

He hurries off, and I put my phone away. Maneuvering my arms under her, Lindsey's right arm gets pinned between us when I stand. She moans again more loudly. Fearing it's also injured, as gently as possible, I carry her to her vehicle. Jeff has reclined the front passenger seat, and I ease her onto it. It's better that she's sitting up slightly—if I remember head injuries I've seen in movies.

"Drive carefully," I tell him. "I'll lead you."

"I can't drive a stick," Jeff says.

I don't waste time berating him for missing out on one of life's pleasures and, in this case, necessities. At least now I know why he was trying to make a call instead of bringing her back to town. Since I have to push the driver's seat back to fit behind the wheel, he can't go in the Jeep with us.

"I'll drive her back. Take my motorcycle."

He gives me a strange look.

"It doesn't matter if you've never driven one." I give him the thirty-second tutorial, basically how to turn it on and how to brake. "If it stalls or you can't handle it, then leave it." I don't give a damn. "I'll pick it up another time."

I don't even wait to see if he can start it. After holding my breath the way I've seen Lindsey do, I turn Bella's key. She doesn't start on the first try, but I send up a little prayer, and the second time, the engine sputters to life.

I floor it, probably driving faster than anyone has ever driven on Murray Island. The rain beats down on the soft top, which leaks in a couple places, and both headlight lenses must have oxidized because they're dim as fuck. I'm pissed off at Lindsey for this entire boneheaded adventure.

Utterly unnecessary. And her wipers are shit, too, which just makes me madder.

However, since the island is barely larger than my backyard in North Carolina, we're at the health center in less than ten minutes. Thinking it better not to move her again, I run in and get the PA.

"Lindsey fell at the fort. She knocked herself out. And she may have injured her right arm."

"And she's bleeding," Jenny says, gesturing to my shoulder.

"Shit," I exclaim, seeing my shirt. I hadn't even noticed the blood since it wasn't on my hands.

By the time we get back to the Jeep, Lindsey is trying to sit up and groaning. Now I can see blood smeared on the seat from the back of her head.

Relieved she's awake, I open the passenger door, but she can't get out on her own. Before I can help her, she turns her head and vomits into the street.

"We're not equipped for severe TBIs here," Jenny says, exchanging a worried glance with the nurse who came out into the rain with us. "Hopefully, she's just got a mild concussion."

"Hopefully," I mutter, as the PA lifts each of Lindsey's eyelids and shines a light into her eyes.

"Not good," she says, then puts her fingers on Lindsey's right wrist at a pulse point. My fear is ratcheted up by the expression on Jenny's face. "I'm calling for a MedFlight. Just stay with her. Don't let her move."

Breaking out in a cold sweat, I crouch down beside the passenger door, not caring what I'm standing in. I squeeze Lindsey's right leg for comfort. I want to hold her hand, but now she's cradling her right wrist with her left arm.

"Hang in there, beautiful," I say.

Her blue eyes flutter open, but she doesn't focus her gaze on me before they slam shut.

"Vision's blurry," she whispers, then licks her lips. "Gonna be sick again."

I've never felt so fucking helpless in my entire life. Despite what the PA said, I help Lindsey lean over, with the nurse, saying, "Go slow. Be careful," in my ear.

By the time Lindsey has finished throwing up again, Jenny returns. I can see the news isn't what I want to hear.

"No MedFlight in this storm. Let's get her inside."

"What can you do for her?" I demand.

"She needs a brain scan, possibly surgery to relieve pressure. Neither of which I can do here."

"I'll fly her to Boston," I say the words even as I'm thinking up my plan. "Have an ambulance standing ready at Logan. Just make sure they've been told to take her to the best hospital."

"Wait. If MedFlight won't risk it—" Jenny begins.

"I'll be flying away from the storm," I insist, not even knowing or caring if that's the truth. Closing the passenger door, I rush around to the driver's seat. "Tell her parents what's happening."

"Hold on," the PA says, frustrating the hell out of me. "I'm going to give her a medication to ease brain swelling if she has any." She nods to the nurse who dashes off to get the injection.

We wait what feels like hours but is actually about a minute for her to return and administer a shot.

"It's Acetazolamide," Jenny says. "That's the best I can do for her. I'll tell the hospital what I've given her."

"I'll look up Lindsey's partner and have her records and info sent," the nurse says.

"Her partner is Jeannette James," I tell them.

With that, I'm playing racecar driver again.

In a few minutes, we're at the airstrip, and I ready my plane for takeoff. I just have to get Lindsey into the passenger seat. Even in her woozy state, she starts to put up a fight. I wish I'd asked Jenny or the nurse for a knockout drug, but it probably wouldn't have been safe to give Lindsey in her condition.

"Oh, shit. Oh, shit," she repeats through gritted teeth when she realizes what's happening, but she keeps her eyes closed.

"You need to calm down and let me get you to the mainland. Trust me."

"Nooooo," she moans.

But I have strapped her in now, and she has no choice. I did it as gently as I could because of her wrist.

We pick up speed and take off with our wings dipping and bobbing in the wind. It's not going to be smooth, by any means. In fact, these are nearly the worst flight conditions anyone could go through, short of a hurricane. I'd rather fly through a blizzard than the atmospheric hijinks of a thunderstorm.

We slice into the dark clouds, reach our cruising altitude, and never find a break in the thick, rain-filled masses. The tops would be too high, and the bottoms too low, so we maintain our flight path right through the thick of things. The storm's pressure is creating wind shear regions, mimicking sporadic roller coaster climbs and drops, a thousand feet here, another thousand feet there. And I battle to keep us level, feeling a sweat between my shoulder blades because of my precious cargo.

Thankfully, my wipers work about a billion times better than the ones on Lindsey's Jeep. Still, it's one of the worst flights I've ever had, and flying doesn't scare me in the least. Today's journey, I would say, is putting me on the serious side of nervous.

I try to think positively, that it's a blessing she has drifted off again, either to normal sleep or into healing unconsciousness. The entire trip should take twenty minutes tops, but it's dragging on.

Through the entire tense flight, all I can think about is Lindsey's wonderful brain and doing whatever I can to safeguard it. Yeah, in my opinion, her thinking has been a little fucked up lately concerning me. But if she hates me for flying her to the mainland, it's no different from how she's been hating me lately anyway.

Suddenly, we break out into an open area, a clear pocket surrounded by clouds. The eerie green light tells me this is not good. Sure enough, up ahead and to my left, toward the south, a tight, dark green-gray area indicates a T-cell. To my mind, it looks "angry."

As we re-enter the clouds, skirting the monster, we switch amusement park rides. Apparently, we're now in a giant blender.

"Hang on," I say, not knowing whether she can hear me. And then I offer up my second prayer of the day.

30

Marcus

For five long minutes, the endless turbulence feels as though giant hands are beating on my plane from every direction. I'm making constant adjustments and notice the proverbial white knuckles where I grip the controls. Glancing over at Lindsey, I question my rash choice to bring her up into this maelstrom.

When I start to wonder how much more the fuselage can take, the worst of it is over, and I start our descent through rain. And hail! We cannot catch a break. Although since the hailstones are not golf-ball sized, I suppose something is working in our favor.

My state-of-the-art communications system doesn't fail me. Very quickly, I'm given permission to land and a runway number. After all that, our wheels touch down uneventfully at Boston's Logan Airport, where air traffic is almost zero because most of the flights have been delayed or canceled. Jenny has an ambulance waiting on the tarmac.

Just like that, Lindsey is whisked away and out of my care. If they'd let me go with her, I would've abandoned my plane. Instead, all I got was the name of the hospital, and the ambulance doors closed in my face.

I taxi my plane to the hangar set aside for private jets, even though mine is the saddest looking of the bunch. Not because I don't have a sleeker, bigger jet that could blow these others out of the water back home in North Carolina, but because I brought my sporty, German-made CTLS, that's fun-to-fly, with plenty of leg-room for my height.

Fun to fly, indeed!

Robin texts me where to find the car she's reserved. Not a chauffeured limo this time. She followed orders so I can drive myself, which I find preferable in an emergency to sitting in the back seat like a child.

Time stands still until I reach the hospital's ER, give my keys to a valet, and rush to the nurse's desk. Somehow, I need to impart to the staff that this woman is special, not only to me but to everyone who knows her, and that I have all the money they need to give her the best care.

And that I will be broken if I've failed her.

$♥$♥$♥$

B etween Jenny and Robin, everything had been arranged for optimal results. A neurologist is already with Lindsey, and I'm escorted to a private waiting area where the doctor will come speak with me. I'm told about an MRI and also X-rays for her wrist.

Her wrist! I'd nearly forgotten about that.

Then I wait. By myself. Nothing but my swirling thoughts over why she took Chef Jeff to Fort Mercy in a storm.

Questions pile atop other questions about why she dislikes me so intensely.

I don't even care if I ever get any answers, as long as she comes through this OK. I want to see her blue eyes in perfect focus, even if she's glaring at me with steam coming out of her ears.

An interminable amount of time later, maybe two hours, during which I've paced and sat and closed my eyes and bargained with God and fielded calls from her parents, as well as from Mel and Robin—all pointless since I have zero new information—one of the double doors swings open.

"Mr. Parisi?"

I spring to my feet and read his badge with his name and the word "Neurology" under it.

"How is she?" I ask, foregoing any chit-chat. "I want to know about her brain." It sounds weird when I say it.

His smile releases the twisted knot in my chest.

"Miss Cooper's brain is going to be fine. There was very minor swelling but no bleeding. Basically, a concussion. Her wrist, on the other hand, is broken."

I'm still processing that her head is OK, when the doctor adds, "I suggest postponing the surgery needed to set her wrist for at least twenty-four hours. But you can discuss that with her orthopedic surgeon and anesthesiologist."

"She'll have no lasting effects from the concussion?" I press him, wanting reassurance.

"None. She'll be fine," he says.

"May I see her?"

"A nurse will come get you in a moment. If you have any more questions, call my office."

He doesn't bother to give me a card, and I don't know his name, but I'm only thinking of getting to Lindsey right now anyway. I wait about a minute after he leaves, and then I go toward the double doors. Pushing them open, I'm in a short corridor, which I follow to a nurse's station.

She frowns at me.

"I'm Marcus Parisi. I just spoke with the neurologist—"

"Neurosurgeon," she corrects, imparting all the gravitas and respect a top brain surgeon deserves.

"He said I may see Miss Cooper *now*." I emphasize the last word.

She doesn't exactly roll her eyes, but she doesn't spring into action, either. Unless I get satisfaction in the next five seconds, I'm going to start throwing my financial weight around. Lucky for her, she picks up a chart and runs her finger down it.

"She's in Room 324." After indicating the direction with a nod of her head, the nurse gives me a look. "You're family, right?"

"Yup." And I keep walking.

Pushing the door open, I peer around into the room in case she's asleep. In fact, her eyes are closed. No one has ever looked prettier in a hospital gown. I stare a moment, drinking her in, with every intention of backing out quietly when she opens her eyes and turns her head.

I release the breath I was holding. "Hi there, beautiful."

Lindsey's face goes through an easily readable series of expressions. First, she smiles with all the lovely warmth I'm used to. Then, as if she remembers she doesn't like me, her smile dims and disappears, replaced by a frown. Finally, she switches to distant and neutral.

"Sorry if I woke you," I say taking the few steps necessary until I'm beside her bed.

"I was awake," she tells me.

"The doctor said your brain wasn't injured. Nothing permanent anyway."

She nods, then raises her arm, which is in a brace. "The ol' wrist isn't so good though."

"Did someone explain that you need surgery? I'll make sure he or she is the best orthopedic surgeon in the area."

She shrugs. "Not necessary. I bet they see breaks like mine all the time."

"I don't care. You'll have the best."

"When?" she asks.

"Not before tomorrow. You have to spend tonight letting your brain settle down. I don't think they want to give you anesthesia yet."

"Will my parents be here by then?"

I feel guilty for not thinking of them. As soon as I leave Lindsey's room, I'll give them an update and make sure The Rough Rider brings them over in the morning.

"I'll get them here soon," I promise.

Lindsey nods. I can see she'll be asleep again in a minute.

"I'll be close by. And I'll leave my number with the nurse's station."

She doesn't speak, merely looking at me with those big blue eyes, her face remaining impassive.

"Before I go, tell me why you went to Fort Mercy in a storm. I know you're not a reckless person."

Her cheeks turn pink, and my stomach dips. Maybe she's going to tell me she went there to make out with Jeff. It's a ridiculous, juvenile thought.

"I lost an earring when you and I were there," she says. "Found it on the second floor. I hope it's still in my shorts' pocket. Otherwise, it was all for nothing." She gestures at her arm.

I'm flabbergasted. "Was it a family heirloom?"

"No, but I like the pair. Sterling silver with a dolphin."

"A dolphin," I repeat, stupidly. "You risked your life for a cheap earring."

"If you hadn't knocked it off my ear—"

"When we kissed," I interrupt, reminding her of how she used to be fond of me.

Shrugging again, she looks exhausted, and I bite my tongue against any more outbursts.

"The storm came up faster than I expected," she explains, her voice quiet, "plus I showed Jeff a few sights along the way."

Just like how she showed me the island before she knew who I was.

She yawns broadly, not bothering to cover her mouth, looking like a kid who has stayed up way past her bedtime.

"I'll let you sleep." I want to brush her hair off her forehead, or just touch her shoulder, any contact whatsoever. But I have a feeling she will flinch. Instead, I turn toward the door.

"Wait," she says softly, making me freeze in place.

Oh, I'll wait, darlin'. I'll stand right here for the rest of my life, if that's what you want.

The next moment, her eyes flutter closed. I don't move a muscle until they open again a few seconds later.

"Marcus," she says, her voice dropping to an even softer tone. "Thank you."

I wonder if she remembers fighting me when I put her in the plane.

"You're welcome." Her eyes shut again, and she turns her head away.

Still, I wait in case she needs me or has anything else to say. But she's out like a light. Maybe that's why I feel safe telling her those three little but humongous words.

"I love you."

31

Lindsey

Well, this is an unexpected crappy turn of events. One minute I'm bemoaning all my life choices, past, present, and future, not realizing how great I have it. And the next, my right arm is in a cast. I won't be able to wash my hair by myself, write legibly, or even drive my stick-shift Jeep for about six weeks.

That's what I'm thinking while my parents chat about their ride over to the mainland on Marcus's yacht. For some reason, it was decided that Sam's fishing boat wasn't good enough. By Marcus! My dad actually wishes he could have a trip on his plane, too, having never flown in something that small before. I'm simply glad I was unconscious for most of the flight and don't remember it.

Knowing I was thousands of feet up, over water, in a tiny tin can makes me want to throw up. I've been told I already did that *before* I got on the plane, but I don't remember that, either. I interrupt my mother, who's still talking about taking a turn at the helm of The Rough Rider.

"Did I vomit inside Bella?"

"No, dear. *You* were inside, but you managed to lean over."

I nod. My arm is in a tight cast that goes almost to my elbow, and it's set in such a way that my hand is ever-so-slightly curved, like it should be attached to a Barbie doll. The surgery happened about nine this morning.

The orthopedic surgeon who Marcus deigned acceptable to set my badly broken wrist wasn't available until today, which was fine since everyone seemed to want to wait as long as possible before I was anesthetized. Also, they did a bunch of "stuff" to get the swelling to go down. Not in my brain, which was fine, but in my forearm.

Yesterday, while waiting for my parents, I alternately watched TV and slept. They arrived just before lunch. Marcus had already visited the night before and twice more in the morning. I'm pretty sure I thanked him each time. Because even though I think he's a backstabber, he has always treated me like a princess—apart from lying to me.

He even found my shorts when I asked him to look in the narrow cupboard. After digging around in the pocket, he produced the earring. The symbol of our last kiss.

We looked silently at one another. Then I said, "You can put it back. I just wanted to know it was there."

He was quiet, picking up on my lack of enthusiasm for all things Marcus, including his presence in my hospital room. I can't be friendly because, for all I know, he's ready to fly somewhere to screw some congressman's wife, just to get even. But I couldn't bring myself to tell him I overheard what a sleaze he is. It's too embarrassing for both of us.

If he defends himself, I won't believe him anyway. That's why instead, I mentioned his big lie.

"You told me you were leaving Fort Mercy alone."

He shook his head. "No, I never said that. Not the day we were together at the fort, nor any time afterward."

"You let me assume though."

After a brief hesitation, he agreed, "I did."

"Why?"

He crossed his arms, casually letting his muscles bulge and looking unapologetic. "For purely selfish reasons."

"That's what I thought," I said. "And it kinda makes you a scumbag."

His eyebrows shot up. "Hardly! I'm a hundred percent right, and you being here in that hospital bed is proof."

I thought about that. "I've been waiting for you to say, 'I told you so.' And now you have. Anyway, all my accident proves is that I wear old sandals with slippery soles. And you're not a scumbag for wanting to tear down the fort as much as for lying to me about it. Although I'm not thrilled about either."

When I add these sins to what I heard about his shady treatment of the congressman, I'm surprised I've been ablet to speak to him with a civil tone.

The last time he came in yesterday, my parents were with him. I refrained from thanking him again. I barely looked at him. I hope he got the message and has gone back to the island. Or wherever. I don't care.

I *do* care, but I don't want to.

I really, really don't want to care if I ever see him again.

"Do you?" my mom asks. I haven't heard a word of her question.

"Do I what?"

She laughs. "My poor girl. It wasn't important."

"Did you fill out your meal card?" my dad asks. He thought the food was yummy yesterday and is eager to taste what the hospital is making tonight.

I think of my night in Boston with Marcus and how delicious the food was. And how great the company. And what came after. I sigh.

"We should leave you," my mother says. "You're a hundred miles away in your thoughts."

Try a billion, I think. "You don't have to leave," I say without too much gusto because the surgery has left me tired again. "What will you do in the city?"

"Marcus owns a hotel," my dad says.

"The Ritz-Carlton?" I ask, shocked.

"No," he says, looking at me as though my brain might've been damaged after all. "It's called The Parisi on the Square."

"It's gorgeous," my mom says. "From the thick, squishy carpet to the amazing sheets to the heated lap pool to the croissants we had for breakfast to—"

"I get the idea," I say, wondering why Marcus hid his hotel from me the last time we were here. Then it clicks—because I didn't know he was a Parisi yet. *Bastard!*

"Every detail has been thought of," my father agrees. "If Murray Island turns out to be as well-planned, then we are going to outshine Nantucket and Martha's Vineyard."

His enthusiasm is genuine. "We'll let you get some rest, baby girl," he says, but then he adds, "Did we tell you about the lunch we had on The Rough Rider?"

I roll my eyes. "Glad you had a pleasure trip on your way over to see me."

"We barely enjoyed ourselves," my mother said. "And that was only because Marcus had already given us the good news from the doctor about your head."

"You should be nice to that one," my father says.

My mouth drops open slightly until I clamp it closed.

He shrugs. "The man obviously cares for you. And it's just as easy to fall in love with a rich man as a poor one."

If I could throw a pillow at my father, I would.

"He's not all that and a bag of donuts," I protest. "There are things you don't know about him."

"Maybe not," my father says. "When I heard he'd bought The Lady, I started scouring the Internet. Parisi, Inc. has an A plus rating with the BBB."

"And his parents seem like lovely people," my mother adds.

"Not you, too?" I complain. "Do they have a five-star rating as well?"

"I don't know what you mean," she says. "What does she mean, Nate?"

"It's her concussion making her loopy," he says before kissing my forehead. "We'll let you rest. But he didn't have to sit in that waiting room two days ago to keep us posted or stay here in the hospital all day yesterday. Not unless he cared about you personally. Otherwise, he has people to do that."

"Dad," I half whine, half yawn. "He does not have people to sit in hospitals."

"He could if he wanted," my father persists. "Marcus is a *self-made* billionaire. He did not inherit. Repeat: He did *not* inherit!"

"I know that," I say, before I yawn again, a full face-splitting one that I try to hide behind my left hand. My father's not the only one with Internet. Marcus Parisi built his fortune with a vision that grew into an international company. He's one of the youngest billionaires on the planet. But if he has the entire world to play around on, why has he zeroed in on Murray Island?

I drift off to sleep and dream about Marcus walking on the warm sand with me.

$♥$♥$♥$

When I wake up the next time, he's silhouetted by the late afternoon light coming in the window. Actually, since it stays light until eight now, it may be any time of day or early evening, but my stomach isn't growling, so I think it's not any later than three.

Without turning my head, I can study him. He's in the chair that my father said was uncomfortable. Dad thought the hospital did it on purpose to make visitors leave.

Marcus is typing away on his phone. I swear the man is always working. Which begs the question, why is he still in my hospital room in Boston? I haven't been warm and welcoming. I tried to brush him off without being overtly rude. Then I told him point-blank that he's a scumbag. That was risky. I don't know him that well. He could have snapped and been vindictive when he realized we weren't ever having sex again.

Maybe he wants to destroy me the way he does the congressman. That's silly. My brain may be muddled after all. He's hardly going to be worrying over me if he also feels vengeful.

Looking at his focused expression, his topaz-brown eyes, and his slightly parted lips, I'm awash with sadness. He got to me. For a little while there, I basked in his attention, sizzled at his kisses, enjoyed mind-blowing sex, and generally enjoyed his company. And he made me laugh.

I should have known he was too good to be true.

It's easier to fake genuine goodness and kindness than to be the real deal twenty-four hours a day. At least, that's what I think happened. Otherwise, I can't explain how I could have fallen for his bullshit.

I can't refrain from a groan of distress at never kissing Marcus Parisi again, and he is up and at my bedside quicker than I think humanly possible.

"Are you OK? Does something hurt? Shall I get a nurse?"

"No," I say. "I'm fine." Everything is, in fact, pretty painless at this moment, except for my heart. It's still hard to fathom how fast and hard I fell for him. I didn't even realize how deep I'm into him until I have to steel myself against his easy charm at this moment.

It's fake. He's fake.

"Why are you here?" I demand, sounding peeved.

He smiles. "Because you're here."

I sigh. He's like a puppy. It's really hard to tell him to go away. But he's also like a wolf, and for that reason, I decide to rip off the Band-Aid.

"I don't want you here."

He sighs. "I guessed that, but I still don't understand why. I withheld the fate of Fort Mercy, which I see now was a shitty thing to do. But I didn't lie to you. Even so, that doesn't seem like enough to make you wash your hands of me entirely. Is it Chef Jeff? Do you have the hots for him?"

"What? No, that's not it. Besides, he has a girlfriend, and she's moving to Murray Island soon."

It's weird how that cheers him up, but it obviously does. "Great."

"Jeff has no bearing on anything. You own an old yacht," I point out.

He frowns. "I do. And?"

"Then you're not averse to history? The fort is Murray Island's history. It should stay."

"Says the woman who sustained a concussion and now wears a cast."

"Rain and crappy sandals," I remind him.

"If boat or a building was expertly crafted and has been not only maintained but improved with modern amenities, like The Rough Rider, blending the best of the old with the new, then I'm all for it. That's what's going to happen to The Lady of the Light and to the cottages, bring modernity to the historical. But the fort is just some stone and wood that no one on the island has given a damn about for well over a hundred years."

Tears prick my eyes at his harsh words. I gave a damn. Lieutenant Cooper gave a damn. "I suppose you're tearing it down while I'm trapped in this hospital."

He sighs. "Murray Island needs a new wastewater treatment plant more than it needs that deathtrap of an eyesore. Or eyesore of a deathtrap. Take your pick."

I say nothing because there's nothing left to say.

"I think we could have something," Marcus continues. "We already do. Or did. I enjoyed every minute of being with you. Apart from almost getting burned to death. And flying in a storm wasn't too much fun, either."

That distracts me. "You had no right to risk my life."

"The PA talked about brain swelling and bleeding on the inside. We all know that can turn deadly real fast. And you were bleeding on the outside, too. You have stitches back there. Do you know that?"

"I do. My mother told me."

"Seeing your blood on my shirt was not a highlight of my time on your island. If you think the short flight was a bit bumpy, imagine a couple hours on Sam's boat. It would've been agony and risked your brain."

"My brain is fine," I snap. "But we are never going to 'have something.'" I fail at air quotes, looking like I'm just making bunny ears with my left hand.

"You owe me an explanation," he says, crossing his arms.

I nearly say, "I don't owe you a thing." But I suppose I do. If I don't explain where I'm coming from, he won't believe we're finished. But I refuse to bring up the congressman's wife because I don't want to talk to Marcus about his past with other women. Besides I want to leave a measure of dignity between us.

"You have misrepresented who you are," I say, knowing I sound lame. That hardly sums up all the issues of a lying, womanizing, fort-destroying billionaire.

He frowns. "Are we back to the beginning again? When I paid in cash at your shop?"

"No. After I discovered you were a billionaire, you made yourself out to be a nice guy."

"That's your perception," he says. "I never said I was Saint Marcus."

Weird he uses that phrase. I flashback to thinking he was a saint for not jumping my bones the night of the fire when

I was particularly vulnerable. But there's so much other garbage.

"You lied about having a hotel. Why did we stay at the Ritz-Carlton?"

"Christ!" he says. "You don't give up on someone, on me, merely because I didn't want to freak you out. You were already nuts about a limo and went weepy seeing a standard two-room suite. You would have disintegrated into a puddle of hysterics if I tried to take you to my Boston hotel, seen the luxury, and had all the staff rolling out a red carpet for us. Besides, I never said I didn't own a hotel. I have a few, in fact. They usually make superior investments. But I didn't lie to you."

Marcus is splitting hairs. And he's also plainly annoyed as he continues, "OK, what have we got? I'm not a tourist, I'm a billionaire real estate developer. True. I think the fort should be razed and replaced with a safe and useful treatment plant. True. I didn't take you to my Boston hotel. True. Am I accused of any other unforgivable crimes in the court of Lindsey Cooper, judge, juror, and executioner?"

"Did you sleep with a congressman's wife?" I blurt, immediately wishing I could take it back. Hadn't I just told myself I did not want to hear about him and another woman?

His expression is priceless. Stunned, befuddled, confused by my information. Guilty!

"No," he says quietly. "I did not."

"And now you *have* lied to me," I say. "Go away." I close my eyes to hide the disappointment. I fake yawn to make him leave.

"I'm not lying, Lindsey. I don't know how you found out about my issues with Dan Bradley but—"

"Did you sleep with someone important to him?"

"I slept with his *girlfriend* when we were in college."

"If not lying, then parsing words. And you're willing to sleep with his wife now to get back at him."

"No, I'm not."

"That's not what it sounded like." There, now he knows I heard him with my own ears. I open my eyes again to see his grim expression.

"Basically, you're not who I thought you were," I say. "That's a recurring theme when it comes to you. In any case, you're definitely not someone I want to be around. I appreciate what you're doing for the island, although I question your motives. And of course I'm grateful you brought me to this hospital. But that's all. We had fun sex, and now we're done with that. You're too complicated and not what I need in my life."

Inside I'm trembling when I add, "I have to figure out my future, but one thing I do know. You're not in it."

He stares back with his tawny eyes, and the little muscle at his jawline jumps. When he says nothing more, I plead with him, "Will you please just leave me alone?"

32

Marcus

Just like that, she dismisses me.

I told myself as long as Lindsey was all right, I wouldn't care if she glared at me. She's not exactly glaring, but if a person could be made of ice, it would be this woman right now, lying in a hospital bed.

After what she's been through, she ought to be fragile, but she seems more kick-ass than ever. And the ass she wants to kick is mine.

As it turns out, she has taught me a lesson: Even a billionaire can't have anything he wants. Or anyone. I'm seriously thinking about arguing with her, but her characterization of us as "fun sex" is so belittling, I decide not to.

If that's all it was to her, then who am I to assign deeper meaning to sinking into her wet and willing body in her bedroom with the sound of waves in the distance. Makes me sound like a sappy romantic.

In the end, I walk out with a cursory, "Take care."

In the elevator, I scan the guide for all the floors. The one thing this hospital lacks is a bar. When I think about it, a hospital seems like the exact right locale for one. People are stressed, waiting for patients to come out of surgery. Why not give loved ones a place to drown their sorrow or soothe their anxiety?

Since I am not a *loved one*, I guess I wouldn't qualify for the bar anyway.

Reclaiming my rental car, I do, in fact, head to a bar, The Fed at The Langham, advertised as British-inspired. I've never been there, but a phone search indicated I'd like it. At first sight, I do. Since it's five o'clock and sunny, they have the good sense to dim the lights and pull down the shades. Shelves display glass globes and some brass . . . I think the word *whatnots* and am ready for a stiff drink.

Settling into a wingback leather chair, I can pretend I'm a Victorian nobleman at a men's club in London. My mistress has just kicked me out of her life, and I need to lick my wounds. After ordering a signature cocktail called the Aeroplane, just to torment myself, I'm torn between a cheese toastie and a lobster roll. When I find I can combine them and put lobster on my grilled cheese sandwich, I go for it.

Three hours later, during which time, I've sent Robin at least thirty texts about all manner of pressing items, then I send Congressman Dan Dickhead a brutally frank email. Using Stan Brie's term, I tell Bradley I know his *tentacles* are in everything that's going wrong at my Iris, North Carolina, development. And I'm prepared to release to the media a goddamned Excel spreadsheet of his corrupt activities if he doesn't stop immediately. I'll even throw in a colorful pie chart of his bribes and threats.

I've also downed a drink called Frozen A$$ets—it's like this place was made for me—and a sticky toffee pudding that gives me a sugar high. The bar has filled up and become loud. I've switched to whiskey, preparing for a headache in the morning.

Predictably a few young women come in and sit at the center bar like they're on display. One in particular is stunning with cat-eye makeup, full lips, and a skin-tight, silver tank top with a short black skirt. After twenty minutes of trying to make eye contact with me, which I admit, I'm encouraging by way of occasionally looking over at her, the leggy brunette strolls over and drops uninvited into the matching wingback chair.

"Hi," she says. "Would you like to buy me a drink?"

"Sure," I say, ready for lighthearted company. This is what I'm used to, not having to work hard to get a woman's attention or have her simply be nice. "Why not? What would you like?"

"You choose for me," she says.

It's the stupidest thing I've heard all day. "No, seriously. Tell me what you want to drink. Why would you force down something you don't like? It's meant to be enjoyable. Life is meant to be the same. So is sex and boats and airplanes," I add, letting the alcohol run away with my mouth.

She smiles. "OK, then. I'll have a glass of the Champagne Taittinger."

I know it's the most expensive drink on the menu because I've studied it a few times, searching for my next poison.

Getting the server's attention, thinking of Lindsey in her Dave's bar T-shirt, I order one for each of us.

"What's your name?" she asks.

I realize I should have asked her first. I'm off my game. But the tagline for the bar, written along the cocktail menu, is distracting me: "The Fed is the perfect place to celebrate all of life's moments."

I wish Lindsey was here. She might feel uncomfortable at first. She definitely wouldn't have ordered the expensive champagne unless I forced her to. And she wouldn't be leaning forward to show off her cleavage, with breasts pushed up and nearly out, while wearing a skirt that barely covers her ass. Although I would very much like to see my island girl her in this outfit.

It wouldn't matter. Lindsey's a dime-piece even when wearing her usual shorts and a T-shirt.

"Marcus," I finally say. It seems I've been ogling the woman with unconcealed appreciation when, really, I've been comparing her to Lindsey and finding her obvious sexuality not nearly as appealing. Even the thick, red gloss on her lips makes them look armored and unkissable.

"I'm Vanessa," she says.

I don't know why it strikes me as made up, but suddenly I wonder if she might be a hooker. I've had a lot to drink because I almost ask her outright before I rein in my curiosity.

Still, I find myself asking, "What do you do in Boston?"

"I run a tourism company," she says. "I'll escort you wherever you'd like to go."

I was right. It strikes me funny, and I can't hold back my laughter. Luckily, she doesn't take offense. Our drinks arrive, and she sits back to enjoy whatever the night brings.

"Are any of the other women at the bar part of your company?" I ask, idly wondering if I can help her scale up her business.

Her smile dies. "No. Only me."

I guess she's offended at the notion that I might want someone else.

"Sorry to tell you, but I'm not a tourist."

She shrugs and licks her lips. The gloss doesn't shift, smear, or smudge in the least. "That doesn't matter to me."

If this were a movie, I'd give her a shit-ton of money to finish her law degree or whatever her heart is dreaming of, and she'd never turn a trick again. Better yet, we'd fall in love.

Suddenly, I'm tired and having her beside me makes me lonelier than when I was by myself.

When her high-heeled foot touches my calf, I glance at her slender ankle. She has to angle her leg to stroke me, but she manages to run her foot up my pant-leg.

It elicits nothing.

I down the drink that was meant to be sipped. Reaching for my wallet, I wave the server over again. I don't wait for him to hand me a bill, I just give him my card. When he sees it's an American Express Black, his eyes widen. He moves fast to get me rung up.

I give the guy an obscene tip because I can, and then I stand. Vanessa seems to think she's going with me because she gets up, too. I hope she's not going to make a scene.

"Please enjoy your drink and the rest of your evening," I say. She looks befuddled and slightly annoyed, probably how I looked when Lindsey dismissed me.

And then I walk out. I decide to leave my car wherever the hell I parked it and get a room upstairs, here at The Langham.

Because, dammit, I'm a billionaire.

$♥$♥$♥$

Three days later, I stand at the dock, arms crossed, sunglasses on, watching as Lindsey's new Jeep is driven off the ferry. I bought it in a happy turquoise color. Automatic, of course.

She and her parents came back on my boat yesterday. I'm sure she put up a fight until she heard I wouldn't be on The Rough Rider. Naturally, I flew my plane back to Murray Island. It was a much smoother flight. However, as soon as I returned, I decided I wouldn't be staying.

All the revitalization plans are set in motion. Robin and I decide to work around the visitors this summer, inconveniencing them as little as possible while getting a head start on some of the projects like the marina.

The vacant shop I purchased in the middle of town is going to be transformed into a real tourism office, with menus, lodging prices, info on rentals and leases, a yet-to-be-written guidebook, and more. My capable assistant will stay another week to wrap up loose ends, some super important and some just threads. After that, the contractors, both local and those coming from the mainland, will answer to the manager she's hiring.

Meanwhile, I climb into the new Jeep and drive to the Coopers' saltbox. Not surprisingly, it doesn't feel like Lindsey's house any longer. Her mother is outside weeding under the front windows. I talked to her parents extensively when we were hanging out at the hospital.

I hired Barbara to write the official Murray Island guidebook with all the stories she can dig up about its history, and all the details about its natural and manmade features. Robin will send a photographer to help. By next year, it'll be in the new tourism office, as well as copies sold in other stores around town.

The other thing we talked about was Lindsey. As soon as she makes her decision about staying or going to the mainland, they'll know whether they're selling their Portsmouth home. I have the absurd desire to put a tracking device on this infuriating woman or insert a microchip under her skin, in order to keep tabs on her whereabouts. Absurd and scary possessive. Not like me at all.

I honk the horn, as I drive up.

"Marcus," Mrs. Cooper exclaims and rises from a pad she's kneeling on. "What have we here?"

Pushing the ignition button, I turn it off and climb out. "A gift for Lindsey, which she can drive while her arm's in a cast."

"That is unbelievably thoughtful of you."

I like how she doesn't protest or say it's too much because she understands that it's not that big a deal. Lindsey's parents are cool about my wealth. Duly impressed but not weird about it.

"Do you want to come in for some lemonade?" she asks.

And receive more irritated looks from her daughter?

"No, thanks. I just came to drop this off. Registration and title are in the glove compartment. It's insured for a year. And two key fobs are on the seat."

Mrs. Cooper now looks confused. "You don't even want to see Lindsey and tell her about it yourself? I'm sure she'll be very excited, not to mention grateful."

"I have to be going," I say. "Tell her I said *hi* and I hope she's feeling better," I add rather awkwardly. It's not like the house is a mansion. Lindsey's probably peering out a window at me, and I bet she can hear every word. If she wanted to come out and gush with excitement and gratitude, she would.

But I don't want either. I want her looking at me with red-hot yearning like she did before, and her lips in a small sexy smile, begging to be kissed.

I start backing away, but Mrs. Cooper says, "At least let me drive you back into town."

"No need," I assure her. "I'll enjoy the walk on the beach." I decide against telling her I'm leaving soon because she'll make a fuss and start trying to force Lindsey outside again. "Tell Mr. Cooper I said hello."

"Maybe you'll see him in town," she says. "He's meeting with our architect and putting his plan together for the store."

With a wave, I'm gone, deciding to take the beach route to the hotel, practically feeling Lindsey's eyes on my back when I head for the path. I've barely cleared the beach roses when I hear her call my name.

My heart starts racing because this can only be a good thing. Why would she come after me except to apologize, thank me, and be reasonable again? Maybe it was the painkillers talking in the hospital. I hope I get to sweep her into my arms in the next minute or two, tell her what she means to me, and taste her succulent lips once more.

"How dare you!" is her opening salvo, as she fast-walks across the sand.

Well, shit!

"You're welcome," I answer.

"What are you trying to do?" she asks. "Buy me? Ingratiate yourself with my parents? Or simply a bribe to keep me quiet over your dirty dealings that the congressman is rooting out."

Wow! I am not a man quick to temper. I never have been, but she is dancing dangerously close to my last nerve.

"I just wanted to give someone I care about a way to drive around."

Her blue eyes are snapping mad, and it's as though she cannot even hear me.

"Take your glasses off, please. I don't like speaking to someone when I can't see their eyes," she says.

Must be tough living on a vacation island in the summer, I think. Obviously, she's being bitchy because it's me, not because she can't speak to someone wearing sunglasses. But I push them up on my head.

"Better? Can you see my devious nature now? Is it obvious, deep in my eyes, how all along I planned to blow a bunch of money on this beat-up little island so I can rule the world from it? Or maybe you can see what value I place on your silence. With a friggin' Jeep! Is that your price to . . . what did you say? . . . to keep quiet? About what exactly? Because I'm trying to employ my builders and give seniors affordable housing on a golf course in North Carolina? Or because I'm fighting back against a corrupt asshole with a vendetta? Or maybe you're jealous because I screwed a girl in college who came onto me in a bar?"

I have definitely hit my limit. Lindsey has no answer. She's angry for the sake of being angry because she doesn't want to admit she likes me and wants me. Or at least, that's what I'm telling myself.

"You're selling yourself short," I tell her. "If you really think someone wants to buy you, at least demand a Maserati next time."

After she rolls her eyes, and tries to cross her arms, thwarted by the cast, I take a step closer. I give in to impulse that's as natural as breathing. After all, it's been too long since I claimed her soft lips.

She reads it on my face and takes a step back, swinging her cast wide at the same time to thwart my approach. Or maybe to keep me from crushing it between us. Meanwhile she raises her left hand, pressing her palm flat against my chest to push me away.

I think that's her intent. I'm not entirely sure because in the next moment, when my mouth covers hers, her fingers curl into my shirt and hang on.

With that small invitation, I thrust my tongue between her lips and into her warmth, ignoring the danger of being bitten. While our tongues dance and stroke, my hands go to Lindsey's waist to snug her against me. I want to take hold of her ass, but I resist the urge. We're not about to sink onto the sand and have incredible sex.

We're simply kissing because we're both still here and because it's so effortlessly awesome. There's no miscommunication when our mouths are fused, when I'm tasting her and breathing in her perfume.

Eventually, however, even the hottest, best kiss has to end.

As soon as I draw back, she pushes hard with her left hand.

"You can't do that!" Lindsey protests. "You can't kiss me whenever you want."

"I just did," I mutter, like an entitled billionaire . . . or a barbarian.

Her mouth is very red. It's as enticing as a ripe strawberry. I nearly say "fuck it" and kiss her again. But she's backing away.

"You're impossible. Neither a car nor a kiss will change anything," she vows. "I wouldn't need the damn car if you hadn't kissed me at the fort. I wish you'd never come to Murray Island."

I have to admit that stings. I've left a few women wanting more, but I don't think I've ever left one wishing she'd never met me.

I put my hands up in surrender, letting her know I won't reach for her again.

"I'm not sorry I met you," I say because it's pointless to start lying now. "But I won't bother you again. I'm done."

With those choice words, I turn and walk away.

33

Lindsey

I watch Marcus leave with mixed feelings, predominantly misery. My stomach sinks like a stone in the ocean, having never mastered skipping rocks across its surface.

I needed to come after him and let him know his grand gesture of a new car doesn't make a damn bit of difference. Even if it *had* been a Maserati, which I can't picture in my mind since I don't know exactly what one looks like. But I know it's sporty and Italian and expensive.

No doubt the perfect car to remind me of Marcus Parisi. And I'm glad I don't own one.

When I heard him outside my house and saw what he bought me, I nearly turned into a mushy puddle of astonished gratefulness.

Then I realized that was the point of him buying me a car. Manipulation 101! But when I called him on his shit, he acted dismissive and hurt. Besides, as he just reminded me, a Jeep is small potatoes to him, an easy throwaway gesture that he knew would mean more to me than him.

I guess he would've done a helluva lot more if he truly wanted me to stay silent about the problems he's having with the North Carolina congressman.

My head is spinning, and not from the concussion. Despite everything, my stupid self wants to trust him, but I also don't want to. If he turns out to be a stand-up guy, then I'd have no defense against giving in to the love that's rooted in my heart and growing as fast as dandelions in May.

And where will that get me? *Duh!* Broken-hearted. Because while everything is changing around me, one thing is still the same. He's returning to his real life sometime soon, and I'll be left with nothing but memories. That is, until he flies back. He mentioned coming again next summer, like I'm part of the seasonal entertainment. Although now that I've made myself clear, I'll keep my fingers crossed he never returns.

How awkward and painful would that be?

Besides he's not a great guy. He's still tearing down my fort! It makes me crazy, knowing there's nothing I can do to stop him.

Not only that, he just declared he's done. As in Finished. With. Me.

So, there's that.

I don't remember when I lowered myself to the sand, but I am sitting, watching the ocean and feeling defeated. I never should have been friendly and taken him on a tour. I certainly shouldn't have given in to loneliness and the sizzling chemistry between us, stupidly sleeping with him.

And I ought to have kept my emotions out of it, like every other summer fling I've had. OK, there was only one before Marcus, but still.

Damned if I do love him and damned if I don't. Either way, it sucks. And it hurts more than falling down the slippery steps of Fort Mercy. I can't imagine anyone else will ever come close to the force of nature that he is.

Not to mention the panty-drenching kisses and the mind-blowing sex and the sheer happiness.

Eventually, I go home, having spent so much time ruminating on Marcus, I'd forgotten about the gorgeous turquoise-colored Jeep in my driveway.

Before I go indoors, I can't help sliding into the driver's seat. I've never experienced the mythical new car smell before. It's amazing. Probably toxic and designed to alter your brain waves into feeling good.

Not only won't I have to shift gears, I don't even have to turn a key in the ignition. It has a big, freakin' "on" button.

Eventually, after I get tired of playing with all the knobs and dials and imagining I'm going somewhere, I head inside.

"Where were you?" my mother asks.

I'm still not used to them being back after three years. They had zero qualms about behaving as if the house is entirely theirs. Which it is. I get that, but it's weird to be interrogated like I'm sixteen.

"Why?" I ask without answering, sounding curt.

My dad comes in from the living room. "Your mother was worried because you were recently in hospital, and you left your phone charging in the dining room."

I'd run out in such a hurry to catch Marcus I'd forgotten.

"Did you need me?" I ask my mother, softening my tone. Just because I'm on edge after talking to Marcus doesn't mean I should take it out on her.

She smiles, and I love her so much that I decide not to mind if she questions me.

"I'll always need you, baby girl."

I laugh. She's called me that my whole life, long after I stopped being a baby.

"But in this case," she adds, "it's because your phone rang while you were out."

"It never rings," I say, heading for the outlet to check. Sure enough, there's a voicemail. Not Marcus, as I feared for a second, but a number I've never seen before.

When I play it back, the female voice identifies herself as Robin LaPointe, and it takes me the first fifteen seconds of her message to realize she's Marcus's assistant. The woman with the flawless shape and dark skin setting off her bright pink bikini. The woman from Dave's patio talking about hitmen.

And she wants to meet with me. Tomorrow afternoon.

$♥$♥$♥$

I cross the short gangplank to The Rough Rider, having been assured that Marcus will not be on board. In fact, when I phoned Robin back, figuring it was to do with her boss, she laughed.

"I let him make his own mistakes," she jokes. "Do you want to come to the yacht? If not, I can meet you in town."

Agreeing to come to the stateroom, I can't help being curious since she wouldn't tell me why she wanted to see me until we met in person.

"There you are," she says, rising from the table where she's working. "The island's best spokesperson."

I can't help my small smile, even though I question her motives. She's obviously devoted to Marcus from what I heard on the patio. "Am I?"

"Do you remember meeting me last year when I came into your shop?"

"Of course. You bought two large candy bars and a water."

Her mouth drops open slightly.

I feel my cheeks grow warm. "Sorry, that was weird of me. I have a keen memory for certain things, like what people have ordered at the bar I work for, or what they bought in my store. Former store," I amend. "I guess knocking myself out didn't ruin it, either."

"Keen is an understatement," she says. "Is it only the sales and orders you store in your brain, or do you recall more?"

"Last year, you asked me a lot of questions about Murray Island, which made me happy and suspicious, to be honest. You didn't seem like a casual tourist, since you were dressed too nicely. I suspected you were here to buy."

She laughs. "And you were right."

"Since we had some empty houses, and I knew the owners had left, I was happy to point them out to you. I never imagined you'd advise your boss to buy the hotel you stayed in."

She puts up her hands in defense. "The hotel is going to be amazing when we're finished. As will the new marina. And a bunch of other improvements and changes I hope you approve of."

That word I hate, *changes*, gives me pause. I wonder how many things I don't know about. I also wonder what Marcus has told Robin about me.

"Why does it matter whether I approve?"

"Take a seat, and I'll tell you." The saloon has a long sofa and two easy chairs. We each take one of them. "It matters because I hope you'll become the new project manager for all things Murray Island."

I must look like one of our island deer caught in the headlights of my Jeep.

"Are you joking?"

She frowns. "Of course not. You're the perfect person. You know the island like the back of your hand. You love it. You'll care for it. You have its best interests at heart. And you are a hands-on businesswoman, who earned all A's while getting your degree. I checked. You won't get taken by overruns, upcharges, and add-ons that we didn't agree to."

My brain has fizzled and cannot believe what I'm hearing.

"And maybe most importantly," Robin adds, "the locals trust you. They won't throw up roadblocks for the sake of stymieing us."

"*Us* meaning Parisi, Inc. You want me to work for Marcus?"

She nods. "It's a great company with a top-notch benefits package. I've worked for him for four years."

"First job?" I ask, wondering if she got brainwashed by her first employment and has no idea that not doing things above board is frowned on. That sleeping with someone's wife to get even and take the upper hand isn't exactly cool beans. I know I've been sheltered, but I've dealt with the store's suppliers for years, and no one tried to sleep with me because I would or wouldn't stock their potato chips.

Robin tilts her head and sends me a smirky smile. "Hell no. How young do you think I am?"

I don't want to say, so I shrug.

"Go on. It's good for my ego," she says.

"Like twenty-six," I guess.

"Girl, you have made my day. I'm thirty-three. Owe it all to my family genes," she adds. "And for the record, Marcus was not the first boss to recognize my worth. I don't have blinders on, if that's what you're thinking. But he was the first to treat me like a partner. I mean, sure, he can bark orders, but he also asks my opinion, listens, and knows when I'm right."

I might as well get it out in the open. "I overheard you two on Dave's patio talking about a congressman. It didn't sound like something I want to have any part of."

She frowns. "Since I don't have your brilliant memory, you'll have to fill me in."

"I heard how Marcus slept with the guy's girlfriend previously. How he wants to destroy a sitting U. S. congressman. How he will basically do anything to get a development done, even if it means breaking the law or playing dirty and sleeping with the man's wife to annoy him."

Robin's eyes widen. "Hold up, girl. You have it ass-backwards and upside-down. Dan Bradley is the bad guy here. He has been sabotaging our project for six months. It has cost Marcus a fortune, and some days, it seems we're no closer to the goal posts. This guy is using his dick instead of his brains, still carrying a vendetta against my boss over some college chick. That and sheer jealousy since they came out of the same graduating class. Marcus reached the moon while Bradley is still rolling in the mud."

"Being in congress isn't the moon?" I ask, although I'm digesting what she said.

"Bradley is trying to turn his two-years in the House into a moneymaker for himself, like so many politicians do, because power isn't enough. But the congressman is failing, which means he has too much time on his hands and is turning his attention to Parisi, Inc. Previously, he asked Marcus for a massive 'contribution' in order to grease the wheels on the project."

It does sound as though I got it wrong, and I want to believe her. I'm simply not sure. It's difficult to entirely let go of a belief that has caused me to be uncharacteristically rude to the man I've fallen for, as well as given me a lot of sleepless nights.

"Marcus mentioned bribery and ruining a man's reputation any way he could," I say.

"And I used the word *hitman*," Robin says, "but I promise you I've never ordered anyone killed. We were blowing off steam. That's all. Bradley is a jerk, and Marcus has been more than patient, but the congressman keeps phoning in favors to cause delays."

"And Marcus hit the wall of patience," I guess.

Robin nods. "It takes a lot for the boss to reach the end of his rope."

I wince because I think I cut the rope the other day on the beach. And maybe I need to offer him an apology.

"He's especially eager to get the golf course and housing project underway. It is the first in the nation that will have reasonably low housing prices on a golf course. His uncle is a veteran who loves to play golf but could barely afford a crappy apartment until Marcus generously gifted him a house with no mortgage. Of course, he included membership to a golf course. It gave the bossman the idea for a development based around a high-qual but affordable golf course, not elitist, which many still see the sport as being."

I take this in and slowly start to do a paradigm shift as to what I think of Marcus Parisi.

"He's already planning a similar project with a ski resort. He's buying a run-down ski lodge, the acreage with trails and chairs, and a terrain park. Sometimes I still can scarcely believe my job and the amount of money at our company's disposal."

"Marcus is buying an entire mountain resort." I can't get my head around it.

"Do you know how expensive a ski ticket is nowadays?" Robin asks. "It's ridiculous. Regular people struggle to enjoy a single day of skiing. Marcus's place will be family friendly and inexpensive, with the most adorable condos. I'm not much of a skier, but I may buy a condo and learn."

"Sounds thoughtful and necessary," I say, feeling like the worst human being ever.

"Now that I know you've got a photographic memory, or whatever it's called when you can remember my candy bar addiction twelve months later, I'm even more certain you're right for this position. I'm attached to my laptop, and Marcus is always on his phone, making notes. But you can simply walk around and store it all in your head."

For a moment, she looks at me as though I'm a cross between a circus freak and a mad scientist.

"So, are you interested?" she asks. "Because Marcus said you were feeling a little constricted as a shopkeeper and that you have as many creative ideas for the island as he does. Might as well make them happen when you're given a chance."

She's right. But I need to think this one over. The islanders might see me as sleeping with the enemy. And they'd be right. Or at least I have slept with him. I could get labeled as a traitor or a stooge. On the other hand, Parisi, Inc. would no longer be the enemy if I had a hand in guiding the renovations and making sure improvements weren't destructive.

"You're offering me a job working for a fairy godmother," I say, using the word I'd heard her say outside Dave's to describe Marcus.

She laughs. "Wow, you do have a sharp memory. Yes, I am. But regarding Murray Island, it's a two-year commitment."

I'm floored by this opportunity. Mostly because it awakens in me some real excitement over what I could accomplish. And the ideas are popping into my head faster than I can breathe. Suddenly, change seems like it could be a good thing.

"Two years seems like a long time to work on upgrading Murray Island," I point out.

"You'd be surprised by how long it takes to handle every detail of multiple projects. The wastewater treatment plant alone is going to be a massive undertaking. The contract has a built-in six-month extension if there are unavoidable delays. Also, the job comes with a house. No one expects Parisi, Inc.'s newest project manager to live with her parents, unless you want to. You can pick anything that's for sale. Just let me know."

She cocks her head and appraises me while I'm looking for a downside to this incredibly generous, out-of-the-blue job offer, not to mention the perks. Then I wonder if this is Marcus's way of getting me onboard with destroying Fort Mercy. If I'm working for his company, I could hardly protest whatever Parisi, Inc. is loaning the town money for. But what if, as project manager, I could decide on the plant's placement. Maybe *I* could be the one to save the fort.

Would he offer me this job if it came with that power?

"May I look at the survey of viable locations for the wastewater treatment plant? Marcus and I disagree on razing the fort," I tell her truthfully. "If it turns out there's another place to put it, yet I'd be forced to destroy the fort, then I'm not interested."

"Scrupulous, too," Robin says. "I have the survey here. And you are free to speak with the surveyor himself. You'll be talking to all of the people involved. It's a really big job. Marcus must trust and believe in you to offer it. However, as you said, it might not take up every work hour. If you found spare time on your hands," she continues, "then Marcus was hoping you'd handle getting the new tourism office up and running. It's actually the perfect place to locate your office as project manager, too. Right in the middle of town."

"My mother is writing a guide book," I say, although Robin probably knows that already, since Marcus was the one who hired my mom.

"We're lucky to have Barbara Cooper at our disposal," she gushes. "I'd read her books before I ever came here last year and realized this used to be her home."

I'm impressed that my mother has an actual fan besides those of us on the island.

"Even after the project finishes, I can run the tourism office?" I ask.

"Or hire a replacement. Marcus seems to think eventually you might want to move away from the island. If you like the work and are successful, then you could go other places for Parisi, Inc. and do the same thing, as a project manager at other developments. That's up to you, of course."

The considerate man who captured my heart turns out to be genuine, after all. I want to thank him. And apologize profusely. Maybe grovel a little. A lot, in fact. And I hope to end the apology with a kiss.

"Do I need to speak with Marcus about the job?" I intend to go over to the hotel and talk to him one way or the other.

"Are you taking it?" Robin asks.

If anyone had told me I would one day be helping with the Parisi polish, I'd have said they were crazy.

"I would be foolish not to," I tell her.

"Awesome. Is it late enough for champagne?" She grins. Then she sticks out her hand, which I shake. "Welcome to Parisi, Inc. I have some documents for you to sign."

I hope I can live up to Robin's expectations. I actually feel pretty confident that I can.

"Then you're hiring me on the spot, and I don't need to speak to Marcus?" I'm still hoping she'll call him over from the hotel or wherever he is in town.

"You don't need to. He trusts me to make decisions. And soon, you'll be empowered to make decisions, too, with the full backing and trust of Parisi, Inc."

It sounds daunting, exciting, and challenging.

"It's five o'clock somewhere, as they say. I'm going to grab us a bottle of champagne from the galley fridge. I'm celebrating, too, because initially, I was going home by way of stinky ferry and crowded commercial flight. Instead, I'm going back the way I came, and it's a magnificent trip along the coast."

Robin gets to her feet, and I wonder briefly why Marcus doesn't want to keep his yacht here. "I'll grab the paperwork off the printer, too," she says. "I printed it out in case you said yes."

She reaches the doorway before adding, "Besides, you couldn't talk to Marcus even if you wanted to. Not in person, anyway. He's already left the island. Flew away this morning." She links her thumbs and makes wing motions with her hands.

Inside, silently, I gasp, realizing the chance to say I'm sorry in person and properly thank him for the Jeep has escaped me.

What's worse is having him continue to think of me as an ungrateful bitch. His last words come back to me: "I won't bother you again. I'm done."

34

Lindsey

Marcus is not coming back. That much is clear. What I've gleaned in the past two weeks from Robin is that my new boss is a hands-on guy, and he has a lot of projects over which he wants to sprinkle the Parisi fairy dust before giving it a good polish. And not only in the U.S.

At this moment, Marcus is in Sicily at one of those villages that advertises the sale of their vacant homes for a single euro, desperately trying to revive their economy. The buyer has to commit to a couple years' occupancy and some renovation money. He thinks he can provide a better way.

I have no doubt that he'll have wild success. But I miss him, and I don't know what to do about the crushingly heavy need to make things right between us, not to mention the endless longing.

As soon as I disembarked from The Rough Rider, I texted him briefly. *Thank you for the job.*

He responded just as briefly. *You're welcome.*

That was it. The entirety of it. I shouldn't have expected more, but *he* certainly should. He can rightly expect a full-throated apology. I've been considering my options. A super long text? *Ugh!* Seems so minimal, even if I add a bunch of emojis.

Fly to Sicily? No can do as I've been thrust into a busy job that resembles whack-a-mole. I love it, but I now see why it will take me two years.

A phone call? At least he'll hear the sincerity in my voice when I explain how sorry I am for not believing him about Congressman Bradley and for thinking he was being a mean jerk over the fort.

Finally, I breathe deeply, try to calm my racing heart, and dial his number. But Marcus doesn't pick up. With that satellite phone of his, I know it isn't a cell service issue.

Is he really finished with me?

I leave him alone for another few days, and then I text again. *I am truly sorry for what I said, and I hope we can talk person-to-person sometime soon.*

I don't know if I expect him to fly back to Murray Island, but nothing happens. Not even a return text this time. What if he didn't get it?

I may be the newest employee of Parisi, Inc., but I have a sneaky idea about how to contact the boss. Robin, who went back to North Carolina in The Rough Rider a week ago, has grown tired of not being able to reach me due to poor cell service, and she shipped me a satellite phone. She even apologized for not sending it sooner.

New phone *and* new number. If Marcus Parisi is dodging me, he'll be caught by surprise. I've decided to do a video call. It's the next best thing to being there, except I'd give anything to press my lips against his mouth or his skin or even his hair.

Yup, starting to feel desperate. I drink down half a glass of wine to take the edge off, even though it's not quite two o'clock. It's already eight where he is.

Here goes . . . everything.

I click the video symbol on my phone next to his number. Fast, almost too fast, the screen changes from the placeholder graphic I use for him—a cartoon airplane, since I never took his photo—to his actual, live, handsome face. He isn't smiling when he appears, looking puzzled, until he sees me.

Then his face relaxes, and I swear I see a softening around his eyes. He's still not smiling, but I can tell he's not annoyed.

"Hi, beautiful," he says, which makes my toes curl.

"Hi, yourself." Not exactly how I intended to start. *Nothing sassy, Lindsey, or confrontational.* I intend to come across as sincerely apologetic because I totally am. "I hope this isn't a bad time to have a chat."

"Well," he begins and looks over his shoulder.

My stomach sinks. It's only been two short weeks. On the other hand, it's been two whole, terribly long weeks, and he's a wicked hot billionaire in Italy. I am such an idiot.

He speaks to someone out of view. In Italian! What if he's asking some gorgeous babe to strip off her clothes or to hang onto that burgeoning climax or—

He leans aside, and I can see four other people in a small dining room. Their median age is about seventy-five years, and they're holding wine glasses.

"We're about to sit down to a big Sicilian meal," he says. Then he adds, "I'm the guest of honor." He rolls his eyes, and I think his tanned cheeks turn a bit ruddy.

"Oh, well," I say. This isn't the ideal time to tell him what's in my heart. "I'll let you go."

"Is something wrong on the island?" he asks.

Yes, you're not here.

"No. Everything is going well." Then I fall silent. The people behind him are chatting, but he waits. I'm enjoying the sight of him, even though he's far away.

"What did you call for?" he asks into the awkward silence.

I blurt it out. "Marcus, I needed to tell you how sorry I am. I was way out of line, and I misunderstood what I overheard. I should have just asked you and let you explain."

A loud burst of laughter erupts behind him, which I'm sure is unrelated to our conversation. He ignores it.

"That would have been appreciated, but we didn't know each other that well. I'm sure it sounded bad."

I nod, then quickly shake my head. He's letting me off the hook, but that's bullshit.

"No. I knew deep down you were a good guy. I just didn't want to believe it. It was easier to think the worst. Safer, too, I guess, especially since we . . . you and me, I mean . . . had an end date. After all, there you are in Sicily and last week you were in Germany." I'm startling to babble. Plus, I sound like a stalker, so I finish with what I know to be true. "I should have been more mature about the whole thing."

About having a mad-passionate, short-term, sizzling affair with the nicest guy I'll ever know.

He blinks those golden topaz-colored eyes, like a wise tiger. I don't even bring up the other source of my anger, Fort Mercy, since that's being settled to my satisfaction. Besides, it would sound like I'm making excuses and trying to justify how awful I was to him.

"Anyway, I'm truly sorry for becoming unhinged. I hope you'll forgive me."

Suddenly, the way he's looking at me, it's as though we are in the same room and there aren't four merry Sicilians behind him drinking wine and waiting to eat.

"I don't think we have an end date," he says quietly but firmly.

I gasp and tears well up. *What?!* I want to ask him more. I sniff once and then get my emotional shit together. This moment is not the right one for blubbering about how much I miss him, nor how much I love him.

"Marcus," comes a man's voice from behind. "La pasta sta diventando fredda."

"Scusa. Sarò lì tra un attimo," he replies.

Whatever he just said in that sexy, romantic accent has made my lady parts start to throb. I'll think of his tawny eyes and his firm mouth and him speaking Italian when I use my vibrator tonight.

He's still looking at me. I fear he can read my thoughts because he gives me a genuine grin.

"Sorry, the pasta's getting cold, and they take that seriously around here."

"That's fine. I told you what I needed to." Then I think about what he said. "You didn't accept my apology yet."

"Lindsey, listen to me. I accept your apology. Thanks. I do appreciate it, but I gotta go."

"OK, I—" But he has already disconnected the call.

I set the phone down on the table and drink the rest of the wine in my glass. I can pretend I'm at that dinner with him.

He doesn't think we have an end date. What does he mean? He's not here, and Robin said he has no plans to come back anytime soon. *What the hell is he talking about?*

I ruminate on his words a lot over the next few weeks while becoming fully involved and, occasionally, getting in over my head as the project manager. But the work is exciting and fulfilling, as well as downright exhausting. When I have a question, I text Robin who is back at the Parisi, Inc. home base in Charlotte, North Carolina.

Until one time, when I ask her a very particular question about the plans for the boardwalk, she tells me to text Marcus as she can't picture what I mean.

"He's in California," she responds. "Three hours difference, but ask him."

I scoff to myself because I know the time difference. I'm not that much of a rube. I've even had Caesar salad! But after I think about it for a few minutes, even though I wish he had texted me first, I send him a quick, professional text.

RE: Boardwalk. Builder said you had expressed a plank preference. Please explain.

Marcus responds almost instantly with a particular width and even snaps a photo of a sketch he's done. There's nothing flirty, though. It's. All. Business. And then, out of the blue, the following day, he sends me a brief text about the fort.

Congratulations on saving Fort Mercy. New site is better.

I chose one of the surveyor's alternate sites for the treatment plant. Marcus is lucky I did because, as it turned out, the entire board of selectmen voted against destroying Fort Mercy.

Once they realized how big the island's rebirth would be, our town officials wanted to honor its history. Once the fort's renovation is finished, we're going to put in a replica cannon and furnishings, along with historical markers telling Lieutenant Cooper's story. It may grow from there, too. Who knows?

As the weeks go on, I try not to abuse the privilege of having the boss's personal cell number. But it's hard. Sometimes, I text an inane question just to see his number when my phone pings.

And then, one day, he stops responding. Two texts go unanswered. I imagine every possible and impossible reason. I know he's not dead. I also know he's in the states. In fact, I learn from Robin that our fearless leader is taking some time at his home near Tryon.

I consider this for a few days and realize that I, for one, cannot go on like this. I'm not a magical carton of milk that doesn't sour or expire. End date or not, I need to know what he's thinking. Or more importantly, what he's feeling.

And that's when I make a decision, pack up my car, and take the ferry to the mainland.

35

Four months later . . .

Marcus

"Marcus," comes her voice, whisper sweet but also alluring without trying.

I nearly jump out of my skin. Weirdly, I had no warning, which might be why I react so strongly. I didn't hear a car engine because I'm an acre away from the main road, hanging out in the stables. Building them was a passion project, as are my horses.

And today, I have the place to myself. In fact, there's almost no staff on the entire property on a Sunday, which is why no one gave me a heads-up that I have a visitor. One minute, I'm talking to Wilder, one of my two-year-old colts, and the next, Lindsey is saying my name.

With my hand still resting on the horse's neck, I turn toward the woman who has insinuated herself in my thoughts and dreams since the day I met her. Although the stables are climate controlled, the only thing necessary to keep my horses comfortable on this perfect, early-October day is the gentle North Carolina breeze. Everything is open. And framed by the wide-open barn doors fifteen yards away, Lindsey is silhouetted against the afternoon sun.

Nothing much has ever rendered me speechless, but the sight of her momentarily takes my breath. With her hair down and sunglasses pushed up on her head, she's wearing a lightweight, casual *dress* for one thing. It's flattering and some shade of blue, although I can't make out the exact color due to the light behind her.

With its scoop-neck bodice that hugs her breasts and ending above her knees, the dress shows off a lot of tanned skin. And because of her position and the bright sunlight, it's also absolutely see-through.

Before I've finished drinking in the sight, she's already closed half the distance and is coming closer.

"Hey, there," I say. *Smooth, Parisi. Real smooth.*

"Hey, yourself. You didn't answer my texts," she says, coming right to the point. I like that about her. No mincing words, for good or for bad. But from experience, I know it's not very pleasant when it's the latter.

"You came all this way because I missed a couple messages?" I guess it worked better than I thought, but I wasn't sure what I'd hoped would happen. Knowing her, however, I figured it would shake her tree.

Lindsey gives a long sigh. It's a sound that goes straight to my groin, especially after all these months apart.

"Not only that," she says, holding up a paper bag. "Mrs. Macey sent this."

Reaching out, I take what she offers and look inside.

"No way!" I exclaim, already excited when I see it's a jar. Drawing it from the bag, I read the label. "Mrs. Macey's Wicked Delicious Beach Plum Jam."

"The name's a little long," Lindsey says, "but that's just the prototype. She was wondering whether you wanted to invest."

I'm staring at my honey-blonde island girl, still not believing she's here. "Tell her I most certainly want to have a stake in this."

Lindsey shrugs, and I can see by her piercing blue gaze that there's a lot going on in her head.

"OK, the jam aside, you came to North Carolina because of my lack of text messaging?"

"I couldn't stand not seeing those tiny, impersonal characters come across the phone screen," she says. "Every other question I've had, every decision I've second-guessed myself on, you've helped me through. Granted, you were on the brief side of chatty but helpful. That's why your silence on professional questions seemed out of character."

"Professional questions?" I ask. Lately, her texts had been about increasingly minor matters. I got the feeling she was texting just to keep in touch, which made me not want to rock the boat. It was adorable, and I kept up my side of the mating dance.

At the same time, I needed to cool it and make sure I hadn't fallen hard for a vacation-mirage woman. The one time I went to Hilo, Hawaii, I was so relaxed and happy and bowled over by the island's beauty, I forgot that wasn't my real life, and I asked Greta to marry me. Big mistake on the Big Island.

Since leaving Lindsey, I've experienced the opposite. I want this woman more than ever, missing her every day while giving her all the space she once demanded. We've spoken once since I flew away from Murray Island, and it was a weird, raw, utterly welcome yet necessarily short conversation while I was in Sicily. Since then, it's been all business and only texting.

"I think the last text was about carpet color. My answer was 'Beige.' No wait, that was the one before. The last message was concerning the font size for the fort's historical signage. I think I said, 'A legible size.'" I can't help smiling as she blushes.

"Did I miss something crucial?" I ask. "Hang on a second." Reaching in my back pocket, I slide out my phone. "This is Wilder by the way."

"Hi, Wilder. You're very tall," she says, speaking directly to the chestnut horse.

I snort out a laugh because he's undeniably *not* tall. The two-year-old is on the small side, but he's got amazing spirit.

I start thumbing through my texts to see the last couple from her. I recall they were random and mundane, I never thought she expected an answer. I certainly never imagined my silence might make her travel this far to talk to me in person.

"You texted me that your father has been allowed to design the island's new tourist maps." I look up and grin stupidly just because she's standing in front of me, and I'm damn happy about it.

"Go on," she says.

"And you texted that you're keeping all the names he invented and even putting up signage to lead tourists to them."

I look at her again, and she's studying me while stroking the colt's velvety nose. I want her fingers on me, anywhere. More importantly, I want my mouth on hers.

"I didn't realize either message held a question," I confess.

"You mean you have no input on my dad making his laminated maps again?"

I think about this. I didn't realize she meant the same weird plasticky maps. Is it worth a showdown and making her mad? Definitely not.

"If you think he'll do a good job," I say, wondering how long she'll stay at my home and whether I can convince her to start over. Perhaps, once we kiss and I get her naked, Lindsey will be infused with what flowed between us before—an instant connection, rich, deep, emotional and physical.

She frowns. "And you have no problem with the signage, pretending we have a Pirate's Cove and a Dead Man's Dune?"

"That's a new one, isn't it?" I ask.

She nods. "He's also turning Kathy's stable into Unicorn Meadows and the marina is Minke Marina."

"Minke?" My voice rises slightly.

"For the minke whale, because he'd already used the word *mermaid* for the bay, and he likes the alliteration."

I swallow, trying to imagine wealthy clientele who want sophistication and superb cocktails gelling with Nate Cooper's goofy place names. But we did say we wanted the island to be family friendly, too.

A glance into her intense dark-blue eyes, and I would say anything rather than have her look disappointed and betrayed the way she did on the beach that day.

"If you and the board of selectmen are fine with all that, then that's your decision."

"Wow!" she says.

"What, wow?"

"You really don't give a shit about the island anymore, do you?"

"Is that what you think?"

She nods. "You used to be bubbling over with ideas and enthusiasm. You had opinions, pretty strong ones, too. Now you have nothing to say if I let my father make official tourist map placemats? What if I'd said we're renaming the streets after fish and painting murals of pirates on the sides of buildings?"

"Wait, are you just making shit up to get a rise out of me?"

This time, it's not a sigh so much as a sound of exasperation that comes from her pretty mouth.

"Marcus, I've spent a billion months without you in my life and barely a month with you, but they were a great thirty-one days."

"Thirty-three," I correct her. "Not that I was counting how long exactly."

She smiles slightly. "Mostly great," Lindsey corrects herself. Some superb highs and abysmally low lows. Through all of them, you were interested and persistent. With the island plans, I mean." She blushes again but continues. "And then, you were gone. Do you know how long it's been since we've seen each other?"

I nod. "Yes, ma'am. Since the video call. Too long."

"Yup," she says. "Too long. Knowing what awful things I said, I'm not surprised you washed your hands of all of us, particularly me, and never came back."

"That's not what happened." I reach up and tuck a strand of her soft, pretty, blonde hair behind her ear. "I've been waiting."

Her blue eyes go from staring into mine to darting a peek at my mouth. But all she says is, "Waiting for what?"

"For you to decide what you want. You had a lot of upheaval all at once. I didn't want you to feel pressured by me when you had a lot of other stuff to work out. I hope I made it easier."

"By leaving me alone?" she asks.

I wonder how I would have been able to give her so much time to think if I hadn't had a few spies on the island telling me how she was doing. Her mother being one.

"By offering you a challenging job, two actually, affording you the opportunity to stay on Murray Island without having to be a shopkeeper or a server, if that's what you chose. And you did."

"And I appreciate it. I promise you I'm not ungrateful. But I also want to be dead honest. I was hoping you would return."

Not gonna lie, that's what I'd hoped to hear. I can't help my smile.

"I'll be honest, too. I've thought about coming back every day."

We stare at one another.

"What stopped you?" she asks finally.

"I wasn't sure you were ready."

She frowns. "Meaning?"

Wilder chooses that moment to whinny, and I realize I have no idea how long Lindsey has been traveling or whether she's hungry, thirsty, or tired.

"Have you been inside my house yet?"

"Nope. Your housekeeper told me where to find you. She buzzed me through the gate, and told me I could walk back here. I could use some water."

"Come with me," I say. Patting the colt again, we walk between the stalls, down the length of the stables to the riders' room. It has a small kitchen because most days, someone is out here for hours.

Heading for the fridge to grab a bottle of water, I still can't believe she's here. Turning quickly to confirm I'm not dreaming, I catch her staring. "Were you eyeing my butt?"

This time, her cheeks turn scarlet, but she confesses, "I was. You look good in your jeans and boots."

"Not as good as you look in that dress." I tamp down thoughts of how much better she would look out of it and hand her the water bottle. "How long did you drive today? You hungry?"

She takes a long drink, then wipes her mouth with the back of her hand. Lucky hand.

"Thank you. Four-and-a-half hours, and yes."

Without hesitation, I open the fridge again to see what Harvey, my stable manager, has squirreled away in here. He's super-organized, and has a loyal crew who keep everything clean and my horses healthy. The sandwiches have tags with dates and made by my personal chef up at the house every other day.

"Peanut butter and jelly, BLT, or turkey and cheese? They were all made yesterday."

"Yummmmm," she says, dragging out the *M* like a small moan, which makes me want to forgo feeding her and find an empty stall.

"I'm starving," she admits. "I skipped breakfast and just had coffee and an apple on the road." Then she bites her lip, which nearly does me in. As she considers her choices, I have to hold back from kissing her.

"BLT, please. No, turkey and cheese. Wait—"

"How about both?" I offer. "We can combine them." I think of the delicious lobster and grilled cheese last time I was in Boston. "We'll make something even better."

Soon, we're seated at the stable hands' table, eating the massive combo, mostly in silence. And after she slows from wolfing speed to nibbling, she's ready to talk again.

"Meaning?" she asks.

I have to catch up. Robin told me about Lindsey's superior memory, and I'm surprised I didn't notice before. I guess I was too busy enjoying her other assets. But I remember where we left off.

"I wanted to give you time to see whether you liked the job, and if you did, then also time to succeed or fail, although I guessed you'd do really well. If I came back while you were still proving to all the contractors that you were in charge, it would have undermined your authority. Also, I wasn't sure you'd want to take up where we left off."

I pause, because I intend to lay all my cards on the table. Making sure I have all her attention, I add, "And if I spend time on Murray Island, if I'm in close proximity to you, I'm going to want to kiss you. I want to kiss you right now."

"Oh," she says softly. Then she shakes her head. "We just ate. I would need to brush and floss. And by the time I walk back to my car and find my bag, then the kiss would seem too premeditated."

I'm catching flies with my open mouth. "Glad to know you haven't changed at all. Hold on." I jump up and go back to the fridge. "No lemonade, but iced tea. Will that do?"

She nods. In two seconds, we're both rinsing and swishing and spitting into a bucket.

"Better?" I ask, hoping that wasn't too much of a mood killer.

"Better."

She steps closer, and I take her in my arms. It seems as though we've never been apart. Except for the serious ache that reminds me how long it's been since we had sex.

But I'm getting ahead of myself, thinking of stripping her out of her dress. When her hands slide up my chest, I lean down and kiss her. As soon as my lips touch hers, she relaxes against me, and I grasp hold of her ass, pulling her hips against mine. At the same time, I slip my tongue into her mouth.

Stunned by how right this woman feels in every way, I don't break the kiss until my pulse is thumping from my heart to deep in my groin. Naturally, my cock is at attention, too.

It's too late to ask if I may kiss her, so I ask the next logical question. "May I take you to a soft bed of fresh, sweet-smelling hay and . . . ?" I manage to stop before I finish with the crude phrase that's in my mind—*fuck your lights out.*

I guess she has missed me as much as I've missed her, because she nods. I sweep her literally off her feet.

"Oh!" she exclaims as her sunglasses nearly slide off her head. She catches them. "No narrow staircase, I hope."

That makes me chuckle, thinking of trying to carry her up her ancient stairwell. I realize the ladder to the hayloft is not a good idea either.

"We'll skip the ladder to the hayloft," I promise. I also avoid the narrow cot we take turns napping on when there's a troublesome foaling. Instead, I carry her toward the end stall while she threads her fingers in my hair and kisses me. I can't see where I'm going, but it's not a problem. I've fantasized, more than once, about taking Lindsey somewhere in this stable, and I could make it happen blindfolded.

In a few steps, we're in the stall that I use for storage when necessary. It's never housed a horse and is pristine except for a stack of thick blankets and bales of clean straw for bedding.

Her kiss is so damn hot though, I don't want it to stop, not even to set her down. And I don't. I let her mouth stay fused to mine for as long as she wants, until my biceps are burning.

Eventually, she needs a big gulping breath of air. And when she does, I set her on her feet, pull out my pocket knife, and slice the twine to free some clean straw. In seconds, I send two blankets flying onto the nest I've created. In the next instant, I drag her down onto it.

It's not the bed at the Ritz-Carlton, but, man, does it feel great to be lying beside her again.

36

Lindsey

I can't say I'm surprised, but I am delighted to find myself on my back in a horse stall with Marcus less than an hour after sneaking up on him.

He is the sexiest cowboy I could ever imagine, with his T-shirt molded to his upper body and his worn jeans proving he really works in his stable. And then there are his boots. *Jeez!* I'd like to see him in nothing but the boots. But I wasn't sure what my reception would be when I showed up uninvited.

Right now, I can tell by the way he's undressing that he's glad to see me. He whips his shirt off over his head, giving me a view of lean muscle and broad shoulders. I get to pull at the button fly, which is surprisingly easy to open, before he tugs his jeans down. His enthusiasm is even easier to see then, with his erection tenting his boxer briefs.

It makes me want to giggle, how obvious a man's desire is. But I'm not as smug after he pounces. In a heartbeat, I'm flat on my back with him pushing my dress up to my waist and pulling my panties down.

With a little kick, I send them flying. Without warning, before I can even be nervous or embarrassed, he kisses the heart of my lady parts.

"You are so ready for me," he says.

He's right. I'm wet, which is as easy a sign of how much I want him as his hard cock shows how much he wants me.

I start to tug at his hair, wanting his body up and covering mine.

"Wait," he says, his mouth against my inner thigh. "This is where we left off, remember?"

I realize he means before the fire. But he's wrong. He made me climax with his mouth and tongue and teeth, *then* we smelled smoke. However, when he parts me and dips his tongue against my most sensitive part, I don't bother to fight. I'll let my superior memory shut the hell up.

I guess it's the four months of missing him, but I am on the edge of a climax almost immediately. The way he holds me open for his wicked kisses, the way he flicks his tongue over my pulsing clit before sucking on it, blowing my mind, and destroying any illusion that I have control, the way he tugs at it with his teeth, I—

"Marcus," I say his name.

"That's right," he whispers against my mound before sliding a finger up into my drenched channel. Then another. "Say it again."

But I can't. While I'm mid-orgasm, his fingers stroke my G-spot, and I swear I've never felt a climax blossom and multiply as this one does. Soon, I'm squirming and shuddering, when he says, "Easy, girl," like I'm a horse.

As I crest, not the least bit afraid of the thrilling height I reach, he's already pushing my dress up higher and undoing my bra.

"Ooauh," I exclaim with some crazy sound of gratitude and awe and satisfaction, still in a haze and light-headed.

Barely pausing to look down into my face with a smug smile, he latches onto my right nipple. It's pearled from all the excitement. When he teases it and pulls on it with his teeth, the sensation zings right back between my legs. Like magic!

I grab both sides of his face with my palms and make him lift his head and look into my eyes.

"What the hell was that? Some kinda fancy billionaire move?"

He laughs. "Yes, exactly. Only taught after someone's bank account reaches one billion dollars and not a penny less. You bucked like an unbroken mustang, by the way."

Embarrassed but also pleased, I push his head down to my other breast. This makes him laugh against my skin.

Then I give him a gift. "I'm on the pill."

He blows his warm breath against my nipple, muttering, "Thank you," and I can feel his erection twitch against my thigh.

Then I add, "And I'm . . . you know." I can't believe he had just buried his nose between my legs yet I can't discuss my sexual health without feeling my cheeks turn scarlet.

"No," he says, lifting his head again and looking at me with those dazzling golden-brown eyes. "I don't know. Are you an alien? A mermaid? Vegetarian?"

I smack his shoulder. "I'm saying I'm *clean*."

"Ohhh," he says. "I didn't doubt it. And to put your mind at ease, I haven't been a man-whore. Much. Lately. And I've been tested, too."

"Then please," I say, "proceed." After that ridiculous statement, I'm glad when he does, in fact, continue.

He gets down to business, rising up over me, leaning on one arm, and fitting his erection to my ready-and-waiting opening. When he hesitates, I can't help lifting my legs and wrapping them around his hips.

Marcus leans down and kisses my mouth at the same time as he slowly enters me. Using my calves, I press him closer and grab onto his shoulders with my fingers, imparting my urgent need for him to be greedy, to take me hard, impaling and ravaging.

He gets the message and quickens the pace of his rocking hips, filling me with each forward thrust. *Yes, please!*

Straw pokes me in the back, right through the blanket. I don't even flinch. This is exactly where I want to be and with whom. It seems the perfect place for a man to ride a woman, hard and fast, the way he does now. My skin dampens with a sheen of sweat from the heat of his body and the ramping up of my heartbeat.

I'm going to come again if he can just last another few strokes. I feel his body tense, and know he's close. Luckily, I'm right there with him. As I feel Marcus shower my core with hot seed for the first time, no condom between us, I fly over the edge into ecstasy.

$♥$♥$♥$

After he proudly introduces me to a bazillion horses, each one with its own backstory, each one proclaimed his favorite, we walk hand-in-hand on the long dirt road to his house. North Carolina in September is green and lush and warm, and Marcus's place is idyllic with the stables, a riding ring, fenced paddocks, the vineyard he once mentioned, mature sweetgums, magnolias, and yellow poplars, among other trees. Not that I know what any of them are, since our flora and fauna is limited on Murray Island, but he tells me about everything I point out and ask.

He'd make a great father in that regard.

"Black walnut," he says in response to my most recent question about a copse of trees. He plucks something that reminds me of a mottled, round lime or maybe a small unripe apple, and hands it to me. Then he grabs another.

"Press your thumb into the husk," he says while doing precisely that, causing the slightest impression in the green skin.

When I press, nothing happens at all.

"Nearly there. Another couple weeks and we'll harvest them. But let's take these inside and open them up so you can see the nutmeat."

For some reason, that makes me snicker. "Nutmeat," I repeat childishly, making him grin at me. Then I slip the walnut into the pocket of my dress while his disappears into his jeans' pocket, too. Next to his other nuts!

This feels almost too normal and ordinary, strolling his land together, having just had sizzling sex, and now going indoors to hash over the future. At least, that's what I think will be the topic of discussion. I'd rather have sex again and again, or just keep kissing. Anything to keep us from having a serious talk. Talking can lead to problems.

Anyway, why wait until we're in his mansion? Which is daunting to say the least, even from the outside. It's both elegant and rustic, a blend of stone and brick and wood.

"How big is," I gesture around us, "all this?"

"Thirty-nine acres," he says. "Want to take the tour on horseback?"

"You'd have to drug me first," I say.

"How about if we rode the same horse with my arms around you?"

I think about that. I'd be so distracted and happy, I might not be afraid of being that far off the ground. "Maybe." Then I look ahead at the buildings looming large as we get closer. "That has to be the biggest house I've ever seen."

"Really?" He looks at it as if he's never noticed before.

"Did you build it or buy it?"

"Designed and built," he says, a touch of pride in his voice. Then he says, "I hope you like it."

Funny how he sounds like he means it, as if my opinion matters. I think of my new house on the island. A perk of the job. There were a number to choose from. Naturally, I chose the one closest to my favorite beach and near my parents. Why not? Having my family back is comfortable and fun. Living nearby but *not* together is even better.

And if I could've handled the closeness of living with my parents, I wouldn't have anyway. I've been hoping Marcus would return. If he did, I wanted my own place to bring him. Of course I was thinking about where to have sex with him. But he never came. Regardless, I nested in my own place. The house wasn't the largest of those available, nor the smallest, but it suits me fine. I hope he comes back and gets to see it someday.

I tug on his arm as we reach the landscaped back of the house. There's a sparkling pool and hot tub. A few outbuildings, one of which I assume is a shower and changing area, are dotted around. There's an outdoor kitchen with a massive grill and a smoker. And I think the other building, about the size of my Murray Island home, is a guest cottage. There's also a large greenhouse, full of plants. I can see ripe red tomatoes through the glass.

"*Um*, how about we sit out here for a while?" I suggest. "Too nice a day to go inside."

In truth, I'm nervous about entering Marcus's home and experiencing its sheer wealth and luxury. Earlier, I didn't go inside. Pressing an intercom beside the front sliding gate and telling some guy my name, I'd been told to park my car in front before being sent on a long walk to the stable.

What if I'm so intimidated by the billionaire-style interior, I can't look Marcus in the eye again? After all, he's seen my parents' only bathroom!

Without answering, he pulls out a chair at one of the tables by the pool and gestures for me to sit.

"The lady's request is granted." He drops into the chair beside me, not opposite, and once again takes my hand, threading his fingers through mine.

"I had a week of time blocked out for the end of the month," he says. "Flying to Murray Island to check on my favorite employee."

I catch my breath, happy to know he was coming back. "Then I jumped the gun a little."

"Glad you did," he says. "Actually, a lot more than glad. Easier to talk and get some clarity away from all the action."

That makes me laugh. "Murray Island has never been considered a place with much action before, but you're right. Lately, it's been like a bee hive."

"You've been reporting to Robin, and she's kept me up-to-speed on the progress. Now that the high season is over, I expect your job will get even busier."

"Yes, we have a lot of irons in the fire and most of the renovations have simply been waiting for folks to vacate."

He rubs his thumb over mine. "Lindsey, you have exceeded my expectations as a project manager." Then he smiles. "Except for shirking your responsibilities and going AWOL. But since you came here, I'll let it slide."

I take a deep breath. Enough joking and teasing. "I missed you. Obviously, I didn't need to send half those texts, but I did it to keep in contact."

He squeezes my hand. "So, what do you think? For the future, I mean."

"What are my options?" I ask because the man confounds me. "You know how much I like choices and upheaval and change."

Marcus throws his head back and laughs. When he looks at me again, the gleam in his eyes steals my breath. "Option one, you finish out your contract with twenty months to go. Then take over the tourism office full-time. Option two, you finish out your contract, then let me assign you somewhere else in the world to work where I need your business acumen and efficiency. Option three, you quit because I'm a taskmaster and you hate Parisi, Inc. You decide to become a beach bum and sit on Siren Sands, watching out for minke whales."

I smile at him, although I'm worried. I haven't heard any option that brings us closer together yet.

"Option four, you become my woman officially, and we figure out the rest of it around whatever works for us."

That's the one I've been waiting for.

"Officially?" I ask.

"You'll have to take your sunglasses off," he says. "I can't talk to someone when I can't see her pretty blue eyes."

Touché, I think before pushing them up on my head. He has a pretty good memory, too.

"Better," he says. "*Officially*, as in exclusive, expecting and planning for a future together, spending a lot of time in one another's company, and going at it like a stud stallion and a mare in heat whenever we get the chance."

I'm laughing again until he adds, "But I can't make my permanent home on Murray Island because I need to meet with people, shake hands, walk on job sites. Which means, if we're together, you wouldn't live there year-round, either." Then his thumb is stroking my palm once more, sending shivers down my spine. "And if you keep working for me, then you may eventually have to fly."

Two downsides to tying my heart and my future to Marcus. But at this point, I have no choice.

"While I finish my tenure as project manager, will you come visit me?"

"When I can." He's giving me that intense stare that makes my skin prickle. "For the next twenty months, I'll fly to Murray Island whenever possible. Waste of time for you to ferry and drive to where I am."

I nod. It sounds promising. "But sometimes, you might want to relax here when you have downtime," I point out. "I know you love your horses."

"Yes, ma'am. If there's a longer stretch of time, can you see yourself coming here?"

"I don't know if the place is up to my standards," I joke.

He barks out a short laugh. "I think I'm going to regret offering you that project manager job. It ties you to the island for another year and a half. But eventually, I hope the majority of your time will be spent with me." He looks thoughtful. "You know, you could quit now. You don't have to work at all, or you can find some other job you like that keeps you by my side."

That's sweet of him but doesn't sit well. "I'd like to finish what I started. But when the contract's over, who knows?" I have, in fact, been thinking about starting my own business, but my ideas are still percolating, and it's way too premature to tell him about my pipe dreams.

Besides we're still feeling one another out. Neither of us is saying the words that make this "official," or binds us to one another. Since I drove him away, and was a total bitch, I guess I can go first.

"I love you."

His eyes widen before his expression turns serious. Still holding my hand, he pulls me from my chair onto his lap.

"I love you, too."

And of course, we kiss, long and passion-filled until my nipples are pearled and I'm wet between my legs.

Fitting my life into Marcus Parisi's is clearly going to be complicated. With travel and sometimes being apart. But loving him is easy, simple. Essential, actually. A necessity to my continuing happiness.

When he withdraws his tongue from my mouth, I say, "Is that a walnut in your pocket, or are you happy to see me?"

He laughs so hard, he nearly dislodges me onto the pool deck.

"Both," Marcus says finally. Then after stroking my thigh, making me think we might be doing something right here, right now, he orders, "Get up, darlin'. I'm counting on using what's getting crushed."

I scamper off his lap.

"Let me show you the home you're going to get to know very well in the next . . . ," he pauses. "How long do I have you for?"

"Forever," I say dreamily, as he takes my hand.

"That's perfect," he says. We skirt the sparkling blue pool with a golden horse design at the bottom of the shallow end. "But I meant, how long are you staying? A month? Two?"

I shake my head, knowing he's kidding. "Sorry, my boss expects me to keep the renovations running smoothly. Not to mention the progress on Minke Marina. My boss wants to be able to dock his yacht there in the spring."

"He does," Marcus agrees. "But if it's called Minke Marina, you're fired."

"It was two days of driving, and two nights because I didn't want to show up here late yesterday. And I'm putting it all on my expense report."

"I'm going to make you love flying," he says as we walk along a curved, yellow stone pathway to four shallow steps up to another veranda, this one shaded. A large table and eight cushioned chairs are situated under giant paddle fans.

I point up at them. "Safe?"

"I get the wiring checked weekly."

Funny man. But now I'm looking through the arched windows and suck in a shocked breath. I can already see the interior is light and polished and gleaming. It looks like the home of *smooth* people. Of beautiful, rich people. I run my hands down the front of my wrinkled cotton dress.

But this man caused the wrinkles, and he loves me.

"You know," Marcus says, "I could give you a horse tranquilizer and put you in an airplane whenever I want. You'd thank me for cutting out hours of travel time."

"For now, I'm happy to go everywhere in Dammit," I say, still looking through the streak-free glass.

"Dammit?" He stops outside the double French doors, with his fingers grasping the handle.

"The name of my turquoise Jeep. Every time I get in, I say, '*Dammit*, I can't believe he gave me a car.' Or 'he can't just go around giving people cars, *dammit*.' Kinda stuck as a name."

"Lindsey Cooper, I love you."

"I do recall you just said that."

"You won't have to use that amazing memory of yours because I'm going to keep saying it." He opens the door and ushers me inside.

I knew it was going to blow me away. The rustic décor has been left at the stable. I step backward onto his foot before he guides me forward with his hand on the small of my back, into the marble and chandelier interior. My head is on a swivel. Is that an elevator?

Well, shit! I guess he really is a billionaire.

EPILOGUE

Twenty months later . . .

Marcus

My fiancée is late. Again. She still works too hard. I'm standing on Siren Sands, looking at the sea, with a picnic catered by The Clamdigger on a blanket at my feet.

Pulling out my cell, I'm too impatient to text. I call.

"Hey there," comes her voice, but not through the phone. She's behind me, her phone ringing in her pocket. Her arms slide around my waist, and she presses her cheek against my back and I disconnect.

"Why were you calling me?" she asks.

"Because our food is getting cold."

"And you're hungry?" she asks. "Big boy gotta eat."

I grin. She loves to tease me. We are always laughing and happy together. Life is damn good.

"You work too hard," I say, turning in her grasp. Sliding my fingers into her hair, being careful of her earrings, I kiss her.

Long minutes later, we sit on the blanket. Now the food is officially not hot, but I no longer care.

"It's my last full week here," she reminds me like I don't know. "I have to make sure I've done my best."

"You've been doing your best for two years." I open the cover on one of the take-out containers.

"Smells delish," she says. "I'm starving."

Silently, while enjoying the beauty, we devour Chef Jeff's signature roasted magret of duck and fingerling potatoes. When we've eaten all the main dish, we slowly eat our salads of field greens and goat cheese. My personal chef in North Carolina couldn't do a better meal.

"Are any projects going to trigger the six-month extension?" I ask. I hate to be selfish, but I want Lindsey finished as Murray Island's project manager. I want her free to be with me wherever I need to be. So far, we've made it work, but sometimes, we're apart for weeks, which we make up for as soon as we're within kissing distance.

"God, no," Lindsey says. "And the new tourism director is working out well. Who could've guessed that Stan Brie loves the island enough that he not only learned all of its history, but he's friendly to tourists, too?"

Stan Brie, from bitter motel owner to head of the island's tourist office. Amazing! And something else worked out well, too. Namely, the Island Treasures revamp.

"I noticed your old lover's place was hopping."

"My old lover?" Lindsey begins, wrinkling her nose. "You can't mean Conor." She laughs, then she reaches for my hand. "I wasn't a virgin when we met, but I never had a *lover* before you. You know what I'm saying." Then she wiggles her fingers, letting her engagement ring catch the last rays of sunlight. "I certainly never had a billionaire fiancé."

"Point taken. But my idea is working, right?"

"Oh yes. Island Treasures is the most popular shop on the island, but don't let my father hear that. Selling all the artists and crafts people's wares in one place was brilliant.

No one is missing the old plastic crap Conor sold before. Dad was mildly annoyed that Jeannette decided not to put her stuff back in Whatnots, but it didn't make sense to be in both shops."

"I could sit here all night and talk island business," I say, lying through my teeth because I have a surprise for her, "but I'd rather take my future wife out on The Rough Rider."

Lindsey nods enthusiastically. She has developed a penchant for cruising and more importantly, for having sex on the high seas. The rocking motion produces an especially exquisite sensation during the deed, or so she claims.

"Why didn't you say so before?" she asks, jumping to her feet. "We could've eaten on board."

I gather up everything, and we walk back to our home. The beach is our front yard. I like the house she picked. It's a cape, not a saltbox, although I never told her that I don't like the look of the latter. She'd get all defensive about her parents' house and then spout historical facts telling me the superiority and necessity of its design.

Grabbing coats for when it gets chilly, we have everything else we need on the yacht, even toothbrushes for emergency pre-kissing cleaning. When we have more time to go farther, like around the world, I know she'll appreciate the luxury of my superyacht with its resistance pool and gym, as well as room for both our families. I'm thinking that would make a nice wedding and honeymoon trip.

We could take everyone with us on the Bliss to somewhere for the ceremony, and then enjoy a week of continuous festivities onboard, celebrating my love for this woman. And then our guests can fly home and leave us to enjoy a long cruise.

On the other hand, she may want to marry here on Murray Island, which has taken well to the Parisi polish. The natural beauty combined with all the new amenities is making it a destination place.

We walk along the beach toward the hotel and the new state-of-the-art marina where The Rough Rider is docked in the midst of other boats, both small and sporty and stunning yachts.

The blue-and-white sign welcoming visitors to the marina makes me roll my eyes, though. Frankly, it's embarrassing.

But I know she's going to love the gift I have on board.

$♥$♥$♥$

Lindsey

Marcus cringes when we go past the sign proclaiming this as "Parisi Marina." But the town unanimously decided to honor him because without Marcus, Murray Island would be all-but sunk. Instead, two years on, it's thriving.

I am honored to be such an integral part of the new economic revival, the town's renovations, and mostly, I'm shocked to be Marcus's fiancée. He asked me last Christmas, when my parents were with us in North Carolina. Even my father didn't mind letting his star employee, Chef Jeff's girlfriend, Jackie, run Whatnots for two weeks while they spent the holidays with us. It'll be our new family tradition.

As it turned out, loving Marcus is not as complicated as I feared. We make a great team. It's seriously hard to be away from him, but I've been tied to the island while he jets all over the country and sometimes, the world.

Occasionally, I go with him, more often lately, during the last few months as most of the projects are winding down. The lighthouse has its own guidebook and a more professional tour than what Andy first gave to Marcus. The native settlement of the Abenaki has been partially reconstructed and visitors can speak with reenactment actors and learn about the first language of the island.

Fort Mercy is amazing, with the entire structure rebuilt and housing the cannons Marcus thought necessary. A reproduction of the encampment on the side away from the beach shows how the soldiers would have lived. Best of all, industrially laminated historical plaques tell all the fort's history, from its beginning to when it was decommissioned, including Lieutenant Cooper's important role.

Of course, The Lady of the Light is a jewel of an historic hotel. The town has lampposts and flower boxes. Anything rundown has been fixed up. Whatnots and Such is another gem. Dad's redesign is perfect. Light, airy, historically fitting with the town, but modern, too. Very much Marcus-approved. Not that my family is happy about the destructive fire, but the store looks better than what used to be there. The island does, too.

Our hotel and two motels are at capacity, and more lodging is being built farther from town up near the lighthouse, necessitating new cafes and shops out that way. Bed-and-breakfasts are popping up, the marina is filled with yachts and sailboats. Marcus's horses, on loan to Kathy, are being ridden along the beach. Bicycles are zipping everywhere. There's a hum of happy activity.

Even with all that's happened, thrilled as I am by Murray Island's success, I always crave the sight of Marcus's small plane, dipping its wings as he circles the island before he lands.

Sometimes, I wait at the airfield to watch him come in. He's super sexy as a pilot. Super sexy in a car, on a motorcycle, on horseback, vacuuming our house, loading the dishwasher. And, of course, in bed. I'm a very lucky lady.

Whenever we reconnect, it always starts with an incredibly hot kiss. We must have had a billion of them already. Just thinking about how he makes my body sizzle, I tug his hand, stop him on the dock, and look up into his eyes.

He smiles, knowing my thoughts, and then his mouth covers mine.

"Mmmm," I sigh, muffled by our melded lips.

Surprisingly, he breaks it off first. "Come on, slacker. Let's go."

I hope he's not growing tired of kissing me because I could stand still and suck face for hours with this man.

We board The Rough Rider. The name always strikes me as sexual. I've never asked about the women he had on board before me. As long as I'm the last one to enjoy a rough ride in the master cabin, I'm satisfied.

In the stylish saloon where I first met Robin, Marcus grins. "Ready?"

"For a short cruise? Sure." I look out at the sky to make sure I don't see any clouds on the horizon. "It'll be a gorgeous sunset cruise by the time we circle back." And I hope we'll be in our cabin, not noticing the last orange rays of light while we devour one another.

"Woof."

I spin around in place and look at my fiancé. "Did you just bark?"

"Woof." This time, I realize it's coming from the galley.

Marcus can't stop smiling, and my heart starts to pound. "Wait right there."

I swear my hands grow damp, and I have tears in my eyes. He didn't, did he? I've been talking about getting a dog. Thinking about it. Deliberating and debating myself and ruminating over it. Yearning and wanting, but thinking I was too busy. And then there are all the times I jump on the ferry and drive for two days to see my man. Is it the right time for a canine buddy?

He reappears holding an armful of floofy black-and-white cuteness. Definitely not my big ol' Max, and I feel a twinge of sadness. No dog will ever be Max. Then Marcus thrusts the puppy into my arms, and I fall in love.

"He's a terrier mix," Marcus explains. "I thought travel size would be good for now, given our lifestyle. He'll only get to be about twenty pounds, even if you spoil him with treats."

He knows I'll spoil him the way I do the horses at his stables. I've learned all their names and what they like as a special snack.

But he also knows how I feel about puppy mills. So, while my heart has instantly bloomed for this little guy, my thoughts go to all the homeless dogs waiting for their forever family. In fact, I've started to concoct a plan about starting my own rescue on an acre of our North Carolina home once we settle.

Being a rich man's wife would give me the freedom to create a passion project of my own. I'd name it for Max, of course, Max's Sanctuary, because I clearly recall the day my parents and I took the ferry to Boston, went to a shelter, and picked him out. There's a perfect spot between the stables and the Scuppernong grape vineyard.

"Before you get all weepy," Marcus says while petting the pup's head, "I know what you're thinking. And I promise you, this three-month old came from a shelter. And he's a happy traveler. He flew with me from Tryon."

This man knows me through and through.

I look down at the squirmy creature in my arms and then tuck him up against my shoulder. With his soft head in nuzzling distance, I give him what will be the first of a billion kisses.

And when my future husband leans over our new fur baby to get in on the action, I give him equal time and treatment. Our lips meet in the hottest of hot kisses.

The End

ABOUT THE AUTHOR

Jane McBay is the pen name of *USA Today* bestselling author of historical romance, Sydney Jane Baily. She wanted to write about strong, sexy men who know how to treat a lady BUT who aren't wearing top hats and Hessian boots.

Trading carriages for limos, she's dreaming up mouthwatering billionaires with big . . . hearts. They're paired with clever, passionate females who have a hard time resisting these intriguing men. *So why bother?*

Give in, have fun, fall in love.♥ They do. And you will too! *NO* cliffhangers. *NO* frustration. *ALL THE FEELS*. You're welcome!

Contact her through her website, JaneMcBay.com.

Made in the USA
Columbia, SC
31 July 2024

39748245R00219